Demon

In The

Window

Book 1 of the Watchers Trilogy

By

Judah Swann

Acknowledgements

I cannot express enough thanks to my brother Christopher for his unwavering support, and to my friends Emerald, Robert, Melissa and Ashley for their continuous inspiration. Thank you all for your critiques, criticisms and encouragement.

Completing this first project would not have been possible without my illustrator Scott Edward; thank you for your unceasing patience, and for bringing my characters to life through your striking visual interpretations.

Finally, to my caring, loving, amazingly supportive soul mate Bianca: Without you, I would not have had the courage, focus or drive to make it to publication. Thank you for your unyielding love and encouragement, for acting as my northern star to guide me home, and as an anchor to keep me grounded.

Cover art by Scott Edward:

scott-edward.deviantart.com

"This matter is by the decree of the watchers, and the demand by the word of the holy ones, with the intent that the living may know that the Most High ruleth in the kingdom of men, and giveth it to whomsoever He will, and setteth up over it the basest of men." Daniel 4:17

Chapter 1

Death comes to us all, and whether we choose to contemplate or acknowledge death, there is little we can do to delay its inevitable arrival. The presentation of death often invokes feelings of terror, even to those who believe in the existence of an afterlife or count themselves among those destined for an eternity of peace. Jericho Coleman found himself seized by the terror of impending death, and although he was only a mere boy of six years old, the reality of death had already branded itself to his psyche.

As he lay curled up on the floor and hidden momentarily underneath his father's desk, he prayed that the darkness would protect him from discovery. He understood that if he were to be found, death would quickly follow. With each passing second the sound of clicking footsteps grew louder and louder, signaling the approach of his destroyer, intensifying the terror and confusion in his young mind. He could not comprehend why fate had carried him to such a terrible moment, for his life had been far simpler only but a few hours prior.

It had been a typical autumn Sunday afternoon on the day Jericho's world drastically transformed. The air was cool and crisp as leaves of red and brown drifted and swirled in the breeze, slowly descending toward the deadened lawn of 1326 Black Mouth lane. The leaves sprinkled down on him as he lay quietly on his stomach and played with plastic army men in the dirt. His cheeks were rosy from the cool air, his hair blonde and tussled without much regard for style. There is little room for style when one is lost in his imagination, as the boy was intensely focused on advancing his toy forces to fight evildoers and protect the innocent civilians of his imaginary town.

While the heroes of his story were more uniform in their hard green plastic shells, the foes they battled were far more diverse—two ninja turtles and a power-ranger action figure towered over the little green soldiers, daring the tiny army to try and stop their reign of terror. In spite of the imposing size of their opponents, the little boy's army was undeterred and battled on; the little soldiers defied physics in their dramatic assault, always victorious and never faltering in the face of fear. The boy was lost in his world; he would have been perfectly content to stay there forever if given the opportunity, but, as his soldiers surrounded the last remaining ninja turtle and began their final attack, he heard call of his mother,

"Time for supper, wash up, and come inside, Jericho!!!"

Snapping out of his daydream world, the boy stood quickly and brushed the dirt from his trousers in a semi-rushed fashion. As he collected his toys, he suddenly realized how hungry he truly had become, and, with his focus now singularly on the rumble in his belly, he made haste towards the back door of the house at his mother's beckoning. The sun was just beginning to set in the west as dusk descended upon the world.

The home was an old Victorian-style two story, located on a section of secluded real estate near the outskirts of Richmond, Virginia. While the home retained its dated style, several updates to the interior had been completed over the years to give it a more modern functionality. The home was large, with 5 bedrooms, 2 ½ bathrooms, a living area, and a study which was a bit offset from the rest of the home. The study was added later by Jericho's father and was joined to the house by a long hallway with multiple glass windows on either side that allowed for ample natural lighting during the day. The hallway connected to the dining room which created two entrances into the study, one from the hallway which led to the dining room, and one in the study which led out into the backyard. The isolation of the study was an intentional feature as Jericho's father cherished his privacy and would spend the majority of his home life busily working away within its private confines.

Jericho quickly washed up in preparation for supper; the warm water nurtured his hands which had become rough and dry from his long and busy day of play. Long days are usually reserved for those seasoned in years, yet to a child every day seems long and drawn out, while to an adult every drawn-out day still seems far too short. His nostrils were filled with the inviting smells of his mother's cooking. He finished drying his hands and headed quickly to take his seat at the table, eager to enjoy his mother's food and company. Absent from the table was his father, an occurrence which had grown all too frequent over the past several months. Yet, regardless of how often it would occur, the boy's heart would always sink with equal disappointment. In what had become a suppertime ritual, Jericho asked his mother when his father would be getting home.

"Soon, my sweetness, your daddy has much to do. Many people are counting on him." She smiled through her answer as she had done so many times before, yet every time, there was a hidden pain behind her eyes which the boy was too young to recognize.

The boy loved his father very much as most children do, but he had begun to notice changes in his demeanor which had become more pronounced over the previous months. He noticed that his father never seemed to be happy anymore, and his patience more quickly gave way to anger and punishment rather than understanding and guidance. Jason Coleman excelled as a provider, although it seemed that the higher he climbed in financial success, the farther he climbed away from his wife and son. Jericho enjoyed his somewhat privileged lifestyle, but if given the choice, he would have gladly traded all the nice things his father had given him, if it meant just a bit more time with the man himself.

The telephone rang loudly, piercing the silence as Jericho waited quietly at the table to be served by his mother. She quickly answered the phone, and, upon hearing her respond, "Hi Babe," he knew it was his father on the other end of the line. His mother's voice resonated a reserved frustration; her tone lowered, she asked when he would be getting home and then quickly said goodbye. She put the phone down and walked past Jericho, stopping briefly to give him a kiss on the top of his head before returning to the stove to ladle beef stew into a bowl.

"Your father is going to be a little late tonight, but he's promised to wake you up to say goodnight when he gets home." His mother smiled and placed the bowl of stew in front of him. "Now eat up sweetie, you're a growing boy!"

Jericho scooped warm spoonfuls of stew towards his lips in a hurried fashion, eager to quickly satisfy his appetite. The steam drifted upward and kissed his cheeks, warming his face as his mother drifted about the kitchen in elegant fashion. She was an exceptional physical beauty, with soft blue eyes and long, flowing black hair. Her lips were full, and her figure was thin yet healthy, much like the body of a dancer. She moved with grace and speed, gliding about the kitchen in a hurried yet focused ballet of preparation.

The boy slurped stew and watched his mother work with quiet fascination. To Jericho she seemed know everything and anticipate any trouble. As he peacefully enjoyed his supper, he heard the grandfather clock in the living room begin to chime out, signifying the arrival of another hour. Six chimes danced through the house, six times a crystal ping rang out to interrupt the quite calm of the home. He anticipated each tone, and as he had done hundreds of times before, he quietly counted the chimes to signify the hour.

The boy finished his supper, bathed, and was ready for bed by nine. Warm and cozy under the covers as his mother tucked him in for the night, Jericho worked to calm his mind as he often experienced both trouble falling asleep and struggles with nightmares. The room was dark, as his father did not allow him to have a nightlight. Jason felt that the accommodation of Jericho's nocturnal fears would do nothing to help his son build courage, but his mother disagreed and cracked the door ever so slightly to allow just a bit of light to pierce the darkness.

9

She sat on the edge of the bed, combing through his hair with her fingers as he looked up at her while she serenaded him softly to help lull him to sleep. It was a familiar song, a lullaby his mother had sung many times before, but on that evening her eyes glistened with a hint of tears as she sang to her boy . . .

"I sing for the morning, the night is so young,

I sing for my sweetheart, salvation will come.

If trouble should find you, between night and day,

I'll send you an angel, till dawn finds the way . . ."

She planted the most gentle of kisses on his forehead, wished him goodnight and quickly swept herself away. His eyes were heavy; he felt a sense of calm wash over him as he drifted far, far away into a deep sleep.

Jericho found himself transported instantly to a familiar dream; he was standing in a graveyard, with tombstones draped in green moss surrounding him. He began to walk among the stones and panned his eyes around before looking up into the sky which was overcast with ominous clouds that bubbled with instability. It was a sky which had a violent appearance yet yielded no rain, no lightning or thunder.

He walked calmly through the graveyard until he happened upon a pool of water, where he knelt at the edge and gazed down into the glassy, undisturbed surface. The boy stared back at his reflection, and as he did the water in the pool slowly began to boil. The water bubbled with growing intensity until his reflection could no longer be seen across its surface, and as Jericho continued to stare into the boiling pool he heard the chime of a music box begin to drift through the air.

His eyes turned quickly towards the source of the music, and as they did they fixed upon an old man who was slumped against a gravestone with a music box at his feet. The music box was small yet elegant, with gold leaf designs adorning its exterior. A beautiful antique, it played a tune familiar to him, so familiar yet he could not pinpoint where he had heard it before. The old man looked up and met eyes with Jericho, and with a look of exhaustion upon his face, he uttered these words,

"I hunger, yet am not satisfied, my lips are parched, yet my thirst cannot be quenched." The old man reached down and picked up the music box as he continued to speak. "I thought she would love this . . . thought she would love me . . ."

His eyes were glossed with tears, his expression reflective; with a broken smile across his face he clutched the music box with both hands and gazed into it as its tune chimed through the air. "Perhaps it's time to leave the world behind, time to atone for past mistakes," With that, the old man curled up and turned over onto his side as a steady rain descended upon him.

Jericho continued to walk through the graveyard alone, and, just as in the many other times he dreamt the dream before, he felt no fear, Continuing along through the gravestones, he then came across a beautiful woman who stood alone; a slender beauty with long black hair which curled and wove gracefully down her shoulders. Wearing a blue gown and adorned with fine jewelry, she held in her hand an old pair of brass scales, the kind once used for weighing gold or precious gems. She turned and spoke,

"The old man gave me many beautiful things, but his value is now lost forever." The scales in her hand shifted, and the right side which was laden with gold pieces began to rise as if its weight had instantly diminished. The eyes of the woman were empty and distant as she turned her head and looked around the graveyard. "I think I'll look for someone new." With that, the woman drifted away deeper into the graveyard and disappeared from sight.

Jericho continued onward until he found himself standing in front of a large mausoleum. A wide set of thirteen steps led up to a stone enclosure, where a large pair of wrought iron gates stood as the only point of entry. In all the times he dreamt this particular dream, the gates to the mausoleum were always sealed. He would slowly walk up the stairs until he reached the top, where he would then place his hands on the bars of the gate and peer into the darkness which lay beyond. He would look about and strain his eyes to try and catch a glimpse of what was inside, but it was useless; he saw nothing but shadows. On this night, however, the dream was remarkably different.

As Jericho approached the mausoleum, he saw a man sitting at the bottom of the steps with his feet in a wide stance and his elbows resting on his knees. His arms dangled down in a limp manner, his shoulders were hunched and his head was bowed so that Jericho could not see his face. The boy did notice that the stranger was wearing a rather expensive black pinstripe suit, and that he had long, claw-like fingers with sharpened yellow nails. The boy's gaze moved up from the stranger to the top of the stairs, and then to the entrance of the mausoleum, and he was surprised to see that the gates which had always been sealed were now wide open. Suddenly, the stranger spoke with a strong, eloquent voice,

"It would seem I am about to trade one prison for another."

A scream shattered the dream and startled Jericho awake, causing him to sit up with a gasp and look about the room as his heart raced wildly. With panicked eyes he searched for the source of the scream, but saw nothing out of the ordinary and heard nothing but silence. Fear gripping him, he jumped from his bed and began to run to his mother, for in many times past he would seek her comfort when he was haunted by nightmares. Jericho hurried out of his room and into the hallway, bolting through the darkness and cutting across the dining room toward the stairs which led to the upstairs master bedroom.

As he was about to exit the dining room, another scream pierced the darkness and froze him in his tracks. He knew that he was no longer dreaming, and yet he heard the bloodcurdling scream of a woman followed by stumbling footsteps which grew in volume as they approached the dining room. Frightened and confused, he turned away from the sound of the approaching footsteps and retreated into the hallway which led to his father's study.

The hallway was well lit from moonlight due to the large number of windows which ran the length of its walls, giving Jericho a path through the darkness as he hurried down the hallway to the study.

"Sweetness,"

Jericho halted when he heard his mother's voice, and turned toward the sound to find her standing at the other end of the hallway. Her majestic figure was dressed in a white nightgown which illuminated as she stepped forward into the beams of moonlight which pierced the hallway windows.

The look on her face was one of terror, with eyes wide and expression contorted in a frightening fashion; the source of her agony was quickly revealed, as suddenly a crimson fountain of blood poured from her neck, rushing as if an unstoppable river had overflowed its banks. Her hand curled about her neck in an effort to stop the flow, but the attempt was futile as blood rushed between her fingers and stained her once pristine gown. She collapsed in a heap on her side, her beautiful blue eyes locked in a penetrating gaze with her son. Her hand extended out and reached toward Jericho as she attempted to call out again, but her words were gargled through her wound and could no longer be understood.

Frozen in shock, he then witnessed the author of his mother's destruction appear from the darkness. Stepping over the body and into beams of moonlight was his father, a man forty-two years of age, with salt and pepper hair, and a scruffy, unshaven look. Slightly overweight, he wore the white dress shirt and red tie of a businessman, yet his clothes were very much disheveled, with his tie loosened and overall appearance shaken from what had surely been a terrible struggle. His expression was blank, cold, and focused as he knelt over his wife and lifted his hand to reveal a large, silver antique straight-razor. With a brutal swing, he plunged the razor down into her limp body, chopping repeatedly with maddened intensity as his son looked on in horror.

Jericho felt panic pour over his heart; it traveled through his body as he turned in retreat down the hallway. He was running for his life as the sound of his father's furiously barbaric efforts echoed after him in an unrelenting pursuit. He was running away from love, from evil, from death, from the collision of emotions which had manifested at the other end of the hall while feelings of fear and guilt clawed at his mind. He bolted through the doorway into his father's study and made haste towards the heavy wooden desk at its center, where he crawled underneath in an effort to conceal himself.

He scooted as far under as he could, with his body curled and his back resting against the back of the wooden desk, and his eyes facing toward the opening. There he waited, trembling with tears pouring down his cheeks before hearing the unmistakable sound of footsteps clicking down the hallway as they approached the study. Somewhere, within that moment of fear and confusion, his young mind was gripped with the cold revelation that death had arrived, and now was only a few feet away. In that instant the boy longed for his mother, and, in his heart, he knew that they would be reunited momentarily.

The sound of clicking steps on tile were replaced by lightly thumping steps on carpet, and, in a matter of seconds, a pair of shiny dress shoes came into view just a few feet in front of Jericho. His body shook with fear and his heart pounded with such force that he felt himself becoming lightheaded as he waited for death to pull him from his hiding place. Suddenly, a voice shattered the darkness, a voice all the more surprising as it did not belong to his father.

"Jericho... You have no need to hide, nor cower in darkness."

The voice was as familiar as it was surprising, providing a strange relief to Jericho in the midst of the chaos.

The man to whom the shiny shoes belonged crouched down and came into view from Jericho's vantage point under the desk. The boy silently recoiled for a moment as the stranger spoke once more, "Hello, my young friend."

The stranger who stood before him was the man from his dream, the one who had been sitting on the steps of the mausoleum with his head bowed out of sight. Jericho recognized the voice and clothes immediately, as he wore the same pinstripe suit, black shirt, and black tie from his dream. From head to toe the stranger's dress was stylish and professional, which contrasted sharply with his physical characteristics. His face was unmistakably demonic, yet remarkably handsome with strong chiseled features, high cheekbones, and full lips crooked into a sly smile, His brow was lined, and his eyebrows seemed permanently furrowed in a noticeably angry, aggressive expression.

The stranger's eyes were unique as they contained beautiful golden irises which carried the slightest glow, a feature which made him both captivating and intimidating as his stare seemed to penetrate deep into the boy's soul. His teeth and nails were sharpened to almost animalistic levels, yet were balanced enough that they very much suited him, and, in a way, strangely accentuated his handsome features.

Upon the stranger's forehead was one feature which seemed very much out of place; an elegant, symmetrical tribal tattoo of thin black lines rested in the center of his forehead. The tattoo was small, but, due to its location, was impossible to miss. Coupled with the animalistic features, the stranger's appearance was a perfect contradiction—handsome and stylish, yet also primitive and monstrous.

Jericho stared back at the stranger; the initial fright had dissipated and was replaced by an eerie calm as the handsome monster knelt before him. The stranger stretched his hand toward him in an offering, his long sharp fingers uncurling like the legs of a razor-sharp spider as they reached out toward the boy.

"Fear not, my young friend, for I bring good tidings of great joy in your darkest of moments. To you I make this pledge: to save, to guard, to guide, and shield you from the shadow of death and from all enemies who would challenge your existence. I will defend you against both enemies in this world, and those beyond it, and in return I only ask for refuge within your heart, mind, and soul. I ask for the chance to touch the world once more, with you as the vessel to grant me life. Take my hand, and, in return, I offer my service, power, and the means to survive."

Jericho was calm; he felt no fear as he knew not the face of sin. In all the bedtime stories he had ever heard, none had ever spoken of well-dressed demons who offered rescue. Time stood still, as in that moment he could hear the words of his mother's lullaby ringing through his mind:

"I sing for the morning, the night is so young,

I sing for my sweetheart, salvation will come.

If trouble should find you, between night and day,

I'll send you an angel, till dawn finds the way."

Remembering his mother's words, his innocent mind believed in the promise of her lullaby, which carried a truth that could not be denied in the mind of a child. This man, this thing which knelt before him, must be the angel his mother had sung of; come to guard him from the evil which would be upon him momentarily. Jericho slowly reached out his hand and met the long, sharp nails of the stranger, whose face lit up with a broad, sly smile. The deal had been struck.

"Jericho!!!!"

A deep, throaty shout echoed from down the darkened hallway, followed momentarily by Jason Coleman, who rushed into the study and abruptly halted at the doorway to scan the darkness for his son. His eyes were maddened, his hands and clothes bloodied from their exercise in murder as the beautiful silver straight-razor dangled from his right hand. A small stream of blood ran down the handle until it formed a tiny drop at the edge of the blade, which grew until its weight became too much and it broke free to plummet down to the carpet. The carpet became dotted with crimson spots as Jason wildly glanced about the study, unable to locate his son who sat quietly on the floor in the back corner of the room.

The stranger instead would answer the father's call. He stepped forward and revealed his presence, invoking a look of terror from the father as the demon's face illuminated from the moonlight which invaded through the study window. The father's grip on the razor tightened as he lifted his arm and slashed forward at the approaching devil, who, in response, reached his left arm forward to stifle the blow.

When the razor connected with the demon's arm, the blade suddenly shattered like glass into dozens of tiny metallic shards which rained down upon the carpet. The demon was uninjured by the impact, unfazed and undeterred in any way while the father was frozen in shock from witnessing the ease of his weapon's destruction. The right hand of the demon fired forward and caught him around his neck; advancing forward he pushed the father backward until he was pinned against the bookcase which lined the wall of the study.

The demon lifted him into the air by his neck without the appearance of effort, and held him against the bookcase with a single hand. The long fingers and sharpened nails tightened their grip as Jericho's father struggled to free himself. He struck wildly with his fist while using his other arm to brace himself on the strangling arm of his attacker, yet every blow was an exercise in futility; the stranger was as unflinching as a statue, unaffected by the man's helpless counterattacks. Staring into the face of the murderer, the stranger spoke with a calm hushed tone,

"This is where your story ends, my friend. Judgment is now upon you."

Jericho took in the sight with silent horror as his past and future violently collided. A quiet rumble rattled through the house, and as the sound grew, he watched as a pair of massive black wings, like an eagle's wings, protruded from the back of the stranger and unfurled with beautiful grace. He beheld the promised angel, with wings so dark yet elegantly beautiful, tighten his grip with a measure of finality as the life of the father melted away.

With a faint smile adorning his face, the stranger loosened his hold and stepped backward. Rather than dropping to the floor, the father's body remained dangled in the air. A noose, tightly wrapped around the neck, was attached to a hook in the ceiling and was the only thing which kept him in suspension. The body swayed ever so slightly, and a small end table could be seen toppled over on its side no more than a foot away, Silent tears ran the length of Jericho's face; the stranger was gone, and two lifeless bodies remained in the home. He was still huddled in the shadows as the stranger's voice issued parting words from inside the boy's mind,   "And, young Jericho, this is where your story begins . . ."

Chapter 2

The next few years which passed after the night of carnage at 1326 Black Mouth Lane were a whirlwind of change, as Jericho's world would continue to drastically transform in the aftermath of his parent's deaths. Prior to his demise, Jason Coleman had been a successful investment banker, well respected in the community. His status among his peers had exponentially grown over the years along with his lifestyle of wealth and luxury. Mr. Coleman's undoing was the byproduct of a series of poor ethical choices, choices which ultimately led to a tax evasion indictment that pushed the man past his breaking point.

The fear of losing everything, and the prospect of starting over had weighed heavily on his mind. Coupled with the shame of impending social judgment, the stress became too great for his fragile psyche to handle. In an effort to escape the judgment of others, Jason instead chose to pass his own judgment in an attempt to control his destiny, all the while being entirely unaware that destiny had other plans in mind.

Jericho was an only child, with no family who were willing to take him in after the tragedy had occurred. Naturally, social services stepped in and he ended up on the foster parent circuit, rotating from home to home with no true place to call his own. The boy also spent a large portion of his first years attending psychiatric counseling, which, of course, was understandable given the amount of trauma he had been made to endure. The official coroner's report from the autopsy stated that Jason Coleman's cause of death was suicide by asphyxiation, as Jason had proceeded to hang himself by the neck from a rope which was mounted on the support hook in his office ceiling.

The little boy's repeated accounts of the demon's arrival and intervention was believed to be a coping mechanism, attributed to the intense trauma of witnessing both his mother's murder at the hands of his father, and his father's subsequent suicide. As the years passed, Jericho himself even began believing that perhaps he had truly imagined the encounter, as in the time since his father's death he had not again seen or heard from his mysterious rescuer.

He would not see the stranger—whom he would come to know as Mavado—again until many years later when, as a young teenager, he began to dream of the graveyard once more. Mavado would be sitting on the steps of the mausoleum with his head raised and a blank stare upon his face, while Jericho would stand before him and quietly stare back.

At first, they would say nothing to each other, but as the dream would re-occur, Jericho began to ask questions of

Mavado, questions amounting to: who he was, if he really existed, why he was there, and many other general questions which seemed to fall upon deaf ears. Mavado always remained frozen in his position, motionless on the steps as he stared back at Jericho without acknowledging the boy's presence. Jericho would awaken from these dreams in a tense, frustrated state of mind which began to be reflected in his real world behavior.

The sum of his experiences over his rather short lifetime had transformed him into a bit of a loner who was prone to heated outbursts, which ultimately resulted in his developing a reputation as a troubled and violent youth. He began to isolate himself at school, which made him the target of bullying from some of his less-than-sympathetic peers, yet Jericho welcomed the confrontations. He would happily oblige anyone who chose to cross paths and challenge him, regardless of the time, place, or situation. He did not engage in verbal altercations; when a classmate would begin taunting or threatening him he would instead quickly approach the aggressor without saying a word in response, and upon reaching the perpetrator, he would immediately commence a violent physical attack.

The first time this occurred, the bully was so surprised that he had no time to react to the assault and was quickly knocked unconscious in seconds. To Jericho this was justice. If someone threatened to hurt him, then he believed it would be foolish to allow them to simply walk away without first instilling enough fear to prevent the bully from returning later to make good on his threats.

This rule also applied to anyone whom he saw bullying other students, as the act of dispensing justice on someone else's behalf gave him a sense of purpose. He felt as if he was doing his part to make the world a better place, although both guardians and school officials did not share Jericho's views on the world, and so he was branded a troublemaker. Ultimately, the results of his actions were that he found himself expelled from three schools for this type of aggressive behavior.

When he turned sixteen he was shipped off to the Northwestern Academy, which was primarily known for its work with troubled teens. It was during his time there that Jericho met Michael Bradshaw Jr., who was an old friend of Jericho's current foster father. Michael, who had been a career military man before retiring after serving his twenty years, was very direct and pulled no punches. Whether you liked it or not, he would tell it like it was, and offer his opinion, regardless of if it was asked for.

A life of military service had aged Michael considerably. His face was lined with wrinkles and his hair was fully gray despite the fact that he was only forty-eight years of age. Although having already lived as a civilian for almost ten years by the time he first met Jericho, Michael still struggled with assimilating to civilian life and kept many of the military habits that a lifetime of service creates. His physical appearance was stereotypical as his hair was a pristine crew cut which he had trimmed weekly, and his clothes were pressed daily. His shoes were always shined, and everything he owned was organized and in good order; Michael had the firm belief that without order the world suffered chaos, and chaos should be avoided whenever possible.

Recognizing Jericho's tendency for aggressive behavior, his foster father introduced him to Michael, who ran an after-school boxing program which was intended to build discipline in otherwise undisciplined and aggressive teens. Upon meeting Michael, Jericho immediately felt that the man held a measure of apprehension and distrust towards him. Nevertheless, Jericho was hungry for combat instruction and joined the program without hesitation, for he believed in his heart that he needed to do everything possible to become powerful, and training with Michael was viewed by him as being a tremendous opportunity.

Jericho was ruthlessly aggressive right from the start. Immensely strong for his age, he fought with rage, and carried no concern for his sparring partners, operating only at full speed whenever he fought. Michael immediately noticed that Jericho did carry a bit of natural talent for boxing, and while sometimes reckless, he was still proficient in utilizing brute force to overpower his opponents.

His raw physical ability and overly aggressive style was too much for opponents of equal experience, yet against a more seasoned fighter, Jericho would succumb to superior technique and skill. It was a rather glaring chink in Jericho's proverbial armor, and so Michael spent hours working with him to hone his pure boxing skills, all the while using the opportunity to try to mentor the rather unruly boy and provide some form of fatherly guidance.

As the two continued working together over the next few years, they became almost family-like; Jericho grew in trust and respect for Michael and began to seek his approval and acceptance, while Michael looked out for Jericho, showed concern for the boy's welfare, and did his best to instill discipline. In spite of their growing friendship, Jericho could never seem to shake the feeling that Michael didn't fully trust him. Not by any particular action of the man, but sometimes Jericho felt an inkling of suspicion swirl in the back of his mind when he was in his presence; a feeling which would be quietly pondered and quickly dismissed, yet nevertheless, seemed to return from time to time without warning.

Life continued on its course for Jericho in a rather routine way until he turned seventeen, at which time the dream which haunted his childhood made another transformation. He dreamt one night that he was back in his old childhood home, and to his awe, every detail of the house was just as it had existed in reality. Jericho walked about the house in his dream and marveled as he took in all the perfect details which he had forgotten over the years, details which invoked nostalgic memories and grieved his soul, for due to his constant change in living arrangements, he had all but forgotten the feelings of belonging and stability which a singular home provides. It was a bittersweet emotion to behold the sight, for it reminded him of how drastically his life had changed, and how far from normal he had become in his own eyes.

Jericho continued through the house until he found himself in the hallway which led to his father's study, a realization which, when achieved, immediately settled in the pit of his stomach like a frozen stone, while his heart raced in anticipation of the room which lay ahead. He had not seen the room since the night his family died, and the thought of what this dream had in store for him beyond the door to the study was almost more than he could stand. Jericho slowly began his walk down the hallway; with each step he took, his knees trembled, and the hairs on his arms and the back of his neck lifted as if they were fighting to abandon his body. Stopping at the doorway, he took one last deep breath in preparation and stepped forward through the entrance.

Jericho entered the study and looked about the room in utter amazement, for it was exactly as he remembered it from his childhood. Every detail was picturesque, except for one significant difference. Mavado now occupied the study and was seated in a large leather chair with an identical empty chair positioned directly across from him. Sitting with one leg crossed and his hands clutched to the arm rests of his chair, Mavado remained still with his head turned slightly to the right as he blankly stared out the study window. Jericho, of course, was surprised to see Mavado, and at first he merely stood and watched as the demon silently stared out the window, seemingly oblivious to his arrival. After a few moments of eerie stillness, Jericho spoke,

"What are you doing here?" He posed the question without any expectation of an answer, but to his amazement, Mavado turned his head in response and met eyes with him. "Good evening, young Jericho, please forgive my previous lapse in manners. I do believe you are owed a bit of an explanation for my absence, and, naturally, I am more than happy to answer any and all questions you may have. We haven't conversed since the night we met all those years ago, but rest assured that I have always watched over you throughout the years. Our first meeting was essential to your survival, but the timing was less than desirable, as you were not yet at the age to understand our purpose together. Yet now our time is rapidly approaching, and as such, I decided it would be wise to reacquaint ourselves."

Mavado stretched out his right hand and motioned for Jericho to take a seat in the empty chair across from him, while Jericho remained a bit stunned and unsure of how to respond. Understanding that he had nothing to lose, he approached Mavado and took the offered seat.

This began a series of recurring dreams for Jericho where the two would sit facing each other in his father's study and engage in conversation. Sometimes they would debate theology for what seemed like hours, sometimes they would discuss life and philosophy, and sometimes they would merely sit and tell jokes, laughing like the best of friends. Jericho found the dreams to be both haunting and comforting in a strange way. To him, Mavado was an illusion, a figment of his imagination, or another coping mechanism which his mind had generated to offer him an explanation for his unusual life.

Yet Mavado also seemed to possess a great deal of knowledge—too much knowledge which was beyond Jericho's understanding—and more than any figment of the imagination could ever know. It was this knowledge which began to imprint the notion in Jericho that perhaps this phantom was something more, something greater than an illusion.

When Jericho reached the age of eighteen, he evolved yet again as his conscious thoughts began to be invaded by impulses and ideas which seemed foreign to him. These thoughts slowly grew in frequency and clarity until Jericho could actually hear an auditory response within his own mind while he was still awake. The voice he began hearing was that of Mavado, which naturally frightened him fiercely the first time it occurred. Flashes of the demon's voice would ring in his ears, whispering advice and comments with growing frequency during times of particular stress or duress. It reached its peak one afternoon when Jericho was training at Michael's gym, during a particularly intense sparring session. By this time Jericho had become Michael's most talented pupil, and Michael would use him for class demonstrations or to break in new students.

Michael trusted in Jericho's abilities, as he believed his skills as a fighter would protect him from harm, and that Jericho's mental strength and discipline would protect a new student who still had much to prove, Such was the situation on this day; Jericho was sparring with a new fighter named Beau, who in a bid to impress and build a fearsome reputation in the gym, had decided to try and make an example out of Jericho. Michael had already instructed both fighters to spar at half speed, as the intent of the session would be to practice footwork and put together combinations properly, rather than do any real damage to each other.

The session began as planned with both fighters circling and throwing combinations as Michael called them out. Beau and Jericho would pepper each other with soft, quick shots in a turn-taking approach, yet as the session progressed, Beau began to add more power behind his punches. With a clever smirk he would tag Jericho with a heavy shot and then quickly ask him if he was all right. Jericho was unfazed at first; he knew exactly what Beau was doing, and, as they were both wearing headgear no real physical harm was being done.

"Sorry dude, guess I don't know my own strength, huh?" Beau chuckled out the insincere apology and circled away while Jericho began to feel his temper getting the better of him.

Michael continued shouting instructions, followed by the occasional, "Cut that shit out, you're not fighting for a title here!" He continued to hold his temper, but with each snide remark and each cheap shot thrown, Jericho felt Beau gradually chipping away at his patience. The two circled each other, with Jericho now beginning to follow suit and increasing his intensity to match Beau.

Jericho began to move faster and faster, and slipped every punch Beau would throw while counter punching quickly in return. Beau's frustration with every miss quickly became evident; Jericho fed off the emotion, dropping his hands to brazenly taunt Beau to try and hit him on the chin. Jericho continued to grow in both confidence and anger, as he focused on putting the bully in his place, The actions were most evident to Michael, who had shifted his ringside criticism away from Beau and toward Jericho.

"Knock that shit off, the both of you!!"

Jericho heard Michael's instructions but dismissed them completely, for he had a new mission of justice, and had reverted back to the former approach to dealing with bullies which had served him rather well in his youth. Over Michael's instructions, which were being shouted all the louder as the session began to spiral out of control, Jericho heard another voice call out,

"Be swift and untouchable. They can never break what they never touch . . ."

Jericho continued to weave back and forth, ducking each shot from Beau with tremendous speed. He heard the voice once more.

"Be unrelenting, the waves show no mercy to the shoreline. Neither should you."

Jericho's fatigue began to wash away; he felt as if he could push his pace forever as the voice rang out again.

"Be powerful, more powerful than existence, time, and death. Death claims everyone sooner or later. It has no equal . . . become as unrivaled as Death . . ."

Jericho threw a vicious body shot to Beau, who clutched his ribs and folded to the ground in considerable pain. He stood over his fallen foe and felt a tremendous power building deep within him, a feeling which consumed him so much that he did not realize Michael had jumped into the ring to push him away from Beau.

"If you can't follow my direction, then get the fuck out of here!!" Michael was enraged and forcefully grabbed Jericho by the arm, yet as he did his expression changed from a look of anger to one of instant concern.

"I'm nobody's punk, Michael! He's got to learn his place, and I don't have to take shit from anybody!" Jericho shouted back, his anger at full boil.

Michael was speechless, and continued to look upon Jericho with concern for a moment before he quietly muttered,

"Go home Jericho, come back tomorrow and we'll talk about all this."

"Go home!? Are you serious?"

"Now isn't the time," Michael muttered again before raising his voice to a louder, yet controlled tone, " Go home, get some rest, and come back in the morning. We'll sort it out then."

Indignant, Jericho turned and began to pull his gloves off as he walked to the ropes and quickly exited the ring. Jericho thought to himself, *"Why am I being lectured and kicked out, when Beau broke the rules every chance he got?"* That wasn't justice to him. Through his anger and self discussion, he continued to feel the swell of power within as the adrenaline rush from his confrontation in the ring was still growing even as he took his leave.

His pace remained hurried as he grabbed his gym bag and headed for the door, hands still wrapped in tape as he was focused on leaving the gym as quickly as possible. He struck the steel door, violently knocked it open, and stepped out into the evening air. His hands burned intensely and inexplicably. At first he did not notice because they always tended to feel a bit sore after sparring, but he was quickly alerted to the strange new feeling which continued to intensify. He wrung his hands vigorously in response as he quickly climbed in his pickup truck and peeled out of the parking lot.

Jericho was incensed with rage, weaving through traffic as his mind raced and hands continued to ache and burn. In spite of the chaos of muddled thoughts and anxiety within his mind, he also felt tremendous physical self-awareness as he reacted quickly and seemed to possess exceptional mental focus. Then, as clearly as if someone was inside the truck with him, he heard Mavado's voice shout out.

"Stop!!"

With a startled reaction Jericho hit his breaks, swerved to the right, and pulled to an abrupt stop in a gas station parking lot. Sitting in the cab of his truck as his mind raced and the burning in his hands grew to an almost unbearable degree, he became overwhelmed with a sudden feeling of claustrophobia. He felt as if the truck was closing in on him, and needing to escape, he reached for the door handle, pulled and took a step out of the cab just as he felt his body suddenly go numb.

He fell from the truck as his body and mind were overwhelmed with the sensation of a crushing weight upon them, a feeling which clutched him and caused his body to crumple to the ground. Lying on his side on the parking lot black top, Jericho scanned his eyes about and suddenly beheld a rather frightening sight. His hands, or, more accurately, what were previously his hands, were now replaced by a new yet familiar pair. The long fingers and sharpened nails of Mavado were in full view, and Jericho flexed the new fingers as he silently marveled at the unexpected transformation. He rolled over onto his stomach and pushed himself up, and in doing so he quickly sprang to his feet with no effort. The crushing force had left him, replaced by new strength which made him feel lighter than air, yet still amazingly solid. Then a voice, ever so slight, snuck across his mind in the faintest of whispers,

"Let me carry your burden today, for while yours has been most difficult, I assure you that my burden is light."

Renewed and energized, Jericho took off on foot and sprinted down the alleyway which ran between the gas station and its neighboring buildings. His speed continued to increase as he bolted through the streets, before suddenly a feeling of lightheadedness seized control of his mind, and pulled him away from consciousness, just as he felt the unexpected sensation of his body being lifted high into the air.

Without warning, he instantly found he was now sitting in his father's study. The same place where he had conversed with Mavado during his dreams so many times before, yet this time the chair across from him was empty and Mavado was nowhere to be found. Jericho stood up and looked about the room and indeed found that he was alone, and, as his eyes panned to the study window behind his father's desk he was quite surprised by what he saw.

The view from the window was now an open sky, as if he were the pilot in an airplane soaring high above the city. He walked to the window and placed his hand on the glass, and as he looked down he observed the city as it rolled by from the elevated perspective. He stood amazed, taking in the view with silent awe while wondering what to make of it; for it was a peculiar dream he found himself in, one which made him question how many of the events which had just transpired had actually only occurred within his imagination.

Jericho watched as the soaring perspective out the window began to descend, and the buildings and automobiles below continued to grow until he recognized precisely what part of the city he was viewing. As if from an eagle's eye, the view swooped down to street level in a smooth gliding motion which then lowered until it seamlessly transitioned into an apparent walk, as the clicking of leather dress shoes against a sidewalk distinctly began to ring out among the various surrounding street noises. He recognized the street, for it was his own.

He stared through the window as if he were looking through someone else's eyes, watching as the view moved into his apartment building, up the flight of stairs and toward the front door of his apartment. As his door was approached, Jericho witnessed the lock click open seemingly of its own accord as the view continued to move forward and into his apartment.

It was at this moment that he finally noticed a faint humming sound coming from within the study. The sound had actually existed during the entirety of the experience and had gone unnoticed until that moment, for he had been so captivated by the view through the window that he had almost forgotten where he was. Nevertheless, the humming had grown to undeniable levels so he turned his attention towards the location of the sound, which emanated from the desk.

His father's hourglass, which was displayed so prominently on the edge of the desk, had been turned upside down. The motion of the sand steadily streaming downward was what produced the unnatural humming sound, which continued to grow in volume until it demanded attention. Jericho walked up to the hourglass, lifted it from the desk, and turned it over to position it right side up. As he sat the hourglass back down on the desk, it made an unnaturally loud cracking sound as if it had crashed down against the desktop with considerable force.

Immediately following the first cracking sound was a second, equally loud crack as the glass in the large study window split from top to bottom. The window remained whole, yet cracks expanded and traveled the length of its surface in rapidly increasing numbers until the view outside was completely obscured. Jericho walked back to the window and reached his hand forward, and as his fingers met the surface of the glass, the window violently shattered outward and he felt a great, unseen force pull him out through the opening.

As if dropped from a plane, Jericho found himself plummeting downward through stacks of thick, gray storm clouds; his vision of what he was falling toward was obscured by the presence of the clouds, while his senses were overwhelmed with the sounds of crackling thunder and the force of howling winds. As he continued his rapid descent, Jericho heard the sound of a voice in the midst of the storm growing louder and louder, as if he were falling directly toward the source. As the voice peaked at an almost earsplitting volume and in a language unknown to him, Mavado suddenly burst through the clouds, flying upwards with his great black wings manifested and passing Jericho within inches, before quickly ascending out of sight as Jericho continued to plummet with no clear view of the ground. Moments later, Jericho heard a final boom of thunder ring out through the storm, which sent a rush of adrenaline shooting through his chest.

He quickly sat up in his bed; awakened by the boom he was startled, confused and looked wildly around the room in an effort to gain his bearings. He was back in his apartment, lying on his bed and fully clothed in his gym attire as if he had merely walked into the room and collapsed from exhaustion,

"It was all a nightmare,"

He clutched his chest in relief, his heart still racing as the images from his dream were still fresh in his mind. Jericho looked at his hands, his attention was drawn to them as they were still immersed with the burning sensation, yet the feeling quickly dissipated as if it were a fleeting production of his dream. Jericho laid back down as a sense of calm washed over him and he drifted off to sleep, and in doing so, he seamlessly slipped into another most vivid dream.

"You really should have destroyed the husky fellow, for he was attempting to humiliate you, Jericho. You should consider defending your status more vigorously, for what will the other fighters think of you if they see you so easily tamed?"

Mavado let out a chuckle as he stood in front of the study window, hands clasped behind his back as he stared out into nothingness. Jericho stood in the doorway and faced the demon's profile; the exterior light which shone through the window hinted at a cloudy day, but condensation glazed over the glass and camouflaged any discernible details outside. He was not sure how to respond, so instead he remained silent as Mavado continued.

"Not all of what you recently witnessed was a dream, Jericho, for tomorrow morning you will step outside to find your truck missing. Not to worry, it was not stolen, and in fact is exactly where we left it. Although I must say, the truck is probably the least of your concerns at the moment, for I assure you that the rest of your world has changed quite dramatically."

Mavado turned and made eye contact with Jericho; his expression was thoughtful and reflective, and even for a demonic figure was a welcoming sight to Jericho. With a hint of a smile, the demon broke his gaze and proceeded away from the window and toward his chair in the study, where he stopped and took his seat.

Jericho followed suit and took his seat directly across from Mavado who sat with one leg crossed over the other and looked relaxed, yet attentive, as he always did when the two would sit and enjoy their subconscious conversations. Jericho broke the silence, as the day's events gave him the feeling that his questions at this moment would gather more information than they had on previous occasions.

"Who are you? I mean, who are you *really*?"

Mavado stared back at Jericho with his expression unchanged, and without hesitation he began his reply:

"Who am I? I suppose that even after all these years I am still just the stranger extending his hand with promises of life. The time has come for revelations, a time which I have longed for, yet waited patiently to arrive as you were not yet ready to hear the truth. I am not a figment of your fractured imagination, for you see, I am every bit as real as you. All those years ago I rescued you, and now I need you to return the favor. I did live once before, just as you do, before passing from physical constraints to wander the earth in exile for thousands of years. Until the day that fate brought the two of us together . . ."

Jericho let out a hearty laugh which interrupted the demon's speech, "You're a ghost? Come on Mavado, when you die you go to heaven or hell, even I know that . . ."

Mavado's demeanor immediately changed in response to Jericho's perceived lack of respect. His tone was now more rushed and carried with it a bit of hostility.

"A young fool like you does not understand the intricacies of death, eternity, heaven, or hell. If you truly believe in heaven and hell, then you must believe the devil is real, that demons and angels are real, that God is real. Do you, Jericho?"

"I've been to church before; I went to Sunday School when I was a kid. Yeah, I believe in God, but I don't believe in you. You aren't real, Mavado . . ."

Mavado retorted in anger, "I was real enough the night I saved your life! I was real enough when I snatched you away from death, from annihilation at the hands of your miserable father!"

Jericho's casual attitude retreated upon witnessing Mavado's reaction; he sat in silence and looked back at Mavado with an almost embarrassed expression. Mavado still fumed with anger, but he also took a moment of silence and stared back at Jericho. His anger restrained, the demon spoke once more in a stern tone,

"Jericho, whether you believe me or not is irrelevant, for tomorrow our enemies are coming for us. You spoke of your time in Sunday School, so this should ring familiar, 'For everything there is a season, and a time for every purpose unto man.' You can call me what you wish—angel, demon, spirit or ghost. I want you to understand that I am as real as you, and that there are many others just like me. You find it so fantastic an idea, but these things are so clearly written. What does the Bible say, 'Our battle is not against flesh and blood, but against the rulers, against the authorities, against the powers of this dark world and against the spiritual forces of evil in the heavenly realms.'"

Jericho responded and completed the verse for Mavado, "Therefore, put on the full armor of God, so when that day of evil comes, you may be able to stand your ground." "Yeah, Mavado I remember that from Sunday School too. It's talking about being committed to God, so that when tough times come around you don't fall apart. I don't seem to remember your name being mentioned anywhere in the Bible. Anyway, we all know how that story ends."

Mavado's tone was unchanged, "Do we truly know?"

"Yes," replied Jericho, "If I remember right, the devil takes over the world, Jesus comes back, the devil and his guys go to hell, God wins, and everybody's happy."

Mavado cracked a smile, "Well, that's a very succinct description Jericho, although those unfortunate souls who lose the Battle of Armageddon probably aren't all too happy. Again, I will pose the question, Jericho. Do we know if that is how the story truly ends?"

Jericho looked at Mavado, not with sarcasm or indignation, but for the first time showed a measure of curiosity, "Okay, Mavado, how do you think the story ends?"

Mavado's mood had returned to conversational, and the subtle smirk still crept across his lips. "Well Jericho, I am no cleric. I do not claim to know the future, but I'll give you some food for thought. First I must ask you, do you believe God is all knowing?"

"Of course I do."

"So, if God knows everything, and has always known everything, did he know the devil would rebel against him?" Jericho leaned back in his chair, placed his arm across the armrest and rested his chin on his hand. "I guess so, yeah."

"In that case, if God knew the devil would rebel, why did God elevate the devil to angelic status? Surely he would have foreseen both the rebellion and the ensuing fall of humanity which took place due to the devil's influence. Why set mankind up for failure? Why not destroy Lucifer and cast him into hell instead of down to earth? There would be no sin, no need for salvation, and for that matter why did God create a tree of knowledge which was forbidden, thereby creating temptation and the means for his creation to fall?"

Jericho interjected—"Whoa, slow down Mavado— Listen, I don't know how things work in heaven, and I'm not going to pretend that I do. Maybe God wanted the challenge, maybe there's free will in heaven too, I don't really know. When I get to heaven, I'll ask God."

"And I encourage you to do so, but as I said before, I have been around for some time so I would like to tell you my opinion on the matter. Being the creator of all things does not necessarily mean you would know everything before it happened. Humans are made in the image of God, and their eyes were opened to knowledge of right and wrong, yet humans cannot predict the future. There is no question that God is powerful, that he has a plan for salvation which the Bible states he will successfully accomplish, and that he also has a plan for how this world shall pass away. I will propose a thought for you Jericho. What if God's plan for the end of days was defeated?"

Jericho was now the one with a smirk creeping across his face, "Who's going to defeat God's plan? The devil who couldn't keep from being kicked out of heaven? Let's pretend for a moment that it wasn't for sure—that Armageddon wasn't a done deal. God certainly wouldn't lose the battle. I think you're giving the devil too much credit."

Mavado let out a laugh. "Ah!!! Perhaps I do give him too much credit." Mavado's laughter calmed, and while the smile still lingered, a serious tone emanated next, "Jericho, all I am suggesting is that the future is not ordained, which means we have the power to change what has been prophesied. That battle, the 'spiritual forces in the heavenly realms' that the Bible speaks of, is a battle which has already begun." Mavado stood from his seat, turned and walked back to the study window behind the desk. There he stood, hands clasped once again behind his back as he stared out the foggy window.

"You said our enemies were coming tomorrow, who are you talking about?"

Mavado responded without breaking his gaze through the window, "Misguided souls who believe they serve a higher purpose. They believe in that purpose with such passion that they serve their master blindly, choosing to kill in his name and failing to question contradiction; they embrace the destruction of those whom they deem unfit for their kingdom. Unfortunately, you and I are counted among those thought to be unfit." Mavado remained at the window with his attention firmly focused away from Jericho, who quickly dismissed the ominous warning.

"I don't have any enemies, at least not any like what you're talking about. I think I'll be just fine." With that, Jericho rose from his seat, turned and headed towards the door.

"Jericho," At Mavado's call, Jericho stopped at the doorway and turned once more to face the demon, who still stared out the window as he spoke a final time.

"I remember when I first saw you in the real world, our eyes met, and you looked back at me without fear or terror, but instead chose to embrace me with trust in your most desperate hour. All that I ask is that you please trust me once more as you did on that day so many years ago. When they come tomorrow, let me help you." Mavado turned his head from the window and the eyes of the two met. "Let me save us."

Jericho's eyes opened and groped at the shadows which surrounded him as he lay in bed. His mind was immersed with confusion due to the abrupt exit from the dream world and quick emergence into the darkness of his bedroom. He sat up and strained to focus his thoughts as reality began sinking in, and with each passing moment his mind became calmer and more rational as he dismissed the idea that anything extraordinary had actually occurred.

He instead chose to believe that everything had been imagined, that perhaps he had blacked out after returning home from the gym or that the entire day's events had actually been an elaborate succession of dreams. The idea of a mystical or supernatural explanation was absurd, a thought which brought on a sense of relief which, as he lay back down on the bed, allowed him to drift back to sleep.

The remainder of the night was filled with dreamless sleep, and in the morning he awakened feeling more refreshed than he had in months. His mind quickly reflected back to the previous day as he began to attempt to separate what had actually occurred from what was only part of his imagination, until a simple answer to his question suddenly struck him.

He leapt from his bed, not needing to dress as he was still clothed and wearing shoes, and made for the front door. He headed outside at a brisk walking pace which transitioned into a light jog as he entered the parking lot and began to look for his truck. The jog transformed into a run as Jericho dashed back and forth and scanned the area for his truck, but it was nowhere to be found. He thought that perhaps it had been stolen, but he also understood that an alternate explanation could exist; one which was far more troubling than theft.

Jericho took off on foot; he jogged down the street and across sidewalks, cut through parks and alleyways, and continued his search as the cool morning air wrapped him like a chilly blanket. He knew exactly where he was going, and as he rounded the corner and the gas station came into view, he felt a chill run though his body which was not produced by the morning air. He approached his truck, which stood exactly where he remembered leaving it before his blackout. He climbed into the cab, put the keys in the ignition and pondered what to make of it all before deciding on his next destination.

Jericho started up the engine and headed back to the gym, as Michael had already requested he return in the morning, and Jericho felt that there was no reason to delay. After all, Michael was his friend, and Jericho felt remorse for his behavior the previous day and was eager to mend fences before turning his attention to Mavado's ominous warnings.

Chapter 3

The drive that morning was filled with anxiety. It was a trip which had been done hundreds of times before yet Jericho dreaded facing Michael after the previous day's events. An apology was definitely in order, but Jericho also felt a need to confide in Michael about the existence of Mavado. In all the years that Jericho had known the man, they had never discussed any of the dreams of Mavado or the presence of the demon on the night of his parent's death.

Michael was generally straight-laced and without superstition, always leaning toward logical explanations and rather dismissive when talk turned to the supernatural. It wasn't that Michael was without religion, in truth, he attended church every Sunday and was never shy about his belief in God, but it was just that he simply did not attribute every supernatural claim or odd dream to spiritual intervention.

Jericho knew this, and the apprehension of Michael believing that he was simply mentally ill or weak-minded was enough motivation for Jericho to keep his nocturnal visits from Mavado a secret. Jericho was acutely aware that Mavado's assessment had been accurate; Jericho's world had indeed changed. The location of his truck was enough evidence that Mavado was beginning to invade Jericho's physical world, and he understood that he would now need an ally to seek guidance from, which was a duty Jericho believed Michael was most suited for.

Jericho rounded the corner and pulled into the gym's parking lot, but was surprised to find it almost completely empty. The notable exception was Michael's motorcycle, which oddly was the only vehicle present; the gym opened at six in the morning, and as it was now ten-thirty Jericho had anticipated the usual contingent of the boxing team to already be well into a training session.

Jericho was actually a bit relieved as there would be no spectators to witness his walk of shame into Michael's office, so he exited his truck and moved swiftly to the front door, pulled it open and stepped into the small lobby where he was again surprised, as the gym lights were switched off. All appearances indicated that the place was closed but the door had been left unlocked uncharacteristically, an oddity as Michael was neither careless nor overly trusting and could probably be labeled as more than a bit paranoid.

"Hello??? Michael???" Jericho's words echoed into the darkness. The gym had two small skylights which provided a bit of interior lighting directly below them and a bit of residual lighting for the gym, however the windows which ran along the walls of the gym were darkly tinted, which made running the lights during the day a necessity. Michael had explained previously that this was done for privacy purposes, as the tinting made it impossible for someone to walk up from the parking lot and observe everything that was going on inside. The other side effect of the tinting was that it always felt as if it were after sunset, which made it a bit easy to lose track of time; in the same way that casinos have no windows or clocks to prevent the occupants from noticing how long they have been inside. Michael felt that keeping focus during training would be assisted by a similar strategy.

He cautiously pressed forward and made his way towards Michael's office which was located in the back of the gym.

"Mike?! It's Jericho! The door was open . . . please don't shoot me!"

He deadpanned the exclamation in a half serious, half joking manner as he continued to head for the office door, and upon reaching it he stopped at the entrance to knock. When there was no response he took the initiative to let himself in and turned the handle, but found that the door was locked.

"I told everyone the gym was closed today!" Michael's voice echoed through the room, surprising Jericho who turned around to find Michael standing in the center of the boxing ring, with the light from the skylight directly above illuminating him. Jericho slowly approached him, and wasted no time in beginning his apology.

"Hey, I know I said some things I shouldn't have. I appreciate everything you've done for me, I just kind of lost my temper yesterday ..." Jericho's tone was bashful as he awkwardly searched for the right words to say, and through his embarrassment he tried his best to scrape together an apology while struggling with whether or not to bring up what he believed had transpired with Mavado. "...I don't really know what came over me, I've just been stressed out lately, haven't really been sleeping too well."

Michael stared back at Jericho, his expression still serious as he replied. "I can relate, because I lost a lot of sleep last night too. You see, there's a reason I asked you to come back today and why I didn't invite nobody else here. First thing I want you to know is that you are, and will always be, my friend. I'm on your side, Jericho. But the truth is that you aren't the only one who lost his temper yesterday, and we got to know which side your friend is on."

Jericho froze; his mind raced and his pulse quickened at the realization of what Michael was saying.

How could he know about Mavado?

The words flashed across his mind as he uttered an ambiguous response,

"I don't know what you mean."

"You know what I mean. He's been hiding within you for as long as we've known each other. I knew he was waiting, and so I waited too. Waited until the day he'd break his silence."

Michael walked forward to the edge of the ropes, and as he did, his eyes suddenly transformed from their usual brown iris to a bright, glowing blue. His eyes burned in the darkness with a supernatural glow, rendering Jericho speechless as Michael spoke once more, yet this time his usual southern accent was replaced with a distinctly different voice which was both powerful and eloquent.

"Did you truly believe you were unique? That you were the only one who possessed a secret?"

"Who are you?"

"What is its name, Jericho!? Where did it come from, and how long has it possessed you!? It is imperative that you answer my questions without delay . . ."

"I'm not possessed! I met him when I was a kid, he helped me once before, and we've been together ever since. His name is Mavado, and I don't know where he's from. He never told me." Jericho shouted back, his voice cracked from the suddenly overwhelming moment.

Michael stared back, eyes glowing ominously as he stood in the shadows at the edge of the ring with his hands clasped behind his back. If anything was clear to Jericho, it was that his friend was now replaced by someone else entirely. An unknown force was moving through Michael, a spirit which used him as a vessel to give voice toward Jericho and which spoke in definitive tones.

"His name is not Mavado, for he disguises his identity from you, Jericho. What delays him from seizing control of you now, from lashing out against his enemy?"

"I told you, I'm not possessed by anything! He's been with me ever since my parents died, but now he only shows up when I dream."

"That is not possible Jericho, for they never relinquish control. They possess and dominate, never sharing power but using others as a means to embrace the world. You are his vessel to control, for he began to reveal himself yesterday when you fought with the boy."

"No, that's not what happened. Beau was fighting dirty, and I let it get to me. Mavado was in my ear the whole time, I was upset, and I followed his advice. But you saw, I snapped right out of it and left the gym when Michael told me to. I control my life and Mavado doesn't tell me what to do. I don't understand it either, but he looks out for me."

"Would he look after you now? For your sake, I hope he is as courageous as you claim him to be." The spirit's reply was short yet abundantly clear. Jericho remembered Mavado's words from the previous night and understood this to be the enemy of which he had spoken. His initial fear upon seeing Michael's transformation had subsided, and realizing the spirit within him was real now empowered Jericho with an attitude of defiance.

"Who the hell are you? So you possess Mike, huh? I guess that makes you some kind of demon, too."

"I am no demon, not like the creature which dwells within you. It is not my place to reveal my true name, but to Michael I am known only as Garrison. I do not possess the man as that is not what I have been commanded to do, unlike this Mavado who exists within you who honors no commandments and wanders without true direction. I am here because God has granted me the opportunity to exist in this time, and I reside within Michael because he accepted me. We have formed this union in order to serve a purpose which is far greater than ourselves, a purpose which most certainly cannot be shared by your devil."

"Look, you don't know anything about me, and you have no way of knowing what Mavado's purpose is, since you don't seem to know anything about him, or you wouldn't be asking me. If Mike accepted you, and the two of you work together, then it's possible for me and Mavado to do the same thing. I don't know what he is but he doesn't control me. He promised to protect me, and he's been good to his word." The frustration in Jericho's voice was evident as he tried his best to defend his union with Mavado, a matter which was exceedingly difficult since Jericho himself did not fully understand the nature of his relationship with the creature.

"He wishes to kill us; you cannot deny this to be true . . ."

Mavado's voice flashed across Jericho's mind, causing him to pause mid-sentence. Jericho felt his nerves begin to get the better of him as Mavado's words instantly instilled anxiety and fear.

"His word is only good as long as it serves his purpose. Yesterday, when he began to manifest from within you I felt his strength. It was not granted by God, Jericho, his strength comes not from a righteous place," Garrison continued to speak, unaware of Mavado's whisperings which had begun to drown out his voice.

"You know what a murderer looks like; you above all people understand that troublesome feeling which bombards one as they look into the eyes of their potential destroyer. We may as well be back in the hallway all those years ago." As Mavado uttered these words Garrison abruptly fell silent; his expression became statuesque and cold as Mavado whispered once more, *"Ah, I believe he heard me this time."*

The blue glow of Garrison's eyes intensified further, burning brightly in the midst of the shadows, "Mavado may have you convinced of his intentions, but the true origins of his power are undeniable. I will do what I must."

Garrison unclasped his hands from behind his back and let his arms drift to his sides. As he did, strands of blue light began to slither down his left arm and wound down toward his hand like a glowing serpent. "I have sworn an oath, and I am charged once again with the responsibility of fulfilling our duty. For, as it is written, our battle is not against you, Jericho, for it is not a battle against flesh and blood . . ."

The blue strands of light continued traveling down Garrison's arm, branched off of his hand and assembled into the open air as they increased in density and formed the handle of a soon-to-be revealed weapon. The blue strands divided and continued spreading downward as Jericho took in the sight while hearing Mavado's voice once more, which now spoke in unison with Garrison's,

" . . . *But against the rulers, against the authorities, against the powers of this dark world and against the spiritual forces of evil in the heavenly realms."*

Garrison lifted his left arm up as the strands of light continued branching and forming outward, filling empty space and weaving until it formed a very large blade. A sword so large that when fully formed rested against Garrison's shoulder, giving the appearance that if the blade were to be lowered to his side it would become impossible to swing. The sheer size of the blade made it look as if it were meant to be wielded by a man twice his size, and although it formed from the blue energy which came from Garrison's hand, it still appeared solid and to carry considerable weight.

Jericho stood in awe of the sight which unfolded before him; he felt fear overwhelm him at the thought of Garrison's intentions, and in response had begun to slowly step backward in a nearly paralyzed retreat. Garrison stood with the great sword resting on his shoulder and stared back at Jericho, before he bent his knees and leapt after him in a great show of superhuman ability. Garrison soared over the ropes of the boxing ring and bounded through the air towards Jericho, with the great sword clutched in both hands and its blade trailing behind his head and wound to strike downward with devastating power.

Jericho extended his hand forward toward the quickly-approaching Garrison and uttered one word:

"Mavado . . ."

He watched as time seemed to slow down considerably, and his outstretched hand grew ever so slightly as it began to transform in appearance and reveal Mavado's familiar fingernails.

A moment of darkness flooded Jericho's vision before washing away to reveal that he had switched places and was now inside his father's study, where he stood in front of the large window which projected the view he had previously beheld only an instant prior.

The spot Jericho had occupied in the gym was now inhabited by Mavado, who stood in his pinstripe suit with his hand still outstretched and Garrison bearing down on him. Garrison swung the great blade downward at Mavado, where

53

it crashed with a booming fury. The blade contacted just short of Mavado's hand as if it had struck an invisible barrier, sending some of the power within the sword fanning outward as its blue light enveloped the invisible surface and revealed a dome-shaped barrier which shielded Mavado from harm.

As Garrison's feet touched the ground, he leaned in with the great sword and continued to push the blade forward as its blue energy burned and crackled around the invisible barrier. Garrison seemed to exert tremendous effort as his expression was strained, while the blue energy continued to pulse through the sword and dissolve against the barrier. Mavado, in contrast, simply stood with his arm still extended forward. His facial expression exuded a calm seriousness at first, but quickly gave way to a subtle smile.

Mavado pushed his hand forward ever so slightly, and in doing so, caused the blue energy washing over the barrier to immediately rebound into the sword, knocking both the sword and Garrison backward. The sword continued on through the air and traveled over Garrison's head, slipping free from his grip and sticking itself tip first into the ground behind him. Mavado slowly lowered his hand as the smile on his face evolved into a full grin. "Garrison is it? I must say, after your speech I was expecting so much more."

Jericho's voice echoed through Mavado's mind, as the two now assumed each other's roles, "Don't hurt them Mavado; just stop them. I don't want anything bad to happen to Mike." Mavado's grin quickly melted away upon hearing this, his disappointment clearly visible as Garrison turned and pulled the great sword from the ground before again advancing on Mavado.

The demon muttered under his breath, "Very well, Jericho, we'll do things your way. I am, as always, your humble servant."

Garrison moved forward and began his assault on Mavado with the sword, chaining together large swings with swooping overhand chops, followed by quick steps forward and sweeping vertical slashes. Mavado's reaction still appeared effortless, even in the face of Garrison's attack; he took small steps from side to side and made slight shoulder turns, followed by quick hops backward to avoid contact. Every swing and slash from Garrison was dodged by the narrowest of margins, yet all the same they were still clearly avoided with very efficient efforts from Mavado.

Garrison continued to press forward and back Mavado toward the wall of the gym where Michael's office was located. He lunged forward with the sword, which stuck fast into the cinderblock wall only a few inches from the left side of Mavado's head. As the sword dug into the wall, Mavado stepped forward and engaged his opponent, throwing a single winding kick with his right leg which connected with the side of Garrison's head and knocked him violently through the air. The sword remained stuck in the wall while Garrison was launched into a large rack of hanging heavy bags; he collided against them with considerable force and dropped to the ground, while the energy generated from the impact continued on through the bags, knocking them from their hooks and crashing them to the floor.

Mavado then turned his attention to the sword in the wall; stepping forward and grasping the large handle with both hands he proceeded to pull the weapon free, but from the moment his hands touched the sword they were immediately bound together by blue strands of energy, which leapt from the handle and wrapped themselves around his wrists before continuing up his forearms. The blade of the sword then transformed as well, morphing into multiple glowing blue chords of energy which shot out and snaked across the floor towards Garrison, who had already stood back to his feet. The glowing chords leapt obediently into Garrisons hands, while the chords which bound Mavado continued to tighten their grip.

"The sword belongs to me, for it was created from the power which has been granted unto me. What did you expect would happen if you attempted to wield it?" Garrison stepped forward, turned his shoulders and whipped the chords to the left, and with the energy of a cracking whip, Mavado was launched across the gym and soared through the air with his hands still firmly bound together. His body struck the tinted windows and shattered them, flooding the darkened gym with sunlight as Mavado continued through the opening and crashed shoulder first to the sidewalk outside.

As he struck the ground, the momentum carried his body forward and he quickly rolled back up to his feet. His expression was rage-filled as he sprang into a standing position, with his wrists still bound together, and began grasping the chords which led to Garrison with his unbound fingers. It was now Mavado's turn, as he gripped the chords tightly and whipped his body forcefully to the right, pulling Garrison after him through the shattered window.

Garrison leapt to his feet and launched toward Mavado, but as he rapidly approached the window, a pair of large white wings suddenly sprang from his back. Garrison sailed through the opening, and upon emerging his wings fully extended outward, catching the air and slowing him down as he collided with Mavado and knocked him to the ground.

56

The slack from the blue chords snaked around the demon and bound his arms as Garrison stood over him, reached down and grabbed Mavado by the collar of his jacket with both of his hands. Garrison's large wings extended high into the air and gave one forceful push downward, sending the two rocketing off the ground together and into the sky like a missile.

As they climbed higher and higher into the open sky, Mavado's expression began to steadily intensify; his yellow eyes glowed and burned with increasing radiance as the blue chords that bound him began to crackle and smoke. Black smoke twirled off his body, and the cracking sound peaked with a loud boom as Mavado suddenly exploded free from his bonds, shattering the blue chords as a pair of great black wings sprang forth from his back. Mavado used his freed hands to grasp Garrison by his shoulders, and lifting his feet up he placed the soles of his shoes against Garrison's midsection and pushed off to break free from his grip. Back-flipping into an upright position, Mavado hovered thousands of feet above the city and stared across the empty void at Garrison.

Mavado's eyes still burned with the golden glow, and black smoke continued to curl and emanate from his body as the sly smile revealed itself once more. "The boy refuses to let me kill you, so it would appear that I am wasting my time with this fruitless struggle."

Jericho stood at the window of the study, and as he viewed the entire scene through Mavado's eyes he became increasingly frightened by what he was witnessing; his mind grasped the reality that his body was hovering a few thousand feet in the sky, which was a notion that made him incredibly uneasy.

"Get us out of here Mavado!" Jericho's shout in the study registered as mere whispers in Mavado ears, but nevertheless were silently acknowledged by the demon as Garrison too shouted at Mavado, "You possess not the power to destroy me. I have destroyed thousands like you in this lifetime, and commanded the destruction of tens of thousands in my first. Tell me why you have possessed this boy!"

Mavado continued to smile, his response calm and casual. "I did not possess him, I offered my services, and the boy accepted. I guide the boy, but ultimately he decides what I can and cannot do. In the same manner that you have done with Michael, I have done with young Jericho."

"Lies and deception . . . the Watchers make an oath to those with whom they unite; an oath which cannot be broken by the spirit swearing it. You and your kind are incapable of making such an agreement for you possess, torment, and destroy everything you touch. You inhabit those stricken with madness, those who sell their souls for the promise of power. You are nothing like me, for I am here to serve the one who sent me and protect his children. You have no righteous purpose, for if you are not for the Lord, then you must surely be against him . . ."

Mavado's humored expression was gone, transformed to one of seriousness as he began his reply: "You claim to know everything about me, Garrison, not very surprising seeing as presumption without evidence is one of the finest traits of the Watchers. If what I am cannot exist, then surely you must be witnessing the impossible. In all the years I have known Jericho I have never mistreated him, but instead have protected the boy and have always bowed to his will. You ask what my purpose is, well I believe it is to show the world that things are not quite as 'black and white' as they may seem. Perhaps it's my affinity towards challenging the status quo that drives me forward, and yes, perhaps I lack the purity of you and your kind, but a demon? I hardly qualify for such a sinister title. You fear what you do not understand."

Garrison, unmoved by Mavado's words, replied quickly, "Spoken like a true servant of the Devil. I see through your empty words demon, for while the boy may hold belief in you, I am wise enough to know the difference between good and evil."

Mavado's smile crept back, "Well, I can see we could debate this all day, but young Jericho requested that I 'get us out of here,' so if you will excuse me Garrison." As he finished speaking the words, Mavado suddenly rocketed downward towards the earth at incredible speed, with Garrison immediately giving chase and plummeting after him.

Garrison closed the distance between himself and Mavado quickly, but as he reached out to grab hold of Mavado, the demon spun around and instead took hold of him. The two plummeted toward the ground as they clinched and threw punches, elbow and knee strikes which impacted with incredible force upon one another. Mavado was getting the better of the exchange, landing more powerfully and more frequently on Garrison who appeared to be just a fraction slower than his opponent.

As the ground approached, Mavado broke free from the clinch and landed feet first, with the force of impacting at such a high rate of speed causing him to drop to one knee and crack the pavement beneath him. Garrison also crashed into the pavement with considerable force, but he did so shoulder first, as he did not have time to re-orient himself before hitting the ground. Garrison scrambled to his feet, visibly injured as he stood to face Mavado.

"That's enough Mavado! I told you not to hurt them!" Jericho shouted, as he watched from his position in the study. He had seen enough and decided it was time to take matters into his own hands. He left his vantage point in front of the window and walked to the desk, grabbed the hourglass and quickly flipped it right side up. As the loud cracking sound boomed throughout the study, the window's glass cracked from top to bottom as it had done previously and obscured his view. He then quickly approached the window and shattered it with his touch before stepping though the opening to resume control.

In his haste to intervene, Jericho found himself plummeting through the darkened sky toward reality, unaware of what was unfolding next. The blue, glowing chords once more wound down Garrison's left arm and came together to form a glowing blue dagger in his hand. Staggered and injured, he flicked the blade with precision and sent it sailing toward Mavado. The weapon found its target without resistance as Jericho manifested back into the world, only to be greeted by a thudding impact upon his chest which was closely followed by a searing, overwhelming pain. The young man looked down and spotted the glowing dagger's handle which protruded from his chest, as its blade was buried deep into his heart.

Jericho collapsed to his knees, a look of pain and confusion in his eyes as he gripped the handle of the otherworldly weapon that had begun to rob him of life. His vision began to fade as he collapsed to his side, and in the midst of his fear he tried desperately to call out for Mavado's help once more. Garrison was now gone, replaced by Michael who rushed to Jericho's side and began to speak frantically to his friend, but his words were indiscernible and muffled as Jericho quickly slipped out of consciousness.

Chapter 4

Jericho felt cold to the core, as if the dead of winter had invaded his mind as he found himself standing back in the graveyard which had been a prominent location for so many of his dreams. He struggled to catch his breath, as each inhalation brought with it a jolt of pain which ripped through his chest; the dagger had followed him into his mind and was still protruding from his body, a symbol of the reality he had momentarily escaped.

He reached for the handle and pulled the dagger free, and as he did the weapon flaked apart and dissolved into fine dust, carrying off into the air and vanishing among the gravestones. He began to shuffle forward and winced in pain as his wound ached with the same intensity in his dream as it had in the parking lot. It only took but a few moments before he heard another voice flash across his mind, not the voice of his dark protector but, rather surprisingly, it was the voice of a woman, unfamiliar yet comforting, which prayed in a language which was unknown to Jericho.

His eyes opened up into consciousness, and Jericho found them affixed towards the ceiling as he was lying on his back. The agony which gripped his body suddenly became an afterthought, as his attention became fully captivated by what moved into view; an exceptionally beautiful woman was seated beside him and slowly leaned into his sight picture. She had a light complexion which was contrasted by jet black hair that curled and billowed down her shoulders, surrounding a face which was the most perfect that Jericho had ever laid eyes on. Her irises glowed blue with the same intensity as Garrison's, yet lacked the same aggression and instead were disarming.

Her lips were pink and full, and they moved smoothly and rapidly as her healing words cascaded down and washed over him. She prayed with thoughtful determination, as if knowing that every passing word would be answered without contest. Jericho was mesmerized by her gaze; everything else drifted away as if this beautiful stranger was all that existed in the world. Her unknown words were his lullaby, and his eyelids grew heavy as she faded into darkness once more.

He returned to his position in the graveyard, still moving forward among the tombstones he clutched his chest just above where the dagger had previously rested; the pain which had gripped him so ravenously was now beginning to subside little by little and he felt his strength slowly beginning to return. He could still hear the voice of the woman in the midst of his dream, her indiscernible words hung faintly in the air as he pressed forward towards the pool of water where in dreams past he had stopped to observe his reflection.

Unlike his childhood dreams, however, it was not his own reflection which he saw when he arrived at the edge of the water; instead it was Mavado who stared back at him through the pool. The two looked upon each other for a moment before the surface began to boil rapidly and obscure Jericho's view. The water continued bubbling and boiling with growing intensity, until suddenly Mavado emerged from the surface, rising up from the boiling pool and into the air like a great winged serpent.

Mavado hovered over the pool, his great black wings flapping slowly but with just enough force to keep him stationary; his eyes burned with their golden glow and black smoke twisted off his body and vanished into the air as he simply floated in position and stared silently at Jericho. The woman's voice, which previously was almost a whisper, was now rapidly increasing in volume. As her voice grew louder, Mavado's face began to transform; his eyes became sunken and dark and his cheekbones grew gaunt as each word seemed to induce decay in his body.

As his appearance continued to deteriorate, he slowly opened his mouth and expelled what could only be described as the most painful, deafening scream Jericho had heard since the terrible night his mother was murdered. Mavado lifted his hands upward and clutched the sides of his head in pain; covering his ears he quickly rocketed into the sky to escape the sound, disappearing out of sight in mere seconds.

"Come back to us . . ."

Jericho heard the woman's voice once more; the unknown tongues were now gone and the voice was crystal clear. He turned away from the pool, and in doing so he came face to face with the beautiful woman once more, who was now standing only a few feet in front of him. She was beautiful in a pure, innocent way, yet in a contradictory manner, also seemed to exude a degree of sensuality. She stepped forward and placed her hands on Jericho's chest, and as she leaned in her lips moved ever so close to his as she spoke again, "Come back to me . . ."

He opened his eyes and the beautiful woman came back into view, but this time Jericho was not dreaming. He was again lying on his back and looking up at her, as she was still seated beside him and leaning in as she pressed her hands gently on his chest. Jericho initially sat up with a startled reaction, but the woman quickly reacted in an effort to calm him.

"Shhhhh, it's all right," she gently whispered as Jericho leaned back down and worked to relax his mind. He was now in Michael's office, resting on the cot which was located in the back corner of the room. Michael had been standing near the doorway; his presence in the room had previously gone unnoticed until he quickly approached Jericho in response to his friend's sudden awakening. The usual relaxed look which would adorn Michael's face had been replaced by one of genuine concern.

"How are you feeling, bro? Looks like Annabel got you fixed up good as new." Michael uttered the words in an uncomfortable, sheepish tone which was a result of the feelings of guilt and relief that equally permeated his thoughts. Jericho looked down at his chest to find his shirt was missing, along with the mystical weapon which had plunged into his body and threatened his existence. He ran his fingers across the newly formed scar upon his chest and remained in quiet awe, admiring the many week's worth of healing which had miraculously transpired in a mere matter of hours.

"I didn't mean for this to happen Jericho . . . I should've stopped him . . . I should've done it sooner. This wasn't supposed to happen, you almost died." Michael was not the type to mince words, but he struggled to express his regret in that moment; his decisions had nearly cost Jericho his life, which was a thought that did not sit well with a man who had spent most of his career ensuring the safety of those he was charged to look after. No long-term damage had been done, but the fact that any harm at all had been done to Jericho under his watch was unacceptable in his eyes.

Jericho felt his strength begin to return, and slowly he sat himself up and looked about the room. Michael's office was as simple and organized as its owner; a wooden desk, three small chairs and the cot were the extent of its furnishings. Important files and bills were locked in the desk drawers, and upon the desk sat a day planner, a reading lamp, some stationary, and probably the most basic home computer known to man. The computer was prehistoric by present-day standards, with a boxy monitor and large tower that hummed loudly when in use. Michael only used it for bookkeeping as it worked well enough, and he had the peace of mind of knowing that any burglars would most likely leave it behind due to its non-existent street value.

Two windows ran the length of the wall next to the entrance of the office and were dressed in gray aluminum mini blinds which had definitely seen better days. The blinds were bent on the edges as if too many visitors had accidently leaned against them, and were always twisted open to allow Michael to see out into the gym floor. As Jericho looked upon the open blinds, he suddenly noticed two strangers through the window who were standing just outside the entrance to Michael's office.

Jericho's eyes were drawn first to the man standing with his back to the doorway, as the sheer size of this man made him quite difficult to miss. The top of his head nearly reached the top of the doorway, which Jericho deduced would put his height around 6'6 or 6'7. The man was thickly muscled with a bodybuilder physique, dark complexion, and long dreadlocks which were pulled back into a ponytail. He stood in gray athletic gear with his arms folded as he spoke to the second stranger in low tones, too low for Jericho to make out the conversation which the two were sharing.

Jericho could see the profile of the second man through the window, who height-wise was very much the opposite of the first man as he could not have been taller than 5'10." The second man was light-skinned with medium-length, sandy-brown hair that matched the sandy-brown scruff which ran across his face and neck. While he lacked the impressive stature of the first man, the second had the appearance of a lean athletic build and a face with strong, rugged features. Dressed in a gray sport coat with matching trousers and a black button up shirt, the second man would lift his arm occasionally to take a drag from cigarette which dangled from between his fingers as he continued his conversation with the first.

Michael himself was a bit of a chain smoker, which made the actions of the stranger smoking within the confines of the building permissible, although Jericho always found the hint of smoke which permeated the gym to be a bit repulsive. Jericho observed the two for a moment before the second man made eye contact with him through the window. The man's eyes darted to the first man and then back to Jericho as he continued to speak. The first man then turned his head to look back into the office, apparently having been alerted to Jericho's now conscious state.

"Don't worry about them, they're friends of mine," Michael continued as the two men stepped through the doorway and approached Jericho. "The big one is named Sunday, and the little one is Reggie."

With a look of amused agitation, the second man replied quickly with a pronounced British accent, "Little one? I'm about as tall as you, Mike; everybody looks little next to Sunday." Turning his attention from Michael to Jericho, Reggie continued, "The name's Reginald Hardy, but you can call me 'Reg' or 'Reggie' or 'Hey You' or 'Fella.' Whatever's easiest, I suppose."

"Sounds good, dude," Jericho replied with a bewildered look which was induced by Reggie's immediate attempts at humor. Reggie then proceeded to take another drag from his cigarette, with the very action inciting Sunday to immediately reach over and snatch the cigarette from Reggie's hand.

"This room's way too small for that poison Reg, you are free to abuse your own body, but leave the kid alone. He's been through enough already." Sunday's voice bellowed out, deep and booming yet still smooth and eloquent; he reached down and put the cigarette out on the sole of his shoe before proceeding to flick the remnants into a nearby wastebasket, after which he turned his attention back to Jericho.

"Hello, my young friend, I'm Sunday Brockington. That's right, Sunday, after the most glorious day of the week, the day in which we congregate to hear the word of the Lord." Sunday spoke the words with a warm, disarming grin as he extended his hand forward in a more formal greeting. Jericho responded in kind, and the ensuing handshake looked more like one between a child and a man as Sunday's hand dwarfed Jericho's considerably, a subtle punctuation to the fact that Sunday was surely a rare physical specimen.

"Tell me, son, do you know the Lord Jesus?" Spoken with great confidence, it was clear to Jericho that Sunday was either a preacher or a preacher's son.

"Yes sir, I do." Jericho's response was a bit reserved as, although he had attended church quite regularly as a boy, through the years he had found less and less time for it until eventually he stopped the practice altogether. Jericho had drifted so far away from a church home that, although he did believe in God, the question Sunday posed actually made him a bit uncomfortable.

Jericho's eyes glanced from Sunday to Reggie, and then back to Annabel who was still seated on the cot beside him. When Jericho's eyes returned to meet Annabel's, he was surprised to see that her irises no longer glowed bright blue but instead were an ordinary brown. She spoke again, but this time her voice lacked the smooth and angelic tone which had previously commanded Jericho's attention. While still appealing in its own right, the sound of her voice was distinctly human.

"Last introduction for now, my name is Delia. I'm glad you're all right; it was a pretty close call, but Annabel's quite the miracle worker." Delia smiled and brushed her hand across Jericho's upper shoulder, gently running her fingernails across his skin as he was still shirtless from having his wound tended to. Her demeanor was distinctly different from Annabel's, as Delia seemed almost flirtatious and carefree, a stark contrast from the focused healer who had entranced Jericho only minutes before.

"Heads up, brother!" shouted Michael as he tossed a t-shirt which had been retrieved from Jericho's locker. Jericho caught the shirt and swiftly put it on as he stood to his feet and turned his attention back to Delia.

"I don't mean to sound rude or ungrateful . . . umm thank you, Annabel . . . and Delia," he turned to face Reggie and Sunday as he continued, "and Reggie, Sunday . . . But why are all of you here?" Jericho felt confusion continuing to build in his mind, which was an understandable byproduct of his near-death experience. The sudden appearance of the three strangers, one of whom was confirmed to possess supernatural abilities, only added to his mounting anxiety.

Reggie was quick to offer Jericho a casual response; "Well, mate, I figured that would be pretty obvious by now. You got stabbed, so Michael had Garrison sound the alarm and we all came running. Annabel patched you up and, well, Delia and Annabel are a bit of a package deal . . . eh, well, I guess you could say we all are, actually."

"So, the two of you are like Delia and Michael?"

"Well, I wouldn't say I'm anything like those two; he's a far more responsible bloke than me, and her knockers are much nicer than mine . . ."

"All right, Reggie, I don't think you're helping anymore. I'll take it from here." Michael interrupted, with frustration building in his voice towards Reggie's continued attempts at humor. Immediately recognizing this, Reggie's tone became more serious as he offered his apologies.
"Sorry boss, you know me. The man almost died after all, just trying to take the edge off the mood a bit." His reply was sheepish as he reached into his coat pockets and

retrieved a fresh cigarette with his right hand and his lighter with his left.

"On that note, I should probably chivvy on home." Reggie excused himself from the room, lit the cigarette and stepped outside the office and back into the main gym floor. As Reggie stepped out of the room, Sunday also chimed in, "I agree, I think it's time we all took our leave. I don't think there's much else we can contribute right now."

Delia stood up from the cot and quickly followed Reggie out of the office while Sunday turned to Jericho and addressed him directly, "Besides, difficult conversations are easier to digest when they occur between trusted friends. We'll let you and Michael discuss things, and if God wills it, you will see us again. I'll be praying for you Jericho, peace be with you." With that, Sunday joined Delia and Reggie outside and the three of them left the gym.

Jericho looked at Michael as his mind flooded with questions, yet struggled with where to begin. "Who are they? Who are you? What the hell are Garrison and Annabel?" While Jericho peppered him with questions, Michael proceeded to his desk, rummaged through the top drawer and retrieved both his and Jericho's keys.

"Bro, I'll tell you everything you want to know. I just need you to take what I tell you seriously, but judging by your experience with Mavado it actually shouldn't be too tough a pill to swallow." Michael tossed Jericho his truck keys, "It's late, and I got to head home and feed my dogs, but if you follow me over we will talk about everything there."

Jericho had failed to recognize the passage of time as it only felt as if it had been a few hours since his arrival, but as the two left the office and walked through the gym floor he saw that the previously broken windows had already been replaced. He glanced over at the wall clock to make note of the time. He had arrived at ten-thirty that morning, and it was now past eight in the evening.

The two stepped outside into the cool evening air, with Michael stopping to lock the door behind him as Jericho continued on towards his truck. He hopped into the cab and turned the engine over just as Michael climbed aboard his motorcycle and fired it up as well. The bike roared to life with a pavement-shaking, ear-splitting sound, and the two headed off down the street with Michael leading the way.

Jericho's stomach churned with anxiety as he reflected on all that had happened, and he grew even more anxious at the thought of what Michael was preparing to tell him. Another thought which also occurred to Jericho was the noticeable absence of Mavado. He had expected to hear the demon begin to whisper deep within his mind the moment the truck door closed, but the spirit was not heard or felt, providing Jericho with at least a measure of peaceful quiet amid the nerves. Peace for now, but peace which would surely be short-lived.

Chapter 5

Michael's home was about a forty-five minute drive from the gym, and the two locations certainly could not have been more contrasting. The gym was located closer to the downtown area, surrounded by office buildings and recessed a bit from the main street, and although the location was somewhat private it was still very urban as it was situated in the heart of the city. In intentional contrast, Michael's home was located in a rural area just outside the city which afforded him far more seclusion. He valued his privacy, and country living provided it far more effectively than city life, which made the longer commute completely worthwhile to Michael.

Jericho followed him down the interstate, exited and turned off onto a dirt road which led them another two miles into the countryside. Jericho had been to Michael's home a few times before when his foster father had visited, as well as with the fight team for an occasional cookout or team-building activity, so he was familiar with the area; his nerves became more rattled as they drew closer to their destination and peaked as the property came into view.

The house itself was a rather large single-story home which sat on one acre of well-maintained property, with only a few neighboring homes dotted along the dirt road. The home had belonged to Michael's father who had passed away several years prior, and after retirement Michael returned to his childhood residence and began slowly renovating the property in his spare time. While it was a large place for a widower to live on his own, the extra rooms were often put to good use as his three sons and four grandchildren would visit regularly. On this day, however, he was not entertaining any guests, which was fortuitous considering the nature of the impending discussion.

They pulled off the road and onto the path which led up to the front door, and after a few seconds they parked and headed inside. The interior of the home was unremarkable. Michael had done extensive repair work to address the wear and tear within, yet did little with regard to performing a modern, updated remodel. The ultimate goal was to preserve the original feel of the home, and the only modernization Jericho could see was the rather large flat-screen television in the living room, as Michael appreciated upgrades in technology when it meant better viewing of football games and boxing matches.

Large, comfortable couches and a simple coffee table encircled the TV, and a medium-sized kitchen was positioned just off the living room. As Michael passed through the house and exited out the back door to feed his dogs, Jericho made himself at home and took a seat at the small, oak dining table in the kitchen. Michael was done in a flash and entered back into the house through the kitchen, stopping briefly to hang his jacket up on a hook beside the door before reengaging Jericho.

"Can I get you something? Water or juice or . . . I think I got tea around here somewhere," Michael walked to the refrigerator, opened the door and began to scan his eyes back and forth.

"No thanks Mike, I'm good for now." Jericho always found it strange how often people seemed to be unfamiliar with the contents of their own refrigerators, as whenever he was offered a drink, the host usually had a hint of doubt in their voice regarding what exactly was available. "Well, I definitely need a beer . . . or ten. After today I think I earned it."

Michael pulled two bottles of beer from the fridge, shut the door and took a seat at the head of the table, with Jericho seated to his immediate left as he continued,

"They're both for me, by the way; you've still got a couple of years to go before you start wrecking your liver." Michael twisted the top off one beer, took a hearty swing, and rested the bottle back on the table before taking a moment of silence to simply stare off into space. The moment was quite brief, as Jericho's anxiety would no longer be held back and implored him to speak.

"What the hell is going on? I can barely believe that what happened today actually happened. Who were those people at the gym? What the hell is Garrison? I almost got killed today, and I'm not even sure what I did wrong. I feel like I should be running and hiding somewhere."

Jericho was not even sure where to begin; he simply poured out thoughts and questions which had been brewing in his mind for the past hour ". . . How long has Garrison possessed you?"

"Whoa, slow down there bud! Those questions all add up to one long story, but first off, I'm not 'possessed' anymore than you are possessed by Mavado. In the end, I make the decision on what Garrison is or isn't allowed to do; I get to decide what happens. Now, the whole stabbing thing today was more bad timing than anything else. Trust me; if I had realized you pulled the reins, I would've done the same."

"Pulled the reins?"

"Yeah, you know, pulled the reins. Took back control; the host decides how long the spirit stays in the world, so when we choose to come back out they don't have no choice. Which means the most important rule is to never, ever trade places during a fight." Michael stood and walked over to the coat he had hung up by the door and retrieved his pack of cigarettes and lighter before returning to his seat at the table. He removed a cigarette and placed it between his lips, lit the end and continued to speak. "Now the real question is why YOU were able to choose at all."

Jericho's expression was one of confusion, as every statement by Michael seemed to generate more questions than answers. "What do you mean? You said that we decide how long they stay in the world."

Michael took a deep drag from his cigarette and nodded his head affirmatively. "Yes 'we,' meaning me, Delia, Sunday, and Reggie. The spirits within us have rules, Jericho; they're not at all like this spirit of yours." Michael took another swing of his beer and continued, "I suppose that don't mean much to you unless you know the whole story, so I'll do my best to explain. I first met Garrison about nine years ago, just a short time after I retired from the army. The service pretty much defined my life, and as much as I had been ready to call it a career I felt like I wasn't making a difference anymore just being a civilian. That's why I opened the gym; it gave me the chance to do some good and keep the neighborhood kids out of trouble."

Michael took a drag from his cigarette and continued as Jericho listened quietly. "One night after we closed, I was locking up the place when I got jumped by some gangbangers; young kids, couldn't have been older than eighteen or nineteen, and there were about a half dozen of them. I did my best to fight them off, got in a few licks of my own too, but they were kicking the shit out of me pretty good. All of a sudden I heard this horn blare out of the darkness, and then a shattering sound like . . . like someone had dropped a jar or bowl or something."

With a reflective expression, Michael took another drink of his beer, and then a smile crept across his face as he continued. "The sound made them stop, and they got all afraid and confused. Then for some reason they turned and started brawling with each other. This went on for a bit before they scattered off on their own separate ways; after they had gone I heard a voice in the darkness ask me if I was all right. I asked who was there, then felt a hand touch my shoulder, and when it did my strength came back all of a sudden and I felt better. I heard the voice again, this time it asked if I was ready to make a real difference, the way I used to. I looked around, but no one was there, and then the voice was gone."

Michael finished the first beer quickly and cracked open the second as he continued his story. "For the next six nights I heard the same voice inside my head during my dreams. I thought I was bat shit crazy and got to believing I was losing my mind—until the seventh day, when Garrison showed up in person and knocked at my front door here." Jericho listened to Michael's story with great interest; his experience with Mavado invading his dreams and lurking within his mind had always seemed unique, so hearing of another who could relate to his plight piqued his curiosity.

Michael took a final drag from his cigarette before extinguishing it in the ash tray on the table, and Jericho used the break to interject.

"What did he want from you? Why is he here?"

"He wanted the chance to touch the world again. You see, Garrison was once just an ordinary man, a military man like me. But since he isn't a living person anymore he needs help from someone who is. You know how the Bible says salvation is a gift? Well it is, but the chance to be something more, something special? That's got to be earned. Garrison is what they call a Watcher, these are people who have salvation and have passed on to heaven, but are given the chance to become honored angels."

Jericho smiled a bit as he responded, "So Garrison's trying to be an angel? This is his audition?"

"In so many words, yeah, that's pretty much it. Some angels are chosen right off the bat, but for others there still remains a responsibility to make up for old mistakes. Before Garrison can be honored, he's got to prove he's learned from the wrong choices he made during his life. To do that he's got to work with, and mentor, someone who's still alive in the world. Garrison chose me, if I would have him of course, cuz if I had said "no" Garrison would've been on his way. Once the pact is made the Watchers can only intervene when allowed to by their host. I choose how long Garrison stays in the world, and the same is true for Delia, Sunday, and Reggie. You already met Annabel. Sunday is joined with a Watcher named Fortunado, while Reggie's goes by the name Ignavus."

Jericho began to chuckle a bit as Michael paused to take another drink, "Fortunado and Ignavus? These guys have terrible names . . ."

"Well, if you haven't realized it by now, the Watchers don't use the names they had when they were alive. They aren't supposed to reveal who they are until an hour of God's choosing, kind of a 'when the time is right' sort of thing."

"So they remember the life they had before they died?"

"Most do, some don't. I don't really know a whole lot about how that works. Garrison remembers his life, but he doesn't share much information. He tells stories to get his point across, and from what he tells me I figure he lived a long way back. But he hasn't let the cat out of the bag just yet."

"That sounds like Mavado," replied Jericho. "He claims to have existed for thousands of years, and I don't think 'Mavado' is actually his real name."

Michael took another drink and responded, "See, now that's what's wrong with your situation Jericho; Mavado

79

wasn't sent by God, but for some reason he acts like a Watcher. Garrison tells me that Mavado's a demon. Now I don't know if that means he's a fallen angel, or somebody who was damned for what he did in his former life, but demons possess people. They usually pick those who dabble in the occult or are mentally ill or psycho, making big promises of power until they are allowed to enter the host. But after that, the host has no say, no control, and basically becomes a prisoner in their own body, being taken over at will and sometimes never getting the opportunity to step back into the world again. Demons are arrogant too, usually using old names they were known by because they want to be remembered and take glory for themselves. That's what I mean by the Watchers have rules. They are here to mentor and atone, to help expand God's army in preparation for that last great battle. As for demons, they don't have a real purpose. Sure you could say they are united in rebelling against God, but for the most part, they have no loyalty to each other or even the Devil."

Jericho looked a bit puzzled as he listened to Michael's explanation. "So since God is all powerful, why doesn't he just wipe out all the demons? Why go through all the trouble?" Michael smiled upon hearing this, and his response was quick and confident. "Well, I don't think I can speak for God, but I would say that God is good to his word. It's like when Jesus said that God could've sent his angels to rescue him when he was being arrested, but God didn't because it was happening that way to fulfill the prophecy. God's got a plan, and I sure as hell am not smart enough to figure it out, but he lets things happen the way he said it would so we will know it's him doing it."

Michael stood up from the table, walked to the stove and switched the burner on under a large pot which was already resting on the stove-top as he continued to speak.

"We're heading towards Armageddon, Jericho. It's coming soon, and like it or not, there's no stopping it. How we get there is a bit foggier, so I prefer to go with the flow."

Jericho's expression was curious and concerned, "So this is it? This is the end of the world? Mavado said the world was changing, but he also said things aren't set in stone, and that the way the Bible talks about the world ending isn't for certain. He told me that God's victory wasn't guaranteed." Michael walked from the stove to the fridge and opened the door, reached in and retrieved a large plastic tub which contained what appeared to Jericho to be a stew of some kind. He removed the lid and poured the contents from the container into the large pot and gave them a few slow stirs with a large wooden spoon.

"Not a guarantee? Ha! There's probably no guarantee more solid than the end of the world. Mavado's just trying to twist your thinking." Michael gave the stew a final stir and covered the pot with a large glass lid. Turning his attention back to Jericho, he continued his thought.

"We all know how the big story ends, but there are a million stories on the road to Armageddon. A million skirmishes which all play their part in setting things right, stories most people will never hear...but that don't make them any less important." Michael walked back to the table and took his seat once more, "That's what we're doing; me and Reggie and Sunday and Delia, and many more like us. We do our part to insure things go according to plan."

Jericho felt his heartbeat quicken at Michael's statement; the man was speaking of true purpose, purpose which Jericho knew had been lacking throughout his young life. "I can help you Michael. I can be a part of this with you,

81

with them. You've seen Mavado, you know what he can do, let me be a part of what you're doing."

Michael shook his head and interrupted, "No, Jericho, that's out of the question. This isn't a club which anybody can just join up with. There's a whole hierarchy, and Garrison has his team who reports to him, and he gets his orders from someone else who gets their orders from someone else. Without getting too specific, Mavado isn't a part of their plan. Hell, he's what we're fighting against for crying out loud!"

Jericho felt his anger and frustration return at Michael's rejection, "What if you're wrong? Not everything is black and white; Mavado is proof of that. If his behavior isn't like other demons, then there have to be other exceptions out there too. What if him being here, joining with me was supposed to happen? He saved me from my father the night I should've died. God didn't stop him from intervening, and Mavado kept his word, and has looked after me ever since. Is it possible he can atone for past decisions, just like Garrison and these others are trying to do?"

Michael stared back at Jericho, mulling over the statement with thoughtful attention before responding. "Well, there's a big difference in what atonement means for Mavado and what it means for Garrison and the Watchers. Whatever choices Mavado made condemned him to damnation, while Garrison is already saved through the faith he showed when he was alive. Mavado's soul can't be saved now. It's too late and he is what he is. Garrison's proving he's learned from past mistakes in order to be elevated to a higher position; his soul isn't on the line. Those are two very different things."

Ever growing in both persistence and frustration, Jericho continued his plea. "You said it yourself that you can't speak for God. Either way, Mavado isn't going anywhere since he and I are stuck together, and if I can use him to do some good, then I want to have that chance. Maybe I can't be a part of the team officially, but what's wrong with me just helping out? Besides, it will give you a chance to keep an eye on Mavado, and if anything goes wrong you and the team can stop him." Jericho took a deep breath, stood up from his seat and concluded his appeal, as he was desperate to sell Michael on his idea. "I need your help Michael, please help me make a difference like you do."

Michael's expression remained unchanged as he pondered all that had been suggested. Taking a few moments to wrestle with his thoughts, he addressed Jericho one final time before he took his leave.

"I'm sure the others won't agree, and to tell you the truth I really don't trust Mavado, but I'm willing to give you a chance. I need you to realize something first, though; what we do is no joke. We fight against some terrible things, the worst of the worst, and you're going to be in the toughest spot possible as you'll be asking Mavado to fight his own kind, and how long do you think he's going to want to do that? Especially since the Watchers won't exactly roll out the welcome wagon for him, and they probably won't think of him as any better than what we fight. You're going to find yourself pretty much alone. I'm worried that the little support you get won't be enough, and when you feel the darkness closing in on you, who are you going to lean on?"

"Look Mike, I've already spent most of my life in the darkness; doing this will help me bring some light to the world, to my world. I need this to make me feel normal, to try and make something good from all the bad stuff that's happened in my life. You are the one who can help me do that, so please help me." Jericho's face was lined with distress as he made the plea to Michael, who looked back at his friend with concern in his own expression.

Michael could only muster "All right," which was all the affirmation that Jericho needed.

In spite of Michael's apprehension, he understood that Jericho did need his help, so he went against both his better judgment and the advice of Garrison, who had been whispering his own disapproving opinions within Michael's mind. Neither of those things mattered to the former soldier, for his friend was in need. Something even deeper within his heart gave him the feeling that, in spite of appearances to the contrary, Jericho was indeed meant to help them.

The two shook hands and spoke a few parting words before Jericho headed outside, climbed into the cab of his truck, and started his trip home. Michael's words still permeated Jericho's mind as he headed down the dark, winding road which would lead him back to the interstate. He knew Michael was an honest man, as good to his word in much the same way he believed Mavado to be. As different in perspective and morality as Mavado and Michael may have been, Jericho believed that honor was one trait the two did have in common. The thought inspired confidence in Jericho; he felt a sense of calm, of an almost excited eagerness and anticipation for the first time towards the possibility of what his future could hold. So he headed off into the night, filled with hope as he returned home with thoughts of a new beginning stirring his imagination.

Only a few hundred miles away, however, an entirely different scene was unfolding; one which stirred not thoughts of hope, but feelings of despair and fear. They were thoughts which belonged to a girl of no more than twenty years, who suddenly awoke from a terrible dream, or what she had hoped beyond all hope was a terrible dream. Regrettably, her newfound consciousness only confirmed her fears, as she found herself lying upon an old mattress in a cold, empty room.

The place was unfamiliar, certainly not her bedroom or any room within her home, and her hands were bound behind her back with duct tape which was wrapped so tightly that she could barely feel her fingers anymore. She twisted her wrists in an effort to free herself as her vision acclimated to the dark surroundings, yet the struggle was futile as she did not possess the strength to break freed from the bonds. A single window provided a bit of illumination, as a few beams of moonlight pierced the window and revealed only shapes and unreadable figures in the midst of the shadows.

She heard the sound of creaking footsteps as something approached the door from outside. The doorknob rattled and twisted forcefully as the door swung open to reveal a large, hooded figure which swept into the room and was upon her in an instant. The hooded figure reached out a massive hand and took hold of her, its fingers seized and intertwined with her long brown hair, digging in down to her scalp to secure a tight grip. The figure turned away from the girl without hesitation and stepped back through the doorway, ripping her body from the mattress and pulling her along the floor behind it.

Her scalp burned with pain as she let out a series of terrible screams into the darkness; she crashed with a thud to the concrete floor and dragged across its rough surface, which skinned her back and arms as she continued to scream for help. Yet her pleas were useless; there was no stirring outside or noise of traffic to hint at an imminent rescue. Only the massive hooded figure, a giant whose total stature was shielded by his cloak and the surrounding darkness, appeared to be within earshot of her cries.

The giant released its grip on the girl, bringing her pain to an abrupt halt in what appeared to be the center of a large, empty warehouse. The windows along the walls were covered in dirt and soot which obscured a clear outside view, but allowed the exterior lighting to provide a measure of illumination to the events which were about to unfold. Tears of agony fell rapidly from the eyes of the girl as she was confronted with an unknown terror, one which would surely be revealed momentarily.

"Please . . . Please, let me go,"

Her words cracked through her tears, words she knew would go unacknowledged and unheeded, but ones which she nevertheless felt compelled to speak.

"Do not be afraid, dear girl, for I intend to release you." It was now a calm, clear voice of a man which echoed unexpectedly from the shadows, yet did not emanate from the hooded figure but from a hidden spectator who in darkness had observed the proceedings. She looked about the room from her position on the floor and searched for the source of the voice, and then saw another shadowy figure was slowly approaching her.

He stepped into the dim lighting, which revealed the face of a balding man in his mid thirties. He was quite plain in appearance with very ordinary features, neither attractive nor ugly but was rather unremarkable; a look which would blend in to any crowd and a face which could be passed a dozen times on the street and never noticed. A type of stealth in plain sight which most would consider a disadvantage, but for those with a more sinister purpose the trait would certainly be ideal.

"I don't know who you are," she replied in confusion.

"But I know you; I know the kind of girl you are. You seek to hold yourself to a higher standard, to be pure in mind, spirit, and body. You wear a symbol of purity on your finger so that all may know of your promise; but naturally, there is only one way to really know if your purity holds true."

With those words the man stepped forward toward the girl, crossing through the beams of moonlight which cut across the warehouse. She recoiled with ever intensifying fear, as the closer he drew to her the more discernible he became, until the presence of a small knife clutched in his right hand was revealed. She again began to scream out for help as he grabbed her by the arm, turned her over onto her stomach and pushed down on her back with his left hand to hold her steady. The knife slashed down and stuck into the back of her jeans, sawing down through the waistband to create a notch. She understood what was unfolding, what she was about to endure from this violent stranger, and so she began to thrash wildly. She refused to go quietly or make things easy for her tormenting captor.

The giant leapt forward from the shadows with surprising quickness, knelt down in front of the girl and put his massive hand on the back of her head and pushed downward, flattening the girl against her right cheek and driving her into the cold concrete floor. She stared out into the darkened corners of the warehouse, unable to move her head or neck as the strength of the giant was too great.

She felt the hands of the bald man grasp at the notch, a feeling which was quickly followed by the sounds of ripping denim. Every sense she experienced overwhelmed her with pain and disgust; her nostrils were filled with the dust of the warehouse floor, her neck and head strained under the force of the hand of the hooded figure while the hands of the bald man clawed to expose her. Her ears were flooded with the unmistakable sound of clinking metal, as his belt unbuckled in preparation for what was next to come. She felt her muscles burning, wilting with exhaustion and strain from her continued resistance. Her spirit was willing, yet her body could fight no more.

She let out a terrible gasp, as pain enveloped her and shot through her body like a dagger. Indeed, the ring she wore was not for show; the girl had remained true to her promise of purity, purity which was now stolen away with each brutal thrust from her attacker. His weight crushed her to the floor, plunging deeper and ripping her apart without mercy until she no longer had even the strength to cry out; she had screamed so much her voice no longer gave sound, but only produced muffled whimpers through her tears.

The hooded giant spoke quietly and rapidly in a language which was unknown to the girl, and while his voice rang out with intense purpose and focus, it was directed at neither the girl nor her attacker. With his free hand, the giant grabbed the finger of the girl which held the small golden purity ring and violently stripped the ring loose. He then clutched the ring tightly in his own hand as he continued to speak quickly and intensely, as the bald man continued his terrible deed.

The girl felt the thrusts of her attacker grow with intensity. They increased in power and speed, and then ceased abruptly; her body was in a state of shock, and fought to cope with the trauma it had endured by growing numb to the pain and to everything surrounding it. It was in that very moment that the girl wished to feel nothing, even if it meant she would be taken from this world. Abandoning her life would be a small price to pay, if in exchange she would instead find peace amid the darkness. The bald man put his lips close to her ear and whispered softly, "We are now one my dear; you and I are a part of each other. All that is yours is now mine, and I thank you for your precious gift of life."

The knife plunged into her side, yet she only felt the impact of the blow and not the pain; a small touch of mercy as the bald man repeated the act again and again. With every strike, he chipped away at her life. The girl felt herself slipping away from the world; with a thankful heart she welcomed eternity, and with it the relief from her suffering which would surely be found. The hooded giant continued to speak with one hand on her head while the other clutched her ring, and as the girl passed from the world his voice grew silent. The ring in his hand had undergone a subtle transformation, and now revealed a faint glimmer which it had not previously carried.

Both men stood to their feet as the giant stretched his hand forward to offer the shimmering ring to the bald man, who took the ring and marveled at its new glimmer with silent exhilaration. The giant spoke again, but this time in English and with a deep, gravelly voice.

"Another success, Lord Monroe; that makes three..."

The bald man rolled the ring between his fingers, still gazing at it in an almost trance-like state. He looked up at the giant and responded, "Three are complete, but three more are needed before we achieve true success. Tell the men to find me another, and bury this one with the others."

Chapter 6

Jericho sat in the cab of his pickup truck and impatiently strummed his fingers on the steering wheel in an effort to speed the passage of time. He was now twenty-three years old, a little more than four years removed from the fight between Mavado and Garrison and the pact that followed which he had believed would bring his life a sense of true purpose. He sat in the truck alone as the chatter of sports talk radio carried on from his speakers, yet the banter from the panel of prognosticators faded into the background as his mind was presently distracted by more important matters.

Four years is by no means an extended period of time, yet Jericho's physical appearance had evolved quite significantly; a reflection of the toll his body had paid for the reckless lifestyle he had gradually adopted. His face was peppered with a fair amount of scruff, his hair was short yet still a bit messy, and his eyes were adorned with lines and dark circles that gave him the appearance of perpetually lacking rest. He was still athletic in build, but had filled his frame out considerably and looked far more formidable than his nineteen-year-old self. Formidable, but far less healthy than in his youth, as he was nursing a bit of a hangover which was the result of the previous night's overindulgences; enjoying the nightlife had become a frequent occurrence, one which started slowly enough, but over time crept up on Jericho until it dominated a significant portion of his time.

He drank for all the wrong reasons; to regulate his mood, and to deal with the inevitable stress which responsibility brings. He also drank to cope with Mavado, as the two had grown to disagree with each other's philosophies more frequently as time passed by, and Jericho had even begun to develop a bit of resentment toward the demon who was so universally spurned by all who knew of his existence. Mavado's rejection naturally had meant Jericho's as well, which ultimately resulted in his adoption of a more isolated lifestyle, as those who knew his secret would always hold suspicion of the demon he harbored within.

Now in most cases, the opportunity to listen in on the latest sports topics and debates would have been an enjoyable prospect to Jericho, yet at this particular moment as he waited in the truck his mind was overly distracted.

"They've been gone way too long; it's been almost an hour. What's the holdup? Maybe something happened?"

Thoughts swirled within his mind as he wrestled with the prospect of leaving his position and tracking down the others, but he also knew that any rogue actions could potentially alienate his greatest advocate in Michael, who had ordered him to remain in the truck unless called for. So he decided to remain in wait, and instead checked his GPS pager to ensure it was still functioning properly; the pager was his only mode of contact with the rest of the team, and he kept it positioned on the dashboard and directly in front of his field of vision so as not to miss any incoming request for assistance.

The consequence of insubordinate behavior had begun to matter less and less to Jericho, however, as he had envisioned an entirely different situation when Michael agreed to allow him to "make a difference." Jericho had imagined he would be commanding Mavado in pursuit of powerful enemies on an almost daily basis, that he would be fighting alongside Garrison and other Watchers in a brotherhood united against evil. The reality could not have been further from Jericho's expectations, as confrontations with demons occurred infrequently and did require a measure of investigation, research, and planning before taking place.

The process was a grind much like any other job, with the key difference being that no one pays you to battle against evil. Everyone on the team retained traditional employment as well, which meant whatever free time they had available was spent together to identify new targets and coordinate assaults. It was a slow-moving endeavor as most demons chose to travel alone, which resulted in significant work conducted for a minimal payoff.

The official team was still small, consisting only of Michael, Sunday, Reggie, and Delia, while Jericho operated as a freelancer of sorts. From time to time they would collaborate with other Watchers or provide assistance to another team, but this was an infrequent occurrence as there was a significant amount of resistance from the other Watchers toward both Jericho and Mavado's inclusion.

While Garrison reluctantly honored Michael's commitment, the same could not be said of other Watchers or of Garrison's commander; Mavado was viewed by them all as a wolf in sheep's clothing, not to be trusted or relied upon. Garrison too held his own suspicions, which resulted in Mavado primarily being kept on standby and only called upon in dire situations.

This sentiment was the very reason Jericho found himself waiting alone in the cab of his truck. In nearly four years, Mavado's involvement in combating demons had been extremely limited. The number of manifestations and interventions by Mavado could actually be counted on two hands, which was a primary point of aggravation for Jericho as he resented being relegated to a "break glass in case of emergency" role. To have tremendous power lurking within him, yet a limited opportunity to take advantage of it, seemed to be a colossal waste to Jericho.

In the times Mavado had been called upon, he dispatched the demons with incredible speed and efficiency. The effortless and destructive nature by which he operated in these confrontations only added to the lingering fear and apprehension the Watchers felt towards Mavado, as he had quickly developed the reputation of being unmatched in power by both Watcher and demon alike.

Jericho believed Reggie's assessment of his situation summed it up best: Reggie always worked to keep the mood light and would affectionately refer to the team as "God's Garage Band," due to the unpaid, informal, night and weekend nature of their work. This description was often scoffed at by Sunday, and resulted in follow-up comparisons by Reggie to justify his unofficial moniker.

One such instance stuck with Jericho, as Reggie stated, "Yeah, we're just like a garage band. Except our instruments are actually magical spirits. Oh, and Jericho's got the nicest spirit-guitar and is probably the best guitar player, but we hardly ever let him play, which is exactly like a real garage band; but we're kind enough to let him tag along and help us set up speakers and unload the truck. So, I guess that makes you 'God's Roadie,' doesn't it Jericho?"

Reggie's words were followed by hearty laughter from all present, including Jericho. While Reggie did not intend to actually cause offense, Jericho found that the comments, while funny and perhaps a bit over the top, were surprisingly accurate. With the alternative to his limited role being complete exclusion, however, Jericho reluctantly chose to obediently wait in the truck until summoned.

The cab of his truck was an absolute mess, a testament to the many hours Jericho had burned away while lying in wait. Papers were strewn on the floor along with various fast food wrappers, which were accompanied by a small pile of aluminum cans and Styrofoam cups. Although the interior was unquestionably dirty, overall the truck was well organized and constructed to meet Jericho's needs.

While it appeared stock and unremarkable, the truck had been highly modified for maximum protection. All windows were replaced with bulletproof glass, and door panels were reinforced with military grade armor plating. Engine, shocks, and suspension were all overhauled with high performance parts as Jericho viewed his truck the way he viewed himself; ordinary to the casual observer yet harboring powerful secrets within. Hidden power to Jericho provided a distinct advantage, as the lack of exposure allowed him to operate under the radar and avoid arousing suspicion.

One other important feature to the truck was the compartment underneath the front bench seat. It was there where Jericho would store items he did not wish for the casual observer or occasional state trooper to discover; notably two Japanese kodachi's, which are more commonly referred to as short swords. Aesthetically speaking they were beautiful weapons; the blades were highly polished and razor sharp, and the hilts were adorned with black and gold tribal designs. Along the length of each blade from hilt to tip ran an inscription in Latin which Mavado himself had mystically added to the blades. Translated into English, the inscription read, "I am the author and father of death, I have no equal," Jericho found Mavado's arrogant addition to the swords to be irritating at best, but there was no denying that when in the hands of the demon, the swords were truly unmatched.

The weapons were almost an extension of his body; Mavado would manifest through Jericho and project a measure of his power through the swords, causing the inscriptions to glow with an orange hue as his power amplified the blades beyond earthly limitation. The strength of the weapons in this state were uncharted; while this ability was not singular to Mavado as all spirits retained the ability to forge and amplify weapons to various degrees, Mavado's talent for possession was notably exceptional.

The relative quiet within the cab was instantly shattered as the GPS suddenly chimed and vibrated across the dashboard, causing Jericho's heart to accelerate at the highly anticipated alert. Although his ears had been tuned and eyes continually trained toward the device, the sound still managed to startle him as he grabbed the GPS and checked the alert. Michael's location within the neighborhood was displayed prominently on the screen, the signal that Mavado's assistance had become necessary. Jericho bolted from the truck with the GPS clutched in his right hand and broke into a full sprint, following the directions which led him down an alleyway that ran between two of the neighborhood homes.

Jericho had been waiting in a low income neighborhood which contained a number of foreclosed or condemned homes, some of which were notoriously used as drug houses or were inhabited by squatters. As demons would typically target addicts for possession, the group would quite often find themselves searching these areas of town first, as they made for a reasonable starting point when the team would go hunting without leads.

Upon arriving at potential locations, the responsibility would fall to Annabel to locate any demonic activity; all spirits shared an ability to sense the presence of other spirits to some degree, yet Annabel's power in this regard was heightened to the extent that she could identify others within a few square miles, and could even determine both the number of individual beings and the strength levels they possessed. The routine of the team was to arrive in the general vicinity of the spiritual activity together, and then Jericho would remain while the rest of the group broke off. Garrison believed it best that Jericho not know the exact location of the team unless absolutely necessary, as this would limit the chance of him taking the initiative to intervene should he be tempted to do so.

Fearing the worst, Jericho continued to sprint as he checked the GPS to ensure he was heading in the right direction. He glanced about to verify street signs as he rapidly pursued the stationary dot which represented Michael's location, continuing on his way and taking a left at the next cross street. When he made the turn, he slowed down his pace to a more relaxed jog as the team came into view. He saw Michael, not yet possessed by Garrison, standing on a lawn in front of a very dilapidated property, with boarded windows and visible structural damage.

Also present were Delia, Reggie and Sunday who were all currently in their manifested state and under the control of their respective spirits. Their manifestation was quickly revealed by their eyes, as Delia and Sunday's glowed with a bright blue iris, while Reggie's were lit by a glowing green hue. The change in eye color was the only notable difference carried by Reggie and Delia, while Sunday's transformation was also accompanied by a change to his hair; normally he sported a grouping of very long dreadlocks which were put together in a ponytail, but when Fortunado took control, his hair would unwind and straighten into a large mane of considerable length. The reason for this particular customization was a mystery, and if anything it created an even more intimidating sight on the already statuesque figure.

In spite of their possessed state, all three calmly stood on the lawn as if they were patiently waiting for Jericho's arrival. The brisk jog then transitioned to a fast walk as he approached Michael.

"I know you're eager to get some action, but pace yourself kid."

Michael's informal greeting was met with a matter of fact answer from Jericho, "Well, you took longer than you said, so when I got the call I assumed the worst," replied Jericho as he bent over at the waist and fought to catch his breath, ". . . so, what seems to be the problem?"

Michael turned from Jericho and faced the building as he began his briefing, "Well, we got a couple of problems.

First one is that Annabel says there are a dozen demons in this piece o' shit building, which is a bit strange as we don't usually find more than half that number of these guys together. The second problem is a new one too; we can't seem to get in the building. Oh, and before you act like a smartass and say, 'call a locksmith,' that isn't what I mean."

Jericho smiled at Michael's statement, as he was in fact planning a similar response before being beaten to the punch. "Well Michael, tell me what you actually mean and I'll do what I can to help."

Michael took a few steps forward to the porch and halted just before reaching the small set of steps which preceded it. "There's some kind of barrier here, and none of us can get any closer than this. It seems the demons inside are combining their power to keep us out, making some invisible field that our spirits can't break through or find a way around." Michael turned from the barrier and walked back towards Jericho. "We were thinking maybe Mavado won't have the same problem as maybe they won't recognize him as their enemy." Michael's gaze left Jericho and drifted back towards the condemned home as he continued to speak. "But you know, that would also mean he'd be on his own in there against whatever's waiting, but we can't get inside until this barrier's gone."

"Come now, Mr. Bradshaw, I did not believe you saw me as one who relied too often on the support of others, especially those who hold me in such little regard." Michael heard the voice and turned his head back toward Jericho to find his physical presence already completely replaced by Mavado, who looked fearsome yet dapper as always in his pinstripe suit.

"My apologies for arriving unannounced, yet the boy implored me to take his place; it would seem that young Jericho believes it better for me to hold the discussion, as I will also be the one assuming the risk. A very limited risk to be sure, but a risk nonetheless . . ."

Michael's eyes quickly illuminated with the glowing blue of Garrison's manifestation, and the voice that followed was the eloquent boom which Mavado was all too familiar with. "If that is the case, then I too will forgo a proper greeting, and instead give words toward your purpose here."

"Ah, and I almost expected you to break from your customary lack of courtesy . . ."

"You are to go inside and destroy the demons within, but leave one preserved for me to question. It is of paramount importance that we discover how they block us from entering, and for what reason they have chosen to band together. When you are finished, return control to Jericho and remain dormant until we summon you again. Are we clear?"

Mavado looked back at Garrison with an amused yet irritated expression; he understood Garrison held no trust toward him, and in truth yearned for his destruction as feverishly as any other Watcher. Even so, Mavado would not allow Garrison the satisfaction of seeing him draw offense from the rather condescending attitude he was being shown.

"I am, as always, a humble servant," said Mavado through his smile as he lowered his head slightly in a mock bow. He then reached into his jacket and searched near the inside breast pocket for a moment before withdrawing an empty hand, an action which wiped away his previously amused expression and replaced it with one of distinct displeasure.

"It would seem the boy forgot my swords in his haste to come to your rescue. Never fear, their absence is inconsequential." Mavado was also missing his large black wings, as Jericho had developed a tendency to limit Mavado's use of power when he was in his manifested state. This was meant to serve as a reminder to all that Jericho was the one who exercised the true control, yet even with restricted power Mavado was still more than a match against lower level spirits.

Slowly stepping forward toward the front porch, he arrived at the position where Michael had previously halted and also stopped. He reached his hand forward to see if it would collide with the invisible force which blocked the team from entering, and as his hand extended the air began to visibly ripple like the surface of a pond. No resistance against the demon occurred though, as the barrier yielded to his touch and his hand easily passed through to the other side. He stepped forward and passed his entire body through the invisible barrier, coming to a stop just in front of the main entrance. He halted momentarily, reached up and adjusted his tie as if he were a door to door salesman making his final appearance check, then lifted his hand upward as if to knock on the door and announce his presence.

As his knuckles touched the surface of the wood, the door reacted in an unexpectedly violent manner; detonating as if struck by a bomb, it exploded forward and splintered into a million fragments which shot through the dilapidated home. The interior was as run down as the exterior and shrouded in darkness, as the windows were covered in sheets of plywood and old blankets which had been taped up into makeshift curtains.

Mavado cautiously passed from the entrance and into the living area, which was devoid of furniture and partially demolished; large sections of carpet were missing, and sections of the wall contained holes or were completely lacking drywall. It was unmistakably a squatter's paradise and appeared to lack any occupants to the naked eye, yet Mavado could sense the presence of the spirits within and his confidence grew with every step, as he did not detect any powerhouses waiting in the shadows.

"Welcome brother, join us in refuge as we prepare to strike against the enemies who lurk outside our walls," whispered a shrill voice from the darkness. Mavado watched as a dozen dark figures suddenly came into view; some were standing while others knelt or were lying huddled on the floor, while still others clung to the ceiling and walls as if the home were a demonic beehive. They had laid claim to the place, infesting any drifters who trespassed on the property as it had been used as a drug house by many of the areas less reputable citizens. Those who chose to invade the home had found themselves invaded as well; it was a cruel bit of irony and a testament to the belief that one will ultimately reap what they sow.

"I had a brother many lifetimes ago, and I am quite certain that none of you are he. As for my safety, I can assure you that it is absolutely not in question. Yours, on the other hand, is most certainly debatable." Mavado's golden eyes glowed ominously in the dark as he responded to the greeting, while Jericho watched the scene unfold through the window in the study and felt the tingle of fear creep up his neck.

"I'm not going hold you back on this one, just do whatever is necessary." Mavado only smiled in acknowledgement of Jericho's comment, and while he appreciated the permission being granted, the demon knew a full exercise of his abilities in this instance was not required. The golden glow in his eyes grew several levels brighter as he channeled his strength; the action not only rattled the foundation of the building, but also shook the souls of its occupants as they realized the demon's intentions.

Garrison, Fortunado and Ignavus stood outside on the lawn together as Annabel stood off to the side a few yards behind everyone, but the rumbling of the house immediately caught the attention of all four Watchers. Annabel felt concern for Jericho's safety, knowing that he was essentially at the mercy of thirteen demons and would be without assistance from the team for as long as the barrier was in place.

She focused her energy towards the barrier and searched for weaknesses, but it had remained unchanged in strength for the duration of time since Mavado had passed through the doorway. Then suddenly she felt a small crack in the barrier; it grew and yielded others cracks which branched out and divided as the strength of the mystical structure began to wilt, sending her heart racing with a measure of relief. Her companions also felt the energy around the house begin to dissipate, and the three of them fanned out and took up positions on the lawn in preparation for an assault.

Annabel kept her position at the edge of the property as she assumed the most important role: containment and support. Her talents as a healer were unmatched, which usually placed her in the position of a field medic during conflicts. Not to say that she was helpless in battle, in fact she was adept at combat and could defend herself quite skillfully, but Annabel also had a supreme talent of illusion; the ability to disguise events which occurred in plain view, thereby keeping the activities of the group hidden from any passerby. Those in the neighborhood or driving down the street would see only an old home on an empty property; a projection of Annabel's imagination that shielded the world from the fantastic things which were about to unfold. The rumbling of the building was enough of a signal as Annabel lifted her hands and veiled the scene, while it would be up to the others to ensure their activities did not spill beyond the borders of her illusion.

The plywood covering the two large exterior windows of the home exploded outward, and the remnants were followed closely by the bodies of several demons which were forcefully expelled by Mavado. The first two were launched through and crashed to the lawn void of life, while the next three retreated of their own accord to escape the unseen carnage Mavado was unleashing inside. Fortunado stood at the ready and quickly engaged the fleeing demons, followed swiftly by Garrison and Ignavus. Garrison carried the great sword he wielded against Mavado when they first met, and Fortunado carried a large hammer which was comprised of a similar blue energy as the great sword. Ignavus, in contrast, carried no weapon at all but instead battled effectively with hand to hand combat.

As the team dispatched the demons outside, Mavado stood before the last remaining spirit inside the home; it possessed an old drifter with long, unkempt hair that was matched by his equally long, unkempt beard. His clothes were tattered and filthy, and his eyes burned with a deep red glow which signified the control the demon exerted upon him. Huddled on the floor in fear, the spirit knew what destruction awaited him as he had witnessed firsthand the power of Mavado exercised against his companions. He also understood that his destruction would mean exile; he would be cast out to wander the earth, powerless and alone. Defeat at this point in time did not result in banishment to an eternity of hell, yet to wander in exile without power was a fate almost equally as cruel.

"Please, cast me into the dogs outside or into the birds which perch along the fence. There is no time left for me to gain back lost strength, not enough time before the end of days arrives to begin anew and yet still stand a chance in the war ahead. Please," Mavado looked at the demon without expression as it pleaded for mercy, seeming to stare through him as Jericho whispered within his mind.

"You can't let him go Mavado; they all have to be destroyed."

Mavado responded back, his voice audible only to Jericho, "Do not forget what Garrison has tasked us with, for he wishes to obtain knowledge from one of these creatures. If a deal can be struck, then it would be better to let this one wallow in the dirt as a mutt or a filthy fowl if it meant our enlightenment."

He extended his hand forward toward the cowering spirit and made his offer, "Open your mind to me and show me all that you know; how the lot of you came to be together and why you bound your power. Tell me all of your secrets and in return you shall find yourself with a vessel to inhabit, and no less power than you wield today."

The lawn outside was draped with the bodies of the fallen, bodies which were void of any human or demonic presence, lifeless and in need of disposal. There was never exorcism when it came to destroying these demons, as the possessed had chosen to be inhabited; exorcism is intended for the afflicted, but you cannot exorcise that which is welcomed in. Instead, those who chose to unite with their demonic spirits were doomed to live with the consequences of their choice. The fate of both demon and inhabitant were intertwined, yet the Watchers ensured that the fate of the living was always disguised in a manner which would keep their activities a secret.

The bodies were to be collected and placed back inside the home, where they would be restored to an uninjured state before a more rational death could be staged; house fires, drowning, carbon monoxide leaks, anything which could be easily dismissed was utilized in the cover-up. On this day they would torch the home to disguise the structure's damages, and the fire would take blame for the expiration of the home's occupants; for the time had not yet arrived for mankind to know the truth.

Fortunado was the first to observe Jericho, absent Mavado's manifestation, walk out of the home through the large hole where the front door had once stood. His voice was as booming as Sunday's, yet it had a coarse, brash tone which lacked the eloquent smoothness which Sunday's possessed. "Where's your demon? Has he grown weary of battle and retreated to cower within a child's imagination?" Fortunado had a knack for condescending behavior, subjecting everyone around him to criticism with the exception of his leader Garrison, whom he held in high regard.

While it was understandable that, like all other Watchers, Fortunado would be critical of Mavado, Jericho also believed that he himself was held in a similarly low regard in Fortunado's eyes. The verbal jab fell short of its mark however, as Jericho's expression remained stoic and distracted, with a buzz of activity behind his eyes that took precedence over acknowledging insults. Fortunado was not the only one who took note of Mavado's absence, as

Garrison swiftly approached Jericho with visible anger in his eyes.

"I instructed the demon to bring me an undisturbed captor, why has he disobeyed me? None have been left alive to interrogate!"

"Mavado switched places after the battle as you ordered. He also says that the demons in the house would not surrender and that you could've captured those who tried to escape through the windows." Jericho uttered the explanation with confidence, yet the words he chose were not entirely the truth of what had transpired. Fearing the consequences that a revelation of Mavado's deal would bring, he instead focused on the critical information which the cornered demon had so willingly provided. "It wasn't a total loss, Mavado was able to read the thoughts of one of the defeated spirits, and he thought you guys might take the news better from me, since you don't find him trustworthy. I think we have a serious problem."

"Speak then." Garrison abruptly uttered, as Ignavus, Fortunado and Annabel closed in to hear what information Mavado had obtained.

"These demons had a leader who united them; that's how they learned to combine their powers together. They're starting to organize like we do." Upon hearing this, Garrison was pulled into Michael's mind, and the host emerged back into the world to address Jericho.

"Who's leading them? Is it here?" asked Michael as Reggie and Sunday also resumed control of their bodies and surrounded Jericho. "No, he isn't here. I don't know where he is, but when I heard his name I remembered it. He was in the news awhile back, Luther Monroe. It could've been lying of course, but I don't see why it would make that up."

"I remember him too; you don't exactly forget the name of a serial murderer like him, but he hasn't been dead long enough to gain the power needed to walk in this world, let alone teach demons anything they don't already know." replied Michael in a matter of fact tone.

"It said that Luther didn't actually die, but that he found a way to bypass death and possess himself; that he somehow found a way to become his own demon. It doesn't make sense to me, but that's what he said. It also seems that Luther isn't content with destroying human beings anymore, but he's decided to take the fight to us. He wants to build an army as badly as we do."

"I don't mean to break up the conversation, but we really need to get a move on. Annabel can't shield us from the neighbors forever," beckoned Reggie, as the three had seemed to forget how exposed their position out on the lawn truly was. "Tell you what, give me a few days and I'll find out everything there was to know about Luther Monroe, and then we'll all meet up at my office. In the meantime, let's finish cleaning up and get the hell out of here."

Reggie's suggestion was well received, and the team scrambled to return the bodies to the house and take their leave as dusk began to fall upon the neighborhood. They disbanded one at a time to avoid raising suspicion; Reggie left first, then Sunday and Michael while Jericho stayed to prep the home for its impending destruction. Delia would need to leave last as Annabel was still manifested to hold the illusion of the home in its previous condition, and would need to keep up appearances until the rest were gone.

The approach was less than sophisticated, as Jericho simply opened the gas line in the house before exiting, and then prepared a very crude ignition system; a tennis ball, lit on fire and chucked through the doorway, would be used to create spark while at the same time minimize the appearance of arson. Annabel's powers also acted as a shield to the other homes during the explosion, and once the deed was done her illusion shifted to rest over both Jericho and her as they exited the scene. By doing this, the bystanders who were now leaving their homes to observe the commotion outside would not be alerted to their presence.

As Annabel would have to remain manifested while the two took their leave, Jericho seized the opportunity to engage the spirit in conversation, an event which seldom presented itself yet was relished by Jericho whenever it arrived. The beautiful spirit had intrigued and captivated him from the first time he stared into her glowing blue eyes. His fascination with her had grown by leaps and bounds since that day, in spite of the scarcity of interactions between them; naturally Delia would assume control of her faculties as soon as business had concluded, so Jericho took full advantage of his chance to steal a moment with his angelic rescuer.

The two of them stepped off the property together, with Annabel waving her hand ever so slightly to wipe away the illusion and reveal the blazing inferno which engulfed the remains of the home.

"I've always been amazed about how easy you make that look," uttered Jericho, in an awkward attempt to engage Annabel in small talk. Annabel turned and the two began walking down the street side by side, with Jericho's comment having invoked a bit of a smile which slowly spread across her face.

"I wouldn't call it easy, but I suppose you could say I have a natural talent for putting a positive spin on things," replied Annabel in her angelic voice as she strolled along with Jericho, her thumbs casually placed in Delia's front jean pockets and her posture very much relaxed.

"Has that always been the case? You know, even back when . . . oh . . . or are you not allowed to say?" replied Jericho in a playful manner. He was fully aware that Watchers were not permitted to reveal their identity until instructed to, but it was also common practice for them to share experiences and offer advice from their previous lives as a way to mentor their hosts.

"Honestly, I really don't know, I don't have any memory of my life in this world, not before I was given the opportunity to come here."

"No memory at all? Is that a common thing?"

Annabel obliged the inquiry as they rounded the corner together and continued on. "I'm not sure how common it is, I didn't really think to ask. Although the other Watchers, and your Mavado, seem to know who they are which makes me think it's somewhat unusual. Don't get me wrong, I have flashes of memory, but nothing substantial. I can't remember people or places, or even my own name." Jericho's curiosity continued to grow with every minor revelation that fell from Annabel's lips, but he also felt the window of opportunity beginning to close as the distance from the home grew and two were drawing ever closer to Delia's car.

"Well then, if you have almost no memory, what made you choose to come back and do this? From what

Michael tells me, Garrison, Ignavus and Fortunado have to prove they learned from old mistakes before they can be promoted. In your case, it's difficult to correct something you don't remember," The two arrived at Delia's car and stopped to face each other, with Jericho looking down into Annabel's glimmering blue eyes. Jericho was a tall 6'2, while Annabel was only 5'4, and although he towered over her in sheer size it was evident that Annabel wielded the true strength over Jericho.

Looking back with a thoughtful yet warm expression, Annabel answered his question. "Michael's perspective comes from what he knows about Garrison and the others. It's not always about correcting mistakes. Growing from where you were can mean a lot of things, not necessarily that you did something wrong, but maybe that you have a chance to influence someone's life or complete something you started. I don't know what that is for me, but I've been told that I will have the opportunity for my own redemption, and it's an opportunity I wanted; helping people seems to be my passion so I jumped at the chance, and I'll be patient and wait until my time comes."

Jericho smiled and continued his gaze into Annabel eyes, hoping the moment could last forever yet painfully aware it was rapidly evaporating. "Well, Annabel, I admire you for what you are doing. You have a lot of strength, more than I do for sure."

"You had me worried today, Jericho."

Annabel's response caught him by surprise, but he listened quietly as Annabel continued. "You are a good person, but I'm afraid you don't fully understand the thing that's inside you. Mavado will always be one of *them*, and as much as you point out what he has done for you, it doesn't erase what he is. I'm afraid you'll lose yourself somewhere between the enemies you fight and the enemy you call a friend. I know it's not what you want to hear, but I'm asking you to please be careful and guard your heart . . ."

Jericho felt himself grow a bit defensive from Annabel's observation, but he refused to allow his perception of her to become damaged. "I appreciate you worrying about be, but trust me when I say that I understand better than anyone what Mavado is. Yeah, he isn't a saint, but he also isn't the monster everybody believes he is. He has helped us accomplish things we really couldn't have without him, I mean just look at what happened today. I understand that's not what you want to hear, but I promise I will tell you if it becomes too much for me to handle. I trust you . . . after all you did save my life . . ."

Jericho took a small step toward Annabel, who reached up and placed her hands on his chest in the same manner that she had done in his dream on the day they met. "It's time for me to go; take care and have a good night." The glowing blue eyes were consumed by ordinary brown, and the right hand which had been touching Jericho's chest quickly reached up and grasped him by the chin. Delia's fingers squeezed his mouth and cheeks together in a forceful yet playful manner.

"Aw! You're so cute! Trying to get to first base with Annabel are we?!" Delia let out a laugh and released Jericho, but was quick to give his face a couple of light slaps on the way out.   "It wasn't like that at all." Jericho retorted casually in response to her teasing, disguising his embarrassment at the realization that she had been observing the interaction between him and her Watcher. Delia and Annabel could not have been more opposite in personality, as

Delia was a rough teaser and generally pretty sarcastic, while Annabel was significantly more mature and grounded in nature.

"Sure it wasn't, I thought I may have to whip out the pepper spray! I tell you, if you two start banging I'm going to start charging her rent." Delia laughed out loud at the thought as she unlocked her car and climbed in. Jericho's mood had now completely soured.

"All right, well, good night Delia!" he uttered quickly before he turned and headed down the sidewalk to retrieve his truck. As he continued on his way, Delia pulled up beside him and rolled down her window.

"I'm kidding, Jericho! Don't be mad at me, okay?" she shouted though a huge smile which traveled from ear to ear.

Jericho couldn't help but smile back, "I know Delia, it's cool."

"Just making sure, didn't want you to stay pissed at me. I'm heading over to Leary's to get a drink with some friends, you want to come? Come on, you know you need to unwind a little!" The prospect of a drink sounded good to Jericho, but the embarrassing moment which had just passed still lingered in his mind.

"Nah, it's been a weird day; I'm just going home to crash out."

"All right, old man, I know you got to be in bed by nine! Have fun dreaming about sexy angels!" She playfully bellowed the words as she peeled off into the darkness, while

Jericho continued on his way towards his truck. He climbed into the cab and turned the engine over, and as he pulled away from the curb the day's events began running through his mind. He had the pleasure of actually being alone with his thoughts, as Mavado had chosen to remain silent; while Jericho had previously utilized Mavado as a bit of a confidant, he now had taken on a more business-like approach and exercised large amounts of control over his interactions with the spirit.

The truth was that the more Jericho matured, the more authority he displayed towards Mavado, until the only opportunity Mavado had for an audience with Jericho was during manifestations or when Jericho dreamed at night. Jericho did understand better than anyone what Mavado was; he saw the tremendous benefit of Mavado's contribution, but he also was not oblivious to the potential risks of his involvement. He had learned to keep him at a safe distance. While he carried a seed of genuine trust in Mavado, the two also continued to rapidly grow apart in philosophy. The years of possession had begun to take their toll on Jericho both physically and mentally, and recognizing this, he did all he could to limit his exposure.

As Jericho headed home, the air in the quiet neighborhood was filled with the sounds of loud barking. The neighborhood dogs were disturbed; not by intruders or passersby, but by each other. Two dogs in a backyard which neighbored the condemned home were barking incessantly at a third, which sat quietly at attention and did not move or respond. A deal had indeed been honored; Mavado had kept his promise, a fact which Jericho had chosen to omit when he spoke with Michael and the others.

The third dog calmly stood up on all four paws and walked to the side gate, where it squeezed between the bars

114

and exited the yard. The two barking dogs retreated into the opposite corner of the yard from the moment the third dog stirred, for they sensed the evil which lurked deep within the animal. The dog continued to slowly walk down the street until it disappeared into the darkness, for its master had called for it to return home at once.

Chapter 7

A few day's time were indeed all Reggie needed, made evident by the stacks of file folders and other documentation which draped the conference room table at J. W. McCormick's Investigators. Two large easels stood off to one side of the room with a number of missing person photographs, and their gruesome corresponding crime scene photos, pinned up for review. Having to view the sometimes horrific results of human nature was nothing new to Reggie, as he had previously served as an Essex policeman and then later joined the ranks of their Major Investigation Team back in his home country of England.

His work in major investigations had been exceptional; Reggie was considered a rising star in the division due to his exceptional attention to detail and unmatched enthusiasm for justice. He was rapidly ascending through the ranks toward what would surely have been a long and successful career, yet his destiny shifted completely on the day he accepted the call to unite with Ignavus and join the Watcher's cause. While all who take up the call inevitably make personal sacrifices, Reggie's was steeper than most; Ignavus was ordered to report to Garrison, which would require Reggie to leave all that he knew, give up his promising career, and leave behind family and friends.

Reggie weighed the cost, and after much deliberation, he decided that the opportunity to deliver justice on an eternal scale was too important to decline. His sense of duty was deep and very much a part of his identity, but it would remain almost entirely hidden to all but his closest of companions as his rather sarcastic and carefree nature tended to brand him as a bit of a loose cannon to the majority of those he knew.

Upon his relocation, he decided to remain as close as he could to his law enforcement roots while still maintaining some schedule flexibility. J.W. McCormick's Investigators would fit the bill nicely, and being a private firm it allowed Reggie to have access to facilities and resources which would aid the Watchers cause when needed. The firm's official office hours ended at six in the afternoon which freed up the use of the building during the evenings, and so on this evening as the employees began to file out, the team began to assemble in the conference room where Reggie was ready to present his findings. Michael and Jericho were the first to arrive while Sunday made his appearance about five minutes later.

The last to arrive was Delia, which was a common occurrence as her immaturity often contributed to her lack of timeliness. It was expected that she would walk through the door anywhere from fifteen to thirty minutes after the agreed-upon time, always with a reasonable excuse which could not be validated for authenticity. This day was no different, as Delia rushed into the conference room to find everyone already seated at one end of the large eight-foot-long oak conference table.

"Sorry! Sorry, there was a lot of traffic and a pretty bad wreck so it took me forever to get here," uttered Delia as she headed to take a seat next to Sunday and slung her purse into the empty chair to her immediate left. Reggie was seated at the head of the table, with Michael and Jericho seated on his right while Sunday and Delia were seated to his left.

"No worries, darling," responded Reggie as he checked his watch. "Your arrival seems to have made me richer by fifteen dollars; you officially sat down at thirteen minutes past the agreed upon time, which makes my guess closest without going over. Pay up gentlemen!"

A sigh of frustration emanated from the defeated, as Michael, Jericho and Sunday reached for their wallets and each withdrew a five-dollar bill which they immediately pitched at Reggie. "We've got to stop playing 'Price is Right' rules, because I guessed fifteen minutes, which is two minutes closer that your guess," chuckled Sunday.

"Not a chance, big man, I prefer this way because I have a better chance at winning. And now that everyone has arrived, let's get down to business, shall we?" Reggie reached for the manila folder which sat directly in front of him, flipped it open and slowly paged through as he began his synopsis:

"Luther Edison Monroe; born April 22, 1973 to George A. and Barbara M. Monroe in Boston Massachusetts.

His father was the George A. Monroe, former governor of Massachusetts who is alive and well and still resides in Boston; Barbara, however, passed away tragically from ovarian cancer eight years ago. Luther Monroe initially followed in his father's footsteps, attending Harvard University for two years before abruptly leaving to pursue theological studies at Duke University's Divinity School. While he excelled there in his first year, he began to display erratic behavior soon after; he openly challenged his professors during lectures on multiple occasions, before eventually being expelled for his continued disruptive behavior.

At the time of his expulsion he had already developed a significant cult following among his fellow students, and upon his dismissal, they also took leave and joined his cause when he founded the 'Reorganized Church of the Living God.' Naturally, Monroe failed to specify that the living God he was referring to was in fact himself."

Reggie closed the folder and sat back in his chair as he continued:

"At this point, the facts get equal parts sketchy and disturbing. He built his church and began delving deep into occult studies, researching and performing ancient rituals with various levels of success. His church purchased a number of old industrial properties, along with a section of farmland which was converted into a compound for him and his followers. It was roughly around this time when the first of the murders began."

Reggie stood from his chair and walked to the easels that contained the photographs, which served as the visual aids for his gruesome presentation. "Forensic investigators recovered the remains of more than thirty women in a mass gravesite located on the compound property. Roughly two dozen have been identified, and the rest are still Jane Doe's to this day. There is a progression in his choice of victim, as the first murders were all runaways, prostitutes, or homeless women; random abductions where the chances of someone looking for them were rather unlikely. Eventually, the women targeted became much more specific and fit a particular profile. All were under the age of twenty and came from affluent families, were highly religious, and dedicated to charitable work, and claimed to adhere to sexual abstinence."

Reggie moved to the next easel which contained a large timeline which was graphed out with abduction dates and continued: "As you can see, the majority of the killings occurred within a few years' time. This was when the cult members would branch out and pick up nomads who weren't being looked for. Later, the abductions slowed down to about two per year, as they carefully selected victims who met the new criteria. It just so happens that this change in philosophy was what ultimately led to their undoing."

Reggie headed back to his seat at the head of the table, and as he sat down he reached forward and retrieved a blue folder from the stack of files.

"The final intended victim was a seventeen-year-old girl by the name of Audrey Decker; the operative word being 'intended', as the men sent to abduct her were careless in their effort. Audrey was leaving her hostess job at a rather popular eatery when two men pulled up beside her in an early model Ford Excursion. As she was unlocking her car door, the men exited the vehicle and tried to pull her into the van, but she put up a wild struggle and called out for help. A few patrons who were leaving the restaurant heard her screams and came to her aid, causing the men to let her go and flee in the van, You can probably guess that the van was registered to Monroe's church; the license plate was quickly identified from security footage which led the police to Monroe's compound and began the infamous standoff we are all very familiar with."

"Three days later, on January 8, 2011, police stormed the compound in an attempt to apprehend Monroe, killing a number of his followers who engaged in a brief shootout before being quickly dispatched. When the smoke had cleared, they were surprised to find Monroe already dead with a deep, self-inflicted knife wound that stretched from ear to ear. Just below the wound was a snug neck-chain that was adorned with a number of small charms and personal items, presumably which had been stolen off the bodies of his victims."

"Luther's body was transported to the county coroner's office for an autopsy, but disappeared mysteriously that evening from the morgue, and was never recovered. His surviving followers claimed the missing body to be a sign of his glorious resurrection. The police, however, contested that his followers had entered the morgue and stolen the body during the night. In the days that followed Monroe's death, his property was excavated and a number of mass graves were discovered. The graves contained bodies with various levels of decomposition which were examined thoroughly, and some were successfully identified. Monroe's personal journals were also collected as evidence and reviewed extensively. In them Monroe claims to have raped each victim only moments before taking their lives, as part of an unnamed demonic ritual. He documented each experience in explicit detail and referred to each girl by name, expressing his gratitude for her sacrifice and contribution towards his pursuit for eternal life. Of interesting note was that he expressed gratitude towards the <u>pursuit</u> in journal entries for his early victims, however the final five entries after he narrowed his search instead thanked the victims for their <u>contribution</u> towards his eternal life."

Everyone had been listening intently and quietly as Reggie presented his research, but it was at this point that Jericho spoke up.

"He wasn't just some lunatic, though. What he was doing actually worked. He found a way to get eternal life." Sunday was quick with a response to Jericho's acknowledgment of Luther's alleged success, "Oh no my friend, eternal life is not achieved by murder or carnage, but only through the grace of God. Whatever he found, it is far from eternal."

Michael was next to chime in, "Hold on everybody. We don't really know what Luther got, if anything. So far, all we have is a long story from Reggie and an ominous warning from Mavado and Jericho, which they got from some demon who possessed a meth addict and couldn't fight worth a shit. Let's not get ahead of ourselves."

"Well thanks Mike, I did try to make the long story more interesting by showing you pictures and stuff," snickered Reggie as he twirled a silver writing pen between his fingers, one of his many nervous habits ". . . but seriously, there are a few facts which cannot be ignored. Monroe changed his M.O. for a reason, and that change was implied to have made the ritual a success, based on his journal entries of course. The neck-chain he wore contained five charms, presumed to have been mementos taken from those five particular victims. Now I'm not really an expert on demonic rituals, but fortunately for us, we happen to have an expert in our midst, so I'm curious as to what he has to say." Reggie's expression was now a bit guarded and serious; the twirling of the pen had come to a halt, and he let it lightly drop from his fingers to the top of the stack of file folders, where it landed with a slight thud.

Michael immediately interjected, "I know where you're going with this. Jericho already told us what Mavado said he saw in the demon's mind, that Luther is a demon and is rallying others to fight us. I don't think we gain anything by asking Mavado questions, because we don't know if he's telling the truth or not. Besides, Garrison already told me he wants to be manifested whenever Mavado possesses Jericho."

"Garrison is already present. You know he can see all this going on through your eyes. I for one would relish the opportunity to pick his brain for a bit, what say you, Jericho?"

Reggie offered the rebuttal as Jericho leaned back in his chair with a bit of an amused look, "Well, I have to listen to him pretty regularly, so it would be nice for someone else to debate him for a change. He'll be happy to tell you whatever you want to know, but he wants me to tell you that he should be the only spirit manifested during this conversation. He says that those who are living now have the most to lose, and should have the opportunity to listen in the flesh rather than behind imaginary windows."

Delia, who had been quiet nearly the entire time, finally spoke up. "I agree, I think if Mavado knows things that could help us then we should hear him out. We already use him for fighting, so it couldn't hurt to hear his perspective." The truth was that Delia found Mavado very intriguing, understanding that she would probably never have another opportunity to personally interact with the spirit if it did not happen at that moment, she offered up her support merely for curiosity's sake.

Jericho looked around the table at his friends, gauging their responses from the expressions which graced their faces. Reggie and Delia had already voiced their approval, leaving only Michael and Sunday on the fence. When Jericho locked eyes with Sunday, he was met with a slight affirming nod. Sunday felt a debate was unnecessary, although he held no admiration for Mavado, he was more committed to understanding a potential new enemy than arguing with the others about the wisdom of engaging the spirit in conversation.

Jericho turned to Michael, but before he could say anything he received his answer,

"I trust you Jericho, if you think it will help . . ."

With that, Jericho shut his eyes and tilted his head forward slightly as small swirls of black smoke began to twirl and twist off of his clothes and body. The smoke did not linger in the room or cloud up near the ceiling, but simply vanished into the air when it had traveled a few inches. Almost seamlessly, as if in the blink of an eye, Jericho was replaced by Mavado, who now sat in the chair with his eyes shut and smoke still emanating out from his body.

The unique nature of Mavado's transformations clearly set him apart from other spirits. With every manifestation he altered not only Jericho's eye color, but his hair color and style, facial features, teeth, and hand structure. The tattoo would appear upon his forehead, and Jericho's clothing would be replaced by the same pinstripe suit and shiny dress shoes on every occasion where Mavado took control. While the relatively subtle changes in Michael and the others' appearances could result in confusion regarding who was actually present at first glance, this would never be a question when it came to Jericho. Mavado had his own distinct style which seemed to further highlight how incredibly different he was from his host, and accentuate the unorthodox nature of their pairing.

The smoke dispersed and the eyes of Mavado opened, revealing the transformed golden irises which quickly glanced about the room at his new audience. Jericho had been leaning back in his chair prior to Mavado's arrival, which clearly did not suit the demon's comfort as he immediately sat forward, lifted his left leg and crossed it over his right. He also moved his hands together, clasped them and let them rest in his lap.

"Mr. Bradshaw, Mr. Brockington, Ms. Rivera, Reginald," said Mavado as he acknowledged each person present at the table. "Thank you for taking the time to meet with me on such short notice."

"Reginald? So you and I are on a first name basis? I'm touched!" Reggie joked, although his surprise with Mavado's choice of acknowledgment was actually genuine.

Mavado smiled back through his response, "Reginald is a fine, strong name which stands well enough on its own, and I do carry additional appreciation for your willingness to include me in your conversation. But if you prefer I will gladly refer to you as 'Mr. Hardy.'"

"No, Reginald works just fine, Mavado. I'm not familiar with your last name so I suppose it's only fair."

Michael was already regretting the decision to bring Mavado into the discussion, as the casual opening words seemed to be an unnecessary time waster. "Well, I'm sure you know we didn't call you out here to talk about names, we got more pressing issues to deal with." Mavado turned his attention from Reggie to Michael, his smile melting away into a stern expression as his penetrating gaze locked with Michael's. When Mavado's eyes were upon someone, they seemed to stalk like a predator. He was a great white shark disguised as a gentleman, equally skilled at dissecting his prey both physically and mentally.

"Indeed, Mr. Bradshaw, you are quite right. We are here to discuss the intricacies of our new foe, and I caution you all against making the mistake of believing that I am not his enemy, for he is equally dangerous to me, you, and the Watchers alike. I asked to speak with you and not the spirits who inhabit you because the consequences of what you do next will impact the living more than the dead. If they are defeated, they simply return to their master to be judged for an elevated status. If you are defeated, then your lives are forfeit, and you proceed to be judged for your sins. You can each weigh the risk and make you own decisions, but you must understand that your days of hunting scattered foes with minimal power have come to an end. Jericho put things very succinctly when he said that Monroe found a way to achieve eternal life, but I will clarify what that truly means."

"Monroe came upon an ancient pagan ritual, one devised with the intent of granting extended life and power to a single being through the sacrifice of others. I am aware of these rituals simply because they are well known by the most ancient of spirits, and Monroe's knowledge of them

126

expanded from his alignment with a number of these beings. They shared with him their wisdom and understanding of the old ways, and he took this knowledge and married it to his notably brilliant mind. He made it new, modified it until it no longer extended his physical life but instead suited his personal needs."

"And what were his needs?" Sunday interjected. His suspicion of Mavado was rivaled only by Garrison, and grew more pronounced with every word which fell from the demon's lips.

"Elevation, to put it primitively; Monroe wished to gain the kind of power his demonic acquaintances displayed, yet he understood that allowing himself to be possessed would not grant him true power or authority. So he devised a plan to possess his own body, passing through death and conjuring himself back into the world to inhabit his own lifeless form, and in the process returning with newly-acquired power. To understand how he accomplished this takes a lesson in spiritual principals, so I shall do my best to explain."

Mavado uncrossed his legs and stood up from his chair, as he had grown weary of his stationary position and preferred to stretch his borrowed legs for a bit. He began a slow walk around the table as his lecture continued, heading in the direction of the easels that contained photos of Monroe's victims. "As you are probably well aware from your childhood days spent in science class, life is comprised primarily of energy. The stars, the earth, and even all living creatures and spirits share this commonality. As we ourselves are all unique, so is the energy of which we are comprised. Some brings life, some takes life, and all have their own special purpose. One energy in particular ties the living to this world, holding each spirit within their fleshy vessel until the day their body expires. At death that energy dissipates, lost to the soul to whom it was tied; gone forever it leaves nothing to hold the soul back as it transitions into the spiritual realm. The plan Monroe devised was to harvest this energy from others and somehow store it away, for the purpose of reuniting him with his body in this world after he transitioned into a free spirit."

Mavado approached the easel containing pictures of Monroe's victims and halted there. He clasped his hands behind his back and his eyes scanned back and forth across the grisly scenes as he continued speaking. "The early victims were all failures. It seemed that the energy could not be simply contained in this world as there was no longer a purpose for it. This energy has a unique quality to it; much like DNA it is individualized and bonds to its originator. The need to create a strong link between that energy and Monroe would necessitate his change in philosophy, and after a little research, the solution became somewhat obvious. The biblical principle of 'two become one flesh' . . ."

"Mark 10:8. 'And the two are united into one, so they are no longer two but one flesh,' a reference to marriage in the eyes of God," Sunday responded, as he was the resident biblical expert among the group.

Mavado turned his attention from the photos to Sunday and addressed his comment directly. "Not only in marriage, for as you know, the sixth chapter of Corinthians speaks of men joining to prostitutes, and yet becoming one flesh, and how such behavior should be avoided as those who join together will take on each other's sin. It is the act of sexual intercourse which creates this bond, and what better way to bond with another person's energy than to be recognized as a part of their own flesh."

128

Mavado turned his attention back to the easel of photographs as he continued. "Once he understood this he put his plan into motion, raping his victims before slaughtering them and attempting to harvest their energy. Alas, more failure followed which led to an inevitable conclusion: the best chance to be recognized strongly by this energy was to become one with someone untainted in body and spirit, undiluted so to speak. And so began Monroe's final siege on the carefully-selected girls who were befriended and observed by his followers, until enough evidence had been gathered to determine if they were a suitable prospect. It was these girls whom he thanked for their contribution, whom he found success with. He gathered the energy which lingered after their deaths and bound it to an item taken from each the girl. The charms remain with him, placed on the chain which still adorns his neck. The five charms indicate he succeeded five times prior to his death."

"I don't mean to interrupt your story Mavado, but why five victims? How much of this energy would he need in order to successfully possess himself?" Reggie's mind had been filling with questions during Mavado's lengthy explanation of Monroe's transformation, and he saw that moment as a perfect chance to satisfy some of his curiosity.

Mavado unclasped his hands from behind his back and returned to his seat at the table upon hearing the question, and sat down as he responded; "This ritual would only require the energy of one, a life for a life. Why he chose more, or what number he hoped to acquire is debatable; his sixth intended victim managed to escape, but obviously was not required as Monroe completed the ritual in haste prior to the authorities raiding his compound. Perhaps he suffered from the same affliction which plagues most men; he simply wanted more. Theoretically, he could repeat the process as long as he had the energy to perform the ritual, so having additional resources would actually be quite prudent."

Michael had remained silent, taking in all that Mavado said with growing concern. He understood that Garrison had seen and heard all that had unfolded in the conference room, yet the spirit did not stir or rebut internally against anything Mavado had said. It was the silent acknowledgment of Garrison that validated Mavado's assessment; it gave Michael the confidence to believe his questions would be answered truthfully by the demon, so he no longer held back.

"So Mavado, why did he need to possess himself? Why not just do what all other demons do and possess somebody else? Seems like a lot of trouble just to get your old body back."

Mavado smiled at the simplicity of Michael's statement, but his smile washed away quickly with the enormity of his answer and the ramifications it was sure to bring. "It was very much a grand and complicated endeavor, but certainly was not for anything as trivial as merely keeping his previous shell. Monroe gained tremendous power through his actions by omitting the need for a host. Possession in itself takes a measure of power; to be able to hold a manifestation, even with a cooperating host, is a drain on any spirit's abilities. Demons must expend even more power, as those they possess are erratic, uncooperative, and unstable. Monroe is of one soul and one mind, existing in both worlds and never conflicted in purpose. He was, and is a true student of the occult. I know this because when I read the mind of the demon at the house I saw fragments, flashes of his power and of the power of the spirits he has already recruited to his cause. Both he and these spirits possess power which rivals that of any Watcher, but most concerning

130

to me is that Monroe's own power has a feeling of strength which rivals my own, and he is focused on destroying all of us as much as we are on destroying him."

"You mean the Watchers and us, why would he have any interest in destroying one of his own?" chimed in Sunday, "If anything, he's more likely to try to recruit you to his cause like the other ancient spirits you claim he has gathered together." In Sunday's mind the lines between demons and Watchers were clearly marked, made even more evident by Mavado's ability to pass through the demon's barricade without resistance.

Mavado looked at Sunday directly with his usual, slightly amused expression as he addressed the comment, "I can see how someone in your position might believe that to be the case, however, in the same way that God said, 'if you are not for me, you are against me,' the demons classify friend and foe in a similar manner. Monroe does not wish to become just another demon, but aspires to become the Master of all. Like many dictators before him, his goal is to instill loyalty in his subjects and to eliminate his rivals, with myself falling into the latter category. The skirmish at the house was only a scouting mission. He wished to know if the rumors were true, that the Watchers had a so-called 'condemned' spirit fighting by their side. Now he has confirmed my existence, putting Jericho and myself as much in the line of fire as any one of you. He will come to destroy us all, unless we take the initiative to strike first."

The room fell silent as the gravity of the situation began to sink in. Michael leaned back in his chair, clutching the armrests for a moment before his eye color swiftly transitioned to the glowing blue which signified the emergence of Garrison. In his powerful and eloquent voice,

Garrison spoke for the first time to Mavado without the usual tone of hostility.

"If what you are saying is true, then this danger not only falls upon us, but upon all Watchers, and even the angels themselves. I will send word to my commander and meet with him to discuss this threat and will summon all of you together when I return with our new orders. Until then, you are dismissed."

Garrison pushed his chair back and stood up, leaving in haste through the conference room doors without returning control to Michael or offering individual goodbyes. The abrupt end of the meeting caught everyone a bit off guard, as Reggie offered up, "Ok, I suppose that means we're done here," to fill the awkward void of silence in the wake of Garrison's rapid exit. "I, for one, could certainly use a drink after news like that, what say you, Del?"

Delia was checking her cell phone for text messages, already distracted although only moments removed from the very troubling conversation. Her response was delayed for a few seconds as she read the text silently while attempting to answer Reggie, but she quickly finished and looked up from the brightly-lit screen as she redirected her focus.

"Umm, yeah for a bit . . . I'm going to meet a friend later, but not until nine so I have time for a drink."

"Perfect! I can only stomach your company for a few hours, so this works out brilliantly. Sunday, I know you can have fun without drinking, and they do serve water, so there's something for everybody. And Jeri, you certainly have the look of a man who needs a drink."

"I'll drive and babysit," was Sunday's slightly annoyed response. Jericho was still in mid-transformation, so his answer was delayed while Mavado retreated back into the depths of his mind. The black smoke swirled off his body as his clothes and appearance returned to normal. His facial expression appeared somewhat stressed as he experienced the usual burning in his hands which accompanied his return to control.

"You got it Reggie, and I'm riding with you Sunday. I need to blow off some steam tonight."

Reggie quickly packed up the files and closed up shop as the others made their way out of the building. As Jericho's physical pain subsided, he began to focus more on his growing concern over Mavado's words and Monroe's alleged intentions. He felt a measure of guilt deep within his mind, as he realized that in many ways his own desires would now be satisfied; Jericho intensely wanted to be a bigger part of the team and to use Mavado's talents on a regular basis, and due to present circumstances the demon's assistance would certainly be demanded.

What Jericho had not expected was the degree of imminent danger which would accompany the fulfillment of his wishes; the need for purpose was quickly being replaced by concern for his friends, both human and spirit alike. And for one beautiful spirit in particular, Jericho found his heart intensely preoccupied with thoughts of preservation. After all, she had rescued him from death's doorstep, which in Jericho's mind made him solely responsible for Annabel's safety. He owed her his life, and in return, felt compelled to do anything required to protect her, even if it meant his own destruction.

Chapter 8

The neon sign perched above the entrance to The Tree House Bar and Grill flickered and buzzed with its florescent green glow, welcoming its bevy of regular customers as it had done countless times throughout the past two decades. To say that it was a popular hole in the wall would be a grand overstatement, but the place did have its own unique following which generated enough revenue to sustain its existence. From the outside it wasn't much to look at, for its walls were constructed from red brick which had been covered with a tan colored paint, which is to say that it was originally painted white and had slowly progressed to tan through extensive weathering and a lack of upkeep. The roof was comprised of brown shingles and had seen better days, but served its purpose of blocking the elements well enough, save the occasional drip which fell from a few heavily stained ceiling tiles during the rainy season.

The inside was more of the same, with a dated look that was in serious need of an update. Chairs and barstools were a combination of wood and orange vinyl, and it was a rare occasion to find one that did not have at least one crack or rip in the upholstery which exposed the yellow foam padding underneath. The ceiling was relatively low, and upon entering most people would duck their heads slightly despite the unlikely possibility of an actual collision. The place was dimly lit, with a large horseshoe-shaped bar at the center of the room which was flanked by several small, square wooden tables with various dings, chips and scratches displayed on their tops. The majority of patrons would sit at or surround the large central bar, so a free table could almost certainly be guaranteed on most nights.

The décor was stereotypical and consisted of banners and posters which were brought in by various beer vendors, and for entertainment the place housed a few large, boxy projection televisions which were pricy in their heyday but now would retail for no more than a few hundred dollars. The jukebox was the best feature of the bar; a classic Wurlitzer 1015 with the volume set way too high, which forced customers to awkwardly shout their conversations at each other in the event that any sentimental drunks decided to fire it up.

Honestly, the place was a dump, but to Jericho it was comforting and was often his preferred destination for post-meeting drinking sessions. Reggie happily complied, as hole-in-the-walls were his kind of places, but Sunday and Delia found the bar to be repugnant and repulsive, respectively. Usually Jericho would head straight to the horseshoe bar if he were drinking alone; the service at the bar was significantly better in comparison to the tables, as there did not appear to be any formally assigned sections which often resulted in cocktail waitresses wandering aimlessly and losing track of who had been helped and who was still waiting. The other advantage of the bar was that the regular bartender knew Jericho, Reggie and Michael well and took care of them swiftly, another trait which was not entirely shared by the waitresses on duty.

On this occasion, however, Jericho had selected a table which was recessed against a window and about as far from the main bar as possible. This was done with the thought that the conversation would probably head toward subjects related to the day's events, and any discussion in earshot of other patrons would create the undesirable perception that they were a group of mental patients who had found their way into the bar. The four made their way to the table and took a seat, with Reggie and Sunday sitting on one side and Jericho and Delia facing them on the other. Reggie of course would use the opportunity to wisecrack that it would appear to the casual observer that he and Sunday were on a date, but comments like this were so frequent that they no longer phased Sunday or even generated a response.

After waiting patiently for a few minutes, Jericho was able to make eye contact with one of the waitresses and raised his hand to flag her down. Her name was Yvonne, and Jericho knew her well; in fact Jericho had spent so much time at The Tree House over the past two years that he knew all the staff by name, a trait which brought humored criticism anytime he attended with company.

Yvonne was only nineteen, petite and thin, with a pretty, round face and straight brown hair which had been pulled back into a ponytail. She was dressed in a black polo shirt and quite possibly the shortest pair of black shorts ever made, which made for a sporty yet sexy appearance which she skillfully pulled off. Her look was completed with a pair of thick, black framed glasses which would give a nerdy appearance to most, but they suited her face well and accentuated her simple beauty.

Yvonne jogged over with a bouncy energy as Jericho stood up from his chair to offer a proper greeting. She flung her arms around his neck and embraced him in an overly flirtatious hug,

"Hey Jericho! How you been? You want the usual right? Bass saw you when you walked in and already started making your drink!" She laughed as Jericho glanced over and witnessed the bartender Sebastian mixing a whiskey and coke as he made eye contact and gave a nod of his head in a silent greeting to Jericho.

"The usual is perfect, what do you guys want?" In truth, Jericho could have ordered for everyone, as each would generally request the same drink every time they went out. Delia was the first to chime in, as she looked down and rummaged through her purse while ordering a bloody beer. Reggie knew Yvonne as well, and chose to place his order next by posing a familiar question to her.

"Hello my love, do you have any English beers other than Newcastle?" to which Yvonne instinctually replied, "Well, we have Newcastle."

"Brilliant, Newcastle it is!" His response was always the same, and always brought himself a laugh no matter how many times he performed this identical verbal exchange with the waitresses.

Sunday was next with, "You guys are probably going to laugh, but I'll have a Shirley Temple." Sunday rarely partook in drinking, and as the designated driver, it was fully expected that he would stick to a non-alcoholic beverage, although the unusual choice did inspire a chuckle from the table.

"Well, the way I see it, a big, strapping lad like you can drink whatever he wants," replied Reggie as Yvonne left the table to put the drink orders in. As she left, a second waitress approached the table with Jericho's whiskey and coke.

"Here you go babe, good seeing you again!" was both her greeting and parting words as Jericho took the glass and offered a thank you as the second waitress quickly headed back to her section.

Reggie, smiling as always, offered his observations as Jericho lifted the cold, perspiring glass to his lips. "You know, it never ceases to amaze me how EVERYBODY here knows who you are. I come here quite often, and I know Bass and Yvonne, but the rest are pretty much strangers."

Jericho took a long gulp from his drink and drained about half the contents of the glass before lowering it just long enough to answer. "Come on, there's like only four waitresses and two bartenders who work here," he responded before quickly returning the glass to its former resting place and rapidly chugging the remaining contents.

"Damn Jeri, getting the party started already! Wait for the rest of us!" laughed Delia as Jericho quickly placed the glass of ice down on the table.

"No worries, she'll bring me another one when she brings the rest of the drinks, no point in having two drinks sitting here at once." Jericho felt the whiskey warming his chest, seeming to temporarily relieve the anxiety which had been building over the past week. He felt his mouth watering for another drink, and looked about the room impatiently for Yvonne as he had hoped to quickly drown his stress and turn his mind toward more enjoyable distractions. Yvonne was already on her way, and arrived in a moment's time to replace Jericho's empty glass and hand out the assorted drinks before heading off to her other tables.

Jericho quickly consumed half of his second drink only moments after Yvonne left the table, while the rest of the group took reasonable sips.

"Do you have somewhere to be, mate? You seem to be doing the equivalent of a drunken forty-yard dash," Jericho looked at Reggie with a smile; he found his banter to be entertaining and had no problem accepting verbal jabs.

"Just trying to take the edge off a little; it's been an odd week, and I don't work tomorrow, so why the hell not, right?" He would never admit it, but there was no denying that Jericho had a pronounced weakness for alcohol; it was his ultimate medication against the demonic juggernaut which lingered under his skin, yet it only dulled his internal torment for a small window of time, until his intoxication reached major levels and instead amplified his internal suffering.

"I suppose that 'odd' would be a fair description; I think I heard more from Mavado today than I've observed over the entirety of the past few years that we've worked with him. It was quite enlightening, actually. Although, I do suppose that if I had Mavado chattering on and on inside my head, then I'd most likely be joining you in slamming drinks at breakneck speed, so I can't exactly judge you now, can I? I must say, though, he is an interesting fellow . . . "

Jericho polished off the rest of his second drink while taking in Reggie's comment about Mavado, and as he returned the glass to the table he took the opportunity to steer the conversation toward a spirit that was not his own, "Mavado is interesting, that's definitely one way to put it. What about Ignavus? I don't think I know anything about him. You don't find him interesting?"

Reggie took a sip of his beer and thought about the question for a moment before answering, "No, as a matter of fact he's not particularly interesting at all. He's hardly a mentor, something which I used to think was a requirement when pairing up, but apparently that's not the case. Not that I need a mentor, but it would be nice to learn some mystery of the universe, or anything useful for that matter. The few conversations we've had always seem to end up with Ignavus ranting about how God should just destroy all the demons and be done with the whole thing. I don't think he has much patience for the process. He's actually the reason I moved stateside. After I agreed to pair up, he was reassigned to Garrison and we were told to relocate. All that 'Take up your cross and follow me' business; well, that's no joke. Sometimes you end up following a very long way."

As a result of his rapid consumption, Jericho already had begun to feel his buzz forming as he spotted Yvonne across the bar and gave her a quick nod to indicate that he was ready for another drink. "Ignavus sounds like a douche bag to me."

The quick generalization from Jericho caused the table to erupt with laughter, with the heartiest generated by

Reggie. "Well, you may be right!" Reggie chuckled through his words as he took another drink and continued his thought in a more sincere tone, "I don't know exactly what his problem is, I think he's just not as invested in what we are trying to accomplish as someone in his position should be, if that makes any sense. Or maybe he is just a douche bag, that's also possible! What about you Sunday? Would you say Fortunado is a douche bag?"

Sunday had hardly touched his Shirley Temple, which looked very much out of place in front of such a physically imposing figure. "Fortunado and I are very different personalities, but we have a good working relationship. He's like an ancient frat boy, and I'm certainly more pious than him, which is very surprising when you consider he was allowed here by God. We don't talk too much, but from time to time he will tell stories of his great victories in battle, and rave about how the world marveled at his strength. At least we have physical prowess in common or we wouldn't talk at all."

Delia sat with her legs crossed and clutched her cell phone, which had almost entirely monopolized her attention during the conversation; she gazed down at the screen and fired her thumbs in a rapid, piston-like motion, churning out text messages at a dizzying speed.

"I'd happily trade Annabel for Ignavus or Fortunado any day," she uttered with a hint of frustration in her voice as she finished the text and dropped her phone into her purse. She looked up and directed her attention back to the company around the table as she continued, "Annabel is like having your mom lurking a few feet away during every moment of your life. She must have been a stuck-up old grandma when she was alive because she always gives advice that I don't ask for. I'm like, shit, it's my life, so let me make mistakes if

141

I want to because I'm probably going to do it anyway, so why bother with the lecture? Hell, I'd even trade her for Mavado, since he seems like he'd at least be fun to hang out with!" Delia laughed as she looked directly at Jericho in an attempt to gauge his reaction, "How about it Jeri? You can have Annabel and I'll have Mavado . . ."

Jericho smirked at Delia's teasing proposition, just as Yvonne seemed to appear out of nowhere to replace Jericho's drink and interrupt to ask if the others were ready for another round. Reggie ordered another Newcastle while Delia and Sunday both declined, and Yvonne was gone in a flash. Upon her departure, Reggie picked up where Delia left off, "Sorry love, but I don't think you could tame the monster as well as Jericho has . . ."

Jericho lifted his new glass and took his first gulp as he contemplated Reggie's words and the implications they brought. "Mavado isn't the monster everyone seems to think he is. He's actually the closest thing to family that I've had since my parents died. I know he's not a Watcher, and everyone has this belief that he's evil, but bad guys don't save kids they don't know, and they don't keep their word either. He's chosen to do both."

"He's done those things to serve his own purpose, not out of righteous responsibility," countered Sunday.

Jericho looked amused, "And your spirits don't? They're only here to gain status and hopefully become angels, so they serve their own purpose too. Don't get me wrong, Mavado can be difficult to deal with, and we disagree on a lot of things, but I don't think he's more selfish than any other spirit. What makes him a bad guy? Because Garrison and everyone say he is?"

142

Sunday leaned forward and put his elbows on the table as he thought of an appropriate response; it was impossible to deny that Jericho's argument was actually quite logical, and it was an irrefutable fact that the Watchers did benefit from their service. "You are right; they all have something to gain from being here. The difference between him and them is this: we know what our spirits have to gain, but we don't know what Mavado seeks to earn from all of this. He will never become an angel, no matter what he does, and his soul cannot be saved as he already lost his chance at salvation when he lived on Earth, so what's his reward? Not knowing his motivation is what makes me uneasy, and because he represents what we fight against, he becomes a villain by association."

Jericho's response was almost Mavado-like, a byproduct of their time spent in deep conversation, "His motivation comes from the belief that things aren't as black and white as people think. There is so much we don't know about God and eternity, heaven and hell that I can't say for sure that his soul is beyond saving. Honestly, he's been around for many lifetimes, so he's got to have a better perspective than we do, and the fact that he's choosing to exist like a Watcher means there must be something for him to gain by doing so."

"That's a dangerous line of thinking, my friend," replied Sunday. "Mavado thinks things aren't black and white because it suits his situation. God speaks very clearly about what is right and wrong, and from what the Bible says He's anything but neutral. The moment we begin to pick and choose what we want to believe is the same moment when the lines begin to blur beyond recognition. Then one day you realize you've drifted so far from where God commanded you to be, that you've become the enemy and didn't even notice. Things are black and white so that there will be no confusion regarding where you stand."

"I don't know if he's bad or not, but he's way cooler than Annabel," Delia butted back into the conversation, attempting to halt the escalating debate over Mavado's personal motivation, which was information that neither Jericho nor Sunday was actually privy to. "Besides, from what we heard today it looks like we'll need all the help we can get." Delia lifted her glass and consumed the remaining contents of her bloody beer, retrieved her phone from her purse and checked the new message which had buzzed in only a few minutes prior. "On that note, I'm going to head out and meet my friend Carrie, so I'll leave you boys to it. Try and play nice please, no more fighting okay?!"

Delia stood up and rifled through her purse in search of her wallet before Reggie volunteered to pick up the cost of her drink; she obliged him and said her goodbyes, then swung the massive purse over her shoulder, turned and headed for the exit. Her figure was petite but curvaceous; this day she was dressed in black, knee high boots and tight, hip hugging jeans which made her exit a sight to behold. The three of them took a few moments to take in the view as she quickly strutted out the door.

"Whew! She is a looker, no doubt about it," Reggie was the first to comment while Jericho quietly stared at the empty doorway, "and she's right; we can use all the help we can get. I'm with you Jericho, we all are, or we wouldn't be here."

Reggie lifted his hand and waved it about in an attempt to signal Yvonne over to their table, "Enough shop talk for today, it's time to let our hair down a bit since

Sunday is officially our driver for the evening." Reggie ordered a shot and another beer to chase it down, while Jericho ordered a shot of whiskey to accompany his whiskey and coke; it was painfully obvious to both Reggie and Sunday that Jericho was on a mission to drink himself into a mindless stupor.

Reggie had not the heart to let Jericho go it alone but decided that, as the two of them were safely under the watch of Sunday, it would be a grand opportunity to strengthen their bonds of friendship. There were no demons or Watchers present in the room, other than the ones hidden beneath the surface who watched silently as the living seized the moment and did their best to enjoy each other's company.

Chapter 9

Sunday arrived at Jericho's apartment complex with a look of weary frustration on his face; his patience had worn considerably from the continued subjection to the erratic and ridiculous behavior of his two drunken companions. Jericho was clearly the worst of the two as his inebriation had reached an epic level, while Reggie followed closely behind yet still remained in relatively good spirits; Reggie had proceeded to sing English drinking songs at deafening levels during the entirety of the car ride to Jericho's residence, much to the annoyance of Sunday who eagerly counted the moments until he was able to drop the two off and head home to bed.

While Jericho had made a few heavily-slurred attempts to join in and sing along with Reggie, he found little success in holding his focus as he teeter-tottered on the edge of consciousness, while also battling against the internal distraction of his own frustrated thoughts. When intoxicated to this level, Jericho was prone to emotional outbursts in the way that many intoxicated people are. His mind would often flood with both memories of the past and concerns of where he was headed; he would attempt to summarize his feelings in a drunken ramble which would make perfect sense in his own mind, but those who were subjected to it would often find nothing but confusion from the bombardment of fragmented thoughts. He felt himself primed to bubble over with emotions at any moment, but decided against sharing his thoughts on that evening; too many had already been expressed, and he was so near to home that the need for solitude had begun to grip him tightly with anxiety.

Relief came when the vehicle stopped, and Sunday beckoned in a tired, direct tone, "All right Jericho, this is you. You need help getting inside or are you good?" Jericho mustered all his remaining energy to perk up and confidently exclaim,

"I'm good, absolutely great!" as he groped for the door handle, which had seemed to camouflage itself somehow and necessitate a clumsy search before Sunday reached over and gladly assisted. The handle pulled and the door swung open, flooding the car with cool air which felt electric against Jericho's face as he lurched out from his seat and awkwardly slammed the door closed behind him. "Thanks for the ride gentlemen, be safe!" was Jericho's drunken farewell as he staggered off in the direction of his building, pursued by Reggie's parting words of, "Goodnight Arsehole! Love you too!" as Sunday drove off into the darkness.

Jericho stumbled through the breezeway toward his apartment door, with his body and mind numb as he felt the full effect of his night spent in excessive indulgence. He fumbled for his keys and began cycling through to locate the one which would allow him his much-needed privacy. On nights like this, the combination of exhaustion and inebriation would labor the simplicity of this act. After what seemed like a never-ending search, he finally achieved success; the key clicked into the lock, and an overly-forceful twist followed by an entrance resembling more a home invasion granted him passage. Jericho was home. With a singular focus, he locked the door behind him and headed straight for the bedroom.

Too much to drink had created a disregard for clean housekeeping, as Jericho began to shed articles of clothing and let them fall to the floor in a laundry trail toward his bedroom. He tumbled into bed face down with most clothing still intact; shoes, jacket and belt were all he could muster to remove before giving in to collapse. He slowly turned over onto his back, where his eyes met the ceiling fan directly above him.

The fan was not operating, but to Jericho it appeared to be just on the verge of beginning to spin. Alas, he knew this was just an illusion. The room was dark, with nothing but a bit of porch light streaming in through the window, light enough to cast shadows and play tricks on an already ravaged mind. His head was swimming with intoxication; his ears buzzed while his mind raced with a disoriented cascade of thoughts and emotions.

He felt the weight of his eyelids increasing as if they were slowly filling up with sand and becoming heavier with each passing second. Although extremely weary, Jericho's heart still pounded hard in his chest, and each thudding beat coursed through his ears like a thousand drums. While most in his condition would welcome rest, Jericho actually despised sleeping alone. Ever since he was a boy, he had suffered from horrifying night terrors which had only grown in intensity as he progressed into adulthood. That tiny window between the conscious and subconscious held a sometimes terrifying world, as reality and fantasy merged together into an indiscernible mess of sometimes shocking and horrifying imagery.

Jericho stared up at the ceiling with his heart still pounding and his breaths short and frantic, almost to the point of hyperventilation. With exhaustion about to swallow him up, he heard a faint yet clearly discernible whisper.

"Jericho."

Adrenaline spiked through his chest, for just as he had feared, this night would certainly not bring him a peaceful sleep. He heard a low rumble in the distance, which steadily grew into an earsplitting roar of sounds as the walls began to shake violently, sending vibrations which rattled though his bed frame and gave the feeling that the room was about to cave in around him.

As the building trembled with ever growing intensity, Jericho suddenly witnessed a great fire pour out from under all sides of his bed; the flames raced across the floor and up the walls which surrounded him, and then just as quickly swept across the ceiling and converged at the fan directly over his head, covering the entire room in a blanket of fire. Jericho and his bed were the only items which remained untouched by the flames, which only seemed to coat the objects it touched and not consume them.

Jericho knew he was stuck in limbo; not quite asleep yet not quite awake as the illusion unfolded before him, so he began to yell out for help and shift his body in an attempt to rattle himself back into consciousness, yet the rumble of sound extinguished his pleas and only grew louder still. He heard a loud cracking sound, and watched in awe and terror as suddenly the room around him began to come apart. As if assembled from millions of pieces, Jericho watched as walls, floor, ceiling, and every object in the room began to flake away and float upward into the sky. As the room dissolved, the space beyond its walls was a vast expanse of nothingness. It only took a matter of seconds before the rumbling silenced and all was gone; no sound, no light, nothing except darkness.

As if the world in a single moment had been wiped away around him, Jericho remained weightless in the void, unafraid and undisturbed as he breathed in the darkness; he longed to deeply experience every second of the calm he had instantly discovered and remained silent and motionless. Then, just as quickly as the quiet peace washed over him, the most unique scent filled his nostrils. It was an odor of candle smoke and fireplace ashes; an almost clean yet burnt smell if such a thing could exist. And then a sound so clear and distinct began to reverberate toward his ears—it was a slow, clicking sound reminiscent of fingernails tapping on a wooden tabletop.

A voice pierced the darkness, "Good evening, Jericho."

Jericho opened his eyes and found himself in an old familiar place, "Hello Mavado."

He was back in the same room where countless meetings between himself and Mavado had occurred, the perfectly imagined replica of his father's study. Jericho's vision was blurred, and he began to blink his eyes in an attempt to clear his vision as the room slowly came into focus. Jericho's attention was immediately drawn to his father's desk, in particular to the foot-tall hourglass which was positioned at its left corner.

He had been fascinated by the hourglass from an early age, where as a boy he would often sneak into the study, turn the glass over, and simply watch as the sand slowly descended and collected at the bottom. Not only was it perfectly designed and always ran on time, it was a thing of majestic beauty; comprised of black marble and adorned with gold leaf accents, it was dark and elegant and a perfect conversation piece. The hourglass was an heirloom which had passed down through four generations of the Coleman family, yet when Jason Coleman took possession he made his own personal customization to the treasured object; installing a golden nameplate which bore his own name.

It was a fairly typical act of arrogance the elder Coleman had become notorious for in the latter years of his existence, before mental instability had led to his violent demise. The hourglass in Jericho's imagined room also contained the golden nameplate, but was blank and bore no name or inscription of any kind as he did all that he could to banish any memory of his father, and the appearance of the hourglass was no exception.

This type of designated meeting place within the mind was not exclusive to Jericho and Mavado; in fact, every host and Watcher also had a unique transition room which reflected the host's individual personality. Jericho had selected the study as a foundation for his room, as it was the first place he met Mavado on that fateful day when his life was saved and logically Jericho always had a mental predisposition toward picturing Mavado in that location.

151

The study itself was truly a thing of beauty; mahogany bookcases lined the walls and were packed with first edition printings. The books in this world, unlike their real world counterparts, only contained memories acquired over Jericho's rather short lifetime, as well as his accumulated knowledge and experience. On the left side of the study stood a desk which was covered with a number of periodicals, strewn about it in an almost intentional mess, and also contained the cherished hourglass along with an old-fashioned typewriter and a vintage reading lamp. Directly behind the desk was the wall sized-window which served as both the eyes of Jericho when Mavado was unleashed into the world, and the gateway for Jericho to exchange places with Mavado via the hourglass.

In the center of the room stood two rich leather chairs which faced each other, with a small coffee table positioned between them. On the table sat a rather expensive chess set which primarily was assembled for decorative purposes rather than actual use; Jericho could not actually recall a single memory from his childhood when the set was used for its intended purpose, although he did find it to be rather aesthetically pleasing and often wished that the particular set still existed in the real world.

On this night, there were a few additional features in the room which deviated from its usual appearance. The coffee table, which traditionally would only house the chess set, also presented a large bottle of whiskey and two glasses filled with ice. The room was dimly lit; no lamps were burning and no light emanated through the study window, but instead the fireplace was the only source of illumination. Burning brightly with a raging fire, it provided all the light necessary to view the room's contents, as well as any and all occupants who were present.

Jericho had come to believe that the room of transition was really more a form of purgatory than anything else, with the unfortunate inhabitants drifting in limbo until they purged themselves from its restricted enclosure. He continued to stare with his eyes fixed on the hourglass, until his gaze was broken once more by the loud clicking sound which had first caught his ears back in the darkened void. They were indeed fingernails, slowly and methodically tapping in succession against a mahogany end table, as if playing a symphony of impatience to anyone who cared to listen. Jericho's eyes were drawn to the hand generating them; unsurprisingly, it was the demon that authored the sound, seated in his usual chair as he waited for Jericho's arrival.

Same suit, same long nails, same teeth, same tattoo, same burning golden eyes. Mavado always looked just as he did the day Jericho met him, absent his beautiful wings of course. The two locked stares from their respective positions in the room, with Mavado seated with one leg crossed over the other, still rapping his nails on the end table, Jericho's curiosity toward Mavado had been replaced in adulthood by ever growing suspicion; maturity on Jericho's part had drifted the two apart considerably, and although he would always defend Mavado from his critics, Jericho had secretly begun to think of the demon as toxic. While necessary, and certainly irreplaceable, Jericho felt his association with the spirit was poisonous to his soul, and only pushed him closer to condemnation with each passing year. Coupled with his inebriated and fragile emotional state, he was not pleased to see the tenant of his mind at that particular moment.

"It is good to see you have not forgotten how to acknowledge my greetings, even though I have been calling you for quite some time now without a response. I will of course forgive the poor etiquette as any proper gentleman would, if you would oblige me by taking a seat and sharing a drink." Mavado took the bottle and poured a shot of whiskey into each glass.

"Cheers,"

Mavado lifted his glass and took the swig of whiskey without companionship, while Jericho looked on as Mavado returned the empty glass to the table. The act of drinking in an imaginary room was purely symbolic of course; as Jericho had shared drinks with his friends in the real world, Mavado felt that extending the invitation at that moment would be in keeping with the evening's festivities.

As he consumed the whiskey and returned the glass to the table, the demon's expression remained blank as if all he had consumed was water. "Then again, it appears as if you have already had far too much to drink, you should really consider a bit more restraint, Jericho. You only live once, after all." The words brought a chuckle from his own lips, as Mavado understood better than most the concept of eternity and the fleeting nature of existence in human form.

"Why have you been calling for me, Mavado? What could you possibly want to talk about now?" Jericho replied with frustration in his voice as he stumbled forward and awkwardly plopped into the chair facing Mavado, the effects of his consumption still gripping him within the confines of his mind.

"What could I want to talk about? Hmm . . . well, I've spent the last several hours watching you indulge in another one of your excessive evenings; as you know I consider such behavior to be a waste of both time and energy, although I do suppose that taking the opportunity to forge stronger bonds

154

with your teammates could eventually provide some benefit. So perhaps tonight was not a complete waste after all." Mavado reached for the whiskey bottle, removed the cork and proceeded to pour himself half a glass worth of whiskey, failing this time to also offer a drink to Jericho as he knew it would not be accepted.

"What's it to you, Mavado? It doesn't really affect you if I get shitfaced or not." Jericho rubbed his face in an exhausted fashion with both his hands while Mavado finished pouring his whiskey, with the faintest of smiles creeping across his face in reaction to Jericho's words.

"Not true, actually. If you were to die of alcohol poisoning, or take a drunken tumble down some stairs and bash your head in, it would put an abrupt end to our time here together. Seeing as neither of those things happened today, I suppose the worst we can hope for is a wasted day in bed tomorrow as you hide from the sunlight." The two met stares yet again, as Mavado's half smirk competed with an indifferent expression on the face of Jericho.

The demon took another sip of his whiskey and continued, "It was interesting to watch all of you interact earlier tonight, although I am surprised that you did not try harder to convince Delia to abandon her plans, and instead drink the night away with you. She is a fascinating creature; she lacks the usual fear and suspicion which most humans project toward me, which is most certainly a welcome change. But clearly, Delia is not the one whom you truly desire; I imagine that if her eyes had been glowing blue, you would have followed her right out the front door," Still clutching his whiskey glass, Mavado leaned back in his chair and crossed his legs again.

"You don't know what you're talking about Mavado. I care for both Delia and Annabel; in fact I care for all my friends and the spirits within them. I know that's a concept you could never understand. That's why I've wanted the chance to fight by their side, so I can protect them from things like you."

Mavado sipped his whiskey casually, his expression still amused. "Well Jericho, first off it is I who intervene and protect your 'friends.' I know, I know, with your authorization, but nonetheless, I do put in the leg work, so you have me to thank for the preservation of those you have chosen to hold close to your heart. And secondly, you speak as if I am nothing but a lonely monster, incapable of caring for anything or anyone. I had friends in my old life, and family whom I loved deeply, and now I have you. Are we not friends?" Mavado grinned from ear to ear, raised his glass in a mock toast and proceeded to take another sip of his whiskey.

Jericho was still slumped in his chair, with a look that was equal parts disheveled and amused; his eyes had closed as if he were attempting to drift off to sleep, but the faint smile on his face revealed that he was still actively listening.

"Nope, you and I aren't friends. You're like that unwelcomed house guest who doesn't quite know when to say goodnight."

"Come now, I think we are friends. I am probably the closest friend you will ever have. I've known you since you were a boy; I know your innermost thoughts, desires, pain, suffering, insecurities, and every once in a while, joy. I like you Jericho, you've got real potential. But like so many other young men, you become easily distracted by lovely women and immature desires. In your case, the pretty girl you truly lust after has already had her chance to live, and now only exists as nothing but an angel wannabe."

Mavado's last words carried with them a hint of malice; a fact not lost on Jericho, who opened his eyes and directed his full attention toward the demon in response. He understood that Mavado was privy to his thoughts and feelings, so the act of insulting Annabel was seen as a real attempt to provoke an emotional response from him.

"Annabel has a real purpose, Mavado. She could've stayed in Heaven and enjoyed eternity, but she chose to come back and make a difference here. In my opinion, what she's doing is way better than being a devil wannabe like you."

Mavado's expression remained amused, and laughter carried in his words as if nothing could be said to stifle his good spirits. "Annabel has a purpose? The poor girl has no memory of who she was, which means you most certainly could not know anything relevant about Annabel either! Hell, I probably have more knowledge regarding her situation than the two of you combined."

Mavado sipped his whiskey as Jericho felt his agitation continue to grow, but he also felt the tiniest curiosity toward Mavado's implication of possessing exclusive information in regards to Annabel. While a part of him believed that perhaps the demon was simply putting him on, he also had a strong desire to probe further.

"Okay then, if you know so much more than we do, then please share. What could you possibly know about Annabel? Was she one of your friends you claim to have had in your old life? Was she your girlfriend? Is that why you're

157

so interested in my intentions?" Sarcasm laced his words; he hoped to return the favor and provoke an emotional response from Mavado, but the demon would not allow him the satisfaction.

"What do I know? Now that is not a question which I have the time to answer now, nor could I fully respond to it if you and I had the rest of your lifetime to discuss it. You forget that I have existed for a very, very long time, and have witnessed the rise and fall of civilizations. As such, I do have a thorough understanding of human nature and the ways of the world. So how much would you truly like to know?" Mavado's expression was now serious, as the smirk had faded away completely.

"Everything; tell me everything you know." Jericho's reply was as serious as Mavado's question, as the smile had vanished from his face as well.

Mavado uncrossed his legs and leaned forward in his chair. He placed his elbows on his knees and clasped his hands together, interlocking his long fingers and sharpened nails. In this position, his intertwined fingers took on the faint resemblance of a jagged cage, and only served to accentuate his sinister appearance. "*Everything,* you say? Again, I'll defer to my previous statement on 'everything' being unrealistic, but I will be more than happy to impart some of my knowledge upon you. As you know, I was once like you and walked the earth as an ordinary human being. This is true for all of us; Annabel, Garrison, Fortunado and Ignavus. Of course, you know this already, as Michael filled you in on all the details when he first discovered you. But do you know why Annabel has no memory of her past? It was not by her choice, but instead was hidden by a higher power for reasons which, in her case, are admittedly a mystery to me. It is

158

possible that, if you knew the type of person she was in her old life, you might be far less infatuated with her."

Where are you going with this Mavado?" Jericho blurted out in frustration, yet Mavado was unwavering and continued.

"It is clear that the two of you share a bond which makes you exceedingly vulnerable. If the time came when your friends turned against you in battle, would you have the heart to destroy your beloved Annabel? I believe we both know the answer to that question, and that is what makes you weak."

Jericho felt his anger intensify as he interjected. "Annabel wouldn't destroy me either; it's not the kind of person she is."

Mavado reached for his glass and took another sip before offering his rebuttal. "Lesson one, Jericho; no one every truly changes; you are who you are, and not circumstance, nor chance, nor anything linked to this world or the next will modify a person's true inner nature. Annabel had a heart to change the world in her old life, to live outside her own needs or desires and make a true imprint on the lives of others, just as she is attempting to do now. No death or loss of who she was could change her heart, which makes her as foolish now as she was then." Mavado chuckled once more while Jericho felt his anger continue to rise, "You're a real piece of shit, Mavado. You laugh at a genuinely good person who still tries to help others even after dying. You could learn a thing from her."

Mavado just smiled between sips of whiskey and replied, "Jericho, she is the one who needs to learn, and that's my point entirely. Sooner or later her memory will come roaring back, and she will become all that she was, and will no longer be the girl you know. She will not look at you with the same compassion and concern she holds now once her perspective comes into line, and certainly will not hold any love for an old demon like me. I believe her purpose here is to act as our destroyer, 'when the hour of his choosing arrives.' You could say she will become our Delilah."

"Enough! I don't have to listen to this from you!!" Jericho jumped from his seat, his face reddened with anger. "What do you want from me?? Are you bored and need someone to talk to? Can't seem to keep yourself entertained in here? All right, I'll shoot the shit with you! Let's talk about something else then. If you're so powerful and mighty, so wise, so unstoppable, why are you at the mercy of a twenty-three year old man? You sit here alone in a dark room, sipping imaginary whiskey and waiting on me like a jilted girlfriend! Is this what you expected when you saved me? Was this your master plan? Tell me!"

Wearisome of Mavado's constant psychoanalysis of all things Jericho, he had endured enough—he decided, in that instant, that he no longer owed Mavado anything, much less courtesy or respect. Upon hearing the rebuke, the smile which was ordinarily so prominent on Mavado's face retreated into a noticeably bothered expression, "All right then, let us speak now about my expectations." Mavado's face was serious; he clasped his hands together with his ring fingers touched at the tips and pointed at Jericho. "I'm tired Jericho, tired of my prison. I'm tired of watching you waste time, waste life, and wallow about without true purpose. If you believe the Watchers are your allies then you are a fool, for they will destroy us when we are no longer useful. Garrison wants me defeated, to be cast out to wander the earth powerless until the end of days, and he is not alone in this feeling. Of course, as my defeat would also mean your death, you, too, have plenty to lose." Mavado stood up, looked at Jericho with a disgusted expression and proceeded towards the study window with deliberate, methodical steps.

The window lacked the usual foggy light which provided illumination to the room, and instead held nothing but darkness behind it. The ominous orange glow from the fireplace permeated the room; the light from the flames flickered and flowed, casting dancing, eerie shadows throughout the study. Mavado reached the window and stared outside into nothingness, his hands clasped behind his back.

Jericho looked on as Mavado stood in front of the window; his anger had retreated and was replaced by feelings of remorse for his previous outburst, "Mavado, I know we both have everything to lose, but I don't think you fully understand Annabel and the rest of the team, in spite of how long you've been around. Garrison could have killed me years ago but instead he chose to save me. Annabel saved my life before they even understood how 'useful' we could be. Isn't it possible that you could be wrong about her? Or wrong about Garrison or the others?

Silence fell upon the room as Mavado continued to stand and gaze out the window into the dark void, unresponsive and appearing completely oblivious to Jericho's presence. Jericho's irritation began to return at the thought that Mavado was now ignoring his words. "What exactly are you looking at Mavado? There's nothing outside that Goddamn window but darkness."

Mavado continued to stare, undisturbed by Jericho's comment before responding in an almost reflective fashion; "I do see things outside this window; I've spent most of your life watching the world through this very porthole. I see freedom, possibilities, potential. I see the world in its most raw and natural form, and the people who inhabit it; all their flaws, perceived strengths, and selfish desires. Through this window I see myself as well; I see how far beyond them I have grown."

Mavado turned his head and met eyes with Jericho. "I am a king, Jericho. I am a king among the demons and Watchers alike, let alone over humanity. You spoke of expectations, well, I expect that you and I will be kings together, serving a far grander purpose in the way that so many of the great leaders of the past once did. And yet I find myself with a true dilemma for which there is no obvious solution."

"What's the dilemma, Mavado?" Jericho's tone was indifferent and his expression dismissive. Mavado broke his gaze and returned his attention to the dark void beyond the window as he continued to speak. "I'm just beginning to realize that you have not the stomach to rule the masses. In truth, you lack the ability to rule your own existence. And, as we are linked together, it would seem that I also lack the ability to govern my existence."

Being lectured by a creature Jericho considered to be of questionable morality was normally a situation which would be casually dismissed. Yet Jericho understood that while Mavado's perspective was distorted from a biblical outlook, his views did carry some elements of truth. Despite Jericho's arguments to the contrary, he had always believed he was on borrowed time with the Watchers, as the interactions he had with them outside of his immediate team were hardly welcoming. Jericho also understood that the changing climate sparked by the appearance of Luther Monroe would surely generate more clearly defined lines between friend and foe. Perhaps Mavado was right; perhaps his time was running out, wasting away when it could be better spent in preparation for what was yet to come.

"Jericho, how do you not see the world as it is? How do you ignore truth as it looks you dead in the eyes? Our destinies are locked together my friend; fate has pulled us together from opposite ends of an immense spectrum. I knew that the moment I met you. I chose you, and you chose me; not out of necessity, or fear, or chance, but you chose me because in that moment you recognized your future. You asked if my current situation was my 'master plan.' It truly was. This was meant to be."

With an expression which could almost be described as exhibiting pity, Mavado turned his head from the window and met eyes with Jericho once more. His tone changed, and with calm words he offered an olive branch to his host. "Get some much needed rest my friend. I offer my apologies for troubling you on a night meant for escaping from the dark realities of coming days. Sleep well." Jericho's eyes were red, his face covered with a weary expression as he turned and slowly walked to the door. Mavado called out after him, "Oh, and next time we are called into battle, do remember to bring the swords, as they are far more useful in my hands than under the seat of the truck!" Mavado's tone was light and humorous, as he uttered the words in an attempt to part ways with Jericho on good terms.

Jericho stopped at the doorway, turned slightly and looked over his shoulder as a smirk crept across his face. "I thought you didn't need any help, Mavado?"

"If you allow me to be all that I am, young Jericho, then you and I will need nothing." In that final moment as they looked at each other, a mutual admiration was shared. As much as Mavado would never admit it, he admired Jericho's loyalty. Jericho was unwavering in his beliefs, no matter how the consequences impacted him personally, and would always make an effort to defend Mavado against his critics. Jericho admired Mavado's talents; he was gifted with tremendous power which gave him the potential to change the world. The motivation behind Mavado's actions, a debatable subject, was the real flaw. Jericho often wondered about the marvelous things he himself could do, if only he were blessed with Mavado's gifts.

Jericho's hand reached for the doorknob. A twist, a click and the door was opened, a hollow feeling washed over him as his hand touched the cold, metallic doorknob, instantly flooding his heart with an unshakable loneliness. He felt as if the cold from the doorknob traveled up his arm and permeated his soul, amplifying the fact that when he stepped through the imaginary door he would again find himself alone. It was enough to make him wish that he had tried harder to woo Delia to join him in drinking the night away as Mavado had suggested. He took a bit of solace however, in knowing that the doorway would also lead to dreams which Mavado would choose not to invade, and to a place where Jericho could spend a few cherished moments with Annabel. For a longing heart, even the chance to share time with an imaginary projection of the thing you love the most, is a welcome opportunity.

Chapter 10

Michael sat quietly in the lobby of Goldstein, Bachman & Brown, his knee bobbing up and down in a dance of boredom and anxiety as he quietly waited for Mr. Albert Goldstein to request his presence. He had only been waiting a relatively short fifteen minutes, yet had already completed thumbing through both the worn-out copy of Time magazine and the scattered remnants of the daily newspaper, which had been thoroughly ravaged by the various clients who had passed through the lobby.

Goldstein's office was located on the eighteenth floor of an expensive high rise office building, and carried a modern, decadent look. The doors which provided access to the lobby were made of transparent glass, and allowed the occupants to view the continuous traffic of employees and clients who traveled up and down the hallways; those who passed by would often swivel their heads and glance into the well-lit area, giving those inside the distinctly uncomfortable feeling of being on display. Michael detested the continued bombardment of curious eyes which crossed his path as he attempted to patiently wait, and for a brief moment he felt imprisoned; all that seemed to be missing was a sign stating to refrain from touching the glass, and a caution to not feed the dangerous animal within.

In truth, he despised all waiting rooms. No matter what the situation, it always seemed that the occupants of a lobby were preparing for bad news; he noticed that they would usually sit stone-faced and silent as the wall clock ticked loudly in an ominous serenade, while any children who happened to be present would take an entirely opposite stance and race from wall to wall, shouting boisterously and without restraint. If it was a doctor's office, you feared your test results, or if it were a bank you feared loan denial or insufficient funds. A legal office, like the one Michael waited in that morning, now that would usually bring a myriad of frightening possibilities to those who were unfortunate enough to find themselves confined within its walls.

Michael's anxiety on that morning was not due to his own transgressions, as the counsel he sought was not of the legal variety. While Albert Goldstein was a wealthy and prominent attorney by societal standards, he was also host to the Regional Commander of the Watchers, who held rank over Garrison's team along with two others. His territory was comprised of the entirety of the state of Virginia, and each of the three teams which reported to him consisted of one captain and three team members, with the exception of Garrison who had taken on one additional member in Mavado's freelance inclusion. This meant that only thirteen Watchers and one demon were responsible for defending almost 43,000 square miles, a staggering fact which brought weight to the biblical concept of, "many are called, few are chosen."

The law offices of Goldstein, Bachman & Brown also doubled as the region's unofficial headquarters, yet it was a rarity for all thirteen Watchers to be ordered to report in together. In most cases the captains would meet with the commander, acquire their orders and return to brief their respective teams on any assigned duties. Such was the case on this day; Garrison and his two contemporaries had been called together for an emergency meeting in regard to Albert's review of Michael's report. Reggie's analysis and Mavado's testimony had been complied together and delivered two days prior, and the content provoked an immediate response due its rather sensational nature.

"Mr. Goldstein will see you now." The smooth words of the secretary shook Michael from his mini-trance, for he had been lost in his own thoughts as he mentally prepared for the conversation ahead. He stewed with internal frustration at the thought that he would be relegated to a spectator role, as he understood that he would only view the proceedings through the window of his imagined room while Garrison discussed the next course of action with the other Watchers. While Michael held Mavado with as much suspicion as anyone else, he actually agreed with the demon on his opinion that the living members of the team stood to lose the most of all the parties involved; if decisions were to be made which would put the group in mortal danger, Michael believed that the mortals should be the ones to provide the most input.

While hosts did possess the ability to boycott any decision made by the Watchers, actual challenges were at best a rare occurrence. Time after time the possessed would simply follow the assigned orders of their commander

167

without regard to personal consequences. Yet in all those previous instances, they had not faced an opponent who was presumed to be as dangerous and formidable as Monroe; the aura of invincibility which the Watchers carried had begun to fade in Michael's eyes, and he knew it would only be a matter of time until his living counterparts would come to share his concern, that is if they did not already hold unspoken apprehensions.

Upon hearing the invitation from the secretary, Michael stood from his seat and quickly headed for Albert's office. As he reached the door, his eyes lit up with the familiar blue iris which signified Garrison's manifestation, as the spirit wasted no time and immediately assumed control before entering the room. Visits to the commander were purely business, and as the hosts for the captains did not know each other on a personal level, meetings always took place with all spirits in a physically manifested state.

Garrison stepped inside Albert's office and shut the door behind him. As he turned his attention to the room, his view was consumed by the sight of Albert sitting behind his desk, along with the presence of three chairs which were positioned directly in front of him. The middle and right chair were already occupied by a dark haired, athletically built man in his mid-thirties, and a red haired, olive skinned woman in her forties, respectively, which made Garrison's seat selection abundantly clear.

"Welcome Garrison, my apologies for keeping you waiting. I wanted to finish briefing Nicholas and Harley on your report so we could all be reading the same sheet of music, so to speak." Albert's voice crackled with a raspy, harsh tone; indicating to those who heard it that the years had not been kind to him. While his eyes were also glowing blue to signify the control of his Watcher, Albert experienced no additional changes to his physical presence, as the commander did nothing to alter his voice or any other aspect of his appearance. Albert's spirit took his lack of individuality further than most Watchers, as he did not utilize any code name but chose to simply be referred to by his host's name, Albert. Michael assumed that this was due to the use of Albert's business as their headquarters; strange voices and rapidly transforming appearances would lack practicality in a high traffic office building, and did nothing to help maintain the low profile which they so earnestly desired.

Albert's face was weathered and leathery, peppered with liver spots which made him look every bit in his mid-seventies. His hair was thinning and gray, with the few remaining strands combed straight back in a style which was surely more flattering in his younger days, and he was dressed in an expensive gray suit and black tie ensemble which looked stereotypical when considering his line of work.

While Albert appeared physically feeble, the spirit within him was every bit worthy of its elevated position and wielded more power that any Watcher under his command; power which often went underutilized as Albert rarely engaged in direct battle, but instead left the field work to the captains and their teams.

Garrison swiftly headed for the empty seat as he responded, "No apology necessary Albert; if everyone is aware of our situation, we can dive right into solutions rather than recount past events. Good to see you Nicholas, and you Harley." Nicholas was the name of the dark-haired man to his right, who was dressed in a black polo shirt, bulletproof vest, khaki pants, and tactical work boots. He had the typical look of a private security contractor, right down to his athletic build and square jaw which were complemented by his overly tactical appearance. Like Albert, Nicholas shared the name of his host and also chose to retain his host's existing physical characteristics, with the exception of the color of his irises—they glowed a florescent green which was reminiscent of when Ignavus's manifested outward from Reggie.

"Good of you to join us, Garrison, although I do not believe there is much more discussion needed in the way of solutions. We will extinguish this threat, just as we have done all other times before," Nicholas had a smug, simplistic tone as he acknowledged Garrison's greeting, and appeared unfazed by the danger which Luther Monroe was presumed to pose to the Watchers. "Monroe is as feeble as the countless others whom we have destroyed over the years; we need only to arrive at his doorstep and do what must be done."

Nicholas' words burned Garrison with their casual assessment of Monroe, whose true strength had not yet been determined. Garrison was a warrior through and through; he understood better than most what an overconfident approach could cost to those who believe themselves invincible.

"With respect my brother, there is a bit more to the process than that. We must track down the murderer and identify the number of his forces, formulate a battle strategy, determine his strengths and weaknesses . . ."

"You are quite right, and in fact, we have already done just that," Albert interjected, bringing an immediate silence to Garrison's assessment. "Monroe has returned to the compound he inhabited during his human existence, so in truth, he is hiding from no one. I am sending the three of you and your respective teams to converge upon him and his followers. Harley and her team have already performed reconnaissance on the area; they detected only Monroe and two other enemy spirits within the structure. He has also recruited a few hundred human followers who frequently travel to and from the grounds, but as you know, an ordinary human poses no real threat to us."

"I recommended using my team only, but Albert believes a more unified show of force will be necessary. Thirteen versus three appears a bit excessive, but it seems our commander is growing more cautious in his old age." Nicholas directed his words at Garrison yet chose not to make eye contact and instead merely looked down and picked at his fingernails in a dismissive manner.

"You will be joining us in the field, Albert?" Garrison was puzzled, as the indication of thirteen spirits signified that the teams of four would be joined by one additional being.

"I will not, but the rogue spirit whom you command will be." Albert's tone was serious, and flooded Garrison with surprise.

"You have never before requested his inclusion; if anything, I have been criticized quite often for allowing his participation, so with all due respect, I would like to know why you are accepting him now." In no way was Garrison disagreeing with Mavado's involvement, as the spirit had proven time after time to be a valuable commodity in battle. Yet the sudden change in philosophy did provoke his curiosity enough to force an inquiry into Albert's intentions.

Albert's expression was unwaveringly serious as he responded to Garrison, with his hands clasped together in front of him and his elbows resting on the desk. "From what your report tells us, the demons are unable to shield each other from entering their own places of refuge. If that is the case, then Mavado provides us the best chance to infiltrate our enemies' territory. If this demon wishes to destroy his own kind, then we should allow him the opportunity, for it has been said that 'a house divided against itself cannot stand.' We would be foolish to intervene against such a favorable prophesy. If it turns out that Mavado does intend to betray us and fight beside his brothers, then the twelve will destroy him as well. In either case, we will have victory over our enemies."

"So, you would send the beast to his demise, but what of the boy who contains him? Have we not been commanded to protect God's children? It is agreed that the demon will someday be judged for his transgressions, but we cannot destroy Jericho because of what lurks within him, even if we would gain from it." Garrison interjected at the behooving of Michael, who voiced his own concerns within his mind to the Watcher. If he would not be involved in the conversation personally, Michael still ensured his thoughts and opinions would make their way into the conversation by one means or another.

"I have not suggested such a thing, nor would I, Garrison. I only expect that we will do what we must if the situation calls for it, and you cannot deny that Mavado's defeat at the hands of his own kind would only benefit our cause. You have insisted on aligning yourself with this enemy, and yet resist when I finally endorse his involvement. What do you believe is the proper course of action, then?" Albert's voice cracked with frustration toward Garrison's reaction. While he respected Garrison's experience and battle prowess, Albert was not keen on having to justify his orders to someone of an inferior rank.

"You have nothing to fear," Nicholas interrupted, as the turn in conversation had reignited his interest and directed his focus away from his improvised grooming. "For we would never intentionally abandon the demon in battle and leave him to be slaughtered. That is, after all, your area of expertise, to leave a 'good' man behind to die in order to serve your own selfish needs. Do not presume us to be fools. You believe that protecting the boy will bring your redemption and see you restored to former glory. I know it must pain you greatly to have fallen so far—from commanding grand armies as a king, to now clearing out damned souls from back alleys and abandoned homes with but a handful of warriors who bend to your will. It is your selfish nature which has failed to change, for it commands you as loudly in death as it did in life."

Nicholas stared across at Garrison as he uttered the venomous words. While each Watcher was called to mask his or her identity from the world, the Watchers themselves were very much aware of whom the others were in their former lives. Nicholas was one who often used that knowledge when it proved beneficial, or when it provided an opportunity to upstage his rivals.

"I am not the only one who seeks to gain, but I am merely one of thirteen. That is the reason we are all here, and not already elevated to more glorious posts. I too am no fool, for I know you seek to be unwavering and inflexible in your time here; a stark contrast from a man once universally loved by the people for his accommodating ways. That admiration you sought led to compromise, which led you astray. I would caution you in your adoption of this new philosophy. In your effort to be rigid, do not forget to yield to the will of the one who sent you, or to the will of those who hold authority over you."

"That's quite enough from the both of you," Albert impatiently chimed in, "Quarrel on your own time if it suits you, but while you report to me you will refrain from strangling each other and stay focused on the assignments you are given. We will not fight against each other, and in doing so conduct ourselves as we expect our enemies to. I expect nothing but the best from you two, understood?" Garrison and Nicholas had both fallen silent, and in response to Albert's question they both uttered a confirming "understood," before Albert continued.

"Now, in three days time your teams will convene here for a final briefing, before proceeding together to Monroe's location. Upon arriving at the compound, you will then engage the murderer and his followers and wipe them out. Mavado will join you to provide any support you may need, and it will be his actions which ultimately decide his fate, not the opinions of either one of you. Nicholas will assume command of the operation, with you Garrison serving as his second. Harley, you and your team will surround the area and provide containment while the others storm the complex. The objective is to destroy Monroe, which means our focus should be nowhere else. Do we all understand what is expected?"

Each of the three uttered a confirming "Yes," before Albert quickly concluded, "Very good. Now, if no other matters are pressing, then you all are dismissed as my host has a meeting of his own to attend to. Worldly matters, of course, but it would seem that even if the world were about to stop, its obligations never do. Good hunting."

With that, the meeting had come to an abrupt end. Albert stood from his chair, and the three quickly followed his lead and each gave a slight nod of affirmation before turning to leave. They headed toward the office door with the

174

glow in their eyes washing away, as each spirit retreated back into the mind of their respective host. Michael emerged with both a sense of frustration over what had transpired, and a dislike for Nicholas which was equal to Garrison's.

He realized that his friend Jericho was fast becoming expendable to the Watchers, and while he understood that he did have influence over Garrison's actions as his host, it was also obvious that the hosts of Nicholas and Harley would not be easily convinced to protect Jericho; Michael believed that they viewed Jericho's potential demise as necessary, merely collateral damage in the war against their enemy which would be easily justified and casually dismissed.

The three proceeded through the lobby and out into the hallway toward the elevators without stopping or exchanging words with each other. Michael was anxious to share his concerns with the two hosts of Nicholas and Harley; he felt a sense of urgency and wished to appeal to them directly in the hope of swaying their opinions toward his own, yet he did not know either one on a personal level as they were all acquaintances at best. Regardless, he also understood that they were all human, and lacked the jaded perspective that hundreds or thousands of years can cultivate in an old soul. It was a thought which gave him the slightest hope, enough hope to inspire him to make an attempt, even if it would turn out to have been in vain.

Harley stepped forward and pressed the button to call the elevator, and a few brief moments passed before the doors opened to reveal an empty elevator car. The three stepped in, and Michael quickly pushed the button to shut the door, realizing that the trip to the lobby would potentially be his last opportunity to address the two without interruption. The doors slid shut with a metallic clink as Michael began to speak in a hurried fashion. "I know I don't really know y'all that well, but—you're Nicholas right?—and your real name's Amanda?" Michael looked from Nicholas to Harley, which was a code name used by her host in the conventional way of the Watchers.

"Amber." she replied in a tone which distinctly lacked emotional interest.

"Amber, well I'm Michael. I know y'all don't know anything about me, but we're all people so we got that in common, and so is Jericho. They got their plans and want to see Mavado gone, but to get rid of him means killing Jericho too, and he hasn't done nothing to deserve that."

The elevator reached the ground floor faster than Michael expected, the doors slid open and Nicholas and Amber silently turned their attention to the lobby and quickly exited, followed in close pursuit by Michael as he continued his plea, "Jericho has control over Mavado, and he's done a hell of a lot of good and sure as hell isn't going to turn on us as long as we don't turn on him." The words seemed to fall on deaf ears as the three of them continued through the lobby with a hurried pace, exited the building and stepped out into the brisk mid-morning air.

"I'm telling you, I feel like nobody gives a shit about killing a good man," Nicholas finally stopped in his tracks as Amber continued her quick walk down the street and disappeared out of sight. Michael halted as well, and Nicholas turned to face him with a somewhat bemoaned expression as he began his reply, "Listen pal, you seem like a good guy, and I'm sure Jericho probably is, too. But it's not my job to figure out who the good guys or the bad guys are; it's my job to follow the orders I've been given." Nicholas's human voice was no different than his spiritual counterparts in much the same way as Albert's, yet the smug tone which his Watcher exhibited was noticeably absent. "We both signed up for this knowing that things wouldn't be easy, but I take the guesswork out of it by doing what I'm told. Let's face the facts: destroying demons is exactly what we signed up to do."

"I know what I signed up for, but he's family to me. I'll always protect my family, against anybody or anything. I don't care about the consequences, I got to do what I know is right, and I'm asking you to think about what's right instead of what someone else wants." Michael's voice was firm; if this was his one chance to reach Nicholas's host then he needed to lay all the cards on the table and find out where Jericho stood among the others.

"Look, I appreciate where you're coming from, I really do. If I were in your shoes I'd probably be saying the same thing. But the truth is, it's not my place to decide what's right, and if we're being honest, your boy was wrong to get mixed up with something like Mavado. He made that choice, and it was his mistake to make. We all made our choices, and now we've got to live with them."

As he finished his thought, Nicholas turned and headed down the sidewalk while Michael remained frozen in place. Nicholas shouted a final offering as he walked away, "It all comes down to choices, bud; sometimes being the bad guy is determined by one or two big decisions in your life. Try not to get too distracted by all the filler in between."

Nicholas continued on his way as Michael turned and headed in the opposite direction. He understood the man's perspective, yet he held within himself a glimmer of hope that perhaps Nicholas would indeed take the same stance if he were in Michael's position. That common ground provided at least a slim chance that Nicholas could be convinced to spare Jericho, should the Watchers plan to eliminate Mavado without just cause.

As Michael returned to his motorcycle to begin the trip back home, he heard the voice of Garrison ring in his ears, "You must understand; it is folly to believe you can convince the others to protect Jericho, much less Mavado." Michael replied back in thought to Garrison, who heard the answer loud and clear; "Maybe you're right; I can't expect much from anybody else. But I do expect your team to protect Jericho. You promised me that you'd protect him, and the others follow your orders. So just make sure you give the right orders."

Garrison remained silent, but Michael knew the spirit was good to his word. He started the bike and headed back to gather the team together and brief them on Albert's commands; in three days time they would come face to face with their new enemy. He also held a bitter taste in his mouth as he silently wondered just how many new enemies would be revealed in the coming days. Lines which had once seemed so clear were now blurring beyond distinction, with the difference between friend and foe nearly indiscernible. It was a thought which plagued his mind and drowned out the city traffic which surrounded him, and a feeling he knew would only intensify over time.

Chapter 11

The passage of time between Michael's meeting with the Watchers and the planned siege of Luther Monroe's compound felt like an eternity to Jericho; he had been informed of their impending mission only a few hours after Michael left the office, and at the very moment when Jericho became aware, an achingly slow, methodical countdown started in his mind which sought to rob him of his rest, appetite, and mental focus. The combination of fear and anticipation chilled him to his core; he felt ill, as if he had swallowed a frozen stone which was now firmly nestled in his stomach. His agonizing wait was mercifully at its conclusion, as the time for battle was nearly upon him. Jericho had made the drive to the offices of Goldstein, Bachman and Brown, but having arrived early he sat in his truck alone, parked at a meter across the street with his anxiety bubbling at peak levels.

It was half past nine in the evening, and darkness had already blanketed the city as Jericho waited in near silence and watched for the arrival of Michael, Reggie, Sunday and Delia. The lobby of the building was still well lit, yet was also almost completely vacant, with the exception of the two security guards who were seated at the front desk. They took turns manning the desk and walking the perimeter in an unenthusiastic routine, one which Jericho found to be a bit ridiculous considering the amount of power which soon would be congregated within the building. While the employment of two disinterested security guards was indeed completely unnecessary, the appearance of normalcy warranted their presence and made them essential if appearances were to be kept up.

Near silence was the best which could be hoped for on this evening, as a massive rainstorm was bombarding the city with notable fury, slapping hefty raindrops against the roof of Jericho's truck with alternating levels of intensity. Jericho had shut the radio off and only allowed the sound of pattering rain to serenade him in his nervous state; he had always loved the rain and the smell in the air which accompanied it, so its presence in that moment provided a small hint of relief from his ever-growing anxiety.

"We are stepping into the lion's den, passing into the valley of the shadow of death . . ." He heard Mavado's voice whisper within his mind amid the sound of the pelting rain, which continued its dance upon the roof and windows of the truck "have no fear, for my promise to protect you is as steadfast now as it was on the day we first met. You will live . . ."

A loud bang against the glass of the passenger side window startled Jericho, breaking him out of his deep thought as he quickly glanced toward the source of the

180

sound; Reggie was standing outside in a long, brown coat and pointing hurriedly at the lock, indicating his desire to be let in from the rain. Jericho hit the switch and Reggie quickly leapt into the cab.

"Thanks mate. With our luck you know it would have to be raining cats and dogs on the night Albert chose to hunt a madman. Let's hope for our sakes that this is the worst thing that happens tonight." Even in the face of growing danger and eminent confrontation, Reggie still managed to keep a lighthearted demeanor.

"I hope you're right Reg, but somehow I don't think I'll be that lucky." Jericho stared out the window in the direction of the office entrance as he spoke, his tone sounding reflective and distant.

"You're not that lucky? Well you're not the only one with bad luck, and you won't be alone either." Jericho continued to stare out the window, fully enveloped by the solemn, uneasy feeling which had completely invaded him. "Ah, I see what this is. You've always been called in, running to the rescue when your pager goes off. But now the pressure's on since you'll be on the front lines this time. C'mon, Jeri, it's not like you haven't gone to battle before. Mavado's done just fine, better than fine actually, and you got me watching Ignavus watching your back every step of the way. Like Garrison said, they are sending all thirteen of us in, so there's not a lot that could go wrong."

Jericho's eyes broke their lock on the entrance and glanced over at Reggie. "I guess you're probably right. Still, you never know."

Reggie's eyes moved from Jericho to the street, prompting Jericho to follow suit and turn his attention back to the entrance of the building. Michael, Sunday and Delia had rounded the corner into view, and were now standing under the canopy which shielded the front doors from the elements.

"Well, I suppose we're about to find out. Better get a move on." Reggie reached for the door handle and gave it a quick pull, followed closely by Jericho as the two quickly exited the vehicle and dashed through the rain until they reached the others.

The team exchanged quick greetings before Michael commenced his instructions. "Now that we're all here we can head on up. Jericho, as this is your first time here, I'll give you the quick rundown of how this works; the guards in the lobby are ordinary folk who don't know about us, so we can't manifest around them, got to keep up appearances. Albert's assistant will come downstairs and buzz us in, and we'll follow her to the elevator and head up to the eighteenth floor. Once inside the elevator, all spirits will manifest in the physical world and will remain in control until the mission is over. This includes Mavado, who will be expected to follow Garrison's orders just like with the rest of the team. When we reach the offices, we'll join the other teams and be briefed on the operation. Garrison will receive his orders in the field from Nicholas, and will pass along his orders to our Watchers. Following orders is not optional, and disobeying orders won't be tolerated. You got all that?"

Sunday, Reggie, Delia and Jericho all nodded their heads affirmatively. Through the windows of the lobby, a young woman dressed in a black, knee length skirt and a powder blue blouse could be seen exiting the elevator. It was Albert's assistant, who swiftly headed across the lobby toward the glass doors while Michael quickly gave his final instructions.

"Remember, above everything else, we look out for each other. No matter what else happens we protect each other from anyone or anything we run into tonight. Never forget to do the right thing."

The young woman flipped the lock, pulled the door open and greeted the group with a smile. "Good evening everyone, Albert is expecting you. Please utilize the second elevator from the left and proceed to his office."

Conveniently, that particular elevator was experiencing technical issues with its security camera, which provided its users with the necessary privacy to manifest prior to exiting on the eighteenth floor. The team walked quickly to the elevator and Reggie reached out to strike the button to call the elevator. After a moment, the doors slid open and the five of them stepped inside. When the doors had closed behind them, Michael turned and faced the others.

"Be safe out there," were his parting words as his irises transformed into the glowing blue which signaled Garrison's emergence. Jericho glanced from Garrison to Reggie, whose eyes were glowing green as he had already been replaced by Ignavus. Where Reggie's expressions were typically humored and casual, Ignavus's were serious and unwelcoming by comparison; Jericho often noticed that the two contrasted so much in personality, even without the minor physical transformation it would be simple to identify who was assuming control. Jericho looked next at Sunday, whose eyes were also glowing blue and whose hair was in the process of unraveling into the long, straight mane of Fortunado.

183

Jericho's eyes then fell upon the final occupant of the elevator, where they met the glowing blue eyes of Annabel which were already affixed upon him. He was always spellbound when he caught a glance of her, yet the moment he wished would last a lifetime was quickly fleeting as the elevator rapidly approached its destination.

"Your turn," she whispered at Jericho, "Don't get lost in there." He understood it was time; he felt Mavado clawing inside him, fully prepared and anxious to make his entrance into the world, so he shifted his attention from Annabel to the elevator doors and closed his eyes. He felt his hands begin to burn, while small streams of black smoke twirled and twisted off his body and vanished into the air instantaneously. Jericho felt the sensation of slipping into unconsciousness; his eyes opened to reveal the window of his father's study, with the view of the elevator doors directly through the window.

The doors slid open on the eighteenth floor and revealed the presence of Mavado, who now occupied the space formerly inhabited by Jericho. The last of the black smoke dissolved from his body as he stepped forward into the hallway, his appearance thoroughly modified and unmistakably sinister. The group proceeded down the hall with Garrison leading the way and Annabel at his side, while Mavado followed directly behind them.

Ignavus and Fortunado walked on either side of Mavado, flanking him in an appearance resembling a prisoner transport; all that would be needed to complete the look would be an orange jumpsuit instead of the pinstripe ensemble, and his hands and feet to be shackled together with chains. The assembly of the group implied that they were either protecting Mavado from someone, or perhaps protecting everyone else from him.

As Jericho watched through the window, he could not help but be reminded of Mavado's earlier comment that they were entering the lion's den, and he wondered what to make of it. If his assessment was in fact correct, then did that make Mavado the unfortunate man tossed to his doom, or the wild animal waiting to strike? Jericho secretly hoped it meant the latter, but his gut feeling did little to put his mind at ease.

The group continued on through the glass doors which led to Albert's office, cut across the vacant waiting room and headed straight through the office door to meet with the other Watchers who were already assembled. As Mavado entered the office, Jericho beheld through the window a sight which he found most intimidating; Albert was standing in front of his desk, with Nicholas and Harley positioned at his right and left. Behind them stood their respective teams of Watchers who were also already manifested; in the dim light, nine pairs of glowing blue and green eyes could be seen as they quickly panned up from their previous position and affixed squarely on Mavado.

The demon simply grinned at the universal attention which was immediately garnered, but chose to say nothing while Garrison stepped forward and took his position directly across from Albert and Nicholas.

"Good evening, Albert, Nicholas, Harley." Garrison gave a nod of salutation as he greeted the three, while Ignavus, Fortunado, Annabel and Mavado remained silent. All occupants of the room had surrounded the oversized wooden desk, which displayed a large map at its center. The map presented the layout of Luther Monroe's compound, along with the surrounding wooded area and countryside, and had already been altered considerably with markings and notations that described the evening's plan of attack.

"Welcome Garrison," Albert responded with his usual raspy tone, "your timing is impeccable, as the moment has finally arrived to hand out orders for tonight's mission."

"With respect, my commander, it would appear that we have presented ourselves beyond the appointed hour, as the rest of the contingent is already assembled. My apologies if we have caused a delay." While Garrison's tone was quite sincere, his thoughts were consumed entirely by suspicion from the moment he entered the room. He had indeed arrived at the agreed upon hour, but seeing as everyone else had already assembled, it was quite reasonable to believe that discussions had taken place in his absence.

Whether his exclusion was intentional or merely coincidental was entirely unknown, but Garrison also understood that any secret discussions would have certainly been focused on Mavado. Michael held the same suspicions, and as he was witnessing the events unfold through Garrison's perspective, he took the opportunity to make his displeasure well known. He whispered of planned treachery from the Watchers, and reminded Garrison of his obligation to protect Jericho from any threat, regardless of who ultimately posed it.

"No apologies necessary I assure you, we were only addressing a few inconsequential items. But now that you are here we can officially begin." Albert directed his attention away from Garrison, looked down at the map which was spread out before them, and began formally addressing the group. "Nicholas, you will lead our combined forces to this wooded area located five hundred yards from the main compound." Albert pointed to a previously marked spot on the map which represented this zone as he continued, "Once assembled, Harley and Annabel will confirm the number of hostile forces within the compound, and when confirmation is complete Harley and her team will branch out and create a perimeter. They will station themselves across from each of the four corners of the complex, and be responsible for engaging and destroying any fleeing demons."

Albert then turned his attention toward Nicholas as he lifted his eyes up from the map. "You will lead the remaining two groups into the facility and destroy Monroe, along with any other spirits who have joined him inside. Our continued surveillance has shown that there are still only two other detectible spirits accompanying Monroe, although there are also approximately one hundred human followers who travel to and from the grounds. We are not to harm any non-possessed followers, but any humans who have chosen to offer themselves as vessels will share in the fate of their demon, without exception."

As Albert spoke these words, Nicholas glanced ever so casually at Mavado, who was already staring rather intently at Nicholas. The glance lasted only a fraction of a second, as Nicholas's eyes quickly directed back to Albert, yet to Mavado and Jericho, a crystal clear message had been sent with the timing of the look.

"Do not be troubled my friend, for there are no enemies gathered within these walls." Mavado uttered the words in a casual fashion towards Nicholas, bringing Albert's instructions to an immediate halt while Nicholas returned his attention back to Mavado.

"I am anything but troubled, demon; perhaps today we are not enemies, but that does not make us comrades either, for if you are not for the Lord, then you are surely against him. And if you are against him, then you are for the Devil, which means it is only a matter of time before we will

187

be called to deal with you." Nicholas's tone was stern, but not exceedingly passionate; it was a matter of fact belief which he carried, one forged through experience as he had dispatched many demonic spirits throughout the course of his service. He did not see Mavado as an exception, but merely as a dangerous animal which would eventually need to be put down.

The demon continued to smile, unmoved by the less than hospitable words, "So if I choose to go about my business alone and do not serve your Lord, I will die? You make him sound like a cruel dictator, Nicholas, ruling without mercy. He seems to be the type of dictator that humans eventually rise up to overthrow in revolution; that countries unite to destroy for the greater good of civilization. Oh, and if I resist him, then by default I serve the Devil? You make it sound so simple. I serve no one but myself, and yes I realize how that sounds. It seems to lack purpose, nobility, honor, but I can assure you that true freedom from oppression is the most noble of pursuits, regardless of whoever happens to be doing the oppressing."

"Spoken like a true follower of the Devil."

"Have you ever actually met the Devil before? I've been around for quite some time, and must say that I've never had the pleasure. Even you can agree it would be most difficult to serve someone you haven't even met . . ."

"That's quite enough from both of you!" Albert strained his raspy voice to its highest level and interrupted the verbal sparring between Nicholas and Mavado, "Your philosophical stance is of no consequence to me. Both of you are in my service for now, and you will fight beside each other and follow the orders I have issued. Any treachery will reap only your own destruction, which will be swift and unforgiving. Is that understood?!"

Nicholas straightened up and gave a formal "yes, commander," in acknowledgement. Mavado, still with the smile etched across his face, gave an affirming nod of his head and replied, "Jericho agrees to your terms, and I am, as always, his most humble servant."

"Good, because the hour is now upon us, go forth and do what you have been chosen to do, for many are called, but few are chosen." Albert reached under his desk and pressed a hidden button, and as he did, the lights in the room lowered completely while the large window behind him began to retract. In mere moments the window was gone, exposing the office to the outside elements; rain sheeted down across the opening, and lightning flashed across the sky to provide sudden bursts of illumination which were followed by deafening cracks of thunder. The Watchers all stood at attention with their eyes glowing ominously in the darkness, before they suddenly began to speak in unison.

"We are the called, saved by grace, and redeemed by blood. By our service we seek to be chosen, to honor the one who rescued our souls and fight in his name when Armageddon comes. May he bless our efforts tonight, and may his will be done."

The Watchers recited their oath while Mavado looked on and Jericho watched through the study window. Mavado silently shared his observations within Jericho's mind; his words echoed through the imaginary room, "The Watchers do enjoy their rituals. They recite pious prayers while secretly plotting schemes, very much in the way that the Pharisees once did." Jericho paced in front of the imaginary window and took in both the view and Mavado's words.

"They won't betray us. Your problem is that you just don't trust anyone."

"Not true my friend, I trust you. And I also trust that you will allow me the flexibility to use my power to its full potential tonight, and not choose to hold me back."

Jericho was now the one with the smile creeping across his face as he leaned against his father's desk and pondered Mavado's request. "Not full potential, but you will have access to all the power you need. From the look of things you'll at least need to fly."

The Watchers turned from the desk and divided into their smaller teams before facing the large opening in the wall where the glass had previously been located. Nicholas's team was first to approach the ledge, with Garrison and Harley's teams taking position on his right and left sides while Mavado stood just behind Fortunado and Ignavus and to the left of Annabel. "We have our orders, time to fall out!" With this final shout from Nicholas, the eyes of all the Watchers glowed with an even greater intensity through the darkness as great pairs of white wings began to protrude and expand from each of their backs.

Mavado followed suit with the others; black smoke began twirling off his body but was nearly indistinguishable in the darkness, rising up and forming into his great black wings which appeared as grand shadows that blended into the night. His eyes burned golden with brilliant radiance, and the edges of his jacket and cuffs glowed ever so slightly as if they were smoldering embers; a subtle byproduct of higher degrees of manifestation which often went unnoticed, yet due to the amount of darkness were accentuated in that moment.

Nicholas pitched forward and dropped from the ledge and into the pouring rain, followed quickly by his team and then by Harley and her Watchers. Garrison's team was last out, with Garrison leading the way followed by Fortunado, Ignavus, Annabel and then Mavado. They plummeted off of the ledge and picked up speed quickly, before abruptly banking upward and rocketing into the black, storming sky.

The group converged and hovered in a pack for a moment, high above the orange glow of the city lights, before Nicholas turned to face the direction of Monroe's compound and accelerated forward at incredible speed, followed closely by the others. They moved together with blinding velocity across the sky, hurtling out of the city limits and into the dark countryside. The trip from Albert's office to Monroe's compound was roughly one hundred and fifty miles, a distance which was rapidly closing as they would arrive at the agreed upon assembly area in the woods within the hour.

Jericho paced nervously back and forth in the study while the scene of the darkened landscape whizzed by in the view from the window. He turned and directed his attention to the desk, which was adorned with the usual assortment of supplies and papers. The hourglass was positioned on the corner of the desk as usual; its sand slowly trickled down and generated the faint humming sound Jericho had become so accustomed to. As he watched it continuously run, it occurred to him that it would only take a flip of the hourglass to melt the window away and seize control from Mavado in this most precarious of moments. As his transition back to control of his body was always represented in his mind as a freefall through a darkened sky, the irony of awaking into an identical reality was not lost on Jericho. With all the amazing power that Mavado possessed, Jericho was comforted to know that it only took the smallest of symbolic gestures to render the demon harmless to the outside world. That was real power, power which, although not impressive or flashy, could certainly not be discounted.

Jericho turned his attention back to window to find the view had begun to descend into a dark, densely-wooded area. The distance traveled was far beyond the thunderstorms of the city, as the sky above the forest was clear and revealed a brightly-glowing full moon which provided a good amount of natural lighting for the upcoming proceedings.

The group quickly touched down and congregated together with wings still manifested, while Mavado's wings dissolved into a billow of dark smoke from the moment his feet touched the earth, signifying the restrictions Jericho had already placed on his powers. The woods were too thick to provide a direct line of sight toward Monroe's compound, but the team was already aware of its presence only a few hundred yards away.

"Harley, Annabel, confirm their numbers." Nicholas sharply barked the order, and the two complied and began walking forward until they were about a dozen yards ahead of the others. They stopped and faced the direction of the compound, reached both their hands up and stretched them forward. From their fingertips leapt sparks of blue energy, which flickered and cast forward before slowly shifting into an invisible energy which scanned the area for the presence of other spiritual beings. After a few moments the two lowered their hands, turned and headed back to rejoin the rest of the group.

"Still the three?" Nicholas' presumptive attitude bordered on casual as he addressed Harley and Annabel. He fully expected his thought would be confirmed, so naturally Harley's response was quite surprising.

"I cannot say for sure," she replied in a calm, yet perplexed tone, "I felt three spirits for a moment, and then I felt five, and then one-hundred, and then only three again. It is not that there are spirits coming and going from the grounds; they are simply there for a moment and gone in the next. There are also many human followers inside as well, but it is not their energy of which I am sensing."

"I felt it too," Annabel chimed in, "they must be manipulating our vision somehow."

"Your vision is perfect, my dear, there is no need to doubt your abilities . . ." The others turned their attention to Mavado, who was slowly approaching Annabel and the group with his hand placed casually in his pockets. "Your error is only that you do not fully understand those beings that rest beyond the walls which you so effortlessly pierced with your mind."

"And you do understand?" Nicholas responded with agitation, "If you have something to add, then you will inform your Captain who will then brief me on your opinions, if necessary."

Mavado simply smiled and continued his casual stroll toward Nicholas, Harley and Annabel, unshaken by the disregard he was being addressed with. "Since time is of the essence, I thought it would be prudent to cut out the middle man. I immediately recognized him from the moment we touched down, and as you did not, it behooves me to impart a measure of my extensive wisdom upon you." Mavado stopped a few feet in front of Nicholas, and the nature of his words inspired the rest of the Watchers to encircle the two of them.

"Recognized who?" Nicholas was still gripped with agitation toward the demon, but his curiosity was willing to entertain a response.

"Well, quite frankly, I recognized them all. Monroe is inside the building, accompanied by a very old, very powerful individual spirit which remains in a significantly close proximity to his master Monroe. Then there is the other spirit which has you so very vexed; Harley actually put it best when she said there were three, then five, and then one-hundred, for this spirit is every one of those things and even more. They are both one and one-thousand, a single powerful soldier and a sweeping Legion of troops. You know of whom I speak, for even Christ encountered it during his time in the world and chose not to destroy them, but instead he mercifully cast them into a herd of swine. His disciples were powerless against them, and now the entities' strength has increased far beyond the levels it possessed so many centuries ago. So ingrained in each other, so united this Legion has become, that unless they possess an entire group of individuals it becomes nearly impossible to recognize the sheer mass of numbers they represent."

Nicholas' agitation, so prominent only moments before, was quickly replaced by thoughts of concern, "If that is the case, then the human followers inside have all become a danger to us. We are now significantly outnumbered."

"You are absolutely right, and that would be a concern if you were actually able to gain access to the compound. The Legion is exceptionally skilled, and Garrison's team knows very well of one talent in particular which was authored by it; when we encountered the demons who informed me of Monroe's existence, they demonstrated the ability to combine their power and prevent your kind from entering their domain. Those spirits were instructed by the Legion, and it is far more powerful than those feeble creatures who so effectively kept Garrison and his team at bay. It would take your combined forces days to break through the barrier he has constructed, so it would seem that unless Monroe extends a personal invitation, he will remain just out of reach to all of you on this night."

Nicholas thought for a moment about Mavado's statement, and then a solution leapt from his tongue. "Well, it is quite fortunate that we brought you along then, seeing as he either cannot or will not prevent you from walking right through the front door."

"I am flattered that you believe me powerful enough to defeat them all, but I would be a fool to throw caution to the winds and battle such a force alone, especially in the current state of regulated power which Jericho has imposed upon me." Mavado responded; his smile still prominently displayed across his face.

"This is not a request, demon. Your host joined with us and agreed to follow orders on this mission, therefore I am ordering you to infiltrate the facility and disable the enemies' defenses. Once you have completed this task, we will storm the facility and provide you support. We will not abort the mission because of your personal insecurities; this is the only available course of action, and we will pursue it. If you refuse to fulfill your duty, you will be counted as one of the enemy." Nicholas saw this as a remarkable opportunity, either Mavado would comply with the order and meet his destruction from Monroe and his company of demons, or he would decline and be destroyed by the Watchers. In either case there would be one less demon to account for, which was fine by Nicholas.

"Sending Mavado in alone would be a waste of resources," interrupted Garrison, who did his best to intervene on the demon's behalf. "If he engages the enemy force alone, there is a strong chance he will be destroyed, and we will be no closer to completing our objective. We must return to Albert, inform him of the Legion's presence and gather additional resources."

"There will be no more discussion! I am in command of this operation, and my orders remain unchanged and will no longer be questioned. Mavado, continue forward, enter the structure and disable their defense long enough to allow us entry." Nicholas fumed with anger, as his patience had run thin from having his direction continuously questioned.

"Very well," Garrison replied with a respectful tone, "if that is the order then let it be done. I only ask that my team and I accompany Mavado to the edge of the barrier and remain there to attempt to break though. Should he be successful, we will be at the closest possible position to enter the building and assist him. May we have your permission to do so?"

"That request is reasonable. You may escort Mavado as far as the barrier will allow. Go now and see it done, and we will be prepared to join you when the demon is successful. Harley, get your team into position."

Harley and her team quickly complied and dispersed to take their assigned positions across from the four corners of the building.

Garrison turned from Nicholas, stepped a few feet toward Mavado and addressed him. "Do not attempt to engage Monroe or the other spirits on your own. Destroy the barrier as quickly as possible and we will regroup with you inside. You have my word, we will not abandon you."

Mavado's smile was gone, and his reply was thoughtful and without hesitation, "I have no doubt that you will do all within your power to ensure Jericho is not abandoned to destruction, or that you will not intentionally repeat your past transgressions. That is, after all, the reason you are here, the reason you need atonement before you can take your rightful place of elevation and return to your former glory. Yes, I know who you really are Garrison, and I thought you should know that the other spirit which guards Monroe, the one which stays close to his side, he knows who you are, too. Steer clear of him, he is beyond your strength, and you will not defeat him again."

The warning, ever ominous, was silently acknowledged by Garrison. Their hosts understood nothing, and only looked on with confusion as they pondered the meaning of his words. Without allowing a response from Garrison, Mavado then turned and headed though the forest toward Monroe's compound, with Garrison and his team following closely behind.

The five traveled the remaining distance together through the forest, with piercing beams of bright moonlight providing illumination as they pressed forward and moved between the gaps in the trees. Garrison lifted his hand and summoned the same blue energy which he used to form his weapons, however, this time the strands of energy which manifested did not continue to branch outward, but instead burned hot in his hand like a flaming blue torch.

The others followed suit, with Fortunado, Annabel and Ignavus channeling their energy in a similar manner. All except Mavado, who's golden irises merely glowed with a higher than usual intensity. He had no need for additional light, for through the centuries the demon had developed a keen sense of sight, one which had evolved to such a high degree that he had become quite proficient at seeing in the dark. It was a skill which gave him tremendous advantage when light was in short supply, and it would certainly be needed on a night so dark and filled with unfavorable odds.

After traveling a short distance they came upon the tree line, stepped out of the woods and into a large clearing where Monroe's compound was located. The compound itself appeared from the outside to be nothing more than a very large, warehouse style building which sat upon a section of undeveloped farm land, with one muddy road which eventually led to the main highway. The exterior of the building was difficult to see in the darkness yet still noticeably dilapidated, as it had been abandoned in the time after the government raid and before Monroe's return.

The five headed across the grassy clearing and approached the main entrance to the building, which was comprised of two oversized wooden doors that were guarded by two dark figures. Each figure stood in front of one of the two doors; while their features were indistinguishable in the darkness, their irises glowed with possession and burned a bright red color which immediately alerted the approaching team to their presence. The figures did not appear alarmed in the slightest, but instead stood quite still and made no attempt to engage the quickly approaching group, or to alert anyone inside the building.

When he had arrived about twenty yards from the entrance, Mavado stopped in his tracks and turned to face the others. "This is as far as you can go," he said, as Annabel approached the spot and reached her hand forward to touch the invisible barrier. It reacted with solidity as her fingertips made contact, sending visible shockwaves that stretched outward and across its surface.

"Attempt to draw them outside, beyond the reach of their protection and we will be ready to attack. We will make every attempt to come to your aid, so you must make every attempt to grant us entrance. I implore you, do what you must, but do not be careless with Jericho's life." Garrison gave his final instructions to Mavado with genuine concern, as Jericho's preservation was indeed of self-serving importance to Garrison.

"No need to fear Garrison, for I swore an oath to the boy, and I am, if anything, a man of honor," Mavado turned from Garrison and addressed Annabel, who was positioned beside him. Their eyes met, with her blue glow competing against his gold burn as he continued his parting thoughts, "I will do all that is required to protect the boy, and I will also ensure that Nicholas is granted the confrontation with Monroe which he so desperately desires."

Jericho stared through the window at Annabel, praying that this would not be the final time his gaze would fall upon her. He believed her eyes were looking past Mavado's exterior façade and instead were beholding him; her expression was the same as it was the day she appeared in his mind and whispered for him to return to her, when she pulled him back from the brink of death. It was a loving concern which tugged at his heart and made him desire his own survival even more, as his safe return would be greeted by the restrained joy and relief which bubbled behind Annabel's eyes. She kept her feelings well hidden; her separation from the world and sense of duty called for it, but Jericho believed that the infatuation he felt towards Annabel was somewhat mutual, even if the degree she shared was merely a fraction of what he felt.

Mavado turned away from Annabel and set his sights ahead as he stepped forward and pierced the transparent barrier, passed smoothly through without resistance and came out safely on the other side. Although only a few feet removed from the others, he and Jericho were now very much alone, for they had crossed enemy lines and were swiftly approaching what was undeniably a most hostile force.

"What's the plan Mavado?" Jericho's words echoed inside his own mind, his fear multiplying by the second as the view closed in on the two shadowy figures which stood guard outside the doors.

"The plan is for you to trust me. Try not to limit my power too much, and certainly do not make the mistake of taking back control until we are out of harm's way. Not until the danger is fully extinguished, do I have your word?"

"Of course Mavado, I trust you." The degree of danger and lack of support from the team had robbed Jericho of his usually controlling demeanor; he understood that he was far out of his element, and that if he wished to survive the night and see Annabel again, he would have to fully place his faith in the demon.

Mavado reached the doors and stopped only a few feet in front of the figures, which still remained motionless as their red irises glowed ominously in the darkness. After a few seconds, they slowly turned to face each other and reached their hands back to grasp the large wooden handles of their respective doors. They pulled the handles and stepped sideways and backward in an almost robotic motion until the doors were fully opened, and then resumed their motionless stance. Access had been granted to Mavado and his host without even the slightest resistance provided against their entry, much to the surprise of both the demon and his host. Mavado calmly walked forward into the foyer, accepting the invitation inside as the guarding spirits then proceeded to shut the doors behind him.

The demon and his host stood alone in what remained of the foyer of Monroe's church, the place where he had built his cult and held his last stand against law enforcement before making his ascension into demonhood. It was nothing but a ruin, badly damaged from the bombardment of firepower on that fateful day. A large, decorative mirror which hung on the wall in the center of the room had been smashed to pieces, with both long shards and small fragments of glass still strewn upon the floor.

There were bullet holes in the walls, and damage from an exploded gas canister which had set fire to a section of the carpet and the sofa in the small sitting area on the left. The foyer was lit by both candlelight and oil lamps, which lined the walls and flooded the room with an orange glow. The flames flickered about from the drafty air and cast dancing shadows along the walls and ceiling, adding to the already eerie ambiance of the room.

The room was quiet and empty, but the same could not be said of the main sanctuary which was located only a few feet away. To the right and the left of the broken mirror stood two doorways which led down the aisles of the sanctuary, and each doorway was covered by a tattered curtain. The curtains were black and badly worn, making them almost transparent through sections of the fabric. A significant amount of light could be seen through these tattered sections, as the sanctuary itself contained a large amount of torch and lamplight.

As Mavado began to approach the doorway on the left, the sound of whispering voices began to register in his ear. The voices were very faint, and the content of their conversations were very much indiscernible, but as he drew closer to the curtain they seemed to multiply in number and grow steadily in volume and speed, until he could hear what could only be described as the sound of one thousand voices rapidly whispering together.

Mavado stepped though the curtain and into the sanctuary, abruptly stopping just outside the doorway to survey the scene. The room was lined with three rows of old wooden pews; one row was centered, with a second row on the right and a third to the left. The aisles which led to the two shrouded doorways divided the rows, which were each about fifteen pews long. The source of the whispering became immediately clear, as each pew was filled with bodies that resembled the two shadowy figures which stood watch outside. They were people of all ages, sizes and ethnicities who sat motionless, draped in filthy clothes and with their irises glowing with the same deep red color of possession. When Mavado entered the room, the whispering quickly ceased and gave way to an uncomfortable silence. His eyes scanned the room and estimated the number of possessed who filled the pews at around two hundred.

From the ceiling dangled multiple iron chandeliers with large fires burning at their centers, and several smaller torches lined the walls which led up to the main platform located at the front of the room. On the platform sat three thrones; the largest throne sat on a slightly elevated platform that rested on top of the main platform, and the two smaller thrones were placed to the right and the left of the elevated throne. The middle throne and the throne positioned at its right hand were empty, but the same could not be said for the throne located on the left.

On that particular throne sat a man who appeared to be in his mid-thirties, with long black hair which flowed to his shoulders and surrounded a face with features that suggested he was of Asian descent. He was clothed in a set of ancient Japanese armor, which was black with gray accents and a large silver crest of a dragon located in the center of the breastplate. The suit of armor was nearly complete and only lacked a traditional helmet, which left exposed the man's face. His expression was one of brooding intensity, adorned with multiple battle scars which served to document his warrior lifestyle to those whose eyes fell upon them.

Mavado recognized his face, for the man had been a great warrior many centuries ago. His legend had grown to such heights, that at the peak of his human existence it was believed that the warrior was indestructible in combat. No one who stood against him could prosper, and this rang true until one fateful battle, a battle where Mavado himself had been present in spirit, only as an observer and not a participant in the carnage which unfolded before him. The man was mortally wounded by a foe he never saw coming, as a sword pierced his back and ripped through his body; dropping to his knees, he was immediately rendered helpless by the ambitions of a hidden rival. Betrayed and felled by one of his own men, he collapsed on the battlefield in a desperate struggle to cling to the life which rapidly slipped from his body.

In the midst of the chaos which surrounded him on that day, he was found by more than just the treachery of men, for the spirits of the Legion has been drawn to the battlefield by their attraction to death, and they swiftly came upon him. The warrior feared his eternity more than words could describe, so in exchange for continued existence on earth he offered his body as a vessel in service to the demons, and in his pact he forfeited both his freedom and soul in a bid to delay his eternal judgment.

The man had not physically aged since the day of the agreement, yet his centuries of possession had begun to take their toll, evidenced by the dark burns which had formed upon his face, neck and hands. His eyes always burned red, and the same black smoke which would twirl off Mavado's body during manifestations would perpetually emit from the Legion's host. As with Mavado, the smoke would simply vanish after drifting a few inches from his body, serving only to reflect the amount of unholy energy which the man harbored within.

The Legion sat motionless upon his throne, hands clutched to the armrests as he remained in a state of concentration. Mavado understood that his present, almost catatonic state was for two reasons: first, the spiritual collective of the Legion was responsible for generating the barrier surrounding the building, which was a feat that took a significant amount of focus. Second, the congregation in the room was also under the possession of the Legion, which stretched their collective powers even further. The higher number of spirits within one host, the more powerful that host would become, yet each spirit which possessed individually was also a formidable opponent on its own. Whether spread among a group, or banded together, The Legion was a mighty force to be reckoned with. The choice of how to possess was based only on which approach proved more advantageous.

Mavado began a slow, methodical walk down the aisle; his shoes clicked loudly against the wood floors and echoed though the now silent sanctuary with every step he took. As he moved forward toward the stage, the possessed who were seated in the pews began to turn their heads toward him as he passed them by. They remained silent and seated, but closely followed him with their eyes which were affixed on his every move. As he reached the front pews, he heard a set of loud, thudding footsteps overtake the echoed clicks of his dress shoes. He came to a stop, his attention drawn to the origin of the sound, and his eyes directed to the doorway of a darkened room positioned just to the right of the stage.

What emerged from the room was a huge cloaked figure robed in black with its face shrouded by a hood. The giant lumbered across the stage to the throne seated at the right hand of the largest throne, and slowly took its seat. It was an impressive and imposing sight to behold, as the cloak and hood camouflaged the giant's individual features, making his appearance reminiscent of the grim reaper.

Two thrones were now filled, and the congregation packed the sanctuary as Mavado looked on. Jericho felt overwhelmed by a sense of helplessness. He could only observe through the window the frightening scene as it unfolded, yet Mavado appeared completely calm despite the hostile surroundings, and continued to whisper thoughts within his mind to Jericho.

"Look at them all, they are sheep without a shepherd, sitting idle and without purpose until an empty chair is filled by someone willing to show them the way. They are not the ones to void our lives, so fear nothing from them. Fear not even the one who sits upon the throne, for the throne holds no power, except what is given by those who choose to serve the one who sits upon it. And neither the masses, nor their master have the strength to overcome us."

"Why are you here?" A voice echoed through the sanctuary, clear and smooth. While it did not originate from the Legion, the Giant or any member of the demonic congregation, the author of the voice was obvious to both Mavado and Jericho.

"I believe you already know why I am here Monroe, it is rather apparent that I have come here for you." Mavado's tone was still quite relaxed as he answered the voice, which was quick with a reply of its own: "No. That is why *they* are here; those powerless fools outside, who cower under cover of the forest. They are too weak to enter this place, so they have called upon you to exercise their will. I am curious though, what reason do you hold for serving the will of insects?"

Mavado's familiar smirk quickly returned and he casually walked forward, turned right and slowly made his way across the front of the sanctuary with his hands clasped together behind his back. "I serve no one outside your doors or anything in this world or the next. I only seek to honor my word, to fulfill an oath I have sworn to my host. That is why I am here, for the boy wishes for your destruction, just as those whom he chooses to follow do." Mavado stopped as he crossed in front of the empty throne and stared at it for a moment, then turned to face the possessed congregation who remained ever still and silent, with eyes which burns like fire.

Mavado continued, "I am a bit surprised that you would mock those outside as 'powerless,' yet you refuse to reveal yourself in spite of the presence of your many obedient servants. And all the while you hide in plain sight, already seated upon your throne. You see, one of those powerless creatures outside is actually quite skilled at that little trick." Mavado was, of course, referring to Annabel, who held the talent of illusion, a talent which Monroe had also developed, but not yet to a level which could fool a spirit as old as Mavado.

Mavado turned to face the empty throne once again, and as he did the view began to dissolve in front of the throne to reveal the presence of Luther Monroe. He was sitting up straight, with his arms draped upon the wooden rests which ran along each side of the throne. In life, he had been a man with a forgettable face, but his ascension had brought with it a degree of physical change; while he was still bald, the rest of his facial features had become sharper and more defined. They retained their original essence, but were significantly more chiseled and attractive. His build was also leaner and more athletic, and his eyes were large and darkened, with pupils and irises completely blacked out. The lack of a glowing iris was a customization allowed due to the body he possessed being his own, which individualized his appearance and distinguished him from other possessing spirits.

He was dressed quite regally and in the fashion of royalty, with a long black coat which was knee length and trimmed on its edges with gold, and matching black trousers with gold trim that ran down the side of each leg. The coat was joined at the waist with a gold belt and was buttoned only from the belt up, which allowed the lower half of the coat to remain open and to not restrict the movement of the wearer. The shoulders of the coat were slightly raised, padded and also adorned with gold. White dress gloves and black boots completed the ensemble, which only seemed to be missing a crown as his head remain uncovered.

"I do not disguise my presence out of fear of the mongrels, or fear of you for that matter. I would not have returned to a place where the Watchers would so easily be able to find me if I believed they posed any real threat. I simply have a weakness for presentation; the more theatrical, the better."

"That you do Monroe. Look at you, seated upon a throne of your own creation, with faithful subjects surrounding you and heaping praise upon your ears. It is all very much theatrical, and also very pointless. You are a king who lacks a kingdom, instead finding refuge within the dilapidated ruins of your old church." Mavado replied, tone still light and conversational.

"This hallowed hall represents my greatest triumph!" Monroe shouted back, angered by Mavado's lack of respect and cavalier attitude. "It is here where I conquered death, delayed eternity, and denied God's judgment for my alleged sins. Here, where I gained a power beyond even the oldest of spirits, and here where I begin my campaign to forge the greatest kingdom ever known! My journey toward deification begins tonight, and I extend to you this one offer: Serve me, swear your allegiance, and join your true brothers against those who seek your eventual destruction. Oppose me, and you will be counted as an enemy and shown no mercy. Make your choice a wise one, and do it quickly."

Mavado's smile had washed away to reveal a more serious, focused expression. Hands still clasped together behind his back, he began his reply. "Curious, I find it very curious that no matter whom I encounter, whether angel, demon, or Watcher, the ultimatum is always the same. Join us, or be counted as an enemy and slaughtered without mercy. I find it vexing that both the just and the unjust share this same philosophy—serve God or be damned to hell— serve the world or be doomed to martyrdom. We are told to fear God and to fear the Devil, and the truth of the matter is that whomever we fear the most becomes the one we ultimately serve. In either case our choice results in both lost freedom and an existence spent in service to a tyrant. If those are my options, then I choose to be free from all tyranny, regardless of affiliation."

The sanctuary was silent, not a soul stirred as Monroe stared back in genuine shock at Mavado's rejection. "You cannot simply choose neutrality! If we were to suffer defeat, God would strike you down without hesitation. When I am triumphant, you will be punished for your insolence! There is no other way, you must choose!"

Mavado unclasped his hands and allowed them to drift to his sides, then slowly approached the front of the stage and stopped directly in front of Monroe. "I'll ask you a question Monroe. Is the pursuit of freedom a sin? I have existed for a very long time, longer than any spirit in this room and nearly all within this world. I have watched empires rise and fall, witnessed dictators hold power until they were overthrown by other dictators, and observed both wicked and somewhat honorable regimes rule with varying success. The one constant, which both saint and sinner in this world can agree on, is that the pursuit of freedom is an honorable cause. We are standing now in a country which was founded on both biblical principle, and the notion that mankind should be free from tyranny to pursue liberty and happiness. Yet we are told that when our time on earth expires, we must revoke this amazing concept and instead exist on bended knee, worshiping for the remainder of eternity? And that if we do not forfeit certain freedoms in mortal life, then we will be burned in never-ending fire and suffer darkness and agony forever? This leads me to the conclusion that freedom is indeed of the world and not of God, making it sinful. Personally, I cannot imagine an existence without freedom, whether it be a sin or not."

Monroe stood from his throne and quickly walked to the edge of the stage, where he stopped and stared down at Mavado with intensity in his face. "Sin is an illusion, my friend, the opinion of a single spirit which conflicts with the wills of an infinite number of living beings. This is why you belong with us Mavado, for through my divinity you will achieve freedom, wealth, and power beyond what you can possibly imagine. Together, we will unite the ancient spirits and wage war upon the heavens. You need only to bow before me in worship, and all these things I will grant unto you."

Mavado looked up at Monroe, who stood in regal clothes which were adorned by a number of fine jewels. Still around Monroe's neck hung the chain which contained the five charms that had previously belonged to his victims; four of the charms still had a subtle glow emanating from them, revealing the energy which was still bound within, while the fifth contained no glow at all and was quite unremarkable. It was the charm he had used for his first resurrection, and it remained only as a symbol of what had already transpired. Mavado and Jericho both zeroed in on the mystical objects, for they understood that if Monroe was to be defeated he would have to be relieved of the necklace, lest his followers use the power within to resurrect him once more.

Mavado's smile crept across his face once more at the thought of Monroe's proposition. "There is nothing in the way of power which you can offer me, and I certainly have no need for wealth. As for your promise of freedom, well I once served a master who offered me protection, health, and prosperity in exchange for my obedience. I gave him my loyalty, sacrificed and served just as he had ordered, and sought to honor him in all my actions just as I had pledged to do. Yet an interesting thing happened, which I never expected."

As Mavado spoke those words, he placed his hands behind his back and clasped them together just above where his belt line ran underneath his suit coat. " One day, my master decided that, although I did all which he had asked of me, I was not serving him as well as I could have been. Such is the way of a tyrant; eventually they become so consumed by power that they no longer honor their own promises." Mavado's clasped hands passed through his suit jacket and clutched the pair of short swords which Jericho had this time remembered to bring along; they had been fastened behind his back along the beltline and were easily concealed underneath Mavado's manifested suit coat.

The demon ripped the short swords out from underneath his coat with blinding speed and launched the sword which had been drawn by his left hand. The weapon shot through the air directly toward the head of the Legion, who was still seated in the motionless trance on the throne to the left of Monroe.

Breaking his stoic concentration, Legion's right arm flew up into the air to shield his face as he pitched himself forward. He narrowly avoided the blade, which came within millimeters of striking its target, but instead stuck fast into the headrest of the throne. Mavado moved with superhuman speed, rushed forward and swung with the sword in his right hand while Legion was still staggered to one knee from lunging out of harm's way. With equal speed, Legion drew a long katana and crashed swords with Mavado, who reached with his left hand and clutched the sword which was stuck in the throne, pulled it free and followed up with strikes from both his weapons. Legion quickly blocked the attacks with his katana, as Monroe leapt up from his seat and retreated backward while the cloaked giant lunged in front of his master to shield him from harm.

The two exchanged strikes which they each quickly blocked as they fought to a stalemate, before Mavado took a great leap backward, sailed off the platform and put several few feet of distance between himself and the Legion. He stood with swords at the ready, as the demonic congregation seated behind him rose in unison and waited for their order to attack. Monroe stepped out from behind the giant, his eyes wild with rage at Mavado's actions. "You fool! You would dare to raise swords against us?! Your attack was futile, and now you will be destroyed by us all!"

Mavado was ever defiant in his response, "I would not dare raise swords against all of you alone, for I am no fool. My intent was only to interrupt his focus for but a few moments, long enough to allow those 'powerless creatures' outside to join me in battle. After all, to fight against me and still possess the congregation, all while holding the barrier outside is an exceedingly difficult task, even for something as skilled as the Legion." Mavado understood that if Garrison and the team were true to their word, the few seconds would be all they would need to exploit the distraction and step inside the barrier. If they were not, Mavado and Jericho would be at the mercy of Monroe and his followers.

A booming, thunderous sound echoed through the sanctuary as the ceiling in the back left corner of the room exploded; it crashed to the floor and sent the demons seated underneath into a frantic scramble, signaling to Mavado and Jericho that help had arrived as promised. Following the debris down to the floor was Fortunado, with his long mane flowing behind him and his large wings fully manifested. He landed with a heavy impact and clutched in his hands a large hammer comprised of blue energy, similar to that which made up the great sword which Garrison wielded. As his feet touched the ground, he quickly stepped forward and swung the hammer, which violently collided with the nearby possessed who had begun to close in and attack.

A second and third section of the ceiling gave way in similar fashion, as Garrison and Ignavus dropped down into the sanctuary and joined the fray. Garrison was already armed with the great sword, while Ignavus was armed with a more traditional looking scimitar which appeared to be comprised of a mix of green energy and polished metal. The three fought wildly in the midst of the crowd, as more pieces of the fractured ceiling crumbled apart and dropped into the room, exposing the open night sky above their heads.

No longer concerned with containment, the Legion removed the barrier outside and called out orders in a language unknown to those in the room. As the words flowed from his lips, a large pair of black, scaly dragon wings rapidly emerged from his back. The possessed crowd also followed suit and heeded the words of their master, as pairs of wings burst forth from each of their backs only seconds before they took to the air, swarming together in attack like a flock of birds.

Six of the possessed rocketed quickly across the room and landed in front of Mavado, where they lined the stage to defend Monroe, the giant and the Legion's host. The six clapped their hands together in unison, and as they did black smoke rapidly poured out from between their fingers and formed into black spears, which they lifted toward Mavado in a show of opposition.

Mavado's golden eyes burned brighter and more intensely as he channeled more of his unholy energy into the world. The energy charged through his body and ran up the handles and blades of his swords, causing the inscriptions which were engraved upon the blades to illuminate with the same burning golden glow. He stepped forward toward the demon directly in front of him, swung the sword in his right hand with an upward sweeping motion, and effortlessly split the spear in two. He followed with the sword in his left hand and slashed the demon from his belly up to his shoulder, nearly cutting him in half. As the body fell, the eyes of his host shifted from their glowing red color to an ordinary brown; the spirit of the demon lifted into the air like a dark mist, but rather than vanish into exile the demon quickly retreated into the body of the possessed host who stood beside it.

Mavado swung his swords at the now twice-possessed host; when they struck the outstretched spear of the host this time however, the swords failed to shatter it on contact as they had so easily done just moments prior. It was that which made the Legion so dangerous and formidable, for a defeated spirit could find refuge by uniting in possession with another, and in doing so would amplify their strength through a union of their abilities.

The remaining five began their combined assault on Mavado, who stepped forward and chained his attacks together with speed and precision; blocking attacks with one sword while counterattacking with the other, he continued to dispatch the demons with relative ease. As he would destroy each attacker, the demonic spirits would continue to expel from their deceased hosts and then immediately retreat into a neighboring body, until only one host remained which was possessed by all six of the spirits. This carried on throughout the battle in the room, as every spirit that Fortunado, Garrison, and Ignavus defeated were absorbed by the possessed around them, increasing exponentially the power of those who remained.

Mavado remained unfazed as the final spirit lunged at him with amplified speed, strength, and durability, for it was still nowhere near a match for him. He quickly dodged the attacks of the last demon before casually taking a calculated swing which violently decapitated the host. As the head of the host tumbled from its shoulders, the collective spirits within rose from the corpse and were quickly pulled back toward the stage, where they rejoined the body of the Legion and the thousands of spirits housed inside.

As Mavado turned his attention toward Monroe and his bodyguard, he suddenly and unexpectedly found himself lifted from his feet by an incredibly loud boom. A brilliant flash of light detonated beside him, knocking him backward through the air until he collided forcefully with the row of pews directly behind him. The concussive blast destroyed the floor and the front of the stage where Mavado had previously stood, and was even felt by Jericho within the study as an invisible impact knocked him backward as well, sending him into a collision with the desk behind him where he crashed to the floor in considerable pain.

Mavado's ears buzzed and rang as he gathered his senses and observed the source of the blast swoop in through the now completely destroyed ceiling. Nicholas and his team had joined the battle, and were targeting Monroe with no consideration for Mavado's proximity to their attacks. Nicholas carried with him a long staff with a crystal globe mounted on top, and it was from the globe where he focused his power and projected explosive orbs of blue energy. The first had struck the floor and sent Mavado flying, while a second and third hurtled more accurately toward Monroe. The cloaked giant stepped in front of Monroe to shield his master from danger. He raised his hand and instantly generated a transparent barrier, upon which the second and third orbs harmlessly detonated against.

215

Mavado leapt back to his feet as the remainder of the Watchers flooded into the thick of the fighting. As Nicholas touched down, large pairs of black wings sprang from the backs of both Monroe and the giant, who then rocketed into the air in retreat along with Legion and the remaining possessed. Jericho watched through Mavado's eyes as his head also rang with disorientation from the explosion. In all the prior instances where Mavado had possessed him, Jericho had never been in significant danger or even injured, so the sensation of feeling pain while he was located inside the study was new to Jericho. The experience was real, and generated within Jericho a true fear for his own safety. Gone was the concern for regulating Mavado's power; he very much wanted to stay alive and wished for Mavado to do whatever he deemed necessary to fulfill that desire.

Mavado felt Jericho's thoughts and was more than willing to oblige his host. The great black wings poured out of his back like smoke and formed instantly as he kicked off from the ground with incredible force. Cracking the floor behind him he ripped through the sky in rapid pursuit of Monroe.

The rest of the Watchers joined Mavado in his pursuit; as they soared into the sky they found the possessed waiting for them high above the remains of the compound. The spirits crashed into each other and fought in a scattered frenzy, while Mavado continued to press forward and use his exceptional sight to zero in on Monroe, who was flying low and fast across the tops of the trees above the wooded area, followed closely by his giant bodyguard. Nicholas spotted Mavado and pursued as well, escorted by two of his team members who flanked him on the right and left.

Mavado rapidly caught up to Monroe and grabbed hold of him so quickly that the giant did not have time to intervene. The giant reached for Mavado, who accelerated away from his grasp and crashed down into the forest with Monroe in his clutches. They struck the forest floor at an angle, and the force of the impact knocked the two apart and sent them tumbling in opposite directions.

The giant slowed to a hover above the trees, where he scanned the ground for his master before Nicholas and the other two Watchers arrived at his position. Nicholas dived into the woods while the two Watchers engaged the giant, who formed a great spear and a shield from a dark smoke-like energy which rolled from his hands. Nicholas headed into the darkness of the forest, leaving the three behind while he continued his pursuit.

On the forest floor, Mavado quickly rolled to his feet with swords drawn and power surging though his body; his eyes burned golden, and the edges of his coat and wings also burned like orange embers in the darkness. The inscriptions on the swords glowed as well and the blades reflected the moonlight, flashing as they shifted angles while he turned and searched for Monroe in the darkness.

Although his physical presence was nowhere to be seen, Monroe's voice pierced the darkness as clearly and loudly as if he were standing right beside Mavado, "It would seem that the boy fears me more than you; you finally show your true power Mavado. You would make an excellent addition to my army, if only you would abandon madness and reconsider my offer."

Mavado continued to scan the trees and cautiously stepped forward with his swords at the ready. "No Monroe, you have not even begun to witness the extent of my powers. It is curious that one who speaks of power so often has yet to show any power at all, although I must say you do seem quite adept at hiding yourself from danger." Mavado spoke the words casually and without emotion; he hoped that his indifferent challenge would lead Monroe to reveal his position out of anger, yet Monroe remained unmoved by the comment as he continued, "Oh I am quite adept at survival, and part of survival is to know when to act and when to lay still. As powerful as you may or may not be, I exceed yours in two regards. First, I am free from the conflicts which come with possessing a host. As much as the boy may wish for you to do all which is required to destroy me, the soul inevitably rebels against control. It is human nature to struggle for freedom, and that internal struggle which resides within you saps your power; power which could be better used for other applications. I command the full extent of my ever-growing abilities which grants me Lordship over even the oldest of spirits. My second advantage is that I have others to do my bidding, for great warriors will always rise and fall, but the kings they serve live on to claim the glory of the warrior's conquests."

"Unfortunately for you, all your warriors seem to be pre-occupied at the moment." Mavado scoffed at the presumed second advantage, but as he spoke the words he also heard a humming sound which was rapidly growing in volume. A blue orb of energy was once again hurtling in his direction, yet this time Mavado was not caught off guard as he moved with superhuman speed to remove himself from its path. The orb struck a massive cedar tree and splintered it completely at its base, sending it down to the ground in a mighty crash.

Nicholas had made his presence known. He swooped down and landed atop the fallen cedar with his staff raised to attack, but saw no one as his eyes groped the shadows in an attempt to locate Mavado and Monroe.

"Reveal yourself demons! You wish to match yourself against a servant of God, to defy his will and challenge his authority? Now is your chance, for I am prepared to destroy either one of you!" Nicholas shouted his open challenge into the darkness knowing that his opportunity to eliminate Mavado had arrived, as neither Garrison nor any other Watchers were present to intervene.

A shadowy figure darted among the trees, too dark and quick to be discernible from Nicholas' position. Seeing the movement, he raised his weapon and fired orb after orb into the pitch black forest, which lit up with brilliant shockwaves as they struck the trees and ground. The impacts did not produce fire, but only flashes of light as they obliterated on contact, smashing trees and forming car-sized craters in the ground and sending debris flying into the air. A dusty cloud quickly formed in the wake of his destruction and obstructed his vision further, as the moonlight reflected off of the floating particles and generated a foggy screen in front of him.

The figure reemerged suddenly, and approached with superhuman speed. In an instant it closed the distance and collided with Nicholas, knocking him from his perch atop the tree. The two fell together to the ground, and upon landing the figure forcefully ripped the staff from Nicholas' hands and stood back to its feet. Grasping the staff by its center, the dark figure poured orange flames from its hands which engulfed the staff completely, and their glow served to reveal his identity; Monroe stood before Nicholas as the flames transformed the staff and swept back into his hands, replacing Nicholas's weapon with a dark staff constructed of sharpened blades on either end. Monroe lunged and swept the blade downward upon Nicholas, yet to his surprise it was unexpectedly halted by a metallic crash before it reached its intended destination.

Like a phantom, Mavado had seemingly appeared from nowhere as if he had materialized from the darkness. He stood over Nicholas and faced Monroe, his two swords crossed and holding the blade of Monroe in its frozen position. The burning inscriptions on Mavado's swords flashed with energy, which traveled outward and upward to the tips of their blades where it detonated with concussive force and propelled Monroe backwards.

Mavado was now on the offensive as he lunged forward after Monroe, striking rapidly and repeatedly with both swords as Monroe backpedaled and desperately fought to deflect the attacks. As the demon repelled Monroe, Nicholas leapt to his feet and began drawing blue energy out from his core, which snaked down his arms like glowing threads until they reached his hands and flashed in a burst of light, instantly forming a large glowing bow in one hand and a brightly pulsing arrow in the other. Nicholas raised the bow and took aim at Mavado's back, and without hesitation he fired the glowing projectile with incredible speed.

Mavado sensed the approaching danger even as he was engaged with Monroe; he crashed his swords down in unison against the middle of Monroe's staff and shattered it in two, and then quickly turned to deflect the approaching projectile. But before it could reach him, the arrow detonated against an invisible barrier which had formed just a few feet in front of Mavado, who was both surprised and puzzled by the unexpected protection. He quickly turned back to engage Monroe, yet his eyes only found darkness. The self-proclaimed king had seized the moment of distraction and fled.

Nicholas was equally surprised by the unexpected interference, but it only took him seconds to locate the source. Annabel had found her way to the forest as the battle had spilled out, and she witnessed the treachery of her fellow Watcher. Calling upon her gift of protection, she had been the one to shield Mavado from his attack, an action which ignited a sense of fury within Nicholas. She had chosen to defy her commander and protect his enemy, which now equaled her with Mavado in his eyes. His response to her perceived treachery was swift, as another arrow quickly formed in his hand and he raised the bow once more, this time taking aim at her.

The impact was tremendous; crippling pain coursed through Nicholas's chest as the arrow which had been drawn back instantly shattered, followed closely by the disintegration of the bow in his hand. He dropped to one knee as his body burned with pain, and, as he trained his eyes downward the source of his agony was quickly revealed; one of Mavado's swords had plunged deep into the left side of his chest. It was embedded almost to the handle with the tip protruding out of his back and the glowing orange energy of the sword slowly pulsing out of the blade and through Nicholas's torso. Each pulse of energy felt like a crushing grip on his body and squeezed the air and life from him with every moment that elapsed.

Mavado slowly approached and stared down at Nicholas as he struggled to catch his breath, his second sword casually lowered to his side as he spoke, "You fancy yourselves to be so noble, so wise, and so unwavering. Yet it is your disobedience which has always condemned your kind to destruction, as you failed to heed Albert's commands just as the first of you rebelled against your master. Did he not tell you that treachery would be rewarded with death? But you have already passed through death. Instead, you have failed to protect the host to whom you swore an oath, and now he is condemned to judgment because of your selfish pursuits."

Nicholas slipped from his knee and crashed to his side, where he slowly rolled to his back and breathed laboriously as he locked eyes with Mavado. He was too weak to speak and could only gasp for air as Annabel reached the two of them and halted abruptly. As skilled a healer as Annabel was, she immediately recognized his injury had advanced too quickly for intervention, and she could only watch as his breathing slowed and the blue glow of his eyes washed away. The host within had now assumed control, and the expression on his face had changed to one of fear at the realization that his final moments had arrived. Another second passed before the body was vacant; both the host and the spirit had gone from the world.

"I remember him— in life he was so different yet so very much the same. A man of the people, he compromised himself to gain favor, to be loved, and he indeed was loved very much. It was this lack of steadfastness as a man which undid him throughout his existence, and he believed his redemption in this life lay with assuming an uncompromising stance. So he chose to never waiver, to do what is 'right' at all times, yet his true folly in both lives was that he refused to be obedient and follow the commands of his Lord, which was a lesson forever lost on him. Both him and his brother,"

Mavado spoke the words as he looked down at Nicholas's lifeless body, for he knew the identity of the spirit and understood its struggles well. Even in death, the demon chose not to reveal who Nicholas had actually been, but instead only shared vague observations which Jericho found impossible to decipher.

The forest was silent, the battle above had ceased, and the air was still as Mavado and Annabel stood over Nicholas's body. The silence was ever brief, as a rushing sound could be heard in the air which grew louder with each passing second. It was the sound of rapidly approaching Watchers; Garrison swooped down through the treetops and landed a few feet from Annabel and Mavado, followed by Ignavus and Fortunado. Garrison looked upon the scene in shock; filled with rage he demanded answers; "What have you done, demon?!" he bellowed as he manifested his great sword in preparation to engage Mavado.

"He has saved me, saved Jericho," Annabel frantically countered to Garrison, " Nicholas turned on him, and when I tried to stop him Nicholas made an attempt on my life as well. I would not be standing here unscathed had Mavado not intervened." Annabel stepped between Mavado and Garrison as she spoke, almost as if she hoped to shield Mavado from an assault by the three Watchers.

"And he had no choice but to kill him? No, he took the opportunity to murder him as he would with any one of us," Ignavus interjected fiercely in response to Annabel, before focusing his attention directly on Mavado " You are as much a danger to us as Monroe and his followers. I would gladly slay you now and be done with this, yet it is only my host's desire for Jericho's protection which stays my hand."

"You flatter yourself, for you have not the strength to do me any harm. And I would have no need to wait for 'opportunity' if I truly desired your destruction." Mavado was ever defiant in reply to Ignavus's accusations. The behemoth Fortunado was next to offer his opinion, as he stood with his glowing weapon still at the ready. "Betrayal can only be rewarded with death. If Nicholas truly chose this path then he reaped the rewards of his pursuit. I would have done the same as the demon, and will not judge him for his actions. Justice was done, so there is nothing more to discuss."

"You would choose sides with a devil?!" Ignavus retorted in response to Fortunado, whose response surprised even Mavado with its lack of bias; "I am on the side of justice. Treachery in any form cannot be tolerated, nor can unwarranted punishment." Regardless of the players involved, Fortunado was assessing the situation for what it was and did not allow personal feelings to sway his reasoning. It was a welcomed change to Mavado from the usual anti-demon rhetoric which was common among the Watchers. Jericho surveyed the scene from his subconscious vantage point and felt a measure of hope generated by Fortunado's words, but the feeling quickly fled as he realized that a larger number of those who shared Ignavus's perspective would soon be upon them.

The air was filled once more with the rushing sound of rapidly approaching spirits as Harley, her Watchers, and the three remaining members of Nicholas's team fell from the sky like shooting stars. They touched down on the forest floor with glowing swords, spears and bows already manifested and quickly surrounded Mavado, Garrison and the others. Harley approached the group but froze just a few yards from Garrison and Mavado; her movement halted from the sight of Nicholas's lifeless body, with Mavado's sword still buried in his chest.

"What has happened? What has he done?" The words had barely fallen from her lips before the Watchers accompanying Harley became aware of who was responsible for Nicholas's destruction. Upon the realization, they raised their weapons and prepared to take vengeance for their fallen commander. In response, Garrison, Ignavus, Annabel, and Fortunado drew their weapons as well and took up positions around Mavado, facing outward in challenge against their fellow Watchers. Garrison was true to his promise, for he would honor his host's request and do everything possible to protect Jericho, no matter who presented as the enemy.

"He did only what he was compelled to do in order to save another. Nicholas chose to defy his oath, to act without honor and according to his own desires. His punishment for this defiance has been delivered." Harley was unmoved by Garrison's words, "It is not the demon's place to dispense justice; he has no authority among us and therefore is not protected by our laws. He will bring destruction to all of us, unless we act now and remove his power!"

"I am now the acting commander, not you! While you may believe our laws do not apply to him, I assure you they do apply to me. Those who choose to rise against me will share the fate of our former commander, so I implore you all to abandon madness and stand down now!" Garrison's voice powerfully boomed through the forest; his words halted the Watchers in their tracks and inspired submission, as their weapons lowered in obedience to their acting commander. "The demon's fate will not be decided here; your orders are to return with us as we escort him back to stand before Albert. He will be judged by our laws and punished according to his transgressions."

Garrison turned to Mavado as he continued to speak, "and you will accompany us without resistance, and upon returning to the tower you will relinquish control to Jericho and await Albert's decision. If you choose to resist, then you will forfeit the boy's life, so if protecting him is your true desire then I implore you to comply."

Mavado looked back at Garrison and addressed him with an unusually serious tone, as generally his smile and more sarcastic demeanor were present whenever he conversed with Garrison, regardless of the situation, "I would never do anything to compromise young Jericho's life; I accept your terms and will accompany you without incident. I am, as always, his humble servant."

Garrison and his team flanked Mavado from all sides as they lifted off the ground together and rocketed into the night sky. Jericho remained in the study, seated in the leather chair across from the second chair Mavado usually occupied during their many nocturnal discussions; no longer interested in viewing the sight through the window he stared blankly forward, with a cold sickness churning in his stomach at the thought of what awaited him upon the return to Albert's offices.

Jericho had no regrets for what had transpired, for he had seen everything and did nothing to prevent Mavado from destroying Nicholas and his host. He understood that Mavado's actions had not only preserved his life, but also insured the continued earthly presence of both Annabel and Delia. Jericho cared for them both, but he loved Annabel more than anything or anyone from the moment they met; seeing the spirit in imminent danger only reinforced his feelings for her, and Mavado's swift intervention generated feelings of true gratitude toward the demon.

As much as Jericho had learned to push Mavado away and hold him in suspicion, he now felt closer to him than he had in years. He thought to himself about all the times Michael and Garrison had warned him about Mavado and questioned his motivations, yet despite their claims he had always been true to his word and looked after both Jericho and those he cared for most. Jericho felt himself renewed in belief in his union with the spirit; he knew that within the hour they would be back at headquarters, and that he would now be the one stepping into the lion's den while

Mavado observed from the study window. It would be Jericho's turn to save the demon's life, and he felt honored to have the opportunity to return the favor.

Chapter 12

Jericho waited in the empty office, seated on a leather sofa he leaned forward and rested his elbows on his knees, which bobbed up and down like pistons and caused his body to tremble rapidly. No longer in the study within his mind, he had traded one lonely location for another as he now sat by himself in a vacant office at Goldstein, Bachman and Brown, while the remaining Watchers congregated outside in the lobby and conference rooms. It was now six o'clock in the morning, and the sun was preparing to break through the horizon and begin a new day. The concept of dawn breaking usually symbolizes hope and new beginnings, yet it was a contrasting feeling of hopelessness and despair which permeated Jericho's thoughts.

The longer he waited, the more nervous he grew; he had believed that the opportunity to speak in front of Albert and defend Mavado's actions would be forthcoming, but as the minutes passed he began to feel as if the demon's fate was already being decided, and without regard to any testimony from the closest eye witness. As his anxiety continued to mount, he wondered if perhaps he should have whispered to Mavado to flee rather than accompany the team back to stand before Albert. He worried that his compliance might possibly have sealed both of their fates, but he did his best to show a measure of faith in both the Watchers and those who served as their hosts.

The door handle jiggled slightly, followed by a twist and a click. The sound spiked Jericho's heart rate as if it were a blast of gunfire, breaking the silence and shaking him out of his train of thought. The door slowly opened and a welcomed sight stepped through.

"Hey buddy, how you holding up?" Reggie stepped into the office and shut the door behind him; no longer possessed by Ignavus, he was the first person to join Jericho in the room since his arrival back to the office.

"Sunday's outside too. Well . . . Fortunado is actually the one outside right now. The big bloke is standing guard outside your door; it kind of makes this look like this is the VIP section." Reggie awkwardly chuckled through his comment; ever the comedian, even he struggled to remain light hearted due to the gravity of the current situation.

Jericho smiled at Reggie's attempt to lighten the mood, "Making sure I don't try to run huh?"

Reggie smiled back as he approached with his hands placed in his pockets, stopping to lean against an old desk which was across from the sofa where Jericho was seated,

"Nah, he's more focused on keeping the others out than keeping you in. I probably don't have to tell you that it's pretty tense outside." Reggie removed his hands from his pockets and hopped up on the desk, using it as seat he casually let his legs dangle back and forth and clasped his hands together, resting his elbows on his knees.

Jericho looked down at the floor and remained quiet for a few moments before he responded, "Do you think I did the right thing?"

"Well, I certainly don't think you did anything wrong at all. You weren't the one who killed Nicholas, but even if it had been you I would say that the outcome would still be justifiable. Don't get me wrong, it is a shame that things ended up the way they did, but given the circumstances I don't think it could've been avoided."

Still looking down, Jericho smiled and raised his eyes to meet Reggie's, "Somehow I don't think God or the Watchers outside will see it that way. Nicholas and his host were destroyed while fighting against what they have sworn an oath to destroy. His intention was to destroy an 'evil' spirit, so it's hard to find justification in his death, even if he was told not to engage Mavado without a reason."

A few moments of silence passed as Reggie mulled over Jericho's statement. His response required little deliberation though, and he began with a question: "You used to go to Sunday school as a boy, right?"

"Yes"

"Do you remember the story of a man named Uzzah?"

"Name doesn't really ring a bell, but if you tell me the story it may jog my memory."

"All right," replied Reggie, "you remember the Ark of the Covenant?"

Jericho's reply was quick, "Oh yeah, from Indiana Jones? It's the box with the poles coming out the sides and all the gold on it, and at the end of the movie a bunch of ghosts fly out and kill all the bad guys?"

Reggie couldn't help but chuckle at Jericho's answer, "Yes Jericho, although Raiders of the Lost Ark was not a documentary and none of that actually happened, but that's the ark I'm talking about. The Israelites carried it with them, and God gave them instructions that it must be carried by the poles and that no one could touch the Ark, and anyone who broke that rule and touched it would die. Well, right away they started doing things wrong; they put the bloody thing on a cart which was not what God told them to do, as it was supposed to be carried by the poles. Anyways, one day when they were moving the cart with the ark on it, one of the oxen pulling it stumbled and caused the cart to start tipping over. When this happened, a man nearby named Uzzah reached out and put his hand on the ark to save it from falling over. And just as promised, God struck the man dead because of his actions."

"Yeah, I remember the story. It never made sense to me that God killed him for doing the right thing. He wasn't touching the ark to defy God, but he was trying to save it from getting smashed on the ground. He was killed for doing the right thing."

"King David would probably agree with you, as he was pretty angry with God for killing Uzzah. But honestly, was Uzzah doing the right thing? The Bible says that he reached out to steady the ark, but it doesn't say the Ark would've fallen had the man not intervened. And I suppose the real question would be why God would need a man's intervention to save the Ark. The creator of the universe is too powerless to stop an object from falling a few feet to the ground? You see, God didn't need man's help, or his good intentions. God wanted them to be obedient, and he made his expectations very clear. Because they didn't obey him, they put themselves in a bad situation. Uzzah chose to do something which sounded noble and courageous and which practically anyone could look at as the 'greater good,' but the flaw in his logic was *believing* that he had the authority to decide what the greater good was."

Jericho still looked puzzled, "So you are saying he should've just let the ark smash to the ground?"

Reggie, still smiling continued, "I'm saying, it wasn't his choice to make. God knows what he's doing, so Uzzah should have honored God's instructions and waited. Uzzah's death was a result of everyone's disregard for God's command. Such is the same with Nicholas, he knew his orders and decided that he could break them for the 'greater good,' but that was not for him to decide, either. That's the problem with living in the world; people begin to believe they understand what God really wants, rather than listening to his word and trying to live obediently." Reggie hopped off the desk and started to rummage through his coat pockets, hunting for his cigarettes and lighter, "With a little luck that philosophy could apply here, and you and your friend may just make it out of this in one piece."

232

Two quick knocks emanated from the door, and the handle twisted immediately without waiting for either Reggie or Jericho to acknowledge the entry. The attention of both was immediately drawn to the disturbance; the door only opened about a foot before Delia slipped through the opening and shut the door behind her.

Jericho stood to his feet as she rushed toward him and embraced him tightly, her arms wrapping around his waist as she buried her face into his chest. She looked up at Jericho, eyes brown and absent the glow of Annabel as the spirit was now recessed into the depths of her mind.

"Thank you, you and Mavado, for saving me. I told them what happened, Annabel did too—about Nicholas and how you protected us, but I don't know what they're going to do . . ." Her voice cracked, her eyes were red and brimmed with tears as she continued to speak while Jericho's arms wrapped around her snugly, "they didn't say anything, they just listened, and after we both spoke they said I could go."

"It's all right, darling, you did well. It's out of our hands now."

Reggie calmly acknowledged Delia's words as Jericho remained silent and just held her tightly; saying nothing he leaned forward and gave her a small kiss on the top of her head. He not only embraced Delia but also the spirit of Annabel that resided within her, so he quietly breathed in the moment. The two were identical in every way except eye color and personality, but as Delia embraced him with overflowing gratitude and concern, he believed that in the present moment both the host and spirit were truly united.

There was no forewarning knock this time as the door swung open again, revealing Garrison and Fortunado who stood just outside. Jericho had hoped to speak to Michael before facing Albert, but the presence of Garrison's manifested form all but assured him that the opportunity would not arrive.

Garrison's expression was ever serious and his tone was formal, "Jericho, Albert is requesting your presence." He released his hold on Delia, and felt a supportive pat on his right shoulder from Reggie as he started on his way. He quietly walked to the doorway and followed Garrison, who turned and led him down the hallway towards Albert's office while Fortunado followed closely by Jericho's side.

As Jericho entered the hall, he observed the other Watchers who comprised Harley's and Nicholas's teams as they lined the walls outside Albert's office. All were still manifested with their eyes glowing blue or green, eyes which immediately focused on Jericho from the moment he stepped through the doorway. They were solemn in expression, but Jericho felt the intensity of their gaze burning through him as he approached.

No matter what was to transpire in Albert's office, Jericho knew that these Watchers held him responsible for the destruction of their leader, and he believed that despite their righteous directives, they would always hunger for vengeance against him. He felt the tenseness of the moment, but remained still in expression with his focus on following Garrison, not daring to make eye contact or provoke an outburst of violence. The short walk felt as if it took ages, but finally Garrison arrived at the door to Albert's office and quickly opened it; he turned and allowed Jericho to enter the office first before joining Fortunado and following Jericho into the room.

A single chair was placed in front of Albert's large desk, with Albert and Harley seated on the other side and facing toward Jericho. Albert remained silent and motioned his hand to indicate to Jericho to have a seat, who complied without any verbal response. Garrison continued forward and took his place in the empty seat at Albert's right, while Fortunado took a position behind Jericho and stood watch over the proceedings. Albert wasted no time getting the conversation underway, as Jericho had barely taken his seat when Albert began to speak.

"I declare this tribunal now in session, witnessed by ranking Watchers Garrison, Harley, and Fortunado. Mr. Coleman, you are here to face judgment for the alleged murder of host Nicholas Baker and the destruction of his Watcher. You will not be permitted to speak on your own behalf, as any testimony from you or the demon Mavado would be understandably biased. There were only two witnesses to the event, the host Delia Miranda Rios, and her Watcher whom you know as Annabel. We will not accept the testimony of Ms. Rios, as her allegiance to you corrupts the reliability of her statement and would most certainly be biased as well."

You can't just assume she would lie," Jericho interjected, an outburst which found a quick rebuttal from Albert.

"Please remain silent until I have concluded my statement Mr. Coleman." Albert continued, "Now, we have accepted the testimony of Annabel, as she has sworn an oath to uphold our laws, and I have no cause to believe she would operate without honesty and integrity. Annabel has testified that the Watcher hosted by Nicholas, without provocation and in direct violation of issued directives, attacked the demon Mavado with intent to destroy both him and his host.

The Watcher in question also made an attempt upon Annabel when she intervened to protect the demon Mavado; subsequently, the Watcher was struck with a single blow from the demon's weapon which fatally wounded both the host and the Watcher. Based upon her eyewitness account, we have determined that the actions taken by your demon were justified, and that the host's death, while tragic, was a result of his Watcher's inexcusable actions. "

Jericho felt a sense of relief begin to wash over him as the words fell from Albert's mouth; "Thank you sir" he uttered quickly, before Albert interjected once more.

"I am not finished, Mr. Coleman. While you are indeed innocent of wrongdoing in this instance, I am saddened to say that those who sit before you are not. It was my allowance of your demon's participation which directly resulted in the tragic events that unfolded. It was my belief that a house divided against itself would fall, and that a demon rallying against his kind could serve our purposes well. Yet the house which divided was our own, and that division will continue to tear us apart if it is allowed to continue."

Jericho was stunned, as his prior elation had been quickly replaced by indignation. "What are you saying? I can help you, we can help you; you saw that tonight. The only way we even had a chance to confront Monroe was because of Mavado's abilities. Without him the Watchers would never have even gotten into the church; they were stuck outside until Mavado got them in."

"And what exactly did that earn us?!" Albert shouted back, cutting him off in mid-sentence, "Monroe and his demons are still at large, one of our own was defeated and returned to eternity, and his former host is now facing eternal judgment. We gained as much as we would have if they were still stuck outside as you put it, and yet we lost far more. I do not place the blame with you, Jericho; I accept responsibility for my choices and now take on the responsibility of correcting my mistakes!"

Silence washed over the room as Jericho sat silently, dejection and frustration simultaneously filling his mind. He looked at Garrison, but was only met with a stern, emotionless expression. He desperately hoped that Michael would seize control from Garrison and side with him against Albert, yet the glowing blue irises remained constant as Albert passed his judgment. "Jericho Coleman, as you freely accepted to join in possession with this demon, we cannot cast him out from you as your fates are united; to do so would result in your own death. I will not cast a death penalty upon you for mistakes made as a child; however, I must cast judgment for decisions made as a man. As of this moment, the demon, Mavado, must never be allowed to seize control of you and manifest into the world. You will be allowed to live out the remainder of your days in peace as long as he remains locked away within you. If the demon manifests outwardly, whether by your choice or by his force, you will be branded our enemy and destroyed. You must also sever all personal ties with the Watchers and their hosts. "

"You can't tell me who I can and can't have in my life Albert! It doesn't matter who my friends are if Mavado's 'locked away,' and I can do whatever I want! " Jericho was furious. It was bad enough that he was being treated like a criminal after having done nothing wrong, now he was also on the brink of losing the only meaningful relationships in his life. All that he knew was being pulled away from him, and he was not content to accept the exile which had presented itself so unexpectedly.

"In the case of the Watchers who serve under me, I most certainly can tell you who you can and cannot have in your life! Their interactions are my business, and interactions with you could potentially alert your demon to our movements and targets. Whether you choose to admit this or not, this demon is our enemy, and I will not compromise our mission so that you can retain your social circle! In truth, Jericho, you are fortunate to be leaving this place alive."

"You might be leaving me alive, but you're taking my life from me." Jericho shook his head as the anger within him continued to mount. Mavado had been surprisingly silent. Jericho had expected to hear him whisper rebuttals or snide comments about what was transpiring, yet the voice never came. He was alone, all alone in a terribly difficult moment. It was a feeling he dreaded would now become very familiar in his coming days.

Albert's tone and expression softened ever so slightly at Jericho's remark, "I am sympathetic towards your situation, Jericho. You must understand that I do this accordance with the oath which all Watchers have made, in order to resist and defeat the enemies of the Lord. I will allow you the remainder of today to properly say goodbye to your former team, but as of tomorrow we will move forward without you. I pray that you and I will never see each other again, and that God will grant mercy upon your soul, despite your union with evil. Please go from this place and never return."

A mix of emotions stirred wildly inside Jericho. He felt anger and sadness, betrayal, and even a measure of guilt for accepting Mavado so many years ago as a child. He looked back at Garrison and was still met with the stern expression and glowing irises which he had grown so accustomed to.

"Got anything to add Garrison? After all this time you got nothing to say?"

Garrison remained silent, and with those as his parting words Jericho stood up, turned and headed through the exit and down the hall with Fortunado in close pursuit, who followed to ensure Jericho safely made it through the gauntlet of Watchers outside. He did not even stop at the office where Delia and Reggie were waiting, but continued onward through the glass doors of the lobby and quickly called the elevator.

His mind raced as he struck the call button repeatedly; his patience had gone and emotions overwhelmed him, he needed to escape as quickly as possible yet the elevator seemed remarkably slow in such a critical moment. He feared that at any second Delia, Reggie or Sunday would leave through the glass doors in pursuit of him, but as he looked over his shoulder towards the office doors he saw no movement to indicate an impending confrontation.

The light above the door lit up and emitted a chime to announce the elevators arrival. The doors slid open to reveal a lonely compartment which was quickly occupied by Jericho, who struck the close button repeatedly with the same impatient effort used to initially call the car. It was early in the morning so Jericho was aware that the building was almost entirely empty. An uninterrupted journey to street level was welcomed and most certainly in order, as the building's various tenants had only barely begun making their way into work, which made the chance for a stop to collect additional passengers on the way to the lobby highly unlikely.

The doors shut and the descent was rapid and silent, with Jericho holding a blank stare with his reflection in the brass doors. Mavado was still silent, and his lack of presence or of any words to offer only added to Jericho's frustration. After all, regardless of whether it had been justified, it was due to Mavado's actions that Jericho found his life upside down. If anything, an expression of regret from the demon or some consoling words was the very least Jericho believed he was owed.

The doors opened a final time and Jericho quickly exited. He walked through the lobby with his head down and avoided eye contact with the office employees who were now beginning to traffic into the building. He aggressively pushed through the glass doors and emerged into the morning air; the warm beams of the rising sun washed over him and provided the slightest bit of comfort as he approached the sidewalk.

He stopped there and took a few deep breaths of the fresh air in an attempt to calm himself a bit, as he waited for a break in the traffic to allow him to cross. As the morning commute whizzed by, he turned his head back to the building and affixed his gaze to the windows which ran along the eighteenth floor. No one was standing at the windows to silently acknowledge his exit, and no one had chased after him or shown any measure of support. He felt completely forgotten; a sickening feeling which knotted his stomach and had finally begun to well tears in his eyes.

He turned his attention back to traffic, saw his opportunity and bolted across the street to his truck. He was in the cab in a flash, and just as quickly he peeled out of his spot and made his way back to his apartment. He needed desperately to get home; his lack of sleep and flood of emotions had stricken him with an anxious delirium that fueled his desire for isolation. He needed to escape, needed to feel safe, and he believed that the sooner he could hide from the world, the better off he would be.

Chapter 13

Never before had Jericho's apartment complex been a more welcome sight than on that particular day. He pulled into his usual parking space, exited the truck, and hurried through the breezeway which led to his front door. He had asked for the day off from his construction job in anticipation of the long night out, so he very fortunately found himself with no particular place to be. As he fumbled with his keys and unlocked the door, he was already deciding his next move; he planned to kill two birds with one stone immediately by getting some much needed rest, and to use the subconscious time to confront the noticeably absent Mavado as he dreamt.

Jericho entered the apartment and immediately engaged the deadbolt, then turned to empty the contents of his pockets onto the coffee table in front of his television. He would not venture any further from this point, and, rather than travel the few extra feet to his bedroom he instead chose to crash on the couch. His head was propped up by the arm rest, and his feet drifted off the side of the couch in what would appear to an outside observer to be a rather uncomfortable position. He did not take the time to remove his shoes, but also refused to put his shoes on the couch which made his awkward sprawl quite necessary.

As he lay with his arms crossed in front of him, Jericho hopelessly stared out the window while the sinking feeling in the pit of his stomach worsened by the second. He was exhausted; having been awake for almost thirty consecutive hours had finally caught up with him, and no amount of anxiety would be able to hold up his heavy eyelids.

His eyes shut for a moment and fought their way back open; with each time they opened Jericho's perspective would fall upon the window and its unchanged view, and then the view would darken and vanish behind his eyelids until he could muster the strength to force them open once again. He continued this struggle until he felt his eyelids shut heavily one last time, and then the weight which had previously crushed them down was immediately lifted.

Jericho opened his eyes to find the perspective had transformed; he no longer held the view of the interior of his apartment, but instead found himself surrounded by the interior of his father's study. The window of the study was bright, yet fogged with condensation which obscured the details of what lay beyond; the light it emitted resembled that of a cloudy afternoon, and painted the room with a grayish glow.

"It is a terrible wrong which they have bestowed upon you; to be exiled and cast out is an immensely difficult thing." Mavado's voice broke across the empty room and caused Jericho to sit up and turn his head in the direction of its origin. Mavado was seated in his usual chair, his left leg crossed over his right and his arms draped across the armrests as he continued, "It would seem that I have now caused two banishments. While my own exile was well deserved, you have done nothing to warrant such a harsh treatment." Gone was Mavado's smirk and exceedingly confident demeanor, replaced instead by thoughtful statements and respectful tones.

Jericho stood and moved to the chair which faced across from Mavado. He took his seat and hunched forward, with his hands clasped together and his elbows resting upon his knees. In spite of his present dream state, his expression in this world still reflected his current exhaustion.

"Why did they banish you?" Upon hearing the question from Jericho, Mavado let slip a sheepish smile and remained silent for a moment. He glanced over to the window and stared briefly before he returned his attention to Jericho.

"It was because of jealousy. Mind you, not from those around me, but rather it was my own which condemned me. I allowed my own jealous heart to get the better of me, and it led me to sin against those whom I had a responsibility to protect. As such, my punishment was severe. I was forced to wander alone through existence, a sentence which was indeed justifiable, but one which I felt I could hardly bear. Yet as the centuries passed by, I witnessed others who sinned in the same manner, or even worse than I, receive the mercy I had so desperately pleaded for."

244

"So how long did your punishment last?"

Mavado's smile faded into his more typical smirk as he responded, "Well, to put things honestly, my punishment is still being served to this day. Yet my complete exile ended one day not too long ago, when a young boy offered me the chance to touch the world again." The smirk disappeared, giving way to a serious and sincere expression as he paused for a moment and then continued , "Regretfully, I have brought exile upon you as well, as they have chosen to punish you for my transgressions, a terrible injustice from those who ironically claim to represent the just."

"No, no, you didn't do anything wrong. I owe you, for saving my life and for protecting Annabel and Delia. You did what you had to do, and you were right when you said they would betray us. I didn't listen to you, but you were right." Jericho could not help but concede the fact that, ultimately, Mavado's views on the Watchers had been accurate. Despite Mavado's demonic status, Jericho could not help but admire the truth and honor which the perceived demon appeared to display. Jericho understood exactly what he was getting in regards to Mavado, which was not something he could say about Garrison or any of the Watchers who had so quickly turned their back on him.

"You owe me nothing my boy, for I have only done that which I gave my word to do. I will always keep my word Jericho, to save, and guard, and guide, to give power and the means to live. I will always be here, and if the time comes when you require my assistance you need only call my name, for I will always be your humble servant. But now is not the time for such things as you only have today before you are pulled away from those you hold dear. Waste not another moment for as I will always be here, the same cannot be said for them."

A loud knocking sound echoed through the study, and in an instant Jericho was again lying on his couch, his shoes still awkwardly dangled off the side and onto the floor. The view of his apartment window filled his eyes, and his groggy and disoriented mind struggled to grasp that he had been rather abruptly awoken from the dream. He lifted his arm to check his watch and was surprised to find that it was now four in the afternoon. The conversation with Mavado had appeared to have been no more than a few minutes at most, yet Jericho had slept soundly for almost nine hours. He heard the loud knock once more, followed by a familiar voice.

"Hey, prick! Open the door!" Reggie had arrived and was now making his presence known to everyone in the building, but he was not alone as Jericho heard Michael's voice from behind the door as well.

"Maybe he isn't home, Reg, I told you we should've checked the bar first."

Jericho stood from the couch, rubbed his face and headed for the door as he heard Reggie's reply,

"That's bollocks, his truck is outside. I've never known the bloke to go for a stroll." Jericho reached the door and began to unlock the two deadbolts; the click which emanated from the release of the locks alerted those outside to his presence.

"See? I told you he was here, probably in the loo or . . ."

"Nope, I wasn't taking a shit," blurted Jericho, cutting Reggie off in mid-sentence. Reggie stood in front of the doorway with Michael beside him, while Sunday hulked behind the two of them.

"Hey buddy! Get changed, we're taking you out for a bender. The least we can do is send you off proper." Reggie's enthusiasm did little to lift Jericho's spirit; he felt conflicted as he still yearned for isolation, yet also knew he would forever regret passing up the chance to say goodbye to those who had become his closest friends over the last two years.

"I appreciate you guys wanting to take me out, but I really don't feel like going anywhere today."

"I was thinking you might say something like that, so I took the liberty of picking up a couple of cases of beer. If you won't go to the party, then the party's coming to you." Michael also spoke up in support of Reggie's suggestion, "Come on bro, you know we aren't going to leave you alone today. You're going to get an extended break from us as it is, so you may as well deal with us now."

Despite his current state of restlessness, he found himself quickly swayed by the peer pressure. "All right, get in here. I could definitely use a drink."

Reggie clapped his hands together in visible excitement at Jericho's response, and took off quickly to the car to retrieve the beers.

"I'd better go give him a hand, unless everyone wants to see Reggie attempt to run with forty-eight beers," said a slightly amused Sunday, who turned and followed Reggie back to the car. Jericho left the door open and headed back to the couch, while Michael followed him in and attempted to engage him in small talk.

"How are you feeling bro? You're doing all right?" Michael's question was delivered awkwardly, as he found himself unsure of how to begin. Jericho sat on the edge of the couch and looked at Michael, and the question provoked a smile across his tired expression.

"No offense, but let's stay away from dumb questions right now." Jericho really did not mean to offend, as the words rolled out with a small chuckle which was shared by Michael, "Well, I suppose you're right. That is a pretty stupid question."

"Who's asking stupid questions?" Reggie interrupted as he barreled into the apartment with one case clutched in his arms and Sunday in close pursuit with the other. Reggie placed his case of beer on Jericho's coffee table and began to claw and tear away at the cardboard which stood between him and the brew he longed for.

"Nobody's asking stupid questions today, so let's keep it that way, all right? Oh, and there's room in the fridge for the other case; no sense in letting them warm up on the floor." Jericho uttered the words as he motioned towards the refrigerator, but Reggie failed to take note and continued to dig into the box.

Sunday headed to the fridge and opened the door to find more than enough available space, as the fridge was relatively barren with the exception of a carton of milk, a few eggs and a couple of tallboy cans which would now be in good company. Depositing the case, Sunday returned the few feet to the living area and surveyed the very limited furnishings which adorned the room.

"Wow Jericho, you really don't entertain guests very often, do you?" The room was rather naked in regards to seating, as it contained a single sofa which could seat three rather snugly but certainly could not accommodate four fully grown adults. "Oh, I got a few chairs in the storage closet, give me a second."

Jericho headed out to his balcony which contained a small storage area, and emerged a few seconds later with two foldable camping chairs. Michael immediately spoke up as Jericho unfolded the metal-framed, fabric-covered chairs and positioned them around the living room.

"Those look a bit small for you Sunday, I'll take one and you can have the couch instead."

"Well, that's no fun. We could place wagers on how long the chair could hold Sunday's weight before giving way," laughed Reggie as he pulled the cans from the case and lined them up across Jericho's coffee table, "Do you actually do a lot of camping, Jeri?" Assuming the unofficial mantel of bartender, Reggie cracked open one of the cans and handed it to Jericho.

"Not really, Reg, but they were on sale, and I do tailgate sometimes." Jericho responded as Reggie cracked open two more beers and extended one towards Sunday, "You too, big man, you got to have one drink with us to at least toast the occasion."

Sunday snatched the can from Reggie's grasp, "I'll have one beer, seeing as it isn't a sin to drink. But it will only be one so I can drive you two knuckleheads home later," he replied, to Reggie's delight.

"Splendid! That's the spirit, although a strapping fellow like you could probably polish off the whole case on your own and still not scratch the surface, but that means more beer for us so, good news all around I suppose!"

"All right, Reg, let's back it down a few notches," interrupted Michael, who was already growing weary of Reggie's overly comedic approach. "In all seriousness, Jericho I know you don't want to talk about what happened today, and seeing as this is your day, I'll respect that, so this is the last you will hear about it from me. But I got to say thank you from the bottom of my heart for all the times you watched our back over the last couple of years. No matter what anybody else says, we will always have your back."

Michael lifted his beer in a toast and addressed Jericho for what he truly believed would be the final time. While he would always count Jericho as a friend, Michael also took his agreement with the Watchers very seriously. He knew it would be extremely unlikely that the orders given against Jericho and Mavado would ever be lifted, which meant that their friendship would be over for as long as he was joined in his agreement with Garrison.

Sunday, Reggie, and Jericho each raised their drinks along with Michael as he toasted, "To Jericho!" with Sunday and Reggie offering an affirmative, "Here here!" in agreement. The four each took a long swig from their cans and then turned to take a seat, with Sunday taking one end of the couch and Jericho the other, while Michael and Reggie each took a seat in one of the folding chairs.

As they sat encircled, Jericho then offered a question of his own. "So where's Delia at?" As the orders from Albert applied to her as well, Delia's absence from the gathering

250

notably concerned Jericho. With every minute that faded into the past, he lost precious opportunity; he yearned to visit one final time with both the girl who he had grown to care for as a friend, and the spirit who had earned his love and admiration.

Sunday was the first to speak up after a brief pause of silence, "Delia actually stayed behind, as Annabel wished to speak with Albert alone. We were all dismissed, and we let her know we would be coming over here. I'm sure she will join us later. She's young, and the day was pretty overwhelming for her. Give her a little time; I'm sure she will be along soon enough."

"Well time is certainly a luxury which we have very little of, seeing as it's a bit after 4:00 pm, and Jeri here turns into a pumpkin at midnight." Reggie interjected his usual humorous tone, provoking a smile from Jericho.

"It's all right, I'm sure she will be here when she's ready. I wouldn't expect her to start being on time now; after all, it just wouldn't be Delia without her being late."

The four laughed at the comment and drank their beers. They turned the conversation away from past events, and instead chatted about anything and everything they could think of as if huddled around a camp fire built from aluminum cans. They laughed and swapped amusing stories, discussed sports, politics, relationships, and family. Everything but religion, or angels, demons, or Watchers—not the spirits which dwelled within them, or the oaths which would send them on their separate ways at the conclusion of the evening, but instead they dedicated the time to those who were living.

And yes, they drank. Sunday was of course true to his word and only partook of the one beer, while Reggie was also true to his statement that Sunday's restraint meant more for the rest. Michael, Reggie, and Jericho downed beer after beer; the growth of their inebriation continued to intensify, and steadily transformed their behavior to levels of frat boy ridiculousness.

The three decided to shotgun beers which caused Reggie to awkwardly attempt to pierce the bottom of his can with his car keys multiple times, with varying degrees of success. Once they had grown bored of this activity, their attention turned to an improvised game of beer pong; a shortage of disposable cups gave way to an assembly of various glasses, containers and even small cereal bowls which were arranged upon the coffee table in a disorderly manner.

The hours passed, and although they enjoyed themselves thoroughly, Jericho could not help but be distracted as he continued to check his phone throughout the evening for signs of Delia. He texted her every so often, asked if she was okay, or if she would be stopping by, and finally merely sent a question mark as his slew of messages had gone unanswered. He heard nothing back, nor did his companions who would quickly turn the conversation elsewhere when Jericho would inquire if they had heard anything from their absent friend.

It was close to eleven when things began to wind down; Jericho was surprisingly the most sober of the three, as his proficiency as a beer pong player had resulted in his opponents taking in considerably more alcohol than he did. Both Michael and Reggie were glassy-eyed and had grown noticeably quieter over the past half hour. This provoked questions from Jericho and Sunday as to whether they were

252

feeling all right, and prompted Jericho to retrieve a plastic bucket in the event that one of them would be overwhelmed by nausea and be unable to make it to the restroom.

Jericho recognized it was time for them to go; granted they technically had about one more hour until the imposed banishment would officially begin, but he knew the two were already spent. With some much needed assistance from Sunday, Jericho spurred them from their seats and started the short, yet intensive journey to deposit the two into Sunday's vehicle for the trip home.

He had both performed and been the beneficiary of this act multiple times over the years, and had come to relate the task to assisting a toddler in taking its first steps. In both cases the individual would awkwardly stumble in an effort to acquire balance, while the concerned third party would provide words of encouragement and physical assistance along the way. All the while that third party would silently worry about a potential tumble to the ground which could result in injury.

The difference between a toddler and a drunk in that situation is two-fold—the toddler's actions and attempts are endearing, and universally considered a moment to be treasured. The behavior of a drunk, however, is considered an aggravating moment, and one which is either quickly blocked from memory or forever immortalized to embarrass the guilty individual.

In another stark contrast from a toddler, the drunk is large enough to make an unexpected tantrum far more dangerous for both parties involved. Jericho could not help but be reminded of the parallels between the two at that moment as he helped Michael forward, and then assisted in holding him upright as the four reached the car and Sunday began to unlock the doors.

Jericho assisted Michael into the backseat as Sunday helped Reggie into the front passenger seat. Michael and Jericho exchanged goodbyes, with Michael's highly intoxicated condition provoking a more sentimental response that usual, "Hey bro, you know I love you, and I'll be here for you no matter what. I don't give a fuck what they say, I got your back whenever you need, bro, you got that?"

"Love you too dude. You guys let me know whenever you need me, and I'll come running; I still have the pager and will keep it just in case," Jericho responded halfheartedly as he gave Michael a hug and shut the door, then headed around to the other side to say his goodbye to Reggie, who had already rolled his window down and yelled for Jericho to get his "arse" over to say goodbye. Jericho approached the passenger door and reached for Reggie's hand which was already extended out the window.

"Aye, mate; this isn't goodbye by any means. It's more like 'be seeing you soon.' Just you wait and see, this will all be sorted in a fortnight, and things will be all dogs' bollocks in no time!"

"Yeah, I don't know what that means, Reg, but I love you, too!" laughed Jericho as he shook Reggie's hand. Sunday stood close by, having deposited Reggie into the vehicle and taken a step back to allow Jericho room to get to Reggie; he now stepped forward and gave Jericho a pat on the shoulder.

"And now, my friend in Christ, it is my turn to have a word." Jericho turned to face Sunday, who's calm and concerned expression was a disarming sight in contrast to his towering stature. "I will pray for you every day in the manner that I have since we first met you back at Michael's gym. I will pray that God will grant you peace from the darkness within you, and courage to resist it. I understand that you have a measure of loyalty towards Mavado, but you must remember who he is, beyond how he presents himself to you. Resist him, and perhaps in time he will flee from you."

Jericho smiled, yet remained silent as Sunday spoke. He cringed inside whenever he was reminded by those around him of Mavado's ultimately 'evil' nature. He had begun to see some shades of grey over the more recent years joined with Mavado, shades which multiplied even further the more interactions he experienced with the Watchers. Defining Mavado's evil in comparison to the 'righteous' actions of a Watcher like Nicholas blurred the lines further, so much so that, although Jericho would acknowledge that Mavado was certainly not a saint, he also appeared no more a sinner than the alleged holy spirits which had so quickly excommunicated him.

Jericho chose not to share his thoughts or engage in a debate, but respectfully uttered a simple "Thank you," in return. "Take care of them Sunday, and take care of yourself while you're at it," he responded with sincerity as the two shook hands in farewell.

Sunday drove off into the darkness as Jericho made the short walk back to his apartment, and once there he began a halfhearted effort to clean up the mess of discarded beer cans which peppered the living room floor.

It had only been a few seconds of tidying up before Jericho unexpectedly heard a loud knock at the door, and immediately turned to disengage the locks. He pulled the door open in anticipation of seeing Sunday, perhaps having returned to claim an item mistakenly left behind by one of his passengers. Yet the sight before him was one which surprised and uplifted his heart. Absent for so many agonizing hours, she finally stood in his doorway, and he found himself lost in her glowing blue eyes once more.

Annabel looked up at him, silently for a moment before the blue glow vanished to reveal Delia's brown eyes. She also said nothing, and quickly stepped forward and wrapped her arms around his waist. Her face buried deeply in his chest, he felt her body tremble as she wept and held him tightly; he said nothing in return, but instead put his arms around her and squeezed back. A few moments passed before she loosened her grip and looked into his eyes. He could tell she had also been drinking, as even in the midst of his own intoxication he could still smell the alcohol which emanated from her skin.

"I was afraid you two weren't going to say goodbye."

"So was I," she replied, "I'm so sorry, Jeri, it's my fault. They are punishing you because you protected me."

"Hey, none of that, you didn't do anything wrong," interrupted Jericho, as he refused to allow her to take blame for what had transpired, "the important thing is that both of you are okay. And I want you both to know that I will miss you very much."

Delia looked up at Jericho, her eyes brimmed with tears, "You need to know how much she cares for you too, and I know I might not act like it, but I care a lot about you Jeri. Thank you for everything."

The two stared into each other as their bodies swam with intoxication. Jericho felt the same enchanted captivation he experienced when in the presence of Annabel seize him in that moment as he looked down at Delia. Her hands released from around his waist, and his hands traveled down her shoulders and back, stopping just at her waist where they clutched firmly and pulled her closer.

Her hands reacted in a similar fashion, they swiftly moved up his chest until they reached his shirt collar, where they aggressively seized hold and pulled downward to draw him closer. At the same moment, she stood up on her toes to close the remaining distance between them; he responded and pulled her body forward until it firmly pressed against his.

Their lips met for the first time. It was a moment which Jericho had envisioned for years, and one which lived up to his fantasized expectations. Her lips were soft, warm, and wet; her tongue electric, her taste exquisite in ways Jericho had not the words to describe. The beautiful girl was every bit the same as the spirit which lingered within her, and the thought that Annabel was certainly witnessing Jericho's advances, and doing nothing to halt them, only aroused him further.

They exchanged long kisses in his doorway for only a few minutes before the flames of his lust were well stoked. He needed more, and the grinding of her body against his signaled her equal desire to delve deeper into the unknown. He slid his hands down until they clutched her hips, grabbed tightly and lifted her off the ground; she reacted favorably, wrapping her legs around his waist and her arms around his neck as she kissed him even more deeply.

He took a few steps back and shut the apartment door, then released one hand and attempted to manipulate the locks to ensure no intruders would barge in. Even in the throes of passion, paranoia would always find its way to the forefront of Jericho's mind. As he locked the door, she released her legs from his waist and slid down till her feet touched the floor. She grabbed him by the buckle of his jeans, turned and moved to the bedroom with Jericho obediently in tow.

When they had passed through the doorway, she turned and locked lips with him again as her fingers grasped his belt buckle and swiftly unlatched it. And so began the mad dash to abandon their clothes; they removed their own shirts, and Jericho wildly kicked his shoes off and sent them flying across the room. Delia had worn long black boots which required assistance to remove, and Jericho was more than willing to oblige her. Lying down on the bed, she lifted her legs together into the air, which allowed Jericho to navigate the zipper and then pull each boot free.

She reached down and unzipped her jeans, and Jericho watched as she grasped her waistband and shifted her body to slide herself free. With each swing of her hips she exposed herself a little more to him; her jeans and panties were shed together in one swoop, and Jericho broke his infatuated gaze just long enough to remove her garments from around her feet. His heart pounded as he viewed her beautiful form draped across his covers, which seemed to cry out for him to join her on the bed.

Jericho quickly abandoned his remaining clothing before advancing after her. He felt her smooth, bare skin graze his for the first time; her touch ignited him and sent goose bumps traveling down his body. His senses were overwhelmed by the moment, she smelled so sweet, her body was tight and curvaceous, and her nails ran aggressively across his back as their lips locked again. He moved his lips down her neck, for he wanted to taste every inch of her at once, and he quickly found that the more he tasted, the more he desired.

She lifted her hips into the air and wrapped her legs tightly around his waist. They was both ready and had little time to waste. She reached down, took hold of Jericho and pulled him toward her dripping wet slit; he could not help but let out an impassioned gasp upon reaching a destination so deeply desired, and lifted his head to look into her eyes before accepting the invitation to enter.

Their reckless passion had given way to stillness, as she held him in silence for a moment before lust would ignite him to push forward. She welcomed him inside, and he bathed in her warmth; he pushed himself deeper and deeper, invoking a loud sigh from Delia which only served to swell him further. Their bodies moved together with slow building intensity, a rhythmic dance which grew more rapid and frenetic with every passing moment.

She swept him from underneath, and Jericho immediately yielded to her movements. She rolled him to his back and instantly mounted him, crying out again in the darkness as she slid down the entirety of his cock. It was her turn to express bottled-up passions which had flickered in her mind for years, and there would be no holding back; she pushed up against his chest, dug her nails into him and rapidly rocked her hips with unbridled intensity. Jericho clutched to her hips as they bounced up and down, faster and faster; he could only hold on tightly and take in her beautiful body as she rode him without restraint, and was grateful for the chance to do so.

He could feel the undeniable need for release growing rapidly, and he did all he could to stave off the impulse which had grown nearly unstoppable in the midst of his sensory bombardment, The more he tightened his grip on her hips, the faster she would bounce and grind against him; her breaths quickened, her sighs intensified, and he felt her hips begin to tremble vigorously. They were both on the edge of climax and he could no longer hold back, for the electricity she carried felt like a shot of lightning through his body.

He moaned loudly and clutched her tightly, feeling the rush of release as Delia's bouncing reached its apex. She felt it too, and the sensation of Jericho filling her to the point of overflow only served to send her over the edge. She dug her nails into his chest and screamed in ecstasy, as her body tightened around him in shockwaves of euphoric pleasure. She crumbled on top of him in beautiful exhaustion, and all was still once again. The two were unmoved, frozen in the moment as they breathed deeply, with hearts pounding wildly in their chests and bodies still pressed together. After a brief moment, Delia slid her hips from their position atop Jericho until they were stationed just beside him, but her head and arms remained quietly rested on his chest.

No words were exchanged, and none were needed. He felt actual happiness in that moment and hoped it would never end, for he was so far from his troubles that he dared not think of anything else; not of the past and all of its ghosts, or the future's impending isolation. He wanted nothing more than to drown in that moment with Delia in his arms. The girl and her Watcher were one in the same, and he felt whole for the first time in years as she rested on his chest.

Jericho closed his eyes for a moment, as the weight of the day's events had finally caught up with him. His eyelids shut with crushing force, but this time he would not fight to keep them open. He felt safe enough to succumb to his exhaustion. As the darkness closed in around him Jericho felt a small kiss, and then heard a faint voice utter the words he had so desperately longed to hear.

"I love you."

No dreams haunted him that night, no visits from Mavado or strolls through the graveyard which had become routine, but for once he enjoyed a sound sleep which felt almost instantaneous. Jericho opened his eyes, and they were immediately met by the sunlight which pierced through his bedroom window. He sat up to find he was once again alone. She had vanished just as quickly as she had appeared, with the only proof of her visit being the smell of her body that lingered on his covers and sheets. His head pounded slightly but noticeably; a small hangover was creeping its way up his neck and had begun to burrow into the back of his skull.

It was a familiar emotion, and one Jericho knew would become common as he attempted to adjust to his new circumstances. The euphoria of the previous evening had been immediately replaced by the harshness of reality, the weight of which squeezed at his chest and made it difficult for him to breathe. Lying back down, he put the covers over his head and tried to remain hidden from the world. In that moment, surrounded by the darkness, his nostrils were met by the sweet smell of Delia. He was in no rush to abandon that moment, so he remained there until her essence had vanished from his bed.

Chapter 14

"You ready for another one?" Jericho panned his eyes up towards Sebastian, who looked back at him from across the bar. He had been so transfixed on the pager and cell phone which were laid out in front of him that he had failed to notice the bartender's return. "Yes please," he quickly replied as Sebastian retrieved his empty glass and proceeded to mix another whiskey and coke, while Jericho returned his obsessive gaze to the electronic devices strewn before him.

It had been almost two months since his banishment, and his life had become an exceptional routine. He spent his days at work on the construction site, while evenings were whittled away at the Tree House, perched upon his favorite barstool directly beside the server station with both his phone and his pager at the ready. He hoped each day he would hear from his former companions, yet the messages were few and far between. In spite of the gag order which had been issued, Michael and Reggie would text him once a week to see how he was doing, but the conversations were always brief and quickly tapered off when Jericho would ask questions about Monroe or the progress which had been made in tracking him down.

Sunday would text less frequently, maybe once a month, while Delia chose not to respond at all. He had not seen or heard from her since the final night they spent together, and his mind struggled with trying to understand why; perhaps she was embarrassed, or maybe she missed him so much she could not bear any interaction.

Or perhaps, even worse, he meant nothing to her, and her actions on that night were out of pity or gratitude for his protection. The thoughts lit his mind on fire, for regardless of how she felt for him Jericho had grown to care for her and Annabel equally, and he missed them both terribly.

His isolation was not limited to the living, however, as Mavado had also been incredibly scarce since the banishment. Gone were the frequent dreams and the whispers inside Jericho's mind while he was awake; no more did they debate or discuss life or religion or the Watchers. If anything, the demon seemed to respect the exile more than anyone, and Jericho tried to find comfort in the belief that this was done in part to protect him from attacks by the Watchers.

From time to time he would call on Mavado during his dreams; the demon would oblige him and serve as a sounding board while Jericho poured out his frustration. During these sequences, Mavado refrained from giving any advice and was more understanding than instructional. When it came time for him to leave, he would always remind

Jericho of his oath of protection and how he could always be counted on to serve whenever called upon. Yet the need for Mavado's manifestation had not presented itself, and Jericho understood that the consequences of any appearance by the demon would provoke the wrath of the Watchers, so Mavado's dormant status could not be altered.

Sebastian returned to the spot in front of Jericho and sat the cold, perspiring glass on the bar top. "You know Jeri, you staring at that phone isn't going to make it go off. You got a date standing you up or what?" Sebastian let out a laugh as he attempted to force a smile out of his usually somber patron, and this time was successful as Jericho looked up with an amused expression, "Something like that, you could say I get stood up every night," he laughed in response.

"Well bro, there's plenty of fish as the saying goes. Hell, look around the room and start up a conversation. No need for you to be alone unless that's what you're looking for."

"I'm fine. Chatting with you and the staff is good enough for me at the moment," replied Jericho as casually as he could muster. In truth, he had no desire to expand his horizon beyond his former circle, for they had shared the commonality of possession which was a bond not easily replaced. It was a bond which kept him transfixed on both his phone, and the GPS pager which had remained completely silent for the past two months. He was true to his word that the pager would stay by his side "just in case," yet he had grown to doubt that day would ever actually arrive.

"Well, if you change your mind, there's a whole group enjoying ladies night over by the pool tables. Not like I'm trying to get rid of you or anything, but it feels like I see you more often than my wife and kids." Sebastian laughed out loud and headed over to the other side of the bar to serve a young couple who had just entered and taken a seat. Jericho removed the GPS from the bar top and clipped it to his belt, then picked up his phone and quickly scrolled through the messages until he reached Delia's name.

He looked over the message trail and was surprised to see the vast number of texts he had sent without receiving a single reply back. As his buzz had already begun to establish, he felt himself undeterred and decided to try once more; his thumbs mashed the keys in rapid succession as he typed a simple message, "I miss you, I hope you are doing well and I'm here if you need me." He pushed send and then returned the phone to the holster attached to right side of his belt; the phone and GPS clipped on opposing sides of his waist gave him the look of a technological outlaw, and had drawn amusing ridicule from Reggie on more than one occasion. Jericho didn't mind the teasing, for he preferred the convenient accessibility despite the odd appearance. He reached forward and pulled his drink to the now vacant spot directly in front of him and took a long swig, as he had learned to rely mainly on booze for emotional comfort in the absence of friendship. And so he waited, and hoped for a response as he drank alone in the same fashion he had done day after day prior.

Only a few short miles away, Delia felt her phone vibrating through the walls of her purse, which was seated on the floor by her feet as she rode shotgun in Reggie's jeep. She reached down, fumbled for a moment before locating it, and then quickly scrolled to Jericho's message. After reading it over silently, she dropped the phone back into the disorganized abyss of her purse without sending any response, but not before Reggie purposely glanced over and recognized the author of the message. He continued to drive without saying anything at first, but his silence only lasted a few seconds before he was unable to contain himself.

"So, when are you going to quit ignoring the bloke? You know he misses you like crazy, and I don't think Annabel will snitch on you for saying hello," Reggie glanced over at Delia with a small smirk, and then turned his attention back to the road, "I know it's tough sweetheart, but I think you will both feel a lot better if you stop hiding from him."

"I'm not hiding. It just is what it is, so why should I stir up feelings which we can't act on? He's just going to get hurt worse if I keep things going between us. The longer we are apart, the more we will grow apart which is what needs to happen, you know? He's just a guy. All it takes is a pretty girl or two and he won't remember me at all, you know what I mean?"

Her tone was calm yet dusted with pessimism, which naturally was not lost on Reggie as he smiled through his words and continued, "Well, thank you for summing up the male species in such an unflattering manner. An accurate statement in most cases, I suppose, but very unflattering, nonetheless. Although, a fellow who thought in the manner you're speaking of would probably have moved on after being completely ignored for two months."

Reggie just smiled and continued driving; he did not dare to pass a glance at Delia after his comment, as he could already feel her eyes burning like a laser against the side of his head. Seeing no need to dignify his statement with a response, she instead changed the subject, "Have you heard from Sunday lately?"

"As a matter of fact, yes I have. He's doing well, seems to be settled in already. If anyone could fill Nicholas' shoes, it would be Sunday and Fortunado. They are actually up in Boston right now, following up on some leads for the elusive Mr. Monroe. The Legion's been sighted there on more than one occasion, but no one has been able to locate Monroe as of yet. That's probably the reason for tonight's briefing. I already asked Michael if he knew why we were called in, but he and Garrison don't know why we are meeting either."

Reggie pulled up and parked at the meter across the street from the building which housed Albert's office. It was a clear evening, and the traffic had thinned out as most of the business district's workers had already headed home for the day. He looked up and down the street for Michael's bike, and was a bit surprised to find it absent from view.

"Huh, I managed to beat Michael here; that's so unlike me, and even more unlike you," Reggie deadpanned as he put on his parking brake and unbuckled his seatbelt, "Well, I don't believe it would be wise for us to keep Albert waiting, so we had better head on up."

The two exited the vehicle, crossed the street and proceeded up the steps toward the glass lobby doors, which were awash in the orange glow of the setting sun. It was early evening, and early enough that the lobby was still unlocked, which meant that Reggie and Delia could see themselves into the building without having to wait for assistance. As they entered the lobby, the receptionist was nowhere to be seen, which made their ability to help themselves even more beneficial as they whisked into the elevator and took the eighteen-story ride up to Albert's offices.

The doors opened and the two took the short walk down the hallway toward the office. They were soon met with a sense of bewilderment, for as they reached Albert's offices they found nothing but darkness beyond the glass doors of the lobby. Reggie checked the door by giving the handle a firm tug, and sure enough it was locked up tight with every appearance that the place was closed for business.

"Are you sure they didn't cancel the meeting, and that's why we beat Michael here?" asked Delia as Reggie reached for his phone and began to text Michael. The message had barely been sent when they both heard the buzzing sound signaling the door lock release, which indicated that their presence was indeed expected.

"Yeah I'm pretty sure, or otherwise we wouldn't be getting buzzed in." Reggie pulled the door open and allowed Delia to step in first, and then proceeded to follow her through the waiting area.

Michael felt his phone vibrate inside his jacket pocket, but was unable to answer as he sat in traffic on his motorcycle, fully preoccupied with navigating his way past the three vehicle accident which was causing his delay. He was confident that either Reggie or Albert was the originator of the message, which made its review rather unnecessary. He approached the scene of the wreck along with the procession of slow moving motorists and did his best to remain patient, and understood that once the wreck was passed he would be well on his way and only about twenty minutes behind.

For a man who prided himself on timeliness, the delay was an unavoidable aggravation which would be easily understood by the others, but nevertheless still filled him with anxiety. Soon enough he rolled past the scene, and immediately accelerated along with the rest of the commuters in a bid to make up for lost time.

Reggie and Delia made their way through the dark lobby and entered the hallway which led to Albert's office. Reggie stepped in front of Delia and led the way as she switched on the light, which flashed their vision for a moment as their eyes fought to adjust to the rapid change in illumination. They moved forward with haste and reached the office door where Reggie again took the lead and clutched the door handle. "Let's hope this one's open already," he said as he twisted the knob, which rotated freely and admitted them without resistance.

The light from the hallway flooded into the office, which was also dark and to their surprise appeared completely vacant. The two stepped inside, Reggie reached for the light switch and flipped it back and forth to no avail; the room remained dark, bathed only in shadows and the patches of light which emanated from the hallway.

"Albert!" Reggie called out as an uneasy feeling seized his mind and provoked him to communicate inaudibly to his Watcher, "Well Ignavus, I better let you take over at this point." Reggie's irises lit up with a bright green glow as Ignavus possessed him, and the voice of the spirit, absent Reggie's British accent, flowed forward from his lips. "I do not sense the commander's presence here," he said as he ventured forward into the darkness, followed closely by Delia who had chosen to remain in control of her faculties for the time being. As they moved forward, a dark yet unidentifiable shape could be seen on the floor near the large retractable window. The two approached it cautiously, and as they drew closer it was evident that the shape most closely resembled a human figure.

It was the body of Albert, absent the soul of both spirit and host, curled up and blanketed in shadows. The two crouched low to inspect the figure, and upon its identification Annabel seized control of Delia; she placed her hands on the body and searched for a sign of life, but found his state to be beyond the healing power she possessed. Ignavus stood quickly and grasped Annabel's arm, "We have to go now, for it was not the commander who allowed us in."

A massive impact unexpectedly slammed Ignavus against the safety glass of the window and sent cracks racing along its surface. Monroe's bodyguard emerged from the shadows and fired his gigantic hand toward Annabel; it found its target and struck with the tremendous concussive force, sending her body to the floor and knocking her from consciousness.

Ignavus gathered his bearings and quickly manifested his wings, which gave a great push and launched him backward as the giant rushed forward and swung again. He narrowly missed Ignavus and instead struck the already damaged window, which exploded into a thousand razor sharp shards that plummeted down to the street below. The giant lunged forward wildly and swung his massive hands at Ignavus, who continued to backpedal and duck the shots which rapidly pursued him. Another powerful strike from the darkness connected with Ignavus, but this one did not originate from the giant; the force struck him from the side and propelled him across the room and through the doorway which led to the hallway. He hit the floor with a violent thud, his momentum carrying him down the hallway briefly before he was able to launch back up to his feet and face toward the darkened office.

Ignavus stood at the ready, his hands lifted up in a defensive position as blue energy charged through his forearms to amplify his attacks. He could hear footsteps as they approached from the office, footsteps which belonged to the second attacker who stepped through the doorway and into the hall.

The long absent Monroe came into view, followed closely by his giant bodyguard. The two stopped at the entrance to the office and blocked the doorway, which placed them between Ignavus and the incapacitated Annabel. Monroe was armed with the double edged weapon he had conjured from the staff taken from Nicholas, while the giant drew energy from his core and formed a large spear out from his fingertips.

Reggie watched the scene unfold through the window in his mind; undeterred, he began to shout orders at Ignavus, "We have to get to Delia and get her out of there; Garrison should be here any minute to assist you . . ."

"No, we must leave and bring back reinforcements. I cannot defeat them on my own, and even with Garrison we would not be a match for one with the power to destroy our commander. If we stay here we will surely perish. We have no choice but to gather the others." With that, Ignavus quickly turned away from the demons in the hallway and began his retreat.

Shocked by the action, and not knowing what else to do, Reggie knew he had no choice but to take matters into his own hands. The wings which so prominently protruded from his back dissolved in a burst of white smoke; the green glow of Ignavus's eyes faded to a very human blue as the body abruptly halted and Reggie put his hand against the wall to stop the rest of his momentum. Monroe and the giant merely stood still and did not pursue, but watched with confusion as

Reggie turned himself toward them and stood at the opposite end of the hallway.

"You have no power against them, they will kill you easily and you will not even slow them down. I will not manifest simply to put off our destruction for a few moments longer, so I implore you to heed my wisdom. You must leave this place now!" Ignavus shouted from the depths of Reggie's mind with indignation towards his host's actions, for the spirit did not believe in acts of heroism when they would appear to result in nothing but loss.

"I'm not going anywhere as long as Delia and Annabel are in harm's way; if you wish to go then I give you permission to leave me. Let your final act of service be to travel from this place and get word to Sunday and Fortunado. Bring them and the other Watchers here to help me. The journey without me would only take a moment, since you won't be tied to the physical world any longer." Reggie answered within his mind, his words inaudible to the demons at the end of the hallway which waited to see what would unfold.

"If this is your will, then it shall be honored. I know you will not be swayed from this course of action, but you must understand that you gain nothing by remaining here." With that, Ignavus was gone. There was no pageantry or display of energy or power, but instead he vanished silently from Reggie, whose mind became calm as it no longer carried the burden of housing a foreign spirit. Despite the nondescript departure, Monroe and the giant both sensed the spirit's evacuation from its host, and were greatly perplexed by it.

"Your Watcher has abandoned you, left you to your destruction in favor of saving itself? You choose to serve alongside creatures that lack any courage and nobility, yet look upon me and my servants as monsters?" Monroe uttered the questions with contempt toward Reggie and continued, "You are a brave man, I'll give you that, yet you lack any chance of survival and face only a swift death if you oppose us now. I am a gracious god, and will honor your bravery with a show of mercy; leave this place now and I will spare your life, as you pose no threat to me. Challenge me, and I will swiftly destroy you. My mercy has its limits, so make your choice quickly."

They both understood the truth of the situation, that regardless of whatever offer Monroe extended, Reggie would never leave that hallway. If escape was what he longed for, he would have done so with Ignavus rather than allow his Watcher to leave. He knew what was to come and feared its arrival, yet he had an even greater fear of living with the decision to leave his friend behind, and it was that fear which dominated his heart.

"I was never all that good at doing what was best for me," he replied, his voice just a touch shaken yet still able to muster a defiant response, "so it wouldn't make a lot of sense for me to change my ways now. Besides, I know someone who can certainly hurt you, and who won't grant you any measure of mercy."

He reached his right hand down and swept his jacket back to reveal the pistol which the former detective kept holstered on his hip. He also reached his left hand down and swept his jacket 'back on the other side to reveal yet another weapon; the pager which Michael had used so many times before to summon Jericho had been kept safely at Reggie's side. He pressed the call button quickly, and then even more

273

rapidly drew his pistol and took aim at the demons down the hallway.

Jericho felt a vibration run across his beltline, one he assumed originated from his cell phone as he took a long drink from his whiskey and coke. He had chosen to remain perched at his favorite seat rather than to venture off and socialize among the other patrons, which made for an immediate realization of the message and an even quicker retrieval of his phone from its holster. He was genuinely surprised to find his phone absent any new messages or missed calls, and took a quick scroll-through as he wondered silently if he had merely been victimized by a phantom vibration.

Finding nothing out of the ordinary, he returned the phone to its designated spot across his beltline and returned his hand to its cold position around the whiskey glass. Perhaps it was his heightened state of intoxication which delayed his response momentarily, but after a few puzzled seconds Jericho felt an even colder chill pierce his chest; one which sent his heart racing at the realization of the other possible explanation for the presumed phantom ring. He reached for the GPS and pulled it free, and as he looked upon it found the long dormant device had finally awoken and was transmitting a very familiar address.

He was surprised at the sight before him and did not know what to make of it. Was there a situation which required his assistance? Was he was being summoned back to the headquarters to have his status reinstated? Or worse still, had the Watchers finally decided that Mavado was too much of a liability, and he was being summoned to his doom? Questions and suspicions flooded his brain all at once as he stood and gestured to Sebastian that he needed to close out his tab. Sebastian was back in a flash with the ticket, of which Jericho was prepared to receive as he stood with a fist full of cash already pulled from his wallet. As Jericho rapidly counted out what he owed, he felt another long dormant interaction grab his attention; one which came in the form of an audible whisper.

"What exactly do you plan to do, young Jericho?"

Mavado's voice was calm, and in a way was comforting to Jericho as he had actually grown to miss the conversations the two had shared so frequently before.

"I'm going to head over and see what they need. It's only a few blocks away." Jericho left the money on the bar, quickly waved goodbye to Sebastian and headed out the door in a hurried walk.

"You cannot drive in your present condition Jericho," retorted Mavado in an unexpected plea of responsibility.

"Then you can fly me there, is that better?" Jericho continued down the sidewalk in the direction of Albert's office, anxiety swirling within his stomach to the point of nausea.

"I would love more than anything to stretch my legs in the world, yet I recall Albert emphatically stating that my manifestation would result in both of our destructions. Unless absolutely necessary, it would be wise for me to remain merely a spectator."

"Then I guess I'll have to go on foot, if that's okay with you!" Jericho shouted audibly in frustration as he picked up speed and broke into a jog down the sidewalk. In spite of his evening of heavy drinking, Jericho began to sober up rapidly as he continued to gain speed until he was practically in a sprint. The rapid spike in adrenaline which resulted from the unexpected change in the evening's proceedings, coupled with the numbing effect of the alcohol in his system, fueled his mad dash through the darkened streets. He began to assume the worst and felt the urge to arrive as soon as possible; if his assistance was needed then time was of the essence, and at his present pace he would reach the office tower in but a few minutes time.

Chapter 15

The pavement trembled under the throaty rumble of Michael's motorcycle as he pulled up to the office tower and dismounted in a hurried fashion. He muttered comments regarding the incompetence of his fellow commuters under his breath, pulled his helmet off and headed up the steps which led to the lobby. As he pressed forward through the darkness he felt the crunch of glass underfoot, which both stopped him in his tracks and fueled his frustration, as he now wondered what possible damage had been inflicted to the soles of his boots. His eyes scanned the concrete and beheld the substantial amount of shattered glass strewn about the front of the building, a sight which both dissolved his personal frustrations and directed his vision up the side of the building and to the shattered panels of the eighteenth floor.

The higher intensity of the unfiltered light which emanated from the floor revealed its destruction and also raised the alarm within Michael, who instantly turned control of his body over to Garrison. His eyes flashed with the glow of blue energy, and his wings were manifested instantly as Garrison kicked off the ground and shot up the side of the building toward the shattered windows. Taking no chances, Garrison began to manifest the great sword of blue energy as he quickly closed in, but was unable to complete the formation before finding himself confronted by a sizeable foe.

The giant dropped from the floor like a black dragon and made contact in a violent collision with Garrison, catching him in mid-air before turning and tossing him through the side of the building. Garrison hit the window and crashed forward into a lower level set of vacant offices. His momentum carried him through the room as he exploded through cubicle walls and continued forward until he collided with the reinforced wall at the front of the office. The great sword still forming in his hand, he rose to his feet quickly and scanned the darkness for signs of his attacker.

"You still carry my sword, even after all these years," a deep, gravelly voice bellowed from the darkness. Garrison looked about the room for the source, yet the giant remained hidden from view."You were once a great legend among men, the boy who defeated the greatest warrior who ever lived. Oh, but it was not you who defeated me and robbed me of an honorable death, it was your God who struck me down that day, who took my life and gave you undeserved glory. Let us see now what power you truly possess, for he no longer favors you by fighting your battles."

Garrison moved forward cautiously, his sword prepared to strike as he searched the darkness for signs of movement. Without warning, the giant leapt forward from the shadows, grasped one of the office desks with one hand and effortlessly flipped it forward through the air toward Garrison, who reacted swiftly by slashing the huge sword forward and splitting the desk in two. The pieces of desk spun in opposite directions and collided with the rows of cubicles which lined the room, while the giant continued to lunge forward toward Garrison.

Garrison stepped forward and swept the sword into the air just as the giant was upon him, striking his foe with tremendous force. The blue energy from the sword detonated against the giant and flowed around him to reveal a shield of dark energy, which extended from his left arm and absorbed the force of the blow. The giant revealed a weapon of his own, producing a large spear of energy from his right hand which he quickly thrust at Garrison, who just as quickly dodged out of harm's way.

The two fought wildly in the darkness and traded shots with otherworldly speed and power. Bursts and flashes of illumination pulsed through Garrison's sword and disoriented the senses as the Watcher and demon battled back and forth with destructive fury.

The giant hurled his spear, which flew like a rocket and stuck into the large blade of the great sword, ripping it free from Garrison's grasp. Both weapons continued forward across the room as the two leapt at each other and fought hand to hand; Garrison unleashed a rapid fire barrage of punches and kicks which found their mark yet did nothing to faze his attacker in the slightest. The giant grabbed hold of Garrison in retaliation and lifted him into the air, spun forward and launched the Watcher toward the front wall of the offices in a show of exceptional power.

Garrison crashed through the wall and continued into the hallway, the momentum carrying him into the elevator doors which split open as his body impacted against them. He plummeted into the elevator shaft and dropped the distance of only a few floors before slamming against the roof of the elevator, where he lay motionless momentarily before beginning to struggle to push himself up onto his hand and knees.

Blood trickled from his nose and mouth and his body felt weakened; the power of the giant was more than Garrison could match, and had begun to wear through the spirit's protective abilities. With Michael's body beginning to sustain injuries, he could now feel the pain of his wounds as he watched from the depths of his mind, and although he realized that they were now in serious danger, both the Watcher and his host understood that retreat was not an option.

The winged giant crashed down against the roof of the elevator and stood over Garrison, who still struggled to right himself. The giant reached out and snatched Garrison by his coat, lifting him up with ease until the two were at eye level, where Garrison dangled helplessly in the air and clutched the giant's arms for support.

"You are weak, always relying on the strength of others to grant you victory. Lacking the power to stand alone, that is why you cower behind a God whom you do not fully understand."

Garrison reached his hand forward and took hold of the giant by his neck; blue chords of energy spun from his hands and snaked around the giant, and then leapt out and wrapped around the large cable which supported the elevator.

"You still come to me with a sword and a shield and spear, but I still come to you in the name of the Lord of Hosts, and He will never leave me, nor forsake me," The words flowed with fury and power from Garrison's lips as the blue energy sliced through the elevator cable and sent the two into a deadly plummet down the elevator shaft.

Annabel's eyes opened, immediately greeted by isolation they darted about the dark office and searched for signs of life, yet found no friend or foe to be visible. The smell of burnt gunpowder filled her nostrils, the presence of which confused her as it seemed completely out of place. Both the mind of the host and spirit were foggy, disoriented as the two struggled to regain their bearings and remember what had happened.

Annabel concentrated intensely to draw her healing energy upon herself and manifest further; her great white wings sprang forth and cascaded down her back, and her blue irises burned a few degrees brighter than usual in the darkness. As she watched from the window of her mind, Delia felt her own thoughts become clearer as Annabel's power coursed through her body and brought with it renewed strength. Annabel lifted up from the floor and floated a few feet in the air, her wings stretched open to produce an occasional push just large enough to keep her hovering in place. The sound of footsteps caught her attention and drew her eyes instantly toward the hallway in anticipation of their arrival.

"We have to leave!" Delia shouted the words in fear, having also heard the footsteps which grew louder by the second. Light still emanated from the hallway, and across the beams which cast upon the office floor, a shadow could be seen. It drew closer and flooded Delia's mind with an intense impulse to escape.

"We cannot retreat, even if that is what I desired," Annabel answered in a stoic, emotionless tone as she continued, " for the same power which held me back from entering Monroe's temple, now holds us here within the confines of this room."

Monroe passed through the doorway and into the room, weapon still in hand and with an expression of satisfaction draped across his face. He walked to the desk located in the center of the room, lifted his bladed weapon and stuck it through the center of the wooden desktop. When he did this, the presence of the invisible barrier was exposed as the surface lit up and glowed like burning embers, revealing an energy field which ran along the walls and ceiling of the room. He turned his attention to Annabel who was still unmoved and hovered in place only a few feet away, bathed in the orange glow of the power which prevented any escape.

"I find myself continuously amazed by the actions of you 'holy' creatures. The Watchers pride themselves on their righteousness, yet I have witnessed two betrayals in as many interactions; one spirit chose to turn on his ally, while another abandoned the host whom he had sworn an oath to protect. Stranger still, I witnessed more courage flow from a doomed and powerless man than from either of these anointed, holy warriors. Are you the same as these charlatans? Are you also nothing more than a coward?"

"I have no fear of you, for you cannot stand against the one I serve." Annabel's response was strong and without hesitation, but was met immediately by Monroe.

"Yet here you are, all alone, and the one you serve is nowhere to be seen, so it would seem that I only have you to stand against. It is also quite obvious that you do not remember me, or you would certainly find reason to fear who I am. Yet I do remember you, and the lovely terror which danced across your face as I accepted your generous self-sacrifice. Your gift was a beautiful one, sealed within a memento of our time together . . ."

Monroe reached his hand up to the chain which hung about his neck, and grasped a small golden locket which gave off a very faint, yet distinct golden glow. Annabel looked on as confusion wrapped her mind tightly, "That never belonged to me."

"Oh, but it did my sweet Rebecca, once upon a time. This locket was indeed yours, and it represents the glorious gift you bestowed upon me, to grant me life anew should my enemies attempt to extinguish my existence. So grateful for your sacrifice am I, that I now present a gift of my own. I will make known that which has been hidden from you, for as it has been said by the one whom you choose to serve, the truth shall set you free . . ."

Monroe stretched his hand forward toward Annabel; darkness swept across her vision and brought with it a flood of images, smells, tastes and sensations which rapidly consumed her mind. Everything fell into place; she remembered her parents, her brother and two sisters, her best friend Amanda and her prior aspirations. Her name had indeed been Rebecca; she had lived with a servant's heart and had excitedly pursued a life of helping those from less fortunate circumstances. Thoughts, feelings and dreams from her lifetime, long hidden away, were suddenly revealed, along with one final memory which would serve to be her last.

She remembered the cold, dark December evening as she took the walk to the bus stop which had become just another part of her daily routine. She could have sworn she heard footsteps following behind her, yet when she turned to check there was no one in sight. Then there was instant darkness, followed by a sudden awakening in an unfamiliar place; the floor she laid upon was cold, her hands and feet had been tightly bound together, and her cries for help went unheard by anyone willing or able to rescue her.

Two men moved from the shadows, one a giant cloaked in black and the other a bald, unremarkable man. She struggled and resisted but to no avail, as her strength abandoned her under the crushing weight of their savage assault. Her screams were blood curdling, but only met by the sound of ripping fabric as the men exposed her body; every moment that passed brought more terror, more tears for what she knew was yet to come.

There was incredible pain which knifed through her thighs as he began to invade her body; she clawed and struck, shifted and twisted in an effort to escape, yet her blows were fruitless, stifled by the agony of brutal thrusts which ripped her open and sent paralyzing shockwaves of pain through her body. His hand reached for her neck, grasped her locket and ripped it free just before the giant stepped forward to deliver the killing strike.

"You see, I do know you very well. I recognized you the night your cohorts invaded my temple, and in return for your blasphemous actions I have come here to destroy your sanctuary, to take back what rightfully belongs to me. Your master has returned my sweetness, and I will now bestow the same honor which I placed upon you to the young girl within whom you now find refuge."

Monroe reached his hand toward the weapon in the center of the desk, and as he did a flame of burning liquid poured from the tip of the blade and flowed through the air, twisting and weaving through the open space until it reached his fingertips, wound around his fingers and traveled up his forearm.

"I never belonged to you, and I will never allow a vile creature such as you to harm anyone else, especially one whom I have sworn to protect," Annabel's blue eyes burned through the tears which had welled within them, igniting her thoughts with a combination of long-suppressed pain and newfound rage, "for I am not the helpless girl who once begged you for mercy, which you only showed by granting suffering and death."

Monroe extended his arm forward, and as he did the liquid flames shot toward Annabel like a fiery wave. When the stream of fire reached her, it found resistance in the form of a barrier generated by power from Annabel; the flames spread out across the invisible surface to reveal an oval shield which protected her from harm. Annabel remained hovered in place, slowly lifted her arms up from her sides, and then quickly clasped her hands together just in front of her face. As Monroe continued to pour fire out against the cocoon of energy in an effort to break through, she calmly shut her eyes and bowed her head in prayer.

"Heavenly Father, I ask for the strength to stand against the tyranny of evil men. Against this evil which now hopes to claim another victim, grant me the power to confront my past and protect Delia's future. Please bless my final act as her guardian and mentor; that my actions would serve as an example to follow, and as inspiration during troubled times which are yet to come . . ."

"What are you doing Annabel?!" Delia shouted as she heard Annabel's prayer ring out through her mind.

"I am blocked from leaving this place, along with you for as long as I possess you. I know now why I am here, and what I must do to attain my redemption. This is my opportunity to right the wrongs which took me from this world, and to save another from suffering as I did. I thank you for allowing me the chance to live again, and wish you many blessings as you continue your journey, for mine has finally come to an end . . . "

A burst of intense light flashed across the room and blinded Monroe, who moved his forearm in front of his face to shield his eyes, abruptly halting the flow of fire. Delia saw the flash as well and shut her eyes in response, but as they opened she was surprised to find the view before her was no longer taken in through Annabel's perspective; she now stood a part of the physical world, in the dark office positioned directly behind Annabel who still hovered in the air with her hands together and head bowed. Monroe stood motionless in front of spirit, with a dome of transparent blue energy incasing both the demon and Watcher. To Delia they appeared frozen in time, but in the midst of the stillness she heard Annabel's voice whisper.

"Leave this place."

Delia looked around the room quickly, and after a brief moment of hesitation, she obediently bolted for the door. When she reached the entrance to the hallway her body froze, for the scene she beheld was a gruesome one. Brass casings from spent ammunition were strewn across the floor, along with a large pool of blood. The walls were dotted with bullet holes and blood splatter, and the smell of burnt gunpowder still lingered in the air.

A body was slumped on the floor and leaned slightly against the wall, with an empty pistol still barely clutched in its hand. Reggie's eyes were still open, but unmistakably void of life. His face was cold and expressionless, a far cry from the man who always had a smile on his face and a joke on his lips. Delia rushed to his side and knelt down beside him, and as she wrapped her arms around her friend for one final time, she felt herself grow numb.

Monroe lowered his arm from its position in front of his eyes; the flash of light which had temporarily blinded him had vanished, and he was perplexed to find he no longer stood within the offices of Goldstein, Bachman and Brown. He was instead alone, in a large, empty warehouse, the same building which had belonged to him when he was still an ordinary living human; it was the warehouse he had previously used to detain and dispose of his victims, dark and desolate, with rays of moonlight which faintly pierced its dirty windows.

His eyes moved away from the surroundings and back to his outstretched arm, where he was again surprised by the realization that his kingly robes were absent, replaced by an ordinary dark button up shirt. He was human, powerless, and dressed in the common manner he had chosen throughout his lifetime; he was in the past, or at least a projection of the past, one surely created by someone with both firsthand knowledge of who he was and an exceptional talent for illusion.

"This place was your domain, an evil world where you imposed your will without mercy." A woman's voice boomed out through the darkness and caused Monroe to immediately turn toward the direction of the sound. As he did his eyes fell on Annabel who had reappeared in her angelic form in the center of the room, where she hovered in space with her arms rested comfortably at her side and her eyes open; eyes which burned brightly with the intensity of blue flames. "But you no longer give commands here, no longer grant terrible fates to those who have done nothing to deserve your cruelty."

"You have no power over me, you miserable whore," Monroe sneered in reply, "for a God such as I cannot be defeated by parlor games and trickery. Are illusions all you can muster in your quest for vengeance against me?"

"Vengeance was never mine to take, for my God shall claim it for me. I only seek to be true to my word and to prevent you from destroying another young life, and to trap you here long enough for vengeance to find you."

Fueled by adrenaline, Jericho rounded the corner and dashed up the steps which led to the lobby entrance of the office tower. His body was still numb from inebriation and his heart pounded from the wild sprint which had spanned the course of several blocks. He was too drunk to notice the shards of glass which were strewn along the concrete, too drunk to be alerted by the sound and sensation of the crunch underfoot as he grabbed the door and darted into the lobby. His rush to the elevator however was abruptly halted at the sight of dust and smoke, which wafted out from between the elevator doors and had begun to cloud around the ceiling.

He reached for the call button and mashed it with his finger several times in futility, then turned and looked about the room for another elevator; unfortunately the building only had a secondary service elevator, which he quickly discovered required the use of an access key. Jericho grimaced at the realization that he now had two choices: either sprint up eighteen flights of stairs, or allow Mavado to manifest and fly them to the top in a matter of seconds. Still unaware of why he had been summoned, and understanding the potential ramifications of Mavado's unauthorized manifestation, Jericho reluctantly headed toward the stairwell door to begin his ascent.

A loud boom thundered through the walls of the lobby, freezing Jericho in his tracks before he was able to enter the stairwell. He turned his attention back to the elevators and witnessed more dust rush from the small crack between the two doors, which was quickly followed by another boom which shook the building and sent the doors of the elevator exploding forward. Following the debris was the body of Garrison, which flew through the air and violently crashed against the lobby windows.

The impact sent cracks racing across the glass, yet the windows were not shattered and kept Garrison corralled within the confines of the lobby. He was bloody and battered, yet the resolve of both spirit and host was not yet broken as he pushed himself up from the floor and stood back to his feet.

"I believe my arrival would not be met with objection by the Watchers, young Jericho, judging by Garrison's present condition." Mavado's words rang through Jericho's mind, just as the hooded giant stepped into view through the gaping hole where the elevator doors had previously stood.

"Do whatever it takes." Jericho's reply was swift, and Mavado's response was swifter still as black smoke swirled from his body and consumed him completely, then rapidly dissipated to reveal a fully manifested Mavado, with large black wings and the burning-ember glow which ran along the edges of his suit and wings.

The giant turned his head toward Mavado, alerted to the demon's presence by the sudden rush of power generated from the manifestation. He turned in retreat and quickly swooped up through the elevator shaft and out of sight. Mavado sprang forward after him in pursuit through the opening and rocketed up to the eighteenth floor in moments, where he found yet another demolished set of doors; it was a path of destruction caused by the flight of the giant which led to Albert's office and Mavado rapidly followed it until he reached the final hallway. The scene which met both demon and host as they entered the hall, however, immediately took priority over the chase. Jericho took in the sight from his helpless position behind the window of Mavado's eyes, and was instantly shaken to his core.

The view from the window was Delia, kneeling on the hallway floor with her arms cradled around the lifeless body of Reggie. She wept uncontrollably in a pool of blood, without regard to the danger which lurked only a few feet away in Albert's office. Mavado rushed to her side and placed his hands on Reggie's body for a moment to confirm the absence of any spirit within.

"He has left this world."

The demon spoke the words, and felt the agony and rage which they produced within Jericho. Mavado's eyes then found Delia's, who reached forward and grabbed his arm tightly.

"Help her, please help her!" Delia shouted through her tears as she turned her head toward the office at the end of the hallway, where Monroe could be seen in a trance-like state through the doorway with the giant at his side. The giant lunged forward and out of sight, an action which caused Monroe to move his head as if he had suddenly been awakened from a dream.

As his head turned, he was surprised to catch a glimpse of Mavado in the hallway, which was a sight that immediately widened his eyes and sent him into action. He reached for the bladed weapon which stuck in the desk and pulled it free, lifted it in into the air and plunged it into the floor. The blade struck the ground and detonated like a bomb, sending a tidal wave of fire outward which filled up the office and poured through the doorway and into the hallway, where it swept directly toward Mavado and Delia.

Mavado remained in his position beside Delia and the body of Reggie, unconcerned by the danger which rapidly approached. He stretched out his great black wings and pulled the two tightly against his body, just as the flames washed over them. The fire flashed through the hall and then vanished instantly, leaving only trails of flames across the walls and ceiling that immediately triggered the building's sprinkler system. The water sprayed down and extinguished what remained of the flames as Mavado stood to his feet; he was unscathed, along with Delia and the body of Reggie which had been shielded underneath his wings. He turned his attention back to pursuit and raced into Albert's office after Monroe, only to discover that the villain was nowhere to be found. He instead found Annabel all alone in the room, still hovered in midair and unaffected by the fire.

She glimmered with radiance never before seen by Jericho as he looked upon her through Mavado's eyes; her wings were larger than ever before and glowed brightly and without blemish, her body was adorned in a beautiful white gown and her hands were covered with gauntlets which shimmered like diamonds. Upon her head rested a small crown, a symbol of her transition from one of the called to one of the chosen few. Her hair was longer, still jet black and wavy, and billowed down her shoulders before assuming a weightless drift in the air.

Jericho seized control of his body and stepped back into the world, as Mavado's appearance dissolved away in twirling plumes of black smoke which spun into the air and vanished. He approached her quickly and stopped only a few feet away, then stared up in quiet awe at the angel which hovered before him.

He was awash in a myriad of emotions; bewilderment, mixed with relief and adoration, was coupled with grief and distress. The body of his murdered friend was only a few feet behind him in the hallway, while the beautiful spirit he had grown to love was now without a host to tie her to the world. He waited, frozen and afraid to speak, yet inside he begged for Annabel to break the silence. She obliged his silent wish; her voice chimed out, as soft and soothing as the day he first met her, "It is finally finished; I have discovered my purpose in returning to this world, and just as quickly it has been fulfilled."

"I don't understand," Jericho was hardly able to muster the words, which Annabel immediately answered, "I know your purpose too, young Jericho, you were meant to stop him. That is why you are here, the reason for your union with this spirit. Go, seek out the murderer and bring him to his judgment."

"I don't know how to find him, or where he is hiding. Tell me where to find Monroe!"

Annabel's voice was calm and unaffected, and her response flowed effortlessly from her lips, "Monroe is not hiding from anyone Jericho. When his home was destroyed, he simply sought out another; one long abandoned but all too familiar to you, for the demon also knows who you are, who you were, and where you came from. You allowed Mavado to invade his home, and he has done the same to you in return. He waits there for you even now . . ."

Jericho felt a sickness permeate his body at the realization of where Monroe had taken up residence. He had not returned to his former home on Black Mouth Lane since the night his world was destroyed and the pact with Mavado had been struck, and in his heart he had hoped to never cast eyes upon the place again. As he contemplated what was yet to come, he addressed the angel once more.

"Will you come with me? Help me bring him to judgment and put an end to all of this."

"No Jericho, I cannot help you, for my time here is over. I was meant to guide and protect Delia, to save her from suffering the same fate as I did. I set her free and faced the one who took my life, and in doing so have set her heart and soul on the path they were meant to travel . . ."

"You were one of the girls."

Jericho's body was overwhelmed with a feeling of suffocation, as if he had been walking across the surface of a frozen pond and suddenly plunged through the ice and into the freezing waters beneath. His words seemed to go unnoticed, as Annabel continued to speak through the interruption, "Delia is destined for incredible things, things which must come to pass to fulfill what has been written. You must look after her now, watch over her and see to it that she finds her calling. I will pray for you Jericho, and I hope our paths cross again someday."

"Please wait, don't leave me,"

The words barely parted his lips before the energy which surrounded Annabel swelled and intensified into a blinding flash of light, and then darkness consumed the room once more. Jericho dropped to his knees as the weight of death and loss crushed down upon him and pulled the strength from his legs. Tears began to flow down his face as emotions overwhelmed him. He shut his eyes and whispered a simple prayer in the darkness.

"God, please help me . . . please hear me . . . Oh God please help me," He sobbed through his words, yet only silence met his ears. After a few moments, the sound of voices could be heard in the hallway; Michael had joined Delia outside, and could be heard offering words of comfort as she continued to weep for Reggie without restraint. Jericho continued to whisper through his agony, still on his knees with his eyes shut and awash in tears. He then turned his plea to the one whom he knew would have no hesitation to answer, "Please help me . . . Mavado . . . please help me."

"I am here my friend, and I have always been here, always ready, patiently waiting, still, as always, your humble servant." Mavado's voice rang through his mind, transforming his feelings of sorrow into ones of furious rage as an unquenchable thirst for vengeance took hold of Jericho's soul. He rose to his feet with a singular focus and headed to the opening where the windows had previously stood, and as he reached it he could see four brightly glowing lights streaking across the sky and heading directly for him. They were Watchers led by Fortunado, who rapidly approached to provide reinforcement. They had been alerted by Ignavus as his final service to his host.

Jericho understood that if Mavado were to manifest and leave the building at that moment, the Watchers could very well misinterpret his actions and view him as an enemy. Knowing this, he turned from the window and instead headed back into the hallway to join Delia and Michael. In spite of his distress, he decided that he would use the few minutes before Fortunado's arrival to comfort his friends. Jericho knew that the time for war had arrived, and with casualties already mounting, it was evident to him that more death would come before the night was through.

Chapter 16

He could see the glow from the eighteenth floor growing in size as he made his approach, and the destruction within became more and more visible the closer he drew. Always battle-ready, Fortunado aggressively swept through the opening in the side of the building and entered Albert's office, flanked closely by the three Watchers under his command.

"Sweep the building, stay alert and together," Fortunado's powerful voice rumbled through the darkness; his eyes were lit with glowing blue energy, as was the great hammer which he clutched effortlessly in his right hand. The Watchers obediently dispersed and began their search of the building while Fortunado approached the fallen body of Albert and knelt down beside it. Ignavus had informed him of Albert's destruction, so the sight was not met at all with surprise. Instead, he only performed a quiet validation of his leader's demise before standing quickly and aggressively heading toward the hallway which led out of the office.

As Fortunado stepped through the doorway, he felt the grief of his host immediately elevated by the gruesome scene in the hallway. The long mane of Fortunado retracted, the great hammer and glowing eyes vanished, and Sunday assumed control of his body and rushed to the side of his fallen friend.

The Watchers had stopped in the hallway to provide assistance, where one utilized his power of healing to mend Michael's wounds while the other two stood guard at the end of the hallway. Jericho was knelling beside Delia with his arms around her; she was still sitting motionless on the floor beside Reggie's body, but upon realizing Sunday's arrival she quickly leapt to her feet and rushed toward him. The two hugged tightly, and the massive size difference between the two gave the girl a childlike appearance as she nearly vanished in his embrace.

Sunday turned his focus up from Delia and found Jericho staring through him with a weathered, blank expression and bloodshot, tear-rimmed eyes. "Reggie paged me, but I didn't know what was happening until I got here." Jericho's words softly tumbled from his mouth, laced with pain and frustration.

"Ignavus appeared to us, told us of the attack and the order he received from Reggie. We got here as fast as we could." The usual boom in Sunday's voice was restrained, lacking the customary warmth he was well known for but which present circumstances had removed.

"Annabel's gone too," Jericho replied, "she sacrificed herself to save Delia."

The Watcher concluded his work restoring Michael's health, then joined his companions as they left the hallway and continued to sweep the rest of the building.

"They aren't gonna find nobody in here," Michael exclaimed as he took a few steps forward and joined the others in the center of the hallway, " Monroe's gone, along with the giant, and we got no way of finding them; hell we don't even know where to begin looking."

"I know where he is, and he's not going to escape again . . . he won't survive the night." Jericho's tone was controlled, but the hatred in his voice was abundantly clear as his eyes remained fixed downward upon the body of his fallen friend.

"Nobody knows where he is, Jericho. We've wasted months chasing ghosts without any luck, and then he just walks in and slaughters us and disappears. We aren't any closer to finding him."

"Annabel told me where to find him, and she told me I was meant to stop him. That's why I'm here, Michael; Mavado finding me all those years ago wasn't a mistake, I know it was supposed to happen. Mavado was meant to help us, but Albert believed he was too dangerous to your cause, and look where that got us; Albert is gone, along with my friend who was abandoned by his spirit. Annabel was forced to give herself up too, and now I'll never see her again, so it looks like things are actually more dangerous without Mavado. I'm not going to make the same mistake as everyone else and hold him back anymore; we are going after

Monroe, so you two can either join me or stay behind, but I won't be stopped."

Black smoke curled and twisted off of Jericho's body as the transformation began; his features shifted into the chiseled face of Mavado, his teeth sharpened instantly, and the tattoo quickly scrawled across his forehead as if painted across by an invisible artist. His irises transformed to their burning golden color, his fingers lengthened and sharpened into claw-like nails, and as the smoke dissipated, Jericho's casual attire was replaced by the signature pinstripe suit and polished shoes. "My condolences, gentlemen," Mavado uttered the words downward, as Jericho's line of sight was still oriented toward Reggie's body during the manifestation. "If you have any respect or love at all for your dead friend then you will join me this night, so that we may bring justice to the unjust."

"Don't talk to us about love, demon; we certainly have more loyalty and love for others than you possibly could. And I will never join with you, because no matter the circumstances, you will always represent all that is wrong with the world. Evil creatures like you were the authors of the destruction which occurred tonight; rest assured that your day of judgment is coming soon." The voice of the preacher's son boomed out with authority, but his passionate words were met by the very familiar grin which crept across Mavado's face.

"You may be right; judgment could be coming to me someday, but not tonight. Perhaps together you and I can usher in a measure of judgment for our mutual enemies, while you eagerly await the arrival of mine. I only ask that you fight beside me *now*, and when it is finished, you can follow whichever path seems righteous to you. I do not believe in destiny in the way that young Jericho does, yet I

299

believe we do all have some purpose which can be realized, given the right opportunity, of course."

"And what would you know of purpose or opportunity? You only work to satisfy yourself." Sunday's tone remained defensive and accusatory, while Mavado's remained calm and collected.

"Quite the contrary, Mr. Brockington, I merely serve the will of Jericho and not my own; I come when I am called, and when my assistance is required—and I leave when I am told to, just as the spirits within yourself and Michael do. Yet I would offer the opinion that my oath to Jericho is far less self-serving than the pacts offered by the Watchers, for the Watchers ask you to upend your lives in service to their cause, to bend to their will, while I have never asked Jericho for anything other than refuge."

Mavado clasped his hands together behind his back and turned his attention toward Michael as he continued. "Now I suppose a debate of such things would be rather unproductive, so I will instead explain why I believe there is a greater purpose behind our unification tonight. I had previously warned Garrison about engaging the cloaked giant that guards Monroe, as he was not, and still is not, a match for this demon. The two have crossed paths before, back when they were both among the living, of course. The Philistine giant who made an entire army tremble, felled by a defiant boy with but a single stone pulled from a creek and launched from a sling. As I'm sure you are aware, the victory was not the boy's but rather belonged to his God; the use of such feeble means to dispatch the greatest warrior of a generation was meant to serve as a reminder of the folly in defying the God of the universe. While the boy did eventually grow into a formidable warrior, and some would say a great king, he was never a true match for his most infamous of foes."

Mavado turned away from Michael and directed his attention back to Sunday, "But there is one among us who is more than a match for the greatest Philistine of all, for within you resides none other than the slayer of Philistines himself, heralded for his unmatched strength and unyielding ferocity. Had it not been for his disobedient nature and rampant arrogance, he would have been unstoppable. Yet instead he found his match in a most unexpected place; the most dangerous trap of all, he was ensnared and defeated by the charms of a beautiful woman. Stripped of his power and humbled to the fullest extent, he was doomed to die in a final blaze of hatred against his enemies. This warrior hides among us behind the name Fortunado, and now has a rare opportunity to live up to his lofty reputation. Just as Annabel informed Jericho that I was meant to destroy Monroe, your spirit was meant to rid this world of the Goliath which protects our foe."

"So where does that leave Garrison exactly?" Michael chimed in and interrupted, which caused Mavado and Sunday to both turn their attention in his direction. "I trust Jericho, and I believe in setting things right and making them pay for all this shit. But you say Garrison is no match for Goliath so what's his purpose?"

Mavado's amused expression melted away as he responded, "To lead. He was a fine soldier, but a far better commander and king which is where his true talent lies. Legion will certainly be shielding Monroe as he did when we first attacked him at his temple. We lacked the combined numbers to stand against them all, so this time we must bring a true army into battle, and Garrison must be the one to lead the assault. While Garrison directs the attack, Fortunado will engage Goliath which will leave me uninterrupted to destroy Monroe, who will no longer be able to run or hide behind his servants. I can assure you that he is truly no match for me."

When Mavado finished speaking the words, Sunday's eyes immediately lit up as his braided hair unfurled into the long flowing mane of Fortunado. "All is well; your intervention is not required." Fortunado's powerful voice bellowed out toward the three Watchers, who had returned to the hallway and had already drawn swords of blue energy in response to witnessing Mavado's manifested presence. "Stand down, for the demon is not here to oppose us. The three of you must go now to the commanders of the twelve tribes, break words with them of what has happened and bring them back to this place. For tonight we will purge our commander's murderer from the world."

"Yeah, I don't think that will be necessary," Michael interjected, as his vantage point allowed him to see through the doorway which led into Albert's office; Harley and her Watchers had already arrived, along with several dozen other manifested spirits who filled up the entire room. "Ignavus brought word to you as well?" questioned Fortunado, who like the others, was surprised by the arrival of so many warrior spirits.

"No, not Ignavus, but a newly-christened angel appeared to us and told of the attack, so we have arrived to provide assistance; yet regrettably it would appear our arrival is far too late."

"Gratitude for your assistance Harley, for it is needed even now," Garrison interjected, as Michael had also seen fit to relinquish control of his body upon witnessing Harley's arrival, "for the hour is at hand for us to strike against our enemy. We know now where they are camped, and if we do not attack now we may lose track of them yet again. How large a force accompanies you?"

"All twelve tribes, so including you we are one-hundred forty-two strong. To where are we headed, and against how many do we stand?"

"The Legion is believed to number in the thousands, yet their strength is derived from their status as a collective; individually we are superior in power, so if we work in unison our combined strength will rival theirs."

"And who will lead us into battle?" Harley replied, as Albert's destruction had left yet another void in the Watcher leadership.

"I will," Garrison spoke the words to Harley and then turned his attention to Mavado as he continued, "and he will show us the way."

"The very presence of the demon here, now, is an abomination and a violation of Albert's decree. We have suffered nothing but death and loss since the moment he was sanctioned to assist us, and in accordance with our orders, he should be struck down even now. He is a shadow of death, one which can no longer be permitted to hide from the light."

As Harley uttered the words, the Watchers who accompanied her instantly manifested an arsenal of weapons; swords, staffs, spears, axes and bows were drawn and raised up in defensive stances. Every eye in view was fixed upon Mavado, who remained ever calm, motionless and seemingly unaffected by the sudden show of hostility.

"Stop!" shouted Garrison, "The boy who hosts this demon has done nothing to deserve destruction. Furthermore, this demon is the only one who can lead us to Monroe and pass freely through his defenses. They must be allowed to live, and as Albert's second in command this is my decision to make. I will gladly accept whatever consequences may come from this course of action. Those who refuse to follow my command will find themselves in betrayal of the oaths we all swore, and will be abandoning their duty to usher justice to Monroe and those who aid his cause. If anyone should wish to challenge me, they may do so now; but it is also my duty to remind them of the price of treachery."

Nobody moved or spoke a word as Garrison's voice echoed through the hallway, and then slowly the weapons which had been drawn so hastily began to lower and vanish from sight. They all understood the finality of their oaths, and none could deny the truth in Garrison's words; they needed Mavado more than he needed them, and Garrison's anointed position was far too respected among the Watchers for anyone to openly challenge him.

"We will defer to your judgment, as the demon's inclusion is unavoidable if we are to locate the killer. As you have accepted the consequences for his involvement, any transgressions committed by him will be upon your head. We are prepared to move out at your command." With that, Harley turned and headed down the hallway and back into Albert's office, followed closely by her Watchers, where she joined the others to wait for Garrison's orders.

All who remained in the hallway were Fortunado, Delia, Garrison and Mavado; Garrison turned his attention back to Mavado and addressed him once more, "It is done, you will lead the way. There is no time to waste, we must leave now."

"What of the girl?" Mavado motioned to Delia, who was now powerless in Annabel's absence. Fortunado spoke up in response, "My men will remain here to look after her and care for the dead. She will be well protected." Mavado met eyes with Delia and replied, "Then the time has come for us all to realize our true purpose, and to meet destiny head on." He then turned from Delia and headed for the office with Garrison and Fortunado at his side.

"Wait!" Delia shouted from her position across the hall, her voice bringing a halt to the three and invoking Mavado to turn and direct his attention back toward her. "Please tell him I'm sorry!" she shouted again in a distressed tone, her expression still pained from her state of shock and mourning.

"My dear, you have no need to offer any apologies," Mavado's tone was calm as he addressed her, "for the boy holds no malice toward you. Your absence has been abundantly difficult for him, but understandable given the circumstances. Although Jericho would certainly struggle to find the words, I know his heart better than anyone and can say without dispute that he loves you deeply, and will do whatever is required to ensure your safety, no matter the personal cost." The words seemed to tug Delia forward from her position in the hall, for as Mavado finished speaking she immediately rushed to him; wrapping her arms around his waist, she pressed her right cheek firmly against his chest and embraced the demon tightly.

He did not react at first; his body language appeared almost uncomfortable and hesitant as his arms remained at his side and slightly lifted to allow room between them and Delia's grip. Ever so slowly, he stretched his arms out and around her until the two intertwined in a quiet embrace.

"I'm afraid I won't see him again," she whispered, " please bring him back to me."

Mavado carefully moved his hands across her back, slid them downward to his waist and softly grasped both of her hands. Gently he pulled them free, moved them up and outward and took a step backward. Standing in front of Delia and looking down at her, his hands held hers up and together just below his chest as he addressed her one last time.

"Let not your heart be troubled, for my oath to the boy is as steadfast now as it was the day our paths crossed. You have my word that I will honor that oath and see that he returns to you." Mavado bowed slightly, lifted Delia's hands to his lips and placed a small kiss upon them. He did not speak another word, but let his hands drop and released his hold as he turned away from Delia.

He moved quickly and purposefully into the office with Garrison and Fortunado falling in behind him on his right and left, and was greeted by a crowd of manifested Watchers who packed the room and left only enough space for a narrow path to the large opening where the retractable window once stood.

Mavado reached the opening and stopped for a moment at the ledge, where he took in the sight of the brightly lit city skyline as the Watchers filled the empty space behind him. It was there where he manifested further; the black smoke spun from his back and formed into large black wings, and the edges of his wings and coat burned like embers in the darkness of the room. His voice whispered to Jericho, who could only watch the events from the study within his mind as they unfolded. "It is time for us to go home, Jericho."

Mavado took another step forward and dropped off the ledge and into the night; he fell a few stories before his wings gave a mighty push downward and propelled him up into the sky. Garrison, Fortunado and the rest of the Watchers followed his lead and poured out of the side of the building before they too launched upward into the night sky like a flock of birds.

The inhabitants of the room did not comprise the entirety of the force of one-hundred forty-two which had been summoned, for as Mavado climbed into the sky he could see dozens more Watchers assembled on the rooftop of the office tower, Watchers who began to lift into the sky and join formation with the others to create an impressive show of strength. He hovered in place for a moment and allowed the contingent to reach his position before beginning the rather brief journey to Jericho's childhood home.

"I haven't been back there since the day we met, I don't even remember the way," Jericho spoke the words audibly from his position in the room, only a few feet away from the large window in the study which revealed Mavado's perspective. Jericho's arms were folded tensely and his feet shuffled nervously as he heard Mavado's voice echo through the room in reply.

"I remember the way my friend, for the world is a small place and the passage of time holds little meaning to someone as old as me. From here, the journey will only take but a few minutes."

The Watchers reached Mavado's position and hovered along with him high above the city lights, with Garrison and Fortunado positioned directly in front of Mavado.

"We will follow you in with a full assault, for there are enough of us to break through any barrier Legion may be conjuring. You will not have to worry about interference or attack from any of our men, for tonight you are one of us."

Garrison spoke the words with great sincerity, words which were silently acknowledged with a slight nod of affirmation from Mavado, who then turned from Garrison and oriented himself in the direction of 1326 Black Mouth Lane. He hovered in place for a few moments as the burn of his eyes and the edges of his coat intensified; the energy he drew amplified even further and caused the individual feathers of his black wings to smolder and burn like embers along their edges as well. The great wings stretched out slowly, then fired backward with incredible power and sent Mavado forward like a rocket across the sky.

Garrison, Fortunado and the others followed suit and bolted after him. They streaked across the blackened sky like a meteor shower and left trails of light in their wake as they hurtled toward their destination. Jericho watched anxiously through the window as Mavado drew closer to his home, and felt himself overwhelmed with emotions which battled each other for supremacy. He felt fear for what lay ahead, sorrow for what lay behind, guilt for having not been able to intervene and protect his friends, and intense rage coupled with excitement for now having the opportunity to set things right. He also felt whole again with Mavado manifested for the first time in months, for Jericho had come to miss his partnership with the demon during his self-imposed exile.

In that moment of jumbled feelings, Jericho felt more whole than he had in a very long time; he once again had a purpose, a chance to prove his union with Mavado was not a mistake, but rather an incredible destiny which was now leading him home. Jericho saw the rooftop of his former residence come into view as moonlight lit up the countryside, and he let out a whisper, "Do whatever it takes my friend, I won't hold you back."

Garrison accelerated forward and pulled up alongside Mavado with the great sword already conjured and clutched in his right hand. He lifted the sword, channeled his energy through it and fired a small glowing orb from the tip which rocketed across the sky toward the house. The orb reached the main house quickly, but impacted a good twenty yards before it made contact with the structure and sent the blue energy out and across the face of the invisible shield which protected its occupants from harm.

Upon seeing the detonation, the regiment of Watchers behind him followed suit and launched hundreds of energy orbs at the barrier, which crashed in rapid fire succession against the surface, flashing and crackling like a mighty thunderstorm as they fought to puncture through the shield. Garrison raised his arm in a signal for his forces to halt; in response the Watchers pulled to a stationary position in the air and surrounded the home as they continued to fire upon the shield and break it apart.

Mavado was undeterred from reaching his destination and continued on through the barrier. He passed through and encountered no resistance just as he had done at Monroe's domain, while Fortunado was forced to halt and survey the surface of the energy field for any weakness which would allow him to break through and join Mavado on the other side.

The shield was in a perpetual state of regeneration as it fought to remain intact under the bombardment of the Watchers, yet Fortunado took notice of a small section at ground level which struggled to remain formed. He raised the great hammer with his right hand and accelerated forward against the weakened spot, and when he made contact the hammer punched through, followed by its master who continued on after Mavado.

Chapter 17

"Their numbers are too great. They have already begun to breach my defenses." Legion spoke with the distorted, echoed voice of thousands uttering in unison. He stood in a darkened corner of the room which had formerly acted as Jason Coleman's study, the red burn of his eyes the only indications of his physical presence. The room had been cleared of all furniture and belongings, with only a few empty bookshelves remaining to line what was left of the structure. The large window which stood at the back of the room was smashed, and holes randomly dotted the interior walls from random acts of vandalism, which had gone unaddressed and sent the once prominent property into disarray. Monroe and Goliath were also present in the room; they stood motionless and watched the flashes of light produced by the Watcher's assault through the remnants of the study window.

"Then we can no longer choose to lie dormant, but must instead rise up against them. Lower the first shield and engage them." Monroe's words were met with a slight bow of acknowledgment from Legion, who rapidly whispered in ancient tongues to communicate the orders to the other members of his collective.

Unbeknownst to the Watchers outside, the home was filled with a large number of Monroe's human followers who had given themselves freely to serve as hosts for the Legion. Each individual host was possessed by multiple spirits in order to amplify their strength against the attacking horde, and their eyes burned red as they lined the hallways and packed the rooms of the home in anticipation of the command to attack which had finally arrived. Every window in the home shattered at once as the possessed swarmed out from the house like a flock of bats. They rose into the air and charged the Watchers just as the energy barrier disintegrated; the sky above the home was immediately filled with a mix of Watchers and Demons, who fought in a wild frenzy as Garrison shouted orders and instructions in the midst of the fray.

Mavado swept around the side of the home and landed on the lawn which faced the long, enclosed hallway that led from the house down to the study. He waited there for Fortunado, who took a few additional moments to arrive at the spot due to his time spent breaching the barrier. He reached Mavado's position and touched down on the ground as well, just as the sky above erupted into battle; the boom of explosions and the flashes of energy overhead gave the night the appearance of a terrible thunderstorm, and provided bursts of illumination across the dark lawn as the two approached the study on foot. As they closed in on their destination, Mavado drew the two swords from underneath his jacket and channeled his power through them. The action ignited the inscriptions on the blades with their burning orange glow, while Fortunado already had the great hammer drawn and at the ready.

They reached the large, shattered exterior window of the study and halted just in front of the entrance. "This is as far as you can go Fortunado. Monroe has not abandoned his shield entirely, for it now only protects those he values the most." Fortunado extended the great hammer forward, and it only traveled a few feet before colliding with a secondary barrier which encircled the study.

"I'll summon help to our position, and we will break through this just as we did the first."

"That will not be necessary, for the one you seek has already arrived." Mavado and Fortunado looked upward and beheld the hooded giant, who was perched upon the roof of the study like a massive gargoyle. Fortunado took a few steps back and lifted the hammer in preparation for combat, and his action was enough of a signal to spur a downward leap from the giant. The fight was on, and the two collided on the lawn with a colossal impact. Fortunado swung with the great hammer, and the giant countered with the dark spear; neither one gave an inch nor had the advantage, for the two were well matched in both strength and skill. Mavado did not stop to observe the battle or lend assistance, but continued on and stepped through the open window and into the study as the fight raged on behind him.

The study was dark, but not dark enough to hide its occupants from Mavado's sight. The Legion's host stood in the shadows, stationary and silent as he shielded the room from the Watchers outside, while Monroe stood in the center with the double-bladed weapon clutched in hand.

"It would appear that the powerless fools have called upon their dog once more, and of course, you obediently came running. A bizarre action for one who claims to serve no master at all . . ." Monroe was ever arrogant and defiant, in spite of the war which raged just outside his doorstep.

"As I have always said, I serve young Jericho and no one else, and will do so until my oath to him is fulfilled. I am here to claim vengeance for the lives you have stolen, and in order to balance things, I will need to take something equally precious from you."

"I am a God, for I have claimed victory over death. I command Legions who fight in my name, and at my call they will strike you down where you stand." Monroe turned to the Legion. "Remove this barking dog from my sight." The words fell from Monroe but went unacknowledged as the Legion did not stir from his position in the room but instead remained unmoved and silent.

"What are you waiting for Legion?! Do as your master commands, and destroy this demon now!" Monroe, enraged at the disregard, shouted the order again to no avail; the Legion still did not stir from his position, but remained statuesque in the shadows.

"It would appear that the God has lost his voice!" Mavado shouted with a hint of laughter, which immediately drew Monroe's attention back to the demon. "You are no God, and the power you believe you wield is nothing but an illusion. Did you truly believe someone as feeble as you could hold authority over spirits so ancient and powerful?"

Monroe's expression was twisted with rage, "I am far from feeble, and more than a match for you! You could not defeat me when we first met, and if the Legion will not destroy you then I will simply do it myself!" Monroe lifted the bladed weapon high into the air and plunged it downward into the floor, and as he did flames erupted from the blade and rushed outward towards Mavado.

Mavado extended the sword in his right hand forward in response, and as he did the fire struck the blade and was consumed by it. Mavado was unaffected, and merely absorbed the attack effortlessly as Monroe looked on in surprise. Undeterred by the failure, Monroe lunged forward at Mavado and swung at him wildly with the bladed staff, yet every attacked was easily dodged and effortlessly deflected by the swords of Mavado. The longer Monroe attacked without success, the more apparent it became that the two were nowhere near an even match; Mavado grew weary of the game after a few minutes, and responded with two moves which abruptly ended Monroe's assault.

He swept the sword in his left hand upward with tremendous force, and when Monroe's staff was touched by the blade of the sword it was instantly shattered it in two. The sword in Mavado's right hand was held in an underhand position and followed quickly after the left; it knifed forward and drove into Monroe chest like bolt of lightning, and the energy within pulsed through his body and drove him down to his knees.

Monroe struggled to stand and gasped for breath as Mavado stood in front of him, with the casual smirk painted across his face. "Do you not see? If I had wanted to destroy you in the forest, then it would have been so. It was not the time for you to die, and it was certainly not the time for the Watchers to know just how powerful I truly am. If I had given them a glimpse of what I was capable of, they never would have let the boy live."

315

Mavado reached down and took hold of Monroe by his neck and effortlessly lifted him into the air with only his right hand, while he held the other short sword firmly in his left. Monroe struggled to break free from Mavado's grip, but the effort was futile; he dangled hopelessly from the position as the orange inscription on the blade of the sword buried in his chest burned brightly and sent threads of energy through his wound and across his body. Mavado lifted the sword in his left hand and quickly slashed at Monroe's neck; the blade sliced through the necklace of charms and sent it crashing to the floor, where it softly glowed in the darkness.

"There will be no second coming for you my friend," Mavado drove the second sword forward and pierced upward through Monroe's sternum, sending a wave of energy through the blade and into his body. The darkness washed away from Monroe's eyes and revealed an all too human stare, black smoke twirled off Monroe's body and lifted high into the air, forming a dark cloud that hovered for a moment in the rays of moonlight before it vanished from sight. His spirit had been exorcised; his body was now but an empty shell which dangled from the end of Mavado's arm.

Mavado lowered the body slowly, carefully moved it into a seated position, and then cradled the head as he laid it down upon the floor of the study. Mavado then lowered himself to one knee and straddled the body, braced his left hand against it and used his right hand to carefully pull the first sword free from Monroe's chest.

"And I thank you for your sacrifice."

Mavado placed the freed sword on the ground beside the body, reached for the other sword, gripped the handle and pulled it free as well. He placed the second sword down beside the first, and then shifted his left hand until it rested over the wounds on Monroe's chest. Mavado shut his eyes, and in doing so caused Jericho's view through the study window to instantly turn dark.

"Mavado, what's happening?"

Jericho felt a sense of alarm drape over him as the view from the window obscured; a feeling which only intensified as he heard Mavado's voice whispering rapidly through his mind in a language which was indiscernible to Jericho. The words flowed from Mavado for but a few seconds before he fell silent, and at their conclusion the view of Monroe's body through the window reappeared before Jericho. To his surprise, the wounds on Monroe's chest were gone, while the body remained motionless and void of life. Mavado spoke once more, but this time in words which were audible and understandable to both Jericho and the outside world,

"The time has finally arrived . . ."

An unbelievable pain ripped through Jericho's chest as he stood in front of the study window, so intense that it dropped him to his knees and caused him to gasp suddenly in an attempt to catch his breath. Every breath drawn felt like a blade driving deeper into his heart; he reached his hand up and clutched his chest in response to the pain as confusion wrapped his mind. He could still see Monroe's lifeless body through the window, but the perspective continued to drop as Mavado lowered his head in the real world, and into view came a blade tip which could be seen protruding from Mavado's chest. The sword of Legion had run them both through.

Legion stood behind Mavado, still gripping the sword as it penetrated Mavado's body, yet Mavado remained unmoved and did nothing to resist the attack.

"Our exile is at an end, my brother."

Mavado spoke the words with slow, labored breaths as the life slipped from Jericho's body. In the study within his mind, Jericho collapsed from his knees and rolled to the floor, turned over onto his back and fought desperately to breathe, yet the effort was futile as his vision washed away and darkness consumed him.

Legion slowly pulled the sword from Mavado and did not strike any further blows, but instead returned the sword to its sheath and began to pray rapidly in the same unknown language which Mavado had spoken only minutes before. Black smoke twirled off of Mavado's body, but this time it did not dissolve into the air as it usually did, but instead lingered in a dark cloud which hovered directly below the ceiling. The smoke finished its evacuation from the body and revealed Jericho's physical form now manifested back in the world, with his shirt and jacket soaked in blood, his eyes closed and body limp.

Legion grabbed hold of Jericho, continuing to rapidly speak in the unknown language as he turned him carefully and laid him down on the floor beside Monroe. As Legion placed the body on the floor, he reached down and retrieved Monroe's broken necklace and pulled one glowing charm free from its clasp. He placed the charm, the small locket which had belonged to Annabel, in his left hand, closed his fingers around it and then lifted his closed fist up to his mouth. He held it just in front of his lips as he spoke louder and faster with the sound of hundreds of voices united, and when they reached their peak of volume and intensity the voices ceased all at once. Legion opened his hand and let the charm drop to the ground where it clanked against the hardwood floor, absent the energized glow which it had previously carried.

Once Legion had fallen silent, the cloud of black smoke which hovered near the ceiling in the office divided into two sections, and each section swirled downward toward the two corpses which were laid upon the floor. The first cloud of smoke rushed over the body of Monroe; it raced toward his head and poured into his nostrils and mouth, until it had completely disappeared within the lifeless body. The second cloud was drawn to the body of Jericho, moving over his face where it was swallowed up through his mouth and nose just as the first had been consumed by Monroe's body, Both corpses remained motionless in the dark, while Legion also remained unmoved and stood at attention.

Unaware of the events which had transpired inside the study, Fortunado and the giant continued to battle furiously in the yard. They had delivered significant damage to each other; blood trickled from open wounds on their faces and bodies as the healing of their injuries, typically a rapid event, had slowed considerably due to the amount of power each had already expended. Even their manifested weapons were no longer a factor, as the great hammer wielded by Fortunado had crumbled apart from repeated shots delivered to the giant, while the spear had been ripped from the giant's hands by Fortunado and lost in the darkness.

They closed the distance between each other and fought toe-to-toe, with the close proximity accentuating the sheer massiveness of the giant in comparison to the physically-imposing Fortunado, who wisely grabbed hold of the giant and tackled him to the ground in an effort to nullify the size advantage. They crashed to the ground with a powerful impact, sending dirt and sod flying into the air and producing a man-sized crater with Fortunado in the dominant position atop the giant.

With all the strength he had left, Fortunado launched the final volley of rapid strikes downward until the hooded giant no longer stirred. A final strike was thrown to the chest of the giant, and the blow sent a shot of blue energy ripping through its body. Black smoke poured from the massive body and lifted high into the air, where it lingered for a moment before vanishing from sight.

Fortunado gingerly stood from his position, racked with pain and exhaustion, but very much aware that the battle had not yet ended. He moved with purpose toward the study, but as he approached he found the invisible shield still in place and the entrance impassable. He took a moment to breathe and focused on regeneration, drawing more energy before manifesting his great wings and launching high into the air; he intended to retrieve the Watchers who still remained and begin the final assault on the barrier in an attempt to aid Mavado.

Jericho opened his eyes and found himself still upon the imaginary floor of his father's study, and in the very same spot he had occupied before he slipped out of consciousness. He grabbed at his chest and felt for a wound, but found neither injury nor the crippling pain which had previously consumed him; instead he felt rejuvenated and quickly rose to his feet.

He looked about the room for a moment before realizing something was missing; the hourglass which controlled his transition into the real world was now gone from the desk, and the large window had been smashed to pieces to reveal a dark and seemingly endless void beyond it. The room was absent sound, and Jericho no longer sensed Mavado's presence within him; a noticeable absence for a mind which had become conditioned to sharing the thoughts of two independent beings for what was almost his entire lifetime.

"Mavado?!"

Jericho called out the demon's name, which echoed through the office as if it had been shouted out in a massive concert hall. To his surprise, the call to Mavado went unanswered and Jericho turned once again toward the broken window, approached it quickly and stopped just at the edge of the opening; he was halted by feelings of apprehension, for although he had passed through the window many times before to reestablish control over his body, he felt hesitant to enter the world as his last glimpse of reality had revealed what appeared to be a catastrophic wound.

He considered the possibility that perhaps he was now dead, and that if he passed through the window he would not return to the world but would instead be sent to immediately to judgment. In spite of his concern, Jericho quickly realized there was no other option before him, so he stepped through the window and plummeted into the darkness.

There would be no drop through a storm-riddled sky, no pass by an imprisoned Mavado as he fell toward reality or any of the other imagery which had become commonplace during transition. Instead, he saw absolutely nothing, and only felt an intense rush of falling, a sensation so pronounced that Jericho felt as if his adrenaline had spiked out of control. He gasped rapidly in an attempt to breathe as panic washed over him; he anticipated the sensation of slamming into the ground at any moment, his fear amplified by his inability to actually witness his descent.

Then it happened, without warning; Jericho felt a body-jolting impact which ripped through him with incredible force and redlined his heart rate, and in that moment the darkness lifted and his vision returned. Jericho continued to gasp for air with deep, frantic breaths as he found he was again lying on his back on the floor of his father's study, yet this was not the room in his mind, but rather the real world version, bathed in shadows and moonlight and absent both furniture and decoration.

He rolled over to his stomach and placed his hands on the floor, where he pushed downward in a labored effort to rise from his position. His body felt unusually heavy and struggled against him as he moved up to his knees, lifted his head and looked about the room. It only took a moment before he caught a glimpse of two dark figures which stood off in the shadows; one was in the far corner to the right, and the other stood against the wall directly in front of him. The figure directly ahead began to move toward him, and as it drew closer Jericho could see a large amount of black smoke was emanating from it, to such a degree that its features remained indiscernible.

The figure extended its right hand forward in a silent offer to assist him to his feet, one which Jericho accepted as he reached up and took hold of the wrist of the figure, which did the same in return and pulled Jericho up quite effortlessly. As Jericho stood, his eyes trained to the hand of the figure which clutched his wrist, which at first was quite ordinary but then immediately transformed before him.

The fingers on the hand lengthened, the nails grew and shaped themselves into sharpened edges, and the black smoke which emanated from the body dissipated to reveal the sleeve of a fine pinstriped jacket. Jericho could not believe his eyes; confusion set in as he ripped his hand free from the grip of Mavado and took a few steps backward to put distance between the two of them.

"Greetings my brother, fear not, for I bring you good tidings of great joy. We have been set free from our bonds, and exist now as Gods among men." Mavado, eyes aflame with their golden glow, stepped forward into the beam of moonlight which cut through the smashed study window.

"What do you mean Mavado? What have you done to me? This isn't possible . . ." Jericho looked down at his chest and immediately took note of the large bloodstain which covered his shirt. He ran his hands over the area, but to his surprise found no wound was present. His hands and body appeared to be the same as always, and he lifted his hands up to his face and felt for any noticeable changes, but found none which were discernible by touch.

He then turned his head in the direction of the broken mirror which dangled against the study wall, and to his horror he spotted a golden glow in the darkness reflecting directly back at him. Jericho rushed to the mirror and took in the reflection with utter shock; his brown irises were replaced by the same burning golden glow which adorned Mavado's, and upon his forehead rested an elegant tribal tattoo, identical to the one which marked the forehead of his former demon.

"Of course it is possible, young Jericho, if someone as weak as Monroe could defy death and stand between the living and the dead, then why not us? It was quite fortuitous that we would share the distinction with Monroe of having joined ourselves with Annabel, by way of her host Delia but nevertheless still just as effective. This commonality provided us with an advantageous position which no others would hold, and which was paramount to our ascension."

"You killed me." The words fell from Jericho in absolute disbelief. Mavado had always been true to his oath in spite of his demonic nature, which made betrayal an impossible scenario in Jericho's eyes.

"I freed us, Jericho!"

"I didn't need freedom, Mavado! You destroyed me, and now have condemned me!"

"You were already condemned Jericho, we all are! I have merely given you the means to defend yourself, to stand up against tyranny and forge your own path!" The words boomed from Mavado and silenced Jericho, who still reeled in disbelief. Mavado took a breath and revised his tone to a more conversational volume as he continued:

"They count us the same, you and I, both as dangerous creatures in need of elimination; you, for allowing me residence within your mind, and me for refusing to bend to the will of my former master. The Watchers are here to atone for their past mistakes in the hope that they will be elevated to heights of glory and ascend to the status of Angels. I too sought atonement for my past transgression in the ways they do, and that is what brought me to you Jericho. I made the choice to unite with you in the same manner the Watchers are called to their hosts, and I have served you faithfully throughout your life, and certainly more faithfully than these so-called holy being serve their hosts. Yet where is my redemption Jericho? Where is my forgiveness?"

"What have you done that God won't forgive you for? All you need to do is ask for forgiveness."

"I begged for forgiveness," replied Mavado, his tone still conversational but very much serious as his typical smile was entirely absent, "but none would come, even when I told him that his punishment was more than I could bear. There have been many others who have been forgiven for the sin of murder; even Garrison searches for redemption from ordering an innocent man's death. I suppose my punishment was greater than all, because I was the first; the author of murder who destroyed the one whom I was tasked with protecting."

Jericho pondered the meaning of the words as they fell from Mavado's lips, and it only took a few seconds for the cold realization to sweep over Jericho. It was a story he still remembered from his Sunday school lessons as a boy, but the comprehension of who Mavado claimed to be was difficult to fathom. "That can't be true, the first murderer was . . ."

"Cursed by God, branded as a fugitive so that all would know what he had done . . ." Mavado motioned to the tattoo which displayed prominently on his forehead, "and exiled to wander the earth alone. I served God faithfully, giving my best offerings, only to be unfairly rejected in favor of my brother. In my rage I committed a terrible sin which I have now achieved atonement for, according to the laws of the Watchers. Yet somehow, I find that both elevation and redemption still evade my grasp."

"How does betraying me earn you redemption? You swore an oath to protect me!"

"An oath which has not been broken, but now stands fulfilled!" Mavado shouted back, "I swore to save you, and offered my service, power, and the means to survive. We are now brothers, and I have bestowed upon you my power, my strength for you to wield as you see fit. I told you before that we could be kings; now the time has arrived for us to claim our thrones together."

The sound of muffled explosions boomed through the night, accompanied by bright flashes of blue light which flooded through the window and lit up the three demons. "They are coming for all of us. Mark my words, they will show you no more mercy than they will to the Legion or me." Mavado stepped forward toward Jericho, and as he did the black smoke curled off Mavado's body and formed his great wings,

"Come with us my friend, for as I have always said, our destinies are tied together." Mavado stretched his hand forward, and as he did the same curls of black smoke flowed from Jericho's back and formed two large black wings which were identical to Mavado's.

Jericho felt the surge of energy pass through him as the wings manifested. It was not energy produced by Mavado but was rather generated from within Jericho; power which was now his to command and control. He focused his attention on the energy which moved within him—as it flowed through his body he marveled at the intense power which was seemingly at his fingertips. It was power he had longed for the chance to wield for so many years, yet his feeling of wonder quickly evaporated under the heat of present realities, as he realized the cost which would be paid for his newly-acquired abilities.

"You're wrong Mavado, you don't know my destiny anymore than I do. And I won't fight against God, or Garrison, or any of the Watchers, because I know it isn't right."

"There is no right or wrong, Jericho, such things are illusions. There are only truth and lies, and the truth is that the Watchers will destroy you unless you come with us now!" Mavado retorted with growing intensity as the Watchers outside continued to bombard the weakened barrier which protected the office.

"You wouldn't join Monroe because you didn't believe in what he stood for, no matter how much he warned you about destruction. You didn't want to be on anyone's side; well Mavado, I have chosen my side and it isn't with you. It's time for you to leave my home!"

Jericho's words rendered Mavado speechless, and a look of confused rage filled the demon's expression. Mavado's eyes burned with golden energy, brighter than Jericho had ever seen before, and the edges of his jacket and wings lit up like burning embers and glowed so intensely he appeared as if he would erupt in flames at any moment. The building started to tremor as Mavado continued to draw energy from his core, energy which finally ignited his black wings and engulfed them in orange flames.

"I will see you again my brother, for fate will allow nothing less." With those parting words, Mavado reached his hands upward and clapped them together as if he were preparing to speak a prayer, and as his hands met a wave of flame poured out from between them and engulfed the room.

Garrison, joined by Fortunado, watched from his vantage point high above the home as fire poured from the windows and doors of the study and consumed the building. The Watchers had defeated all the Legion hosts outside and had concentrated their collective energy against the barrier around the study, blasting the surface with rapid fire bursts of blue energy which sent glowing cracks across the energy field and continued to weaken its integrity.

"Continue the bombardment, for we must break through!" Garrison shouted, but as the command left his mouth he witnessed the fire which had engulfed the study suddenly and rapidly draw back in through the windows as if it were pulled by a great vacuum. Then, without warning, a massive detonation of power erupted; it obliterated the study in a fiery explosion and shattered the barrier outward toward the surrounding Watchers.

The shockwave blast fired outward and contacted the Watchers; its impact sent some tumbling through the air while others crashed to the ground, as most had not the time to react to the unexpected explosion. Garrison and Fortunado held fast in their positions against the wave of energy, and when it passed they rocketed forward to the ground and touched down amid the burning rubble to search for signs of life.

Garrison looked about for a moment before he spotted Jericho's body, which was lying face down on the ground and was surrounded by fire. He rushed to Jericho's side, and as he approached was relieved to see movement as Jericho had begun to slowly push up from the ground until he was crouched on one knee.

Garrison took hold of Jericho in an effort to stabilize him, "Are you injured?" he shouted as he helped lift Jericho to his feet, but when their eyes met it became abundantly clear that Jericho was far from unharmed. Mavado's eyes and forehead tattoo were now prominently fixed upon Jericho's face, but the presence of the demon could no longer be sensed by Garrison; he now felt the energy of a new spirit running through Jericho, and immediately noticed the absence of living humanity within the body before him.

An expression of shock draped across Garrison's face; both he and his host Michael instantly understood what had occurred, for the mark on Jericho's forehead was enough to reveal his transformation. They both knew that the consequences which now faced Jericho were significant. He was no longer innocent, no longer afforded protection due to the nature of his union with Mavado, but now stood before them as one of the very beings they were tasked with destroying.

"This can't be happening," Michael muttered in disbelief as he watched through Garrison's eyes, beholding what his friend had become.

"Where are they? Where have the demons gone, Jericho?" Garrison shouted the words as he clutched onto Jericho, holding him steady on his feet as Fortunado quickly approached the two. Fortunado had also sensed the change in Jericho and quickly manifested the great hammer as he drew near, but quickly found that the action caused Garrison to lift his hand in a gesture to stand down, to which Fortunado obediently complied.

Jericho was groggy, and still very much disoriented as he tried to answer Garrison, "He destroyed Monroe, then he took his place and left me. We have to find him," His words were labored as he held on to Garrison for support, but Jericho could feel himself growing stronger by the second as his body began to heal and reenergize rapidly.

Garrison was lost in the moment; he struggled to decide quickly on a course of action as the other Watchers assembled together and headed toward their position. "Fortunado, gather the others and return to the tower. I will join you shortly and reassume command!" Fortunado did not hesitate or question the order, but instead lifted into the night sky and called together the remaining spirits. They joined him high above the remains of the home, and he quickly led them away from Garrison and Jericho.

Jericho lifted his head just in time to witness the Watchers as they withdrew from the area; it was a sight which immediately filled him with confusion, and caused him to release from Garrison and take a few steps back to view the sky as the Watchers darted away like shooting stars.

"Where are they going? We have to find Mavado, find out what he plans to do and stop him."

"We will find him Jericho, for we are sworn to defeat all those who oppose the Lord. But you will not be a part of this."

Jericho was perplexed by Garrison's words and immediately responded, "But I'm not one of them, I've never been one of them, and I can help you stop him!"

"You *are* one of them Jericho!   The Watchers will destroy you because that is what they have been called to do. It is what I have been called to do!"

"If that is why you are here then what stops you now? If it is my fate to be destroyed by you, then do what you must and fulfill your promise!"

Jericho was incensed as he stood before Garrison, but the next words he heard both surprised and silenced him, "I am fulfilling my oath, for I swore that when I was allowed to return to this world that no innocent man would die at my command, even if his death would be advantageous to my cause. I have protected you in spite of your union with the demon, and will do so in spite of what you have now become."

The wail of sirens could be heard in the distance, as fire trucks and police cars raced through the countryside toward the burning remains of Jericho's former home.

"It is time for us to both take our leave, young Jericho. I pray that the Lord will show mercy to you, and give you purpose and peace. I sincerely hope that if our paths should ever cross again, it would be as friends and not enemies, but that is not for me to decide." With that, Garrison lifted into the sky and rocketed out of sight, while Jericho remained still and looked on from his position on the ground.

He could hear the sirens drawing closer, and as he scanned both the sky and what was left of his old home he found himself all alone. He was at a loss, with no idea of what to do, or where to go, and with a new stillness in his mind as the demon Mavado no longer whispered within his

331

thoughts. All he could think to do was to get away, as far away from that place as he could, so he started to run.

He bolted over the remains of the crumbled walls, past the flames and debris of what was once his father's study and continued into the darkness through the empty lots which surrounded the property. His pace grew more frenetic, and he continued to gain speed, yet found he did not grow weary or become out of breath. He felt the power bestowed on him by Mavado as it pulsed within his chest, and he remembered the feeling he experienced when Mavado manifested the great black wings within the study. He concentrated deeply as he turned onto the road which led away from the property, and as he did he saw the flash of red and blue lights from the fire trucks straight ahead as they rapidly approached. Jericho's focus intensified, and he felt the power within him pour out of his shoulders and back just seconds before the sensation of weightlessness seized him. He lifted from the ground and rocketed high into the night sky, and in an instant he disappeared from sight as the fire trucks passed and continued on toward 1326 Black Mouth Lane.

Chapter 18

It was a stormy autumn Sunday afternoon on the day when friends would gather together to say their final goodbyes. Leaves of red and brown twisted and spun toward the earth, finding rest amongst the gray and white tombstones as the small group of mourners were gathered around a closed mahogany casket, which was prepared to make its final descent into the ground. A white-haired priest in his sixties stood before those assembled and offered words of comfort as the casket slowly lowered, "We therefore commit our Brother Reginald's body to the ground; earth to earth, ashes to ashes, dust to dust; in the sure and certain hope of the resurrection to eternal life. Let us rejoice in the knowledge that our father in heaven now holds him close. For today our brother is in paradise."

Only the hosts were present, as Delia, Sunday, and Michael all stood together to witness their friend's final descent, Delia and Sunday both let tears flow without regard, while Michael did his best to stifle his emotions; yet even one as emotionally strong as he could not help but let a tear slip through as he silently whispered a goodbye to his friend. A few hosts from the other teams of Watchers had also assembled to pay their respects, on a day which had been filled with mourning and reflection. Albert's burial had taken place earlier in the day and had brought hundreds of friends and admirers together; the sizeable turnout was largely due to Mr. Goldstein's elevated status in the community, while the funeral for Reggie was the picture of contrast. Fewer than a dozen friends and acquaintances had lingered to share fond memories, and more than a few humorous stories, of the man they had grown to admire and love.

There was one more soul who watched the proceedings from afar. Shrouded in a long brown trench coat, he stood among the gravesites and did his best to ensure his presence remained unknown. He longed to join his friends; to hold Delia and dry her tears, to greet Sunday and Michael and reminisce about better times, yet Jericho knew this was impossible. Impossible because Reggie was not the only death to have recently been mourned, for Jericho also stood in front of a gravesite which bore his own name.

It was a surreal sight for Jericho, to be able to read his name off a tombstone which rested on a plot beside his mother's grave. He had watched his own funeral from a distance only a few days prior; it was a closed casket ceremony, and the body within was an unidentified casualty from the night of the attack on Monroe. In truth, the staged funeral wasn't exactly a deception as Jericho had indeed passed away from human existence, and since only Garrison, Fortunado, and their hosts were aware of his metamorphosis, the purpose of his funeral was understandably to keep up appearances and protect Jericho.

The Watchers would have no reason to search for him if he was presumed dead; they instead were only aware of Mavado's betrayal and now were focused on hunting down the freed demon and any who followed him. Jericho knew that Mavado was actually right in regard to his status with the Watchers, and that if they were to gain knowledge of his existence, then he too would become one of the hunted.

He watched and waited until all were gone before making his way across the graveyard. By that time the overcast sky had begun to crackle and give way to its contents, and tiny drops of vapor tumbled down and pelted Jericho's coat. He stopped at Reggie's grave, and under his breath he uttered a simple prayer for his friend. A prayer he was certain would never be heard, as he knew what he had become; he wondered silently if the wishes of devils could ever be honored by the holy, but he offered the prayer nonetheless.

"You know, Reg would probably be real pissed off if he knew we were blubbering over him." The sound of Michael's voice caught Jericho by surprise, but even so he remained stationary and did not stir from his position.

"He certainly would. He'd also be pretty pissed if he could see what I've become." Jericho casually offered the reply as Michael approached and stopped just beside him.

"You haven't become anything, Jeri; you're still you, no matter how you might look."

Jericho turned his head toward Michael as puzzled thoughts made their way into Jericho's mind; his transition into a spiritual being had brought many new abilities, some discovered and many still hidden. One which Jericho had immediately become aware of was the ability to sense the presence of other spirits. Naturally, he was taken aback to find the presence of Garrison could no longer be felt within Michael.

"Where's Garrison?"

"Gone, called back to heaven for finding his redemption by protecting an innocent person. It was what he was supposed to do, what he didn't do when he was a man," Michael turned his head and their eyes met as he continued, " I tell you, it's weird; without him my mind seems too quiet, which is something I never thought I'd hear myself say."

Jericho could not help but smile at Michael's statement, "I know what you mean. I spent pretty much my whole life with Mavado in my mind, and now it feels like a part of me is missing."

"He was never a part of you Jericho, and if he was then you're better off for losing him. Mavado don't believe in nothing, he just lives for himself, and that isn't you. He tried to make you something that you're not . . ."

"Maybe he knows what I am better than anybody, I mean, I let him do this. Despite what everyone told me, I wanted to believe him, and I chose to put my trust in him. I believed in him more than anything in the world." With a look of reflective regret, Jericho turned away from Michael and directed his attention back to the grave in front of him.

"Bro, it's easy to believe what's right in front of your face. But it's tough to find real faith, and trust in things which seem far away. You got a purpose, Jeri; you may not see it, and things may seem broken beyond repair. But I think we both know that the impossible can happen; hell, a lot of the stuff that's happened to us can definitely qualify as impossible. You just need to start trusting the right spirit."

Jericho appreciated the words of encouragement, but inside he could not help but feel a sense of hopelessness about his current circumstances. Rather than debate with his friend over the realities of his situation, he abruptly changed the subject, "How's Delia holding up?"

"Bout as good as can be expected, I suppose. She's lost a lot of people who she cared about, most of all . . . you. I didn't tell her what really happened, figured the fewer who know, the better off everyone will be. I'm sure that's not what you want to hear, but it's the right thing to do."

"Nah, you're right. She shouldn't know, and you don't have to worry about me telling her that I'm still around. I don't want her worrying about me, or where I'm going to end up when everything is over. Besides, Annabel told me that Delia was meant for incredible things, things which must happen to fulfill God's will, and that it was now my responsibility to look after her. So that's what I'm going to do. I'll be her guardian angel, or demon, or whatever I am. I'll watch over her in secret and see that she becomes everything she's intended to be."

The thunder began to roll across the sky, and the raindrops which fell upon the two quickly grew in size and intensity. The ever-worsening weather failed to hasten a retreat to shelter by either man, as Jericho then turned the conversation away from his own plans.

"What about you? No more missions, or searches, or battles, or arguments with Garrison. What do you plan on doing with all that free time?"

"I don't know, haven't really decided yet. Maybe do nothing, probably just run the gym for awhile and remember what it's like to have evening's off and get to bed early for a change. I'll keep in touch with Sunday for sure, and have him keep me posted on all the happenings with the Watchers, and I'll let you know if they find out anything about your friend, Mavado." Michael stopped for a moment in hesitation before he continued, "Are you planning to go looking for him?"

Jericho's smile faded away into an emotionless expression as he replied, "No, I don't plan on looking for him. I think he has enough spirits focused on bringing him down right now anyway. Besides, I have the feeling he will find me first; he said when we last spoke that our paths would cross again, and knowing him, he will make sure that no one can call him a liar. So I guess I just need to be patient."

The two exchanged goodbyes, shook hands in the rain, and started off on their separate ways across the graveyard. It was a lonely walk Jericho had done so many times before in his dreams as a boy, and as he took in the sights around him and thought back to those dreams he realized that they had finally become his reality. The gates of the mausoleum were now wide open, and Mavado was free from his prison, while Jericho was once again as a child, newly formed in the spirit world with powers he did not fully understand. Powers which he knew would have to be mastered quickly if he were to have any chance at surviving what was to come. He felt his future was as overcast as the present sky, but rather than wander in darkness, he decided to turn his thoughts toward the preservation of the one person

338

who gave his heart a glimmer of hope that good things still remained ahead.

Jericho left the graveyard focused intently on what he believed to be his new calling: to take up the mantel of Delia's guardian. He would watch from afar and keep his presence a secret from her just as he had told Michael he would, and would wait patiently for both their destinies to be realized. For he knew that it would only be a matter of time before Mavado would present himself again, and Jericho could not help but wonder what circumstances would reunite them. One thing he felt for certain was that, should their paths cross again, brother would surely be turned against brother. It was a thought that both ignited fear and anger within the newly- christened demon. One way or another, Jericho believed he would soon have his revenge against the one who took his life.

www.ingramcontent.com/pod-product-compliance
Lightning Source LLC
Chambersburg PA
CBHW051950240626
47153CB00005B/1703